MERCY RIVER

ALSO BY GLEN ERIK HAMILTON

Hard Cold Winter
Past Crimes
Every Day Above Ground

MERCY RIVER

A VAN SHAW NOVEL

GLEN ERIK HAMILTON

WILLIAM MORROW

An Imprint of HarperCollins*Publishers*

MERCY RIVER. Copyright © 2019 by Glen Erik Hamilton. All rights reserved. Printed in the United States of America. No part of this book may be used or reproduced in any manner whatsoever without written permission except in the case of brief quotations embodied in critical articles and reviews. For information, address HarperCollins Publishers, 195 Broadway, New York, NY 10007.

HarperCollins books may be purchased for educational, business, or sales promotional use. For information, please email the Special Markets Department at SPsales@harpercollins.com.

FIRST EDITION

Library of Congress Cataloging-in-Publication Data has been applied for.

ISBN 978-0-06-256743-7

19 20 21 22 23 RS/LSC 10 9 8 7 6 5 4 3 2 1

This one's for Madeline.
Truth be told? It's all for Madeline.
We love you, kid.

MERCY
RIVER

ONE

NEUTRAL GROUND. THE BEST choice for hostage negotiations, selling stolen goods, and meeting ex-girlfriends.

Not that Luce Boylan and I were on bad terms. Our infrequent conversations had been cautious but sociable. Still, when Luce had called yesterday and asked to meet, I instinctively suggested venues away from her Pike Place bar and apartment, or my usual Capitol Hill haunts. Any other neighborhood in Seattle was open territory.

Any neighborhood with an all-night restaurant, that is. Luce usually finished closing her bar around two-thirty in the morning. That suited me. I was keeping odd hours lately.

Which was how I found myself at the 5-Point—WE CHEAT TOURISTS-N-DRUNKS SINCE 1929—at two on a Thursday morning, watching as the café filled with a staggered and staggering flow of customers kicked out of other joints. I sat at the counter and nursed a pint of Mac & Jack's while I waited. And mused a little more about why Luce might want to meet. She'd avoided answering the question over the phone.

She wasn't looking to get back together. I took that as a given, and the fact didn't bother me as much as it might have a few months before. Luce and I had different goals in life. Different perspectives. She wanted to leverage her ownership of the Morgen and the years she'd devoted to it into a very early and very profitable retirement.

I understood Luce's ambition. I might even have shared a piece of that future with her, at one time. Luce had practically grown up running the Morgen with her uncle Albie and his silent partner, the bar's true owner. My grandfather Dono. Dono had treated the bar less as an investment than as a handy way to launder money from his real profession of stealing art and jewels and any other valuables that provided an adequate reward for the risk. He had been exceptionally good at it. So was I, when I was Dono's teenage apprentice.

Luce had imagined something better, something legit. Dono had slowly come to appreciate that. So she'd inherited Dono's bar, and I'd wound up with his house, and for a while Luce and I had wound up with each other. Only the bar remained, from all those developments.

Was she selling out? Seattle real estate had continued its insane climb toward Manhattan-level prices. Maybe Luce had finally received an offer too good to turn down.

Business, I concluded. That was why Luce wanted to meet. She needed my signature on some tax form that still had Dono's name on it, and she thought sending the papers in the mail would be callous, after our history. I didn't mind. It would be good to see her.

I idly observed the 5-Point's patrons in the mirror. Under the moose head festooned with dangling bras, two couples sat shoulder to shoulder in a booth. One of the men was a cop. I could have picked him out of the crowd even without the mustache that stopped one regulation quarter-inch below the corners of his mouth. There was a foundational suspicion in the way any cop with a few years under his duty belt looked at everyone, even at his friends seated across the table. Like they might pass the salt with one hand and steal his wallet with the other.

It must be close to three o'clock by now. I reached for my phone and realized that I'd left it in my truck. Crap.

My empty pint glass became a paperweight for ten dollars. Luce wasn't outside. I walked down the block to where my pickup waited at the curb. I'd plugged my phone into the cigarette lighter socket—the Dodge was that old—and stuck it into the center console while I ran errands and scarfed a bowl of pho noodles for dinner. Out of sight and out of mind.

One voice mail, from an area code and number I didn't recognize. I hit the button to listen.

"Van. It's Leo."

Leo Pak. A friend from the 75th Regiment. I'd been his sergeant in our Ranger platoon, during one of his tours in Afghanistan. Leo had served as a sniper and fire team leader during his time in our unit. He was a quiet guy by nature and had effectively led his team of four by example. I'd been disappointed when he'd rotated out of the company. Leo and I had fallen out of touch after that, until a year ago when he had unexpectedly turned up in Seattle, only weeks after I'd mustered out of the Army.

On the recorded voice mail, Leo was breathing heavily, his voice strained. There was a sound of quick movement before he spoke again.

"They're coming. I can't make it."

Whatever he said next was incoherent. An engine revved, high-pitched, a small motorcycle or something with similar horsepower.

A muffled voice in the background yelled something like, *Get on the ground.* Then a sharp clack interrupted as the phone struck something, and another man's voice came on the line.

"Who is this?" the voice demanded in between gasps for air. Had they been chasing Leo? "This is the Mercy River police, who is this on the line?"

Another moment passed before the call abruptly ended, mid-gasp.

I checked the time on the voice mail. Leo had called me almost six hours ago. Son of a bitch. I called the same number back, twice. No answer.

Leo had been busted before, for vagrancy and once for assault. When he'd turned up in Seattle last year, he'd been drifting. Sleeping in the wild, avoiding contact with people. Being indoors for even a few minutes had put him on edge. Desperate, he'd reached out to me, but before long I was the one who had needed help. And despite his own pain, Leo had pulled himself together long enough to get me out of a bad situation.

I searched online for Mercy River. The closest place with that name was in Oregon, in the rural middle of the state. There was no direct line to the town cops, but the Griffon County sheriff had a station there. I called it.

"Sheriff's department. Deputy Roussa." A woman, rough-voiced but sounding alert despite the late hour.

"I'm looking for a man who may have been arrested in town earlier tonight. Leonard Pak."

"Are you a relative of Mr. Pak?"

"I'm the person he called just before he was busted. I'm in Seattle. Is he under Mercy River's custody, or the county's?"

"He's here," said Roussa. "The town doesn't have a jail of its own. What is your name, sir?"

"Donovan Shaw. What's the charge against him? If he needs bail, I can help."

"Suspicion of murder and armed robbery," she said.

I inhaled. "Jesus."

"Did Leonard Pak say anything to you over the phone about his situation?"

"He left a voice mail. What happened there?"

"We can't release any details without—"

"Just tell me what anyone in town would already know."

Roussa was silent for a moment. "One of our residents was shot and killed yesterday. Erle Sharples. You can save yourself the trouble on bail. I guarantee you that the circuit court judge will keep Pak in custody at the arraignment later today."

Which meant the evidence was solid enough to make them confident that Leo was the killer. And the victim being a local would make things ten times worse.

"Has he asked for a lawyer?" I said.

"He hasn't asked for anything. He's not communicative."

So Leo wouldn't talk. Or couldn't.

"Is he injured?" I said.

"He's being looked after."

A moment passed. Deputy Roussa had volunteered as much as she was willing to say.

When I spoke, my voice was as cold and even as a frozen lake. "If he's conscious, tell him that I'm on my way. I'll be there in the morning."

"Mr. Shaw—"

I hung up before I said more.

Christ, Leo. What the hell happened to you?

I couldn't let myself believe that Leo had murdered someone. His life had turned around during the past year. I'd helped him get placed in an outpatient program, and regular therapy after. Last I knew, he had decided to settle in Utah to be close to his family.

But he could have relapsed. Gone back to living on the road. I wasn't Leo's keeper, or his shrink.

There was nothing I could do now except get to Mercy River. Fast. I studied the highway map on my phone. The town was a tiny white dot on the map, about six hours' drive from Seattle. Flying would take at least as long, even if I could find a connection through Portland or Spokane to central Oregon in the middle of the night.

Driving it was. I could be at my apartment and packed within half an hour. And then—

"Van."

It was Luce. Standing practically in front of me.

"You okay?" she said. "You seemed a little lost there."

Her long blond hair was pulled back and held with a carved wooden comb. She wore a wine-colored coat, buttoned up against the autumn chill, which didn't prevent it from showing off her figure. The sight of her knocked my mind off track for an instant before it found the groove again.

"Hey," I said. "I have to go."

"Go? I'm sorry I'm late—"

"It's not that. Leo's in trouble." I told Luce the handful of facts I knew. "I'm driving down there now."

She hesitated. "Yes. Of course. Will you—do you know how long you'll be gone?"

"Not yet."

"What can I look after here?" That was Luce. Immediately, incisively practical. "What about Addy?"

"Addy should be okay. She has Cyn staying with her this week."

Addy Proctor was my former neighbor. I still checked in on her every couple of days. She was about as self-sufficient as an eighty-year-old person could be, but eighty was still eighty. Addy had semi-adopted a young teenager this past summer. Their own brand of foster care. Cyndra helped with the house and Addy's massive dog, and Addy kept Cyn fed and out of trouble, mostly.

"I'd stay if I could," I said to Luce. "We can talk over the phone, once I get down south."

She looked at me. Luce's eyes could be the shade of rain clouds at times, but tonight, under the pale light of the streetlamps, they were the blue sky above the storm.

"It can wait," she said. "Call me when you're back."

"Yeah."

She stood there as I started the engine. When I glanced out the window she raised one hand in a soft leather glove in farewell.

Packing for Oregon would take so little time, I left the truck in the loading zone in front of my apartment building. A travel bag. Cash. Maybe a few specialized tools. I didn't own much, not even enough to adequately fill my studio apartment near the rail station on Broadway.

Some of what I did own was hidden behind the small refrigerator. I pulled the fridge away from the wall to remove the baseboard at the floor, and reached inside to pull out three gallon-sized Ziploc bags, each with their own contents. A .38 snub-nosed revolver. A tiny Beretta

Nano, which I'd taken off someone who would never have use for it again. And a much bigger, much older Browning. I'd picked that up for sentimental reasons. Dono had owned a Browning Hi-Power. It had been one of the first guns I'd ever shot.

All loaded. All untraceable. They could easily fit in the hiding space I'd made in the front wheel well of the Dodge. After a moment's thought, I took the Browning and the little Beretta and set the revolver back behind the fridge.

There was no solid reason to think I'd need a weapon. Or my lock-picks and other gear, already waiting in the rucksack. But the way Deputy Roussa had refused to tell me more about Leo's condition had my blood up. How badly was he hurt? And who had hurt him? I might not need to play gunslinger, but neither was I going to stroll into Mercy River and count on a brass band playing to welcome me.

TWO

I HAD ONE MORE STOP to make in Seattle. All the way across the city in Briarcliff, a neighborhood on the little peninsula between downtown and the ship canal. Houses with views of the Sound went for multiple millions, a price that included amenities like stone walls and rolling gates with keycard entry. Keeping the working classes like me from driving through and lowering property values.

At the witching hour, the security gate was unmanned. I picked the lock on the guardhouse and pressed the button to make the candy-cane-striped gate lift out of the Dodge's way. It hadn't required much more time than swiping a card.

I found the right house, a long modernist structure, with two-story glass windows and artful illumination coming from low spotlights at each corner. Knocked twice, and rang the bell. Lights inside popped to life, and after a moment the lamp above me on the front stoop followed along.

"Who is it?" a voice hollered from within.

"It's Van, Ephraim."

Ephraim Ganz opened the door. It was a large door, which made Ganz appear even smaller by comparison. He wore yellow silk pajamas, perfectly fitted, each cuff the precise length for his limbs. As if in contrast, his sparse gray hair stood up in electric tendrils from sleep. Brown eyes bright with anger under startlingly dark and hirsute brows.

"Sorry to wake you," I said.

"I don't believe you are. What the hell, kid?"

I let him have the *kid*. Ephraim Ganz had been Dono's criminal lawyer since before I could remember. Even now, edging out of middle age and into his senior years, Ganz had energy enough to power his whole mansion if you stuck plugs in his ears.

"You remember Leo Pak," I said. "He's been arrested for murder and robbery in Mercy River, Oregon."

Ganz grunted. "Come in."

"Honey?" a woman called as I stepped inside the foyer. The very grand foyer, two stories and a staircase. Her voice had come from somewhere above. I glanced up past the railing to see a flushed and pretty face with ash-blond ringlets framing it. Her eyes widened at the sight of me and she tugged her blue satin robe a little tighter around her.

"S'alright, baby," Ganz said. "Just a client."

She didn't seem reassured. Viewing the scene from her side—four o'clock in the morning, a big guy dressed like a handyman standing in my front hall, with scars like pale creek beds creasing one full side of his face—I wouldn't feel too secure either.

"Ma'am," I said. She frowned a little deeper and disappeared into the shadows of the upper floor.

"Third wife's pretty," I said to Ganz, too low to be overheard. "You are still on number three, right?"

"Funny," he said. "What's this about your sniper buddy?"

He *did* remember Leo. I told him the situation. He listened without expression, interrupting only to clarify exactly what the deputy had told me.

"You're on the bar in Oregon, right?" I said. "You had that big Portland case."

"And in California," he said, his mind elsewhere. "Arraignment's later today, the county cop said? That's not a good sign. They think they can close this fast."

"Yeah. I need you down there."

He sighed. "Come on."

I followed him down a hallway and past a dining room large enough to host the entire platoon Leo and I had served in. The kitchen beyond wasn't quite as ostentatious, only half the size of a tennis court. All of the appliances along the walls were of gleaming burnished steel, a match for the sleek lines of the house. It made the kitchen feel a little like a lab. Or a morgue.

"Leo," Ganz said as he took out a jar of instant coffee and two delicate china cups. "He's the one with the troubles, right?" He tapped a fingertip against his temple.

"He's improved since you met him."

Ganz spooned out coffee into the cups and crossed the kitchen to fill them with steaming water from a slim faucet at the cauldron-sized sink. "And he's been arrested before."

"Yeah."

"You know how this is gonna look. Even if everybody in town hated the guy who got himself shot, you take a suspect with a record, with a history of mental instability, that says something."

"He's got post-trauma symptoms. So do I, and so do half the guys I know, in one way or another. You didn't know him before: He was rock-solid. Leo's Army service record—"

"—will just reinforce what the prosecutor wants. The guy is trained to pull a trigger. More than that, he's among the best in the world at it, a Special Forces sniper."

"Special Operations. Forces are the Green Berets. We're Rangers."

"*Pardon moi.*" He finished stirring and handed me one of the porcelain cups. Loose grounds swirled grayly on the surface of the mixture. I looked at Ganz.

"I got a taste for Sanka in law school," he said. "Living in the coffee capital of the U.S., I drink this."

"Get Leo sprung. I'll buy you a tanker truck full of the crap," I said.

"Add one and one, Van. Whatever the hard evidence against Leo is, it's made them bold. And they have to like the story his personal history tells. I would."

"You want to plea bargain? Already?"

"I want you to temper your expectations. Unless they screwed up the chain of evidence we've got an uphill battle ahead."

"So let's go," I said.

"I'll send Arronow. He's good."

"Ephraim."

"He can be there tomorrow. I'll file for an extension on the arraignment from here."

"How much of a retainer did I give you?"

Ganz rolled the coffee around in his mouth. "And I never asked how that miracle happened. From all your overtime as a bouncer, I'm sure."

I'd come into money earlier in the summer. Some from selling the land on which my childhood home had once stood, and a lot more from less-legal ventures. Enough to buy a house next door to Ephraim's, if I chose. A large percentage of that sudden fortune found its way into anonymous donations to causes and people who needed it more than I did. Another chunk became a rainy-day fund. Which for me included legal services.

"Pack a bag," I said.

"What, now?"

"Truck's outside."

"We're driving? God save me. Your grandfather never gave me this much grief, I knew him thirty years." He ran a hand through his wild hair. "Let me go inform Jeannie."

"Tell her you'll bring her a souvenir."

"Mercy River. God. Tell me that name isn't meant as sarcasm." He padded away down the hall. I checked my watch. If Ephraim moved fast, and the Dodge's wheels stayed on, we could be halfway out of the state by sunrise.

THREE

THE TOWN OF MERCY River lay in a haphazard jumble in the crease between two colliding hill ranges, as if its buildings and houses had been scattered across the land like big handfuls of dice, most of them tumbling to rest on the floor of the valley, with a few dozen strays left on the slopes above. As the two-lane highway wound its way down the final long slope, Ganz and I had a view across a slender mile of fields and gravel roads and barns that marked the northern edge of the valley. Cattle stood on the arid hillsides, waiting placidly for the early autumn rains and the good grazing that would follow.

"Yee-haw," Ganz said under his breath. "Ride 'em, cowboy."

Small forests of pine and juniper topped the peaks in the distance like thatched roofs. On the valley floor, we passed the sheet metal monolith of a grain elevator. The highway led through the fields and gradually straightened as it entered the town proper.

Ganz craned his neck to stare at a sign. "I don't believe it. It's actually called Main Street," he said.

He was dressed casually by his standards, in gray trousers and a blue sport coat over a white dress shirt with no tie. He'd filled two large suitcases with clothes before I'd finally hounded him out of his modernist mansion.

In between calls to roust his people out of bed, Ganz had read me some stats on Mercy River from his iPad. The town's permanent population was slightly more than nine hundred. It was the Griffon County seat, a county with the sparsest population in the state. Its single school served all grades. Mining and timber had been the chief industries a century ago. Farms and ranches formed Mercy River's backbone now, plus a handful of restaurants and stores serving the highway, and whatever cash could be gleaned from day-tripper tourists coming to see the painted hills and buttes west of town. The average annual income per person wouldn't cover my rent in Seattle for a full year.

The name of the town came from the flash floods that had been a serious danger back in the nineteenth century, when prospectors panned the river. One night the water had risen high enough and fast enough to swallow half a settlement. According to the official record, all the tents and sheds had been crushed and swept downstream, but no lives had been lost. Or at least none of significance. It made for a better tale that way.

A sign pointing off the main drag read TOWN HALL / SHERIFF. That was where Leo would be.

"There's a hotel," I said, pulling up to the curb.

"Suite Mercy Inn," Ganz said, reading off the name painted on the pebbled glass of the doors. "Is that a joke?"

"See if your staff can laugh us up a couple of rooms."

We got out, me stretching the knots from my shoulders after the long drive, and Ganz groaning with actual pain. My face prickled in the wind. I tugged a barn jacket from my travel ruck and zipped it over my Henley shirt.

"I have a couple more calls to make before we visit your wayward friend," said Ganz.

I shook my head, unwilling to wait. "I'll meet you at the sheriff's."

At the very heart of the town, the storefronts had flat façades and porches, adding to the Old West feel of the street. It was an unexpectedly colorful stretch. Fresh coats of rust-red and sky-blue paint brightened half of the shops, where the planks hadn't been stained a rich brown. Maybe Mercy River had invested in a quick face-lift for tourist season. A few of the buildings had plaques from the state historical society commemorating their original construction. Post office in 1908, mercantile in 1911. A handwritten placard in a diner window plugged venison burgers. My mouth watered instantly. I added food to my mental list of essential tasks, after I'd seen Leo.

The Griffon County Sheriff's station had been built much more recently than the wood-sided buildings along Main. It might have been an elementary school, long and low, with picture windows to the lobby and American and Oregon State flags fluttering from individual poles on the broad lawn. I opened the door for a family of backpackers as they exited and went inside.

"Here for a license, sir?" said the deputy standing at the front desk. He was tall and lanky and had blond hair that had retreated far up his scalp, even though he couldn't have been more than twenty-five. The plastic nameplate above his shirt pocket read THATCHER. "Right over there." He nodded to a teller's window off to the side, under a wooden sign with words burned into the grain: FISHING—HUNTING—VEHICLE.

"Is Deputy Roussa still on duty?" I said.

Thatcher glanced at a wall clock. The county uniform was a short-sleeved khaki shirt with olive epaulets, and matching trousers with an olive stripe. He wore the full belt, gun and flashlight and radio, ready to walk out the door if called. Thatcher was a lefty. "She'll be back shortly. Can I help you?"

"I'm checking on a man who was arrested last night," I said. "Leo Pak. I'm here with his lawyer."

"He the Chinese guy?"

Leo was half Korean, but it didn't feel like the time to argue his ethnicity. "Is he in custody here?"

"Have a seat." Thatcher's politeness now carried a touch of the same chill as the wind outside. He swiped his access card on a door and disappeared within. While I waited, I examined the station. The central room had an open floor plan. One other deputy was typing at a laptop at his desk. Beyond him was a windowed door, probably leading to the administration offices. Thatcher had gone off to the left, where I assumed the interrogation rooms and holding cells were located.

The sheriff would have assigned a detective to a murder case. When Deputy Thatcher returned, I'd get that detective's name and the details on Leo's arraignment. Ganz could arrange for time with Leo and start building his defense. If there was a defense to build.

The deputy emerged and beckoned to me. "This way."

I'd expected the cops to make me wait for Ganz. I kept my mouth shut and followed before Thatcher thought twice.

He led me through the interior door into a short hallway. I removed my jacket and held out my arms while Thatcher swiped a metal detector wand over my limbs. My keys and multi-tool and phone went into a ceramic bowl on a shelf. He glanced through a small high window on the opposite door before unlocking it. A short row of jail cells occupied the right-hand side of the remaining hall.

"Last one down," Thatcher said. I walked past the empty cells— two bunks and a steel toilet and sink in each—to the fourth in the row. Thatcher closed the steel door behind me and kept watch through the high window.

Leo lay on the lower bunk, his arm thrown up to shield his eyes. Asleep, maybe.

"Leo," I said. He didn't move. "It's Van."

His foot twitched. Haltingly, his leg moved off the bunk, his foot in its hiking sock half falling to the floor. He wore jeans—torn and stained with dirt—and a gray T-shirt over his muscled torso. Nothing heavier, although the temperature in the cells must have been under sixty-five degrees. He rolled to one side.

"Christ," I said. Leo's left eye was swollen shut, a stripe of crusted blood running from his hairline halfway to his eye. That whole side of his forehead had puffed up like he'd been bitten by an adder.

"Howz your day?" Leo said through fat lips.

"The fuck, Leo? Did the cops do this to you?"

I couldn't tell if the movement of his head was a nod or a shake. He sat up, as slow as mercury rising.

"Don't stand," I said. "Have they had you into the hospital?"

A shake this time. "Told them no." Leo didn't like hospitals, distrusted them.

"Who hit you?"

"The firs' time? Big fucker at the Trading Post. I'm sitting there when he jus' walks up and whales on me."

"Out of nowhere?"

"Said I'd killed Erle. Tried to tell him no, but he was kickin' me by then. The owner went to pull him off and got pasted. I had to hit the big guy with a plate. Then more of his buddies came at me, so I ran."

"What about the cops?" I said.

He swallowed and stood up, despite my warning, and shuffled to the sink. With some difficulty, he used the foot pump to splash water into his open hand, and then onto his raw face. "I took off out the back. I'd been running the trails up in the hills the past week. Thought I could ditch them, circle around, and find out what was happening. But they had dirt bikes and ATVs. That's when I called you."

I imagined the mob chasing Leo, like villagers after the monster in an old movie. Small wonder he ran. They might have lynched him.

"Smart move, calling me," I said. "I brought Ephraim Ganz. The attorney."

"What'd I say to you on the phone? I don't remember."

"You didn't have time to say much."

"They caught up to me," he said. The simple effort of standing and talking was burning what little energy he had. "Before I could say shit, the town cop nailed me. Fucker was quick with that baton—" He came to rest by leaning against the bars. This close, I could see a virulent purple bruise ringing a slim island of scabbed blood, where the club had struck him.

"What have the cops told you about the murder?"

"Told me? Nothin'. When I came to in the cell here, they asked me a lot of questions about Erle. I'd been working at his shop since I got here last week. Everybody knows that. Asked me why I shot him early that morning, what I did with the money I took. I didn't say anything."

"Good. How hard did they ask?"

His face moved, and I realized he was smiling. "I passed out. Kinda put a halt to the whole Q-and-A thing."

"Leo," I said. "We're going to help you. But you got to level with me. Did you shoot Erle?"

Leo's one good eye met mine, glaring. "Fuck, no, man."

"Did you have an argument? Why do the cops think you did it?"

"I shouldn'ta called you," he said. Leo wasn't a tall guy. His exhausted slump made him shorter still. "It's a mistake. This'll get sorted out."

"You need a doctor. Are you on any scrips right now?" The damn cops probably hadn't even thought to check.

"Couple. But forget that."

"Where are you living?" I pressed. "I can get your meds."

"I got a room at the inn, but—" He tilted his head. "I been stayin' somewhere else."

Of course. I should have guessed that. Leo had no problem attracting women when his chiseled face wasn't beaten halfway to hamburger. "Where's her place?"

"You should head back to Seattle, Van."

"I'll find out who she is. You know I will."

"South of town. Forty-one Piccolo Road. Just don't—"

"I can be subtle," I began, but the door to the outside swung open. A beefy middle-aged white guy in an olive windbreaker emblazoned with the county badge came barreling down the row of cells. Thatcher and a broad-shouldered female deputy followed.

"You." The cop, a detective or whatever he was, pointed at me. "Get out."

I turned to Leo. "Hang tight. I'll be back with Ganz."

"Out." He grabbed my upper arm. I went along with it, let him bull me out of the cell block and back into the lobby. Thatcher and the woman deputy—Roussa, I saw as we rushed past—stepped swiftly out of the way.

In the main room of the station, the deputy who'd been working at his laptop waited by the front desk. All four of them surrounded me in a loose circle, the florid-faced detective still squeezing my arm. Other than tensing my bicep to keep his grip from mangling it, I didn't make a move. Not with two of the deputies already fingering their Tasers and pepper spray. Only Roussa seemed calm.

"I can arrest you now," the detective said, "or you can tell us who you are."

"Or both or neither," I said, "as long as we're listing the options."

"You're not a lawyer."

"Never said I was."

"That's a lie." Deputy Thatcher stepped forward.

"Shut up," the detective said. He gave up trying to crush my arm and glared at me from six inches away. A high crest of cedar-colored hair topped his round head. He smelled sharply of menthol cigarettes. "What did Pak say to you?"

"He can hardly talk." I looked around at the deputies. "Which one of you assholes tried to kill him with your baton?"

"Get your hands on the desk," the detective said, spinning me around.

I complied, grinding my teeth. He removed my wallet and tossed it to Roussa. Halfway through the detective's overly aggressive frisk, Ganz strode in the front door of the station, attaché case in hand.

"Is there a problem, Sheriff?" he said instantly. "Ephraim Ganz. I'm this man's attorney, and I've also been engaged to represent Leonard Pak, who I understand may be on the premises. Who is your lead investigator on the case?"

The deputies and the detective stood stunned, as if Ganz had produced a live elephant from his chest pocket instead of a business card.

"I'm Lieutenant Yerby," said the detective after another second of silence.

"The man in charge. Excellent. Is Mr. Shaw there under arrest? Or is this simply a security procedure before he visits my client?" He gestured to the circle of deputies around me.

Yerby stepped away, letting me straighten up. "Only the lawyer meets with the suspect."

"Of course. Good to learn the local customs. Now, if you would arrange for an interview room for us . . ."

"Pak was assigned a public defender early this morning," Yerby said, coming around the desk. "Until the court says you take over, officially I don't have to do—"

"Judge Waggoner's office received our paperwork of intent half an hour ago. And signed off on it. Officially." If Yerby towering over him bothered Ganz, he never gave the slightest hint. Just smiled and held up his hand apologetically. "No way you could know until now. But Mr. Pak *is* my client, and I *am* here, and I do need to speak with him about his arraignment. Which has been postponed until tomorrow afternoon, by the way."

Yerby took a long inhalation and then one big step to snatch my wallet away from Roussa. He opened it to read my driver's license.

"Seattle," he said, like that confirmed the worst, and tossed the wallet on the front desk.

"Shaw waits outside," Yerby said to Ganz. "Leroy, put Pak in Room One. He and his *attorney* can talk there." The deputy headed for the cell block. Yerby turned to Thatcher. The anger on his face hadn't dimmed at all. "My office."

Thatcher blanched as he quickly followed his boss toward the opposite side of the station. Ganz's phone rang and he stepped away to start barking instructions into it. I picked up my jacket as Deputy Roussa returned with the plastic bowl containing my keys and other personal effects.

"Thanks," I said. "Van Shaw. We spoke on the phone."

"I remember you hanging up."

"I did. I apologize. It was heavy news about Leo."

Her expression remained flat. Roussa wore her black hair pulled into a bun. She had bronze-toned skin and a stance that appeared as immovable as a concrete traffic barrier.

"What happened yesterday?" I said. "With Erle Sharples?"

"The lieutenant's got the file."

"I'm just trying to understand, Deputy. Leo Pak isn't some rando with fucked-up impulse control. He had his shit together, last I saw him. He said he'd been working for Erle recently. Where? Doing what?"

"Erle's Gun Shop. Up on Larimer Road. Erle brought him on for some part-time help. Hand-loading ammo, I think."

Reassembling fired rounds to be used again, or turning them into specialized higher-quality ammunition.

"That's skilled work," I said. "Not something you'd give a guy who was twitchy."

"Erle said he did it well," Roussa admitted.

"So you and Erle had talked about him. Had you met Leo before all this?"

"It's a small town. I'd seen him. Listen," she said, with a glance toward the door Lieutenant Yerby had left through, "don't put what happened to your friend on our department. It was the constable who laid him out."

Right. The voice on the recording had identified itself as Mercy River police, not Griffon County.

"He's a real cop? Not some security guard?" I said.

"Constable Beacham is law enforcement," said Roussa.

"So what does Beacham do for your town besides beat down suspects?"

"There's over two thousand square miles in this county," she said. "Our resources can't be everywhere. The constable handles most of the patrolling around town and the citizen outreach work. I expect that's why he was first on the scene."

And swinging.

"We looked after your guy," Roussa said, reading my frown. "His pupils weren't dilated and Mr. Pak had already told us that he wasn't feeling nauseous, so I let him sleep. We checked on him every ten minutes during the night. The sheriff is at a national conference in Indianapolis right now, else he'd be here to handle the case himself."

Instead we got what was probably the county's only detective, Yerby. Terrific. It was likely a sign of how open-and-shut they thought Erle Sharples's murder was, that the sheriff wasn't hopping the first plane back.

The other deputy opened the interior door. He beckoned to Roussa.

"Mr. Ganz," Roussa called. Ganz nodded and pocketed his phone.

"Best wait outside," he said to me, "before the lieutenant finds a reason to link you to the Lindbergh baby."

He disappeared with both deputies into the depths of the building.

Waiting, inside or out, didn't appeal. I had to move. I left the station, walking back to Main Street. The breeze shoved the growing heat of the morning around. I took off my canvas jacket and held it clenched in my hand.

That fucker Yerby had stuck Leo in the cell after he'd passed out. Leo might have died right there. I wondered if Ganz could get him transferred to a hospital for detention. Someplace where they could check his head for concussion, or clotting. There must be a hospital with an MRI somewhere in the nearby counties. I could handle the bills. If Leo was forced to stay in the holding cell through arraignment, maybe longer, who knew whether he'd wake up the next time he fell asleep? We could—

My careening train of thought was derailed by the sight of two men walking on the opposite side of the street. Early twenties. Jocks. Polo shirts and jeans and distinctive haircuts—shaved almost bald on the sides with a squared-off wedge of hair left on the top. I didn't need a closer look at their sleeve tattoos to know who they were.

Army Rangers.

And past them, another one, a younger guy crossing the street to my side dressed in full Op Camo ACUs, crisp tab on his upper left arm. What the hell?

"Hey. Ranger," I called. He glanced at me. "What's going on? Street's full of brothers."

"What's your unit?" he said, giving me a once-over that stopped at my facial scars. Everyone needed a moment to take in those. Vets weren't shy about it. They'd seen worse.

"Nine years in the Three," I said. Third Battalion of the 75th, the Ranger Regiment. "I became a free man last January."

"Roger that." He held out a fist for a bump.

"I came to town for a buddy," I said. "What's shaking here?"

"Well, shit." He grinned. He had a face that looked like he grinned a lot, broad and heavily freckled, pink splotches only a couple shades lighter than his red hair. "You lucked out, man. It's the Rally." My baffled expression made him laugh. "A three-day party. See?"

He pointed down the street. Two blocks down, workers had placed ladders on either side of Main. One worker climbed the rungs, pulling a broad fabric banner already held high on the other end taut, so that the banner spread and the words printed on it in green and gold became visible over the street.

Welcome U.S. Army Rangers

"Son of a bitch," I said. And the redheaded kid laughed again.

FOUR

ON OUR WAY TO the center of town, the ginger-haired Ranger told me his name was Moulson. He was active duty, out of the Second Bat at Fort Lewis near Tacoma.

"That's why the Rally's so hot," he said. "West Coast. For us."

I understood. Every two years in July, the Army threw their Ranger Rendezvous, a week-long event for active and veteran Rangers. The Rendezvous offered more things to do than there were hours in the day. Air jump shows, team sports, Hall of Fame meet-and-greets, shooting and fitness competitions, ceremonies for incoming and outgoing COs, family barbecues. I had gone to the Rendezvous a couple of times, when I wasn't deployed and wasn't tired of company. I could remember about half of what I'd seen. Being drunk a significant portion of the time was part of the fun.

But the Rendezvous was always in Fort Benning, Georgia. Home turf for guys in the Third, like me, and only a skip away for the First Battalion in Savannah. Rangers from the Second Bat, at Fort Lewis in Washington State, had a long haul to join the fun.

Was the Rally why Leo had come to Mercy River? He didn't drink anymore, but that didn't mean he was opposed to tearing it up. I was surprised he hadn't called to let me know about the shindig. And a little ticked off.

"The Rally isn't an Army event," Moulson continued. "No demonstration drills, no curfews, no nothing. Just us."

"I've never heard of it," I said. "I was in theater in Afghanistan most of the last few years, but still."

Moulson swiped a hand dismissively, practically bouncing on the toes of his desert boots. "It's only the Rally's third year. And the first time, I hear that was nothing but a dozen dudes sitting around a table drinking beer and talking about how to make the Rally into something. Like, they put it all together, got the town to host it, all of that crap happened last year. This is the big push. Me and my buddy Booker from Lewis, it's our second time around. We are going to *shred* this place."

The actives in town might as well have been carrying signs—all with haircuts to match Moulson's and looking like they could run ten miles before they started to sweat. I counted half a dozen before we stepped onto the wooden boardwalk that fronted the shops at the heart of Main Street.

Ten o'clock in the morning. Lunchtime, on Ranger hours. And while Ganz was seeing what he could do for Leo, I was stuck waiting.

"I need food," I said to Moulson, indicating the diner across the street with its placard in the window. "Call your buddy. The Bambi burgers are on me."

IN FIFTEEN MINUTES WE were sitting at a window table where I could keep an eye peeled for Ganz. Moulson had introduced me to Booker, a black man whose rounded spectacles contrasted with his Greco-Roman wrestler's build. Both soldiers were twenty-three years old and the same rank, specialist. When I told them I'd mustered out as a sergeant first class, Booker raised an eyebrow.

"Couldn't make master?" he said. "Sad." Moulson and I laughed.

Moulson pointed up the street. A shopkeeper at the mercantile was setting out a sandwich board, on which was written *Active Duty Discounts! Lowest Prices in Town!* in blue chalk.

"Funny," said Booker, deadpan. "Every store here says they got the best deal."

"Yeah," Moulson said to me. "Make sure you tell 'em you're with the Rally, or wear something that lets them know. That's why we rolled into town with our camo. Cheap food, and happy hour runs all twenty-four."

"Mercy River really rolls out the mat," I said. "How many guys come to this?"

"Who knows?" Moulson shrugged. "Last year they had a couple of hundred coming through for at least a day apiece. With the talk on the Spec Ops boards, you gotta figure at least twice that many this time."

Almost half the population of the town. It was like an invasion, by actual soldiers.

"Most'll arrive by tonight, for the opening," said Booker. Off my questioning expression he jabbed a thumb up the street. "The town hall is where the general kicks things off. It's the only place in town big enough to hold everybody."

"The general?" I said.

"General Macomber. The big brass. He founded the Rally." Booker took off his glasses to clean a smudge off the lens. "It's more than just slamming beers and talking shit. It's a whole support network. Or it's gonna be."

The waitress arrived, arms laden with giant plates of omelets and burgers and fries. While she was dealing out the meals, I noticed something past the sandwich board sign that I'd missed before. Painted on the side of the building in swooping silver script were the words TRADING POST SALOON.

Leo had said he was attacked in a trading post. Or *the* Trading Post.

"You guys ever hang at that bar?" I said, pointing.

"Shit"—Moulson chuckled—"we closed it down every night last year. Biggest joint in town."

"About the only joint in town," Booker muttered.

"Know the owner?"

They looked at each other. "You want to buy it or somethin'?" said Booker around a mouthful of hash browns.

"Or something."

"I remember him," he said to Moulson. "The scarecrow with the boots."

"Riiiight." Moulson nodded. "Real tall."

"Okay," I said. And for five minutes, none of us said another word. Rangers ate like they did everything else. Aggressively.

GANZ FOUND ME AS I was paying the bill at the register. I'd already seen Booker and Moulson off. They were headed to check in at the only real hotel in town, the Suite Mercy Inn, where they'd booked rooms months in advance of the Rally. The town of Mercy River had embraced the annual event to the point where some residents had begun moving away for the week. Whether that was to earn a couple hundred bucks renting out their houses or just to "get out of the way of the fuckin' hurricane," as Moulson laughingly put it, latecomers still had plenty of options.

"Let's take a walk," Ganz said.

We chose a side road, away from the stream of pedestrians. Apart from Main Street, the town of Mercy River didn't appear to have any zoning restrictions on residential and business areas. We walked by a small house with toddlers playing in their yard, a few dozen paces off Main. An auto body shop took up the remainder of the same short block. Some stores blurred the line even further. A realtor had converted a large family home into her offices. A yarn-and-fabric shop might double as the owner's apartment. There wasn't a single building in town over four stories tall, and I saw nothing like apartments or chain stores anywhere. Everything close to the earth, and homegrown.

"I talked to Leo," Ganz said, "and had a phone conversation with the district attorney who covers major crimes in four of the more rural counties around here. She's down in Prineville. They're handling the case and the evidence from there through your good friend Lieutenant Yerby for now. We'll see the DA at the arraignment."

"Can they move Leo? He needs a doctor, at least."

"Leo in his wisdom refused medical treatment. And no way will Yerby insist on it."

"He's got a mild concussion. Minimum."

"Are you a doctor? Is Leo your patient?" Ganz shook his head. "He's an adult, and adults make stupid choices sometimes. Let's concentrate on what we can do. The DA couldn't wait to share the evidence against Leo with me. She's expecting Leo will plead guilty first thing, and hope for leniency."

"Is it that bad?"

"It ain't good. They have Leo's fingerprints on the shells found at the scene. An eyewitness saw Leo enter the gun shop ten minutes before Erle Sharples's body was found inside. No one saw him leave, so it's reasoned he fled out the back after the shooting."

"Shit."

"There's worse. Flecks of blood were found on the bottoms of Leo's shoes when he was arrested. His hands tested positive for gunshot residue, too." Ganz shrugged. "I can work with the fingerprints and the powder test. Leo was working at the shop, he might have touched or fired anything. The other evidence is tougher to challenge. Lab results will take a while, but we have to assume that the blood on his shoes is going to be a match for Erle's. The witnesses and the blood set him at the scene after the fact. And Leo didn't run right out of that shop and call for help. That's their case."

Yerby had hauled me out of the cell block before I'd gotten a chance to press Leo about Erle's shooting. And Leo hadn't volunteered any details. Had that been deliberate?

"He had no motive to kill Erle," I said.

"The till was open and empty. That's motive enough."

I almost protested that Leo didn't have the kind of loose wiring that would make him murder a man for a few bucks, but stopped myself. Ganz didn't care. Ganz would lay out the legal arguments like a surgeon laid out instruments, deciding what was needed at any given moment. Leo's personality didn't matter. Leo's guilt didn't matter.

Who might have had a reason to kill Erle Sharples? Could it really be as simple as a burglar, startled in the act?

"What we need to worry about now is the arraignment tomorrow," Ganz continued. "I'll read the police report this afternoon, see what holes I can find. Arronow is already working on a discovery demand to the prosecutor's office, to make sure they don't get cute and forget to send us a different witness's statement, or anything else that might place Leo elsewhere during the crime."

"What about the attack on him?"

"What about it? Concerned citizens chasing a murder suspect? They'll probably get citations."

"I mean the fact that he nearly had his brains spilled."

"Get real. Your buddy knocked one of his attackers unconscious, and broke the wrist of another man. A bump on our guy's head from a law enforcement officer doesn't buy us a damn thing."

Lost in our conversation, Ganz and I had followed the side road past a schoolyard and a field to its end, where a church stood facing the town head-on. A Methodist house, with white clapboard siding and a fifty-foot spire at its front. As we paused, bells—or the modern prerecorded electronic equivalent—began to sound the hour. Eleven chimes. It felt like they were counting down instead of up.

"I'll make a pitch for bail," Ganz said, "and we might get lucky. But the likeliest result is that they'll keep Leo right where he is, at least until he's transferred to the big jail in Prineville."

I wasn't sure Leo could hack being behind bars until the trial. He'd struggled with claustrophobia in the past, enough that he would sleep outside without any more than a blanket over him.

Ganz fixed me with a wary eye. "You're thinking of making trouble."

"I'm not going to coerce any witnesses, if that's what you mean."

"Maybe not. But even just poking around—watch your butt. These backwaters protect their own, and that goes double for the police here. You already made an enemy of that lieutenant. I don't want you up on charges of dealing crystal meth after one of those deputies happens to find a bag of it in your truck during a traffic stop. That would be horrible." Ganz's face wrinkled as a farm tractor rattled past us on the street, towing a trailer full of manure. "I'd never get out of this cow-flop town."

FIVE

I DIDN'T HAVE TO PUSH open the batwing doors to know that the Trading Post Saloon had gone all-in on the Old West motif of the town center. The tavern had hitching posts along the boardwalk outside. Who knew, maybe some residents of Mercy River really did ride their steeds right down Main Street to grab a brew.

Inside the saloon, round tables and high-backed wooden chairs would have served equally well for family meals or for dealing faro to prospectors and ranch hands. Barrel ends housed the beer taps. A giant mirror behind the long bar with gold filigree snaking around its edges reflected the entire room, making the already large room appear the size of a basketball court.

The only person in sight was a teenage girl in a fringed rawhide vest and silver star, busily wiping down the bare tables.

"Morning," I said. "The owner around?"

"Mr. Seebright? Um." She looked toward the rear of the saloon, as if her boss might appear from behind the taxidermy brown bear rearing up on its hind legs. "He's in a meeting?"

"I'll wait." I took a seat at the bar, and no sooner had my butt hit the stool than a bartender hustled out from the room behind the mirror, still pinning his own star onto his black shirt. A garter adorned his upper arm. At least he was spared the fringed vest.

I was one swig into a Deschutes ale when two men appeared from the back room. Rangers, both of them, but not clean-cut regimental actives like Moulson and Booker. The man in the lead was rangy, late thirties, and dark in both hair and very tanned skin. He had the chin-up-chest-out walk that only career officers and cherry boots fresh out of basic training hung on to for long. The rangy man dressed like an officer, too. Business casual in chinos and a white button-down, instead of the jeans and polo shirt that were virtually the civilian uniform of younger Rangers. He marched straight for the door, targeting his next destination.

Five steps and ten years of age behind him sauntered the second Ranger. Shaggy light brown hair framed his fox-like face. He wore a tight T-shirt reading MASTODON over a graphic of a bearded skull. As he passed my seat, he nodded to me in lazy recognition. I didn't have a shield tattoo like his, but I guess I was just as easy to classify.

As the mismatched pair of Rangers left the saloon, a third man sidled out from the back rooms. He was a character. Almost a caricature. Six-foot-eight and as lean as a lamppost, in blue denim from head to toe, interrupted only by a big oval belt buckle of polished copper. A leather band encircled his forehead and tied back his heavy gray ponytail. His ensemble was nearly enough to distract from a fresh purplish bruise under his right eye. He was counting a slim roll of cash as he walked.

Part of his height came from cowboy boots made of green python skin. Booker had described the saloon's owner as a scarecrow with boots. Couldn't be two like this one.

"Mr. Seebright," I said. "Got a minute?"

He tucked the roll of bills into his shirt pocket. "Kin I do for you?"

"You had some trouble here last night. A man was attacked."

"What of it?"

"I heard you tried to keep the fight from escalating." I pointed at his face. "That how you got the shiner?"

He lifted a hand to touch his eye, reflexively. "Lester's elbow. Stupid move on my part, jumping into that scrap. You know him?"

"Lester? No. I know the guy he was attacking. The one arrested for shooting Erle Sharples." I held up a hand in peace, as Seebright grimaced. "I wanted to thank you for not letting Lester or whoever it was stomp his head in."

Seebright huffed. "Maybe I woulda, if I'd known."

"Tell me what happened."

"You already know what happened. You just said it."

"I know what Leo can remember, which isn't much. What started the fight?"

He glanced meaningfully at the entrance. "We got lunch folks coming in."

"It won't take more than five minutes of your time. I'll help set the tables, if you want."

Seebright huffed again, but moved to half sit, half lean against the barstool two seats down from me. "I remember noticing your friend before all the commotion started. Real quiet sort. So much so that I supposed he might be a little stoned. He sat over there against the wall"—he pointed a long finger—"and ate his stew and drank Cokes for an hour. Seemed content to just be. It was a slow night, so I didn't mind him taking up the table."

Erle Sharples had been shot in the early morning. Then twelve hours later, Leo walks into the Trading Post Saloon and orders dinner. What had he been doing all day?

"Who is Lester?" I said.

"Lester is . . . well, he's a problem for us. Grew up here in town, and in and out of our jail, too, on account of his temper. I guess he heard about what happened to Erle and went hunting for your friend. Called him a couple names I ain't gonna repeat, your friend being a Japanese or whatever. I was coming around from behind the bar to tell Lester to shuffle his ass down the road, and right then he punched your fella Leo out of his chair. Kicked him, too."

"Then you stopped Lester," I said.

"Stopped, naw. Slowed is more like." Seebright touched his face again. "Haven't been in a fight since I was a young buck. Forgot how much it hurts. Your friend got up and hit Lester with his dinner plate so fast I thought he mighta killed Lester dead on the spot. Those dishes are made not to bust when you drop 'em."

"And then Leo ran."

"Out the back, like he knew the place by heart."

He probably had. Leo would identify the entry and exit points in a new space instinctively, just as I had.

"Those boys—some of 'em friends of Lester's—they took off right after him," Seebright continued.

"One thing I don't understand. How did Lester know to come looking? He found Leo even before the cops did."

Seebright shrugged and stood up. "Small town. Maybe he heard it from his brother Wayne. He's our constable."

Constable Beacham. The town cop who'd bashed Leo with his baton. I was getting very interested in the Beacham family.

The saloon owner must have caught my expression. "I wouldn't read much into that. Our town here, a lot of us live in each other's back pockets. Everybody knows everybody's business. Especially if you go back a few generations, like me. Or Erle."

"If you and he were friends, I'm sorry," I said.

Seebright shifted uncertainly. "Not exactly friends. Erle weren't really sociable. But we were young together."

"Thanks," I said again. "You might have saved Leo's life, jumping in."

"It's my place," Seebright said. "Can't let it be soiled like that." I put out a hand, and he shook it.

"Van Shaw," I said.

"You seem a good sort, Mr. Shaw. I hope your friend is worth it."

Me, too, muttered a sly voice in the back of my mind.

SIX

OUTSIDE, I FOUND MORE heralds of the coming Rally. American flags fluttered over the shops, the folds from their packaging still apparent. A shoe store advertised terrain runs every day at 0600, targeting the active-duty Rangers who had to keep themselves razor-sharp, even on a weekend bender. Someone had hung a butcher-paper sign outside the hair salon calling for volunteers to help with Rally events—*See a Redcap!* it read. I didn't know what a Redcap was, but I could already feel a growing energy in the town, like kids before summer vacation. Or maybe animals before an earthquake.

My new friends Moulson and Booker had told me over lunch that the shooting competitions were the most popular events, and that General Macomber and the organizers offered serious prizes for the top shooters. I guessed that Erle Sharples had hired Leo to get the gun shop ready for the rush of customers. Booker had taken pains to point out that there were entry fees, too, and all proceeds went to a charitable trust. Booker was a convert to the Rally's mission.

The draw of the Rally, the younger Rangers had confessed, was that it wasn't a family event. No WAGs—wives and girlfriends—no kids, no responsibilities, just blowing off steam for the entire weekend. Moulson had claimed that he'd nursed a hangover for two full days after the last one.

Actives like Booker and Moulson couldn't go entirely off the rails. There would be a few officers attending. Rangers were expected to represent the regiment no matter where they were or what they were doing. To earn the scroll—the signifier that we had passed the brutal assessment and selection program and claimed a place in the 75th—every single day. But smart officers turned a blind eye to an acceptable level of madness, and even offered some leniency when that eye couldn't avoid seeing something.

I'd been on the receiving end of that kind of clemency once myself. In the wild celebrations not long after passing selection, I had joined some buddies at a massive beach party on the Chattahoochee River. The beach had been closed, not that that slowed anyone down. Between the soldiers and the locals we had enough beer cans on hand to build a battleship out of the empties. Hardly any of us were old enough to legally drink in the state of Georgia, including me. Someone had rolled oil drums onto the beach. A few gasoline-soaked logs in each made for fine campfires. Happenings got very loud. Signal flares and fireworks may have been deployed. Authorities were called. I had a vague memory of being corralled into an unsteady mass of other Benning soldiers—we outnumbered the available sets of handcuffs by something like twenty-to-one—and ordered to wait for the MPs.

I was just sober enough to be terrified that my career was over before it had begun. The training cadres had pounded the lesson into us that if we were found wanting, the result would be RFS—released for standards. Exiled. What the fuck was I going to do now?

Luckily, a major from the 75th lived close and arrived first. He cut the newborn Rangers out from the milling herd of drunk soldiers, marched us far enough down the nearby access road to be out of sight of the Georgia cops, and proceeded to curse at us so long that some of our group might have been halfway to sober by the time he'd finished.

Our only saving grace was that we hadn't actually destroyed anything on the beach, probably because there was nothing there to wreck except ourselves. An M923 cargo truck rolled up. The major ordered the bunch of us onto its flatbed, which we proceeded to paint with a lot of vomit on the way to a waiting barracks at Benning.

The next day was one of the worst of my military life. A squad of merciless robots disguised as cadre sergeants screamed our bleary troop awake after two hours of sleep. They hounded us out to where the major awaited us at the Darby Queen—the grueling two-mile-long obstacle course that had broken dozens of candidates in our class alone. Our groans could have been heard from back at the mess hall. Having earned our scrolls, we thought we had seen the last of the Darby, at least for a while.

The major taught us better. He and the sergeants ran us in barfing, lurching teams of four through the Darby. Timed. After three hellish rounds, the major began allowing the fastest team to return to base and light duty. All of the other teams had to run the course again. I saw the Darby half a dozen times before my team finally finished in the top spot. Only downing a handful of Aleve allowed me to walk like a Homo sapiens the next day. I heard a rumor that the last team ran the Darby eleven times, which was probably bullshit, unless the major had also arranged for their dead bodies to be quietly buried.

But none of us lost our place in the regiment. No one got busted down in rank or arrested. Smoking us into the dirt and making sure we remembered it forever was punishment enough. If any active Rangers got out of hand in Mercy River, I imagined they would regret it one way if not the other.

Leo had said his gear and prescriptions were stowed at a girlfriend's place. Forty-one Piccolo Road. I checked the map. Piccolo was at least four miles from town, as the crow flew. I walked back to the truck and drove south, following the blue line on the phone's screen. It didn't take long for the crudely paved streets to become gravel roads. Each intersection stretched farther from the last, until the flat sheets of land between each road could be measured in hectares. I passed a series of greenhouse tunnels made of transparent polyethylene sheeting, each a hundred yards long and tall enough for a man to stand inside. A rabbit dashed in front of the truck, missing its tires by a whisker. It vanished into the roadside brush before I got another glimpse.

Piccolo Road didn't even rate gravel, just hard-packed dirt. The first sign of habitation was a steel mailbox with 41 stenciled in cracked white paint on the side. About fifty yards down a lane behind the mailbox, a small gray-green house with white shutters waited, as if shading itself under the broad leaves of the surrounding cottonwood trees.

I drove up the lane. The house was even smaller up close. Three or four rooms at most. A concrete slab in the earth served for a driveway. There were no other cars in sight, and I wondered if Leo hiked into town every day, rain or shine. That would be like him.

I knocked, without getting an answer. Walking around back, I gazed out over the fallow field behind the house. No one nearby. A Suzuki dirt bike rested against the rusty screen door, its knobbed tires and body so uniformly covered in soil I had to look twice to identify its paint as blue. Leo knew motorcycles. Maybe the bike was his.

I tried the front door again. Nobody at home. To hell with it. Leo needed his meds, and I wasn't about to wait for Ganz to convince Lieutenant Yerby to open the house for us. I used Dono's old set of picks to open the Schlage dead bolt in less than half a minute. Easy.

When I'd first returned to Seattle, my extralegal skills had been for shit. Years had passed since I'd so much as stolen a car. But the past eighteen months had knocked off all of that rust. I hadn't been ripping off Clyde Hill mansions or looting customs warehouses like Dono and I used to, but circumstances had given me good reason to regain the old touch.

Maybe it was a mind-set thing. I had a need to be good at burglary, so my fingers recollected how to use the picks. If I wanted to crack a safe, my instincts guided the drill bit.

On one of my first serious jobs with Dono, shortly after I'd turned thirteen, we broke into a transport hub for train cargo. After he'd finished greasing the alarm, he let me take my shot at unlocking the interior door while he unloaded the power tools we would use to bust open the crates inside. I beat the multipoint dead bolt before he had unzipped the second kit.

"*Tá sé ó gcliabhán aige,*" he had muttered, mostly to himself. Meaning I'd had it since the cradle, the Irish way of saying I was a natural. Dono wasn't a man given to idle compliments. I remembered the ones I'd heard forever.

The front door opened directly into the living room. I caught a scent of lavender. The tiny house was almost a shotgun shack. A stubby hallway past the combination kitchen and dining nook led straight to the back door.

Someone had gone to the effort to make the place as cheerful as the scuffed drywall and garage-sale furniture allowed. Bright colors won out over consistency. Wicker stools in each corner served as stands for potted ferns and cacti. A red batik sheet had been pinned up on the largest wall like a tapestry. On the mantel, a painting with no frame leaned against the chimney bricks, showing a sun inside a spiral of golden stars.

All that, and a pink scarf draped over the reading lamp. The jackets hung on pegs by the front door were all women's, except for one anorak that might fit Leo. Below the pegs, a pale blue motorcycle helmet rested by a dish of keys and spare change.

I felt the padding of the helmet. Still warm.

"You can come out," I called into the house. "I'm a friend of Leo's."

Ten seconds passed before a woman emerged into the short hall from what I guessed was the bedroom. It was difficult to see much more than her lean outline in the unlit interior, but I caught brunette hair that descended in spikes to her shoulders and a white tank top over cropped blue jeans and boots. She stood poised on her toes, half turned toward the escape offered by the back door.

"Stay there," she said. "I have a gun."

"Okay."

"I'll use it."

"I believe you. My name's Van."

She risked a step closer, one hand held behind her back. The extra three feet brought her into the light from the kitchen window. Her large dark brown eyes dominated a heart-shaped face that didn't lack for pleasing features. One pierced brow lent her expression an extra measure of doubt.

"I know that name. Let me see you," she said, as if demanding equal time.

I took my own step forward and turned my head to show her the scars. Once in a blue moon, the damn things came in handy.

She relaxed a hair, but stayed where she was. "Why did you break in?"

"You know that Leo's been arrested?" I asked.

She gave a slow nod.

"I've come for his prescription meds, if he's got any. And some clothes."

"You saw Leo? Is he okay?" she said.

"He's banged up, but yeah. He'll be all right."

"They're saying in town that he murdered Erle."

"Leo says it's a mistake." I wouldn't trouble Leo's latest girlfriend with the damning evidence against him. That would become public knowledge soon enough. "I brought an attorney. He's with Leo now."

"Good." She glanced behind me at the door, still ajar. "How did you open that?"

No point in dodging it. "I picked the lock."

Her head tilted, appraising. "Van the thief. From Seattle."

Jesus. I was going to have a conversation with Leo about his choice of pillow talk. How long had he been seeing this girl? The Leo I knew could time most of his relationships with an hourglass. This new one might be in the top echelon for looks, but he'd been in town only a week or two and he was already sharing my secrets along with his own.

"Pepper spray?" I said, glancing toward the hand still behind her back.

She brought the neon-colored can out to confirm it. "Guess I'm not much on bluffing."

"Worth a try." Though someone who'd really held a gun would have shown it, to drive the threat home.

"Leo's medicine is here," she said, motioning to the bedroom. "I had the same idea to bring it to him."

"Leo didn't tell me your name."

"No," she said, as if that choice were obvious. "It's Dez. Short for my last name, Desidra."

"Okay, Dez. I'm guessing I shouldn't say anything about you and Leo around town." The tiny house was feminine from top to bottom, but that didn't mean Dez didn't have another boyfriend somewhere.

"That would be better," she said. "Thanks. We—we keep things private."

"How were you going to explain dropping his meds off at the jail?"

"I was going to find his public defender and tell him that Leo had left these in the bathroom of the coffeehouse. Leo goes there every morning, for his black eye. A drip coffee with two shots."

"No wonder he needs sleeping pills."

"I'll get them." She went to the bedroom and returned immediately with a shoulder bag slung over her back, and a large plastic grocery sack containing shirts and pants. She'd packed Leo's things before I showed up and interrupted. She handed me the sack. It rattled like a pillow-sized maraca with the pill bottles.

"I can't visit Leo," she said. "At the jail. But I want to. Would you tell him that?"

"Sure. You two didn't meet for the first time just this week, did you?"

Dez smiled. It was only about halfway to amused.

"I'm why he came here," she said.

She retrieved her helmet and walked down the hall and out the back door. A moment later the Suzuki engine chattered to life. It revved once and then moved away.

She hadn't asked for any details about Leo's arrest. Maybe she already knew. Mercy River was a small town, as everyone kept telling me.

I walked to the cramped kitchen, no bigger than a sailboat's galley, and looked out the sliver of window. Dez was racing the dirt bike across the fallow field behind the house, blue helmet on her head and the shoulder bag bouncing with each rut she hit. Dust obscured her, yellow clouds chasing her on the wind as the angry wasp buzz of the bike faded into the distance.

SEVEN

GANZ HAD TEXTED ME to pick him up at the county courthouse, a utilitarian building adjacent to the sheriff's station.

"Did the cops screw up the evidence?" I said as Ganz climbed into the truck. "Enough to matter?"

"Hello to you, too. Nice to see you. You're no doubt aware that this entire burg is filled to the brim with extremely lethal individuals like yourself?"

"I've learned."

"Well, the occupying force had secured—I use the military jargon deliberately—every single damn room and rental property available in the county. Probably every dry ditch, too."

"So we're sleeping in the truck."

"God. No. Vivian from my office found an acceptable rental house without a deposit holding it. She outbid the previous tenants by a wide margin, and the owner caved. So if we find a group of angry men with suitcases on the lawn, just smile and keep going. Thataway, pardner." He pointed. I drove.

"The chain of evidence against Leo is solid enough to hold up," he said. "Sorry to disillusion you."

"Is there any good news?"

"Not yet. The circuit court judge for the arraignment tomorrow is known to be a hard case. If Leo was a pillar of this fine community, maybe we could convince the judge to take the risk on bail. But he's not. Turn here."

"I've got Leo's meds and some clothes." I nodded toward the grocery sack on the passenger seat floor. "He'll need those tonight."

"I'll take them to the jail after I shower," he said. "It would be best if you don't show your face at the station while Lieutenant Yerby's around."

"Then you can also relay a message: his girlfriend wishes she could visit him."

I didn't have to be looking in Ganz's direction to know he was rolling his eyes.

At the next stop sign, a band of schoolchildren dutifully checked both ways and moved as one through the crosswalk. No adult supervision, but safety in numbers.

Ganz yawned. "You don't seem tired. Why don't you seem tired?"

"Let me read the police report."

"Reports," Ganz corrected. "One from the sheriff's office, and one from the town constable. An actual constable, can you believe it?"

"Beacham."

"Now, how did you know that? Wayne Beacham Jr. That's how he signed it."

"He's the cop who cracked Leo with his baton. And also the brother of Lester Beacham, the asshole who jumped Leo in the saloon."

Ganz glanced at me, but didn't say anything. In another two blocks he pointed at a two-story house painted rose-pink. I pulled into its driveway, next to a four-door Chevy Malibu.

"I hope this place doesn't have roaches," Ganz said, "because the nearest Kimpton is two hundred miles away."

"But there's a decent dry ditch right over there."

I played bellhop and lugged Ganz's two suitcases to the wooden porch of the pink house. His blazer and trousers were wrinkled. First time for everything. "The reports," I reminded him.

He set his attaché on the porch railing and opened it to retrieve a binder-clipped stack of papers. "I'll need these back tonight."

"I'll leave them here when I go to the Rally's opening." And maybe find out more about how the law worked in this town. I grasped the stack of papers in Ganz's hand. He didn't let go.

"Van," Ganz said, "I can see that look on you. Your grandfather had the same expression when somebody crossed him. It scared me then and it scares me now, I don't mind telling you. A reminder of bad times. Just . . . just remember why we're here, all right?"

I'd never known Ganz to be hesitant.

"I'll keep it clean," I said.

"Good. Excellent." He let go of the papers and went to retrieve a handful of assorted keys from under the mat. He handed one ring to me and held up a Chevrolet key. "With the money we're paying, Vivian talked the homeowners into loaning us their car for a day. I won't be forced to have you run me all over town."

"Only one day?"

"By tomorrow evening Leo will be either free on bail or training the bedbugs in his cell to sit and stay. In either circumstance I will be en route to Seattle. You may keep the house through Monday if you're that masochistic, but one night in Mercy River is more than enough for me. Now I need cleansing and a nap and an uninterrupted night to marshal our defense. Talk to you later."

Ganz unlocked the door and grabbed his attaché and one of the suitcases and disappeared inside. I heard him haul the suitcase in steady thumps up the stairs.

I revised my opinion. Ganz wasn't hesitant. He'd been unnerved. His hand on the stack of papers had trembled minutely. And the torrent of words that had followed had helped him regain his composure. Ghosts of our past, coming back to greet us.

Hello, Granddad. I guess part of you really does live on through me.

BEYOND FINDING THE FIRST-FLOOR bedroom and tossing my travel ruck onto the dresser, I didn't waste time exploring our temporary home. I sat down on the slipcovered sofa in the living room and started poring over the police reports.

The first account, less than a quarter of the thickness of the papers from the sheriff's office, was by Wayne Beacham, the town constable. It was dry to the point of dehydration. Constable Beacham had been parked at the intersection of Main Street and Larimer Road, checking out a report of vandalism at a dress store. Erle's Gun Shop was on Larimer. Beacham and the dress store proprietor had both waved to Erle as he drove past on his way to work, at about six-thirty in the morning. The proprietor had gone to get supplies to board up the window while Beacham checked the store for other signs of damage or theft.

Around forty minutes later, a local man named Henry Gillespie stopped to chat with Beacham at his patrol car, while Beacham was helping board up the broken window. Another man named Zeke Caton had passed them, and Gillespie joined Caton to walk down the road to the gun shop. They entered the shop just before its official opening time of seven-thirty A.M. and found Erle lying on the floor. Gillespie had been the one to call 911, while Caton ran to fetch the constable. When Beacham arrived, he ascertained that Erle appeared to be dead, and that the back door to the shop was unlocked. He then closed the shop and radioed the sheriff's office.

That was the extent of Beacham's report, except for the statements that he had taken from the two citizens. Gillespie had come to the shop to buy birdshot shells and shoot the breeze with Erle, who was a long-time acquaintance. Zeke Caton had wanted nine-millimeter rounds for the Rally shooting competitions on Saturday. Both men had Oregon addresses, Gillespie in Mercy River, Caton on a rural route somewhere outside the incorporated towns.

It was Gillespie who had noticed someone pass them and walk down to the shop while he'd been jawing with the constable. Gillespie estimated the time as only ten or twelve minutes before he and Caton had walked down Larimer Road to the shop themselves. Beacham had shortened Gillespie's description to the bare minimum: "Chinese or Japanese. Athlete's build. Black hair." Gillespie was less clear about what the man had been wearing, except that his jacket had been dark, maybe black leather.

It was feasible that there were other men at the Rally who matched that description, although Rangers of Asian background were uncommon. Maybe not as rare as in Mercy River, which was pretty damn white, from what I'd seen. But Leo had worked at Erle's shop for the past week. Too big a coincidence to imagine another buff Asian guy hanging around Erle's place, a full two days before the Rally was due to start.

The sheriff's report dug that hole even deeper. Past the lead deputy's narrative of arriving at the gun shop and securing the premises for the crime scene techs—who had probably still been cataloging the shop when Ganz and I had rolled into town—I found a stack of written statements from store owners nearby who identified Leo as a recent worker at Erle's shop. One of those stores was a coffeehouse on Main Street, two blocks down from Larimer Road where the gun shop was situated. Leo had become a regular customer. I guessed that was the same coffeehouse that Leo's secret girlfriend Dez had mentioned.

The second half of the stack contained the incident report from the attack on Leo in the Trading Post Saloon. Most of it witness statements. A jumbled lot, but they largely confirmed what Seebright had told me: Lester Beacham physically assaulted Leo, the fight escalated, and Leo was pursued out of the saloon and into the hills. He had outrun the mob—no surprise there—but they'd chased him down with off-road vehicles. Someone had alerted sheriff's deputies to the trouble, but by the time they drove a Jeep up the hill, Constable Beacham had subdued and apprehended the suspect.

Subdued. There was no report from Beacham about finding and clubbing Leo. I wondered if his narrative had been deliberately left out of the reports, or not written in the first place. Maybe Ganz could make something useful out of the omission.

There was also no lab report from the crime scene team who'd driven to Mercy River from Prineville. We couldn't expect that to be completed for at least a day or two. A single sheet, empty but for three lines, listed the items removed from the victim's pockets—a ring of keys and a folding knife and a packet of Red Man. I checked the back of the sheet and flipped back through the reports again. The police didn't mention taking a cell phone into evidence. Had Erle been the type to reject modern gadgets?

The last pages showed Leo's fingerprints, and photographs of the initial print dustings of the .45 shells found at the scene. The lab techs had yet to confirm it, but the prints looked like a match to me. A Vietnam-vintage Colt M1911 had been found on the floor of the shop, apparently wiped clean. On the outside. Rounds still in the chamber and magazine carried more of the same fingerprints.

Add that to the blood found on Leo's shoes, which I couldn't delude myself might turn out to be some other person's than Erle's, and the case against Leo edged past bleak to verge on insurmountable.

The only bright spot—or at least not another black hole—was the absence of any video. An appendix to the report noted that Lieutenant Yerby and the crime scene team had viewed the gun shop's security feed, and determined that Erle had entered the shop at 6:32 A.M., and switched off the cameras himself at 6:40. Nothing had been captured after that. The sheriff's office would be reaching out to the security firm on the off chance that additional footage was sent to the cloud. That sounded like a Hail Mary to me, but it showed that for all Yerby's faults, he was at least competent enough to run down every lead.

Erle had turned off his cameras, and within—what? half an hour?—he'd been shot and killed. With nobody in or out of the shop except Leo, and an eyewitness to prove it.

Damn. I'd been holding out hope that the witnesses had ID'd the wrong man, or that the cops had bungled the evidence. But if anything, the police report had shaken my certainty about Leo's innocence.

Worst of all was his attitude. He must have entered the shop, seen the body, and for some bizarre reason not reported it. His arrest wasn't simply a screwup by the cops, as he claimed. Why hadn't Leo told me that he'd found Erle dead? My friend's evasiveness rang like a missing key on a piano, a hollow note that couldn't be ignored. If a jury saw it the same way, Leo was tailor-made for a fast conviction, and a long stretch in a small box.

EIGHT

I LEFT THE POLICE REPORTS on the coffee table and grabbed my barn jacket and Mariners cap to set out for town on foot. My leg muscles were aching for a walk after all of the driving during the past day. The sun had begun its dive behind the hills, leaving a clear sky and that same steady cool wind that had blown all afternoon.

The walk gave me time to think about Leo. I had to believe he was innocent, despite the evidence and his own strange behavior. He'd told me straight out that he hadn't killed Erle Sharples. If I didn't trust him on that, I didn't trust him on anything.

So who had shot Erle? And why? Whoever the killer had been, they must have arrived at the shop before Leo that same morning. Neither Beacham nor the two witnesses had reported seeing anyone else. The back entrance had been found unlocked. Erle had turned off his security cameras. Had he been doing something that he didn't want captured on the feed, when someone slipped in and shot him? Or had Erle been expecting them? Maybe Erle had let his killer in through the back door himself.

I wanted a look at the gun shop. Its address put it roughly between my path through the residential blocks and the town center, and I changed course to stride past the school's athletic field. Any fall season football or soccer practices had ended for the day. A few high school kids in MRHS Rams sweatshirts and shorts jogged around the track in loose packs, more socializing than exercising.

Erle's Gun Shop and Firing Range lay at the terminus of Larimer Road, a sloped dead-end branch off Main, no more than a hundred and fifty yards from end to end. At the top of the road, I passed the dress store where Constable Wayne Beacham had been investigating their vandalized window on the morning of the murder. Wood slats and cardboard covered the broken pane of glass. From the dress store I could see an unbroken stretch of Main Street for a quarter mile in both directions. The heart of the town to the north, and the long reach south toward residences and farms and eventually isolated homesteads like Dez's.

The short road was quiet at dusk and looked to stay that way. Only one structure stood within a hundred feet of the gun shop. A two-story brick storefront, under renovation, its rooms empty and X's of masking tape still marking newly installed windows.

Instead of the imitation western façade of the town center or the boutique trimmings of its dress store, Erle had limited his design efforts to broad corrugated steel sheets bolted directly onto the shop's adobe walls. There were no windows. An accordion gate extended the breadth of the locked entrance to create a second barrier. Or a third, if you counted the police tape sealing the doorjamb.

Attached to the side of the shop was a simple carport, another large sheet of galvanized steel held aloft by four-by-four posts. A Honda ATV sat within like a faithful hound, squatting low on fat muddy tires, its bright red paint turned purple by the shadows.

From under the narrow awning above the door, a closed-circuit camera stared down at the space in front of the shop's entrance. The housing of the camera had been painted over with the same brown paint as the wooden awning. But the trim shape of the camera was familiar. Distinctive.

I looked around. No one in sight. I risked climbing up to balance on the railing of the front steps and scratched at the brown paint with my car key.

Under the flecks of brown, the side of the camera was emblazoned with the maker's logo. One word crowned by a blue laurel wreath. Kjárr.

I knew Kjárr. Every thief knew it. An alarm firm based in Oslo. Top of the line, for the private sector. Around Seattle, I might expect to find a Kjárr system installed at a Saudi exile's Broadmoor estate, or in a tech exec's penthouse condo in Bellevue. I would not expect to find Kjárr providing a line of defense for what was, at most, a hundred grand worth of merchandise in backwater Oregon. The Kjárr system alone probably cost that much.

Erle Sharples might have been paranoid. Or he'd landed a serious deal on a used system and reinstalled it at his shop. But if that were the case, why not go ahead and plaster the famous brand name on every door to ward off burglars?

No. Erle wanted his shop very secure, and to keep that security to himself. The question was why.

I could beat a Kjárr, given time and some computer-assisted equipment to fool the Wi-Fi signal. But I didn't have to. The alarm had been turned off when Erle was killed. Any man security-conscious enough to want a top-flight system wouldn't trust the local LE with the codes. Odds were good that Yerby and team had simply left the alarm off and relied on the shop's dead bolts to keep things secure.

I'd test that theory later. Right now, I wanted to join the crowd for the Rally's opening night, to see if I could catch wind of Constable Wayne Beacham or his brother Lester. If the constable really had been spouting off about the shooting to his family and God knew who else in town, maybe Ganz could use that as grounds for moving Leo to another location. A safer one.

THE MERCY RIVER TOWN hall was an actual hall, extending for half a block beyond its comparatively small entrance. A bronze plaque on the post by the broad stone steps declared that the original hall had been built in 1898, and thanked the sponsors who'd overseen a renovation in 2005. Those benefactors had opted for a timeless aspect, red brick and white-paned windows, unremarkable but sturdy.

Dozens of men milled around the grass, talking and laughing with language raw enough to blister paint. It took me back. There was something unique about Spec Ops when we got together in large numbers. Even separated by different social classes and generations—I saw motorheads and Hawaiian shirts and businessmen in Burberry rain-coats, ears with gauges stretching their lobes into circles and ears with hearing aids—we all examined the world with similar eyes. Watchful. Assessing. Categorizing everything in our surroundings into threat or opportunity or neither, even as we laughed and hugged one another in greeting. It didn't matter if we were honed like razors off our last de-ployment or carrying twenty years of civilian chow around our middles. Put a hundred of us together, and you could feel a charge in the air like ozone foreshadowing a thunderstorm.

I liked it. I'd missed it.

The average age of the men in the crowd was a fraction below thirty. It might skew even lower as more active-duty men arrived for the Rally on forty-eight-hour passes. Which meant the overwhelming majority of us hadn't known service without being at war. I could have figured that out by counting the number of KIA bracelets adorn-ing wrists. Each ring of black metal engraved with the name of a fallen brother.

I spotted Moulson and Booker, the active Rangers. They had changed from their camos into golf shirts and jeans. Moulson waved me over.

"This the starting line?" I said.

"Just in time," said Booker. No one had given a signal, but the volume of conversation quieted and men dropped cigarettes to crush them out, as the crowd began to move toward the entrance.

The space inside the long hall had been cleared, benches and plastic folding chairs pushed to either side along the walls. A few rows at the very front had been left alone, close to a stage. Three men in wheel-chairs chatted in an open area next to the rows. A portly man in a knit sweater excused himself as we made room for him to pass. He supported his gait with a cane in each hand as he walked slowly toward the seats in front.

Moulson nudged me with an elbow. "Okay if I ask you a question?"

"Sure."

His eyes flicked to the left side of my face. "Is that injury why you left the Army?"

"No. This happened on my first rotation with the battalion, in Iraq. I was twenty."

"Fuck me. And you went back?"

"Seemed like a good idea at the time."

"It was me, I might have packed it in."

"Doubtful," I said. "After earning my way into the regiment, I wanted to do what they taught us to do. I hadn't gotten much of a chance."

Plus the idea of going back to civilian life, with a face still looking like a mountain lion had mauled it, had scared me a lot more than combat at that age.

"I hear that," Booker said. "It would feel like you were getting cheated."

"Plus I missed the sergeants' smiling faces," I said.

A man climbed the stairs to the stage, one step at a time. He was somewhere past fifty, and built like a well-fed grizzly, his limbs thick but short in comparison to his substantial chest and belly. That impression was heightened by his deliberate movements and his heavy chocolate-colored wool shirt and pants.

"That's Macomber," said Booker.

I placed the slight stiffness in the general's gait. At least part of his left leg was artificial. He stepped forward to the edge of the stage.

"You're all veterans," Macomber said, his basso profundo voice carrying easily over the dimming sounds of movement and muttering, "so you know nothing's official unless some asshole gives a speech."

The audience laughed. Macomber smiled, too, his open face growing even livelier.

"Welcome. I see a lot of faces I haven't met yet. And if I haven't met you, that means you're new to the Rally, because every man here last year shook my hand and shared his story. I look forward to hearing yours."

The crowd was hushed, listening. So was I. A small part of that silence was the reflexive attention of soldiers to anything that a senior officer said. But most of our focus was due to the man himself. He stood as solid as a marble pillar, his smooth bald scalp over a ring of dark hair the brightest piece of him, save for his eyes.

"We're growing," Macomber continued. "In numbers, and in influence. Our mission is simple. Even a politician could understand it." Another chuckle from the crowd. Behind me, I felt more spectators pressing into the hall, eager to hear Macomber's words.

"Every support possible, to every Ranger, at any time," Macomber said, reciting it like a credo. "In the past six months alone, the Ranger Rally has contributed thousands of hours and tens of thousands of dollars to hospital and therapeutic services, mental health, family care for Rangers overseas or those out of work, education grants, and career guidance. That's what we've done with only a dozen people on our year-round staff, our volunteers, and a couple of corporate sponsors. Imagine what we'll do this year.

"There are other organizations, with similar goals. The Army runs some of them, and good people have created their own groups to shore up what the Army can't or won't do. Which is a hell of a lot." Macomber held up a hand to quell the hooting. "But the Rally is for us. Just us. Our brothers, and our families." The jeers turned into sounds of encouragement. "Those lost, and those who carry on." The sounds melded into a single shout.

"If you're new here . . ." Macomber waited until the noise quieted again. "If you're new, you might be worrying that I'll hit you up to volunteer." He smiled. "I will *absolutely* hit you up to volunteer. And you'll do it. Not just because it's the right thing to do. Not only because when you need it, the Rally will be there to help you, too. You'll step forward because that's what we do. Rangers lead the way."

"All the way," we answered the regimental motto.

"One of the Rally's guiding principles is that we share our experiences. From combat, certainly, but also life in the service, and your lives stateside since you've left. That's what this is about. Once family, always family. Those of you who have been here before will recognize the Wall of Remembrance we're creating on Main Street, where we record the sacrifices both we and our brothers have made and those that we continue to make. Introduce the newcomers to the Wall. It's important that we know our history, past and current.

"But in the meantime, we have some celebrating to do. This town hall will be our gathering point for the duration. All of the information on the Rally's events will be posted outside. If you have questions or need directions to an event, ask a Redcap."

Macomber waved a hand toward the rear of the hall. We all turned to see a dozen young women, some carrying clipboards and rolls of paper tickets. Each of them wore a scarlet baseball cap with a Double-R insignia on the crown. A predictable chorus of whistles erupted from a few younger men in the crowd.

"Stow that," Macomber said. "Redcaps are Rally employees, and they run the show when it comes to organizing our events and contribution booths. I'll put my plastic foot up the ass of any man fool enough to disrespect them. And I expect all of you to do the same."

I had to admire the pivot. Macomber had turned every right-minded guy at the Rally into the Redcaps' protective older brothers. At least temporarily.

"One last thing," said the general. "You may already have heard that a lifelong resident of Mercy River was shot and killed yesterday. Leaving aside the terrible crime, this town has suffered a loss, and every one of you knows firsthand how that feels. Please treat our generous hosts with the respect they deserve, and play safe out there this weekend. Hard, but safe." That earned another laugh.

"Now, given the forecast is for rain, we figured that holding tonight's barbecue inside the town grange might help keep the sauce on the ribs. Get your butts over there and get some food. You can consider that an order."

Applause and a final emphatic roar gave Macomber a fanfare in his slow walk off the stage.

"Man," Moulson said, "he was even better than last year."

"Who is he?" I asked. "Macomber wasn't a CO while I was around."

Booker nodded. "I talked to one of the older guys last year who served under him in Kosovo, back when the general was just a captain. That's where Macomber lost the leg. He stayed with the regiment another few years after that. The shake-ups after 9/11 put him in the Pentagon for a while, my guy said."

"A hard-charger?"

"He retired as a major general before he hit his thirty."

Unusual. I looked around at the crowd of over three hundred, drifting out of the hall and toward the free food. "So now he does this."

"Don't piss on it," Booker said. "The Rally paid the balance on our buddy Tag's tuition and books last year, whatever the GI Bill didn't cover. I'm aiming for the same help when I get loose."

"No urination at this station," I said. "Macomber knows how to motivate. What was that about corporate sponsors?"

Moulson said something about an auto parts chain with a former Ranger on its board, whom Macomber had convinced to subsidize car repairs for families in need. I wasn't fully listening, distracted by one of the Redcaps handing out drink tickets to eager men. She was striking enough to draw attention on her own merit, with big dark eyes and a toned body.

Dez, Leo's secret girlfriend. Working for the Rally.

And as I allowed myself to flow with the crowd back toward the street, I saw more townspeople wearing red windbreakers acting as guides, motioning the way toward the grange and handing out flyers printed with the weekend's schedule. Volunteers, or maybe another way that the Rally channeled dollars into the sleepy local economy.

The grange turned out to be a short walk away, on a side street parallel from the Methodist church that Ganz and I had passed during our conversation. I smelled the savory aroma of cooking meat long before I saw the Grange itself. Moulson and Booker quickened their steps.

I hung back. A silver-gray Ford Interceptor was angle-parked in the middle of a cross street, blue and yellow lettering on the side. POLICE in capital letters, MERCY RIVER in a smaller type underneath. The vehicle was about ten years off the assembly line, and I guessed it had been bought on the cheap from a larger department, lights and push bumper and all, and repainted for the town's use.

It had to be Constable Beacham's. I looked around and spotted the man through the crowd, half a block away, talking with a local. I'd expected some rent-a-cop with a beer belly, but Beacham was young, wide-shouldered, and clean as a needle in a crisp white shirt, navy-blue pants, and blue cap. His shoes had a mirror finish that was echoed in his service belt.

The belt held Beacham's sidearm on the right and the nightstick that had clubbed Leo hanging on his left. The sight of the baton made me aware of my own pulse.

I walked over.

"Hey," I said. Beacham and the townie he'd been talking to, a bearded guy as broad as an armoire, both turned. "The general told us there was a shooting yesterday, and my girlfriend, she's kind of freaked out now. Everything secure?"

"No sweat," said the big man through the tangle of his beard. He had the solid swell of gut that Beacham lacked, and a bottle of ale in his hand to keep it in tune. His soiled corduroy coat and tattered watch cap completed the look of a man well past giving a shit. "The motherfucker's gonna burn, thanks to Wayne here. He coldcocked the punk."

"I was just first on the scene," Beacham said with a tight smile. He was excessively chiseled—strong jaw, straight nose, long sideburns forming perfect rectangles. So proportional that his left profile could have been a mirror image of his right.

That wasn't the only symmetry about his face, I realized. Beacham and the big guy had the same nose, the same brow ridge and blue eyes. The larger man's sagebrush beard and their differences in size and general hygiene had thrown me off at first.

Brother Lester. My luck was running hot.

"Holy shit, man." I clapped the constable on the shoulder. "Way to kick ass."

"A team effort," said Lester, protesting. "I was the one found the little turd in the saloon."

"Wait." I pointed at Lester. "Was this the bar fight I heard about? Was that part of the same deal?"

"Hell, yeah," Lester said. "*I* was the first sumbitch on the scene, if you get right fuckin' down to it. I tagged that egg roll so hard it's amazing he ever got up again."

"Lester," Beacham said.

"You're like a bounty hunter," I said to Lester. "The cops give you the wanted poster, and you track 'em down."

Lester roared. "Yes! Where's my reward, bro?" He touched his head, prodding at the watch cap with thick fingers. "Hazard pay."

But Beacham was scrutinizing me. "You're here with the Rally?"

"Sure," I said. "Best party anywhere. Not counting your saloon."

"Did I see you around the sheriff's station earlier today?" Beacham pressed.

I was rescued by a Redcap with a blond ponytail pulled through the hole at the back of her scarlet hat, who appeared with a heaping plate of ribs and macaroni salad.

"Wayne, we're bringing food out to all the officers on duty. You want some?" she offered. I wasn't sure she was only talking about the ribs.

"Good to meet you guys," I said, and beat it before Beacham's memory got a firm lock on me.

It might not hold up in court, but I was certain that the constable had—intentionally or not—sicced his big bad brother on Leo. Maybe it had been pure chance that Lester had found Leo in the saloon before the cops did. But it didn't improve my opinion of law enforcement in Mercy River.

Dez crossed my path. She spotted me, and her eyes darted away quickly. I wanted to ask her whether it was normal for Leo to go into Erle's shop so early in the morning, but she had hastened her walk and was stretching the distance between us. Maybe wary of people connecting her to Leo through me. Whatever their relationship was, Dez and Leo both appeared dead set on keeping it private.

NINE

Aт THE BACK OF Erle's Gun Shop, in the deep dark provided by
the hill looming behind the building, I picked my way around wheel-
barrows and stacks of old rebar and other signs of abandoned projects.
Maybe Sharples had planned on expanding the shop or building an
outdoor shooting range. As it was, the clutter made for a slow and
cautious path to the back door. Ahead of me, small animals scurried
away into the safety of the brush. Rats or opossums.

I was ninety percent sure that the alarm and cameras had been left
deactivated by the cops. But safety first. I shielded my face and reached
up to drape a rag over the camera housing.

And paused.

The power line leading from the camera into the shop was twisted
where it met the hole in the adobe wall. I risked turning on my penlight, closing the beam in my fist and allowing a sliver of the light between my fingers to show me more. I tugged the wire away from the
wall. The rubberized housing had been carefully stripped away to expose the wires beneath. Not cut. Cutting the power or the fiber-optic
line to a Kjárr camera would have the same noisy result as kicking in
the front door.

I could make out jagged impressions left by an alligator clip. Someone had been checking the power flow to the camera, before pushing
the line back into the wall to hide the damage. I replaced the line where
I'd found it, and returned to my original task of picking the lock.

The gun shop was dead black inside. The low creak of the door
echoed faintly, hinting at an expansive space beyond. Shining the penlight around, I saw that I'd opened the emergency exit of an indoor
firing range. The exit stood at the end of a row of half a dozen shooting
stations, with the span of the range off to my left. White rectangles of
silhouette targets hung at the far end like shy phantoms.

I closed the door behind me and walked down the row to the front
of the shop. My nose picked up scents of oil and burnt powder permanently seeped into the pine walls.

In comparison to the range, the store section of Erle's business was
small, most of it taken up by the employees-only area behind the register. Erle had kept things orderly. A few tall, tight rows of ammunition
and cleaning sets and other supplies. A pair of homemade plywood
workbenches flanked the main display counter. Each bench had neatly
organized tools hanging on pegboards behind it. The bench on the
right was set up for hand-loading ammunition, with shell presses in
different sizes bolted to its edge and a precision scale for weighing
powder.

That's where Leo would have worked. Taking shells from the firing
range, perhaps, or making custom loads on order. If he'd been loading
.45 ACP rounds, that could explain his prints on the rounds removed
from the vintage Colt that Erle had been shot with. The killer might
have grabbed the handiest weapon in the shop, maybe the .45 waiting on the workbench to test-fire the custom loads, and had used it on
Erle. He'd wiped his prints from the gun but wouldn't bother with the
rounds left in the magazine.

An array of handguns and fancy hunting knives lay on tiered shelves
inside the glass display counter. The counter's surfaces were smeared
with powdery brushstrokes, traces of the lab techs from Prineville.

I was seeing nothing but normal merchandise for a gun shop. Nothing to indicate why Erle Sharples had had such a mania for security.

There was another smell here, a miasma under the higher scents of oil and propellant. Old blood. Not the coppery tang of a fresh wound, which was so sharp you tasted it as much as smelled it. This reek was like the spoiled juice in a Styrofoam packet of hamburger, left too long in the trash.

Coming around the counter, I stopped short. A broad stain, larger and darker than the other scuffs and scars on the poured concrete floor, blocked the way. The discolored patch shone like clotted wine under the beam of the penlight. At its closer edge, the stain was smeared and erratic. Where Erle had thrashed until he could move no more, I guessed.

The wall behind the stain held a selection of holsters and soft-sided pistol cases on hooks. Most of the cases were made of black fabric. Those revealed nothing in the gloom. On the khaki-colored gear, blood spatters and spots were more truthful. A second stain lay thick at the baseboard of the wall. Flesh there, as well as blood. Residue from a large exit wound.

Either the cops or the crime lab had removed the shop's computer. The hardware peripherals remained—the mouse and keyboard, and Erle's flat-screen monitor.

A second monitor sat at an angle to the first. A wireless router leaned crookedly against the back of it, a Winchester rifles decal stuck to its top. I didn't have to peel the decal off the router to know it was hiding another logo from the Kjárr alarm company. Both monitor and router had lines running below the counter, and I followed them down to find the backup battery for the alarm system, which would come into play if the building's power was unexpectedly cut. The battery should serve the cameras, too. I found the switch at the top and turned it on. The monitor buzzed faintly to life.

Four quadrants appeared on the screen, in full color. Or as much color as night allowed through the cameras. The first three images showed the steps outside the front entrance of the shop, a black blankness where

I'd draped the rag over the rear door's camera, and the length of the indoor firing range. And in the fourth quadrant: me, standing at the counter, just a faceless mass in a slightly less dark room with my jacket illuminated by the glowing screen. Almost a fractal image, me looking at myself looking at me.

With Erle's computer gone, there was no danger of the live feed being recorded, or sent out into the cloud. But nor could I search back through the video to verify what the police report had said—that Erle had shut off his extremely expensive security system not long before he was killed.

Below the four quadrants, the bottom of the screen read *CHANNEL1—OCT11—21:41* in a menu tab. There was a second tab reading *C2*. I clicked it. The readout changed to *CHANNEL2* with the same date and time, and the screen changed along with it.

Changed to what appeared to be nothing, a blank square. At first I thought the channel had no camera assigned to it. Then I caught a hint of movement. Staring intently at the dark screen, I made out crooked gray vertical bars at the edges of a black background. I tried adjusting the brightness of the monitor, and the higher contrast brought the image into marginally better focus.

Trees. I was looking at trees. There must be another camera somewhere outside. I'd seen no other cameras on the building's exterior, and there was no grove of trees close by the shop. But out behind the dead-end road, the edge of the nearest small forest crowned the top of the hill.

What was the effective range of the wireless camera? Less than a quarter mile, I guessed. The camera must be positioned within that distance. Sure as hell Erle hadn't run a fiber-optic line into the forest.

Now, why would a man put a camera in the middle of the woods?

I stared at the screen for a time. The movement that had first attracted my notice was erratic, and remained in a single spot on the screen. A loose branch, or something else on the tree trunk, fluttering in the wind. I committed what details I could to memory and took photographs of the screen with my phone for good measure.

With a little hunting I might find that camera. But only after the sun came up. I returned the screen to its previous mode and switched off the monitor and cameras.

My nose was stuffed full of the rotten blood smell. After my strange childhood and time in combat, the shop was just another place where something bad had happened. That didn't mean I enjoyed being there. Retracing my steps through the firing range, I left the building, closed the back door, and inserted the pick and tension bar to relock the dead bolt.

Something scuffed the ground behind me. I ducked as a large arm went around my head, missing my throat and wrapping across my jaw.

I bit him. As instinctual as any dog, and as savage, my teeth piercing fabric and flesh. The man cried out and reflexively flung me forward. My skull bounced off the steel door. The man closed again, grabbing me, trying for the same choke hold. I shoved against the door, first hands, then hard with both feet, trying to bowl him over backward.

It was like pushing a tractor. My thrashing only staggered him for a second. Pulling at his steel-cable arm with all my strength, I barely kept him from fully closing the hold and crushing my carotid arteries. My lights would be out within seconds, maybe permanently. He bore his weight down on me. I was losing. He pushed harder. I folded onto one knee.

My leg hit something metal. One of the short lengths of rusted rebar. I let go with one hand and scrabbled to reach it. His arm closed on my neck like a python. I snatched the bar up and stabbed it down into the closest target, the man's broad running shoe. He yelled in pain and tried to shift his stance. My vision went spotty. Blindly, I speared another, harder stab into the same spot. His arms fell away. I gasped in relief. Someone called out from a short distance behind us.

I fled. Maybe I could have taken my attacker down with the metal rod, but with his size and my uncertainty whether the voice in the dark had been friend or foe, a strategic retreat sounded just fine. I staggered around the corner of the gun shop and took off for the alley running behind the stores on the dead-end road. Within half a minute I was far enough away from the shop to pause and listen.

No one was pursuing me through the alley. No sound of car engines nearby.

Who the hell had that been? Lester? Lester was large, but this guy had been altogether bigger, and much more fit. My neck ached. The son of a bitch had nearly torn my head off. Had he been lurking outside the whole time, guarding the shop? If so, why hadn't he stopped me from breaking in? He wasn't law. Or some citizen wandering past the back of the crime scene in the damn shadows.

One thing was for certain: The big fucker would be walking with a limp now. If he hung around Mercy River, I would find him soon enough.

TEN

FROM EAST OF THE dead-end street I heard the throaty boom of a shotgun, chased by the crackle of its echo off the surrounding hills. I walked in the general direction of the sound, course-correcting with each subsequent blast.

Leo might hear the gunfire from the jail. I hoped not. Being confined could already be pushing his stress factors near the breaking point. Leo's particular brand of hell was the hypervigilance that so many vets couldn't shake. For me, it was nightmares. We'd both reined in our worst symptoms with time and therapy. But those demons lurked just around the corner. Evil, and patient.

By the time I cleared the last building and saw a field a third of a mile down the road, the shotgun booms had increased in frequency. Faint whoops of celebration heralded each blast. A line of Tiki torches illuminated thirty or more men, appearing more shadow than substance at this distance. The long guns they carried lent their silhouettes extra limbs.

I wasn't the only person attracted by the gunfire. A handful of the curious wandered toward the field, some of them still holding cans of beer from their last stop.

The glowing green dot of a luminescent clay pigeon soared into the air at the far end of the field, only to be immediately obliterated by flying pellets of birdshot. Another pigeon, thrown by a second mechanical trap, for a different shooter, followed almost immediately. As I drew closer, I counted four separate traps operated by volunteers, each small catapult loaded with a stack of green disks ready for launching. As each shooter finished, he handed his ear pro to the next in line. Not all of the shooters were Rangers; there were civilians as well, both men and women.

A scattered throng had gathered to watch the show. Flags on posts marked the safety line. I scanned the field, on the narrow chance that my attacker had fled here by car after our fight. A couple of the men were large enough to be candidates, but neither was favoring one foot.

"Hey," a voice called. I turned. The shaggy Ranger I'd seen at the saloon was behind me on the road, a backpack and a shotgun slung over his shoulders. If he was still wearing the heavy metal T-shirt, it was hidden under his bright yellow Gore-Tex jacket.

"From the bar, right?" he said.

"Right," I said. "Van Shaw."

"Zeke Caton."

It was lucky I wasn't chewing gum. I would have choked on it.

"Yeah, I figured that would get a reaction," he said, raising his voice over the ongoing booms of the shotguns. "You're the buddy of the guy they arrested, yeah?"

"Right again." I shouldn't have been surprised by Zeke knowing who I was. People kept reminding me how fast news traveled in Mercy River.

"I was hopin' to run into you. Look, I don't have anything against your guy. I don't even know if he's the one who aced Erle. Shit, it was old Henry who actually saw him there."

"You're local."

"All my life. Except the years where the Army had me by the nuts." He grinned, a mouthful of teeth wider than average in his sharp face. "I grew up right the other side of the county line, and everybody knows damn near everybody here."

"So I've heard."

"What's your bro's name?"

"Leo. Third Bat like me."

"I was First. Still feels like I am," he said.

"I got out last January."

"Then you know."

A rusty white pickup truck roared past us. It honked at a knot of men moseying in the middle of the road, urging them into unsteady retreat. One of the group gave the truck's taillights one middle finger each.

Zeke shrugged. "No hard feelings, all right? I'd shake on it, but . . ." His hands were full of gear.

I nodded agreement. The slight movement made my sore neck twinge. "Give me a rundown of that morning."

"I gotta get this to my bud." He hoisted the backpack. "Come on."

We walked through the spectators, past the four shooters and their staccato symphony of clacking traps and shotgun blasts. A tall wiry Latino knelt in the light thrown by the headlights of a Jeep, setting up a fifth trap.

"Van, Rigoberto. Rigo, Van," Zeke said, lowering his pack to the ground.

Rigoberto glanced up from his work long enough to say hey. Zeke laid his pack out and unzipped it all the way to show stacks of clay pigeons, some painted the Day-Glo green I'd already seen and others in equally bright orange, sealed in plastic bags. He handed a bag of greens to Rigo, who silently set it aside while he completed leveling the trap.

"Not much to tell you about yesterday morning," Zeke said. "I wanted to hit the gun shop when they opened. The Rally always spurs a huge run on nine-mil ammo, so the sooner I got mine, the better. I saw Henry, and we walked down the road together to Erle's. Henry tried the door. It was unlocked, so we went in. And there was Erle on the floor."

"How long would you guess Erle had been lying there?"

"The blood on the walls was still a little gluey. That part flipped

Henry out. I don't know CSI shit. But it couldn't have been long, right? I mean if . . ."

"If Leo had shot him after he arrived. Go on."

"We'd seen Wayne Beacham up on Main Street, so I ran up the road to find him. That's pretty much all."

"Tell me about Henry Gillespie."

Zeke cocked his head. "You know his name, huh? Guess I'm not the first person you've talked to about this."

"Is he reliable? As a witness?"

"Henry's Henry. He's a lawyer, pretty much the only one they got in town. He and Erle got along well. That's a rare fact."

"Erle wasn't social."

"Erle was an asshole. Always tryin' to be the smartest guy in the room, and got his panties in a wad when he wasn't."

"Zeke," Rigo said. Zeke reached down to fish a handful of shotgun shells out of his ruck. He pocketed all but two, which he loaded into the two barrels of the over/under shotgun he was carrying. Rigo unzipped a nylon rifle case on the ground—one of three he'd brought—and removed a similar weapon.

"You shoot a lot?" I said.

"Skeet?" said Zeke. "Hardly ever. I'm killin' time before the pistol competition on Saturday. But Rigo here, he's fucking world-class with a scattergun."

Rigo didn't respond, except to swing his loaded shotgun closed with a smooth click. Like Zeke, he was probably still shy of thirty years old, but his resting expression and high hairline carried the somber quality of someone hitting middle age and not enjoying it. The tragedy mask to his grinning buddy Zeke's comedy.

"Check this out," Zeke said, and loaded two green pigeons into the trap. A double thrower. Rigoberto donned glasses and ear pro like funky old-school headphones.

"You want me to count it down for you?" Zeke said, loud enough for Rigo to hear him through the mufflers.

"Screw off," Rigo answered. It was the most he'd said since we'd arrived. Zeke laughed and pulled the cord.

The two pigeons leapt into the air as if in terror, flying in different directions. Rigo fired, turned, fired again, without seeming to really aim, the sound of the two shots overlapping as if they were one bang heard from a far distance. Against the backdrop of the dark hills, the explosions of the green dust and fragments vanished instantly.

"Nice," Zeke said.

"Too slow," said Rigo, already breaking his shotgun to reload.

"If Erle was such a dick," I said to Zeke, "did he have enemies?"

Rigo looked at me while his hands did the work. "You fishing for reasonable doubt?"

"For anything that might help Leo."

Zeke grimaced. "You gotta be seriously pissed to blow a man's chest apart like that." He loaded the trap with one of the phosphorescent orange pigeons.

"It could have been impulsive," I said. "It was a gun shop, with weapons around. Was Erle arguing with anyone?"

"Shit. Erle had ten quarrels a day. His nature, you know?"

Meaning I either had an endless number of possible suspects, or none at all.

Zeke turned to the line of trap shooters and waved a red flag. After a last shot or two, the volunteers and shooters turned to watch him.

"A little demonstration," he hollered to the crowd. "Rigo, you ready?"

Rigo raised his shotgun to his shoulder, casual to the point of bored.

Zeke pulled the cord and the bright orange pigeon flew skyward. Rigo gave it an extra few milliseconds to get some distance before he fired.

A bright white flash and a bang easily three times the decibels of the shotgun blast assaulted my ears. It made me wince. I wasn't the only one. The first words I could make out were vehement curses from men shaking their stunned heads, even as they laughed over the trick.

Zeke was chuckling, blinking the spots from his eyes.

"Okay, okay." He raised his hands until the crowd had quieted. "Now that I have your fuckin' attention. We're selling these beauties for five bucks each, all proceeds to the Rally. See Her Hotness over there at the Jeep for yours." He jabbed a thumb toward the Jeep with its headlights on, where a blond Redcap waved from the open tailgate. "Buyer assumes all risks and all that bullshit."

I reached down to pick up one of the orange pigeons from Zeke's backpack. "What's in it?"

"The usual nitrate and aluminum, plus thermite so it goes boom with lower-velocity rounds." He made a finger gun and dropped the hammer. "Our buddy's secret recipe."

"Maybe too much in this batch," Rigo said.

"We brought a shit-ton of it," said Zeke. "We'll draft some volunteers at breakfast tomorrow to pack the powder into one-pound cans. Instant flash-bang targets for the rifle matches."

"Good advertising," I said, handing him the pigeon. A line had already formed at the Jeep.

"Wait until I post video of tonight." He spun the orange disk on his finger like a basketball. "We'll be selling these firecrackers nationwide."

I left Zeke and Rigo and pointed my feet toward the rental house. It had been something like forty hours since I'd slept, and I was feeling the weight.

ELEVEN

I WOKE EARLY TO LEADEN light coming through the bedroom window, the sight of it chasing away what little memory remained of the dream I'd been having. Not a full-on nightmare. Those left no questions in their wake, only sweats and trembling. This dream had trailed off into a lingering disquiet, like sensing an unwelcome visitor might be lurking in your house, if your house were your mind.

That unease had become familiar after the trouble last summer. I felt it as often during waking hours as after dreaming. Addy would say it was guilt. I thought it might be something closer to temptation.

My mouth and throat felt dry enough to store rice paper. I downed a bottle of Evian—Ganz had apparently had groceries delivered sometime last night—and filled it again from the tap, which tasted even better. I brought the bottle with me as I showered.

The backstreets made the fastest route to the sheriff's station. Iron clouds hovered low enough to touch. A first raindrop, heavy and arcing on the wind, splatted into my windshield and smeared a line of dirt. By the time I reached the middle of town, the patter of drops on the roof sounded like a drumroll and the windshield was next door to clean. I pulled my cap low to jog from the truck into the station.

Deputy Roussa was in position at the front desk. Her mouth tightened a little at the sight of me.

"On duty again," I said. "Split shifts?"

"The department allows overtime while the Rally is in town."

"Looks like the Rally brings in a lot of revenue, directly or not. Must be popular."

"Enough that we haven't kicked this bunch out." She stopped herself.

"Who'd you run out of town before?"

In place of an answer Roussa reached below the counter for the ceramic bowl. While I unloaded my pockets and mused on what group or groups Mercy River had seen fit to banish, she retrieved a hanging clipboard from a nail by the cell block door. She recorded the time and my driver's license number next to my name, which was already listed on the page. Maybe Ganz had gotten me some kind of preapproval.

"How's Leo been?" I said as she swept the metal detector over me.

"Easy."

"I meant his health."

"Improving."

And that was all I got out of the deputy. I was trailing after her toward the cell block when the door opened and the heavily tanned Ranger I'd seen with Zeke Caton at the saloon walked out. We both stopped short.

"You're here to visit Pak?" he said in a soft Southern drawl.

"Yeah. You know Leo?"

"Not personally. I heard the man they arrested was from the 75th," he said. Instead of chinos, today he wore black waterproof running gear, still wet from outside. "Wanted to meet Pak for myself. John Fain, with the Rally."

We shook hands. I imagined the Rally organizers had their collective asses on fire about Erle's murder. One day before the event, and a Ranger supposedly kills a citizen. Very bad PR.

"Let yourself in once you're ready, Mr. Shaw," Roussa said, and went back to her paperwork.

"I saw you at the saloon yesterday," I said to Fain. "Was that about Leo, too?"

"That was about keeping good relations with the town. We wanted to know if there was any damage, and to slip that tall fella who owns the bar a few bucks for his trouble." Fain spared a glance for Roussa, who was out of earshot. "Pak told me his buddy already got him a lawyer. You moved fast."

"He'd do the same for me," I said.

"Still, it can't be easy to drop everything and come on the run. You staying for the Rally?"

"For as long as Leo needs. He might have a concussion."

Fain's expression hardened. His weathered and somewhat gaunt face reminded me of the cowboys in black-and-white movies that my grandfather would watch on quiet afternoons when there was no European football on television. Easy to imagine Fain's narrowed eyes scanning the plains for rustlers.

"You mean to say these assholes never had him checked out? Pak didn't say anything about that."

"Leo's choice."

"Convince him."

A reflexive order. Fain had definitely been an officer, and not so long ago.

"You're just out of harness, aren't you?" Fain said, as if he'd been thinking much the same thing. "What was your operating base, last cycle?"

"Howz-e-Madad. But I doubt our platoon spent more than a month of nights there."

He smirked, understanding. The relentless pace of the OPTEMPO—the amount of action our battalion saw in theater—had most Ranger platoons spending days on end away from the relative comforts of base life. We operated out of patrol bases, temporary homes in the field that might change every night. If we stopped moving at all.

"Business as usual," Fain said. "Kandahar Province was my last stop, too. Civilian life okay for you?"

"Won't complain."

"But you could, if you chose to." He grunted. "Our troubles don't come off with the uniform. If you need to leave here and get back to real life, you let me know. Drop a message at the Rally office. We can look after Pak."

"I'll keep it in mind," I said.

"And I'll let you get on to your friend. Good meeting you, Shaw." Fain pulled his hood up over his short black hair and left mud-specked tracks on his way out of the station.

Leo was already on his feet when I reached his cell. Maybe because he didn't want me to see how much effort it took to stand.

He limped over and bumped my fist with his.

"You're up and moving, at least," I said.

"I'm squared up." The swelling on his forehead was down, but the bruise had spread and turned sickly yellow around the edges. "Guess you saw Captain Fain."

"I did. The Rally covers all bases."

"Covering their asses, is what I think. Ganz will get me out of here."

"He said that?"

"It's gonna happen."

I left that alone. "I met your girl, too. Dez. She was at the house when I went for your scrips. Did Ganz get those to you?"

"Yeah. The cops bring the pills with every meal, like I'm a mental patient." He leaned against the sink. "I'm feeling fine, man. Really."

"Turns out the constable who clubbed you is the brother of the guy you knocked out in the saloon."

Leo grunted. "I should've guessed. Explains why the cop was so pissed."

"You didn't tell me about the Rally. That was a surprise."

"I didn't?" He shrugged. "It's what's on the calendar. The Rally is Dez's regular gig. Or one of 'em."

"How'd you meet?" I sat down on the hall floor. It gave Leo an excuse to sit down as well, resting his back against the cell wall. In profile, the bruises distending and discoloring his skin, he might have been an entirely different person.

"In Utah," he said. "Dez was going around the state for the Rally. Delivering aid supplies and checking in on local families. I was stuck in a half-day group therapy thing at the West Jordan Med Center, and she recognized I was a Ranger from my ink. She gave me a sales pitch for the Rally."

"So you gave her the pitch for yourself."

He grinned sheepishly. Leo didn't smile a lot, but when he did there was usually a woman somewhere in the story.

"She came out to visit a couple more times," he said. "Then we started talking about her staying, when she could afford it."

"Money's that tight?"

"The Rally's a good job. She wanted to stick with it through this week, when they need the most help. Plus"—he shrugged—"she's lived in this town her whole life. There's shit to deal with before she leaves. I figured making some cash working at the gun shop would help move our plans along."

"You ever see Erle have an argument with anyone?"

"No."

"Because I heard Erle picked fights like some people pick lotto tickets. Habitual."

"Not around me," Leo said, probing his cut lip.

"You always start early? Seven-fifteen?"

"Usually, sure."

"Did you find Erle's body on the floor and leave? What happened?"

He turned his head to look at me. "I told you."

"You told me you didn't kill him. You skipped the rest. Like how you got blood on your shoes."

"I forget what I said." He tapped his head. "Scrambled, yeah?"

"Where'd you go all day? Before the saloon?"

"Hiking. I blew off work. The witness got it wrong."

"Come on. You called *me*. Or maybe you forgot that, too."

"Well, I got it handled now."

I stared at him. "What the fuck's going on, Leo?"

"Nothing. They arrested the wrong guy."

"So you keep telling me."

"Go back to Seattle," he said.

"Not happening."

"Then drink some whiskey, or find your own woman. Who gives a shit?" Leo spat pink on the floor. "I know you. Coming at me sideways, looking for the angle like with everything else you do."

"I'm trying to help you."

"Nobody needs it. Get out of my face."

I did exactly that. Leo stayed right where he was, leaning back against the wall, his hand curled around the bars.

Roussa had stepped away from the front desk. I took down the clipboard hanging by the cell block door. Ganz's name was on the list of approved visitors, and so was mine, both dated yesterday. So was John Fain's, in a feminine handwriting dated today.

When Roussa came to give me my belongings, I tapped the clipboard. "Who approved Fain for you this morning?"

"The lieutenant."

"Yerby?"

"Mr. Fain told me I could call him to check. I did. Yerby said yes straightaway."

"Is that normal for Yerby? Allowing visitors on the fly?"

Roussa shrugged, a gesture that said, *No, but I know when not to push back.*

The morning was full of discoveries. Did the Rally swing so much weight in Mercy River that the sheriff's lead detective let Fain walk right in?

"I never thanked you," I said, "for keeping an eye on Leo after he was busted. That was good of you."

"Bad for the department if he'd died." Roussa wouldn't give an inch. Even as pissed off as I was at the whole damn world right then, I had to give that the respect it deserved.

TWELVE

THE WOODS COVERING THE long rise behind Erle's Gun Shop and Firing Range had been clear-cut at one time, leaving a line of trees at the top that looked more like a wooden wall than the organic edge of a forest. Nature was making good progress reclaiming the slope. Bramble thickets and saplings sprouted in a hundred patches.

Shielding my phone from the rain, I examined the photos I'd taken of the security monitor's image. They showed the trees as darker gray lines on a slate background. More like abstract art than a useful picture, even with the one dangling twig or whatever it was that I'd seen moving on the screen.

The camera would be placed high, to show the angle on the images. I guessed the camera had to have at least a rough line of sight back to the gun shop to send its signal. It must be close.

But close was relative. The woods topping the hill included a lot of square yardage. A lot of thick forest. I began to hike up the hill, picking my way around the clumps of brush and the rivulets of water and mud flowing down the slope.

About a hundred steps into the climb, I came across parallel ruts of tire tracks carved into the wet and grassy earth. Only four feet apart, with a wide tread. Made by an ATV. Probably the same one I'd found in the carport beside Erle's shop.

Erle had the ATV. Erle had the camera. One might lead to the other. Hot damn.

I followed the straight lines implied by the path of the treads, onward and upward, diagonal to the slope. Nearer the hilltop, the soil was loose and muddy. My boots stuck with every step. Before long the effort of pulling them free made my stretched hip flexors ache.

But I was rewarded when I picked up the ATV's trail again near the forest edge. Deep channels remained in a patch of earth where the vehicle had turned to enter the trees, through a gap in the trunks wide enough to allow passage.

Inside the canopy of the forest, fir needles and sodden leaves blanketed the ground, interrupting the trail again. My nostrils filled with the heavy smell of moss and decaying plant life. I picked my way slowly through the shaded interior, stopping every few feet to check the ground for tracks or to look upward, hoping to catch sight of the camera. All I found among the branches was a crow. It cawed what sounded like an emphatic profanity before flying off into the trees.

The crow's path arced down and past a thicket of pines. A bright blue plastic ribbon fluttered weakly against one of the trunks in the breeze.

Fluttering back and forth. The ribbon's movement was suddenly familiar. On the colorless camera image, I'd taken its motion for a loose twig on the tree trunk. I crashed through a line of rabbit brush to reach it.

Glancing at the image on my phone again, I checked the angle of the picture against the position of the pine trees, following an imaginary line up to where the camera must be.

There. Nestled under a wide branch and enclosed in a dirty brown camouflage housing large enough to include whatever battery powered it. Only the lens showed from the front, one black staring eye, like a larger version of the crow's. From the side the camera was nearly invisible.

Its lens centered on a patch of ground with a pile of leaves and twigs.

A thicker mass than the natural ground covering nearby. I kicked the leaves aside.

Concrete. I was standing on old, pitted concrete. And there was something else underfoot as well, an edge of gray plastic tarpaulin. I hooked my fingers under it and pulled up. A shower of wet dirt and pine needles fell aside with the tarp, and I was looking at a two-foot square of wood with a handle of weatherproof acrylic rope right in the middle. A trapdoor. A padlock secured one edge of the square to a hasp set in the concrete.

I didn't need more invitation than that. I knelt down and picked the lock, as the rain dripped off my cap and washed the dirt from my fingers. A hard pull on the rope, and the trapdoor swung upward to reveal a ladder leading down to a floor made of the same concrete, eight feet down.

Holy shit. Erle had himself a bunker.

A gun store owner with a hidden underground lair in the woods. I immediately pictured racks of stolen RPGs and squad assault weapons, complete with crates full of ammo belts. I grabbed for my Maglite and leaned in to shine it around the space.

And almost laughed. The underground room was nearly empty. And felt even emptier with its startlingly large size, like a railroad car hidden beneath the wild brush above. Maybe it had been a storage basement for a small house once, crudely built decades ago out of simple poured concrete and rebar frame.

I caught wafts of gun oil and grease, distinctive and dense enough to linger after the guns or whatever had created the scent had been removed from the bunker. Maybe my guess about Erle trafficking in stolen arms wasn't so far off. It would explain why he went to such lengths to conceal and watch his hiding place.

A row of rusted wire shelves stood against one grimy wall. On the topmost shelf, a red plastic container about half again the size of a large file box waited in solitude.

I climbed down the ladder. The air inside was cold but not fresh.

Black mold had formed on the eroded concrete, and water seeped at the corners and dripped down the edges of the open trapdoor. I set the Maglite aside to take the red box down from its shelf.

It was a sealable shipping container, with a clear compartment in the lid to hold papers with the recipient's address and other tracking information. No papers there now. The tape around the lid had already been broken. I clicked the latch and opened the lid.

Inside the box were stacked trays of translucent plastic. Each tray held twenty-four slim rubber-tipped vials, each vial about half the size of a marking pen and filled with a liquid the color of maple syrup. I popped one vial out of the tray to examine its label.

The brand name in big bold letters was Trumorpha. Under that in smaller type was its scientific name, *Oxymorphone*, and a bar code sticker. Each vial held ten milliliters of the injectable solution.

After a long pull in the military, with time spent in and out of hospital wards, and the occasional bout with PT stress on top of that: you learn your drugs. I'd been given prescriptions for—or had acquired by other means—a dozen types of antibiotics and twice again that many painkillers. That wasn't even counting the mood stabilizers widely available, like Leo's Lamotrigine pills, or the sleep aids I still used when my dreams got aggro.

Oxymorphone was in the painkiller family. Powerful stuff, somewhere between fentanyl and pure heroin on the opioid scale. So strong it had become a problem even for Big Pharma, and they'd pulled the injectable version off the market a year or two ago, after one too many accidental ODs from junkies expecting the gentler high of OxyContin. Drink alcohol before a shot of Trumorpha and you might as well be injecting powdered glass.

The Trumo had been yanked from the pharmacies. Why was a box of it here? Was Erle a drug dealer as well as the local gun merchant?

I didn't doubt that rural Oregon was suffering through the same opioid crisis as the rest of the nation. Erle could have found customers. Had he been killed in a buy that went wrong? That might explain why he'd turned off the cameras—no witnesses, even electronic ones.

But how much could the drugs be worth, street value? A few thousand? Less than ten grand, I guessed, even if demand was high after the recall. There were loads of other morphine substitutes to be had. Erle went to a lot of trouble to hide such a small quantity.

Without the shipping information, or a way to scan the bar code stickers on the vials, I was in the dark as to where the drugs had come from, or how long the box might have been cached away in Erle's bunker. There could have been more Trumo hidden here at one time and the red box was all that was left. Maybe Erle had made a deal to sell the rest of his supply and had been murdered for it instead. Or maybe he had anticipated more drugs arriving soon. Plenty of space here in his quiet room under the forest floor. Like a crypt.

If I left the Trumo here in the bunker, I couldn't be certain it would remain undisturbed. Better to hold on to it until I figured out if and how the narcotics were connected with Erle's death. Move it, but without lugging a big red box out of the forest.

Twenty-four vials to a tray. Six trays in the stack. Peeling off my coat and Henley, I removed my T-shirt and laid it flat on one of the shelves.

I left the underground bunker with one hundred and forty-four vials of factory-produced heroin tied up in a V-neck cotton bundle. The empty red box looked incongruously bright in the shadows. It was the last thing I saw of the room as I lowered the lid and pulled the tarp back over, keeping Erle Sharples's secret just between us.

THIRTEEN

As I CAME AROUND the front of the gun shop, I found its doors wide open, making a black square in the gray steel storefront like a moaning mouth. A dented red Chevy Astro panel van had been parked crookedly off to one side.

I'd been wondering about Sharples's relatives. Maybe his family had finally turned up. Under the sound of the relentless rain, a high sustained keening drifted from the mouth shape of the doors. A little closer, and the sound resolved into the whine of a vacuum cleaner. I stashed my makeshift bag full of Trumo vials under the wheel well of Erle's ATV.

I called hello, and a moment later the whine whirred into silence. A woman came out onto the porch. She was old enough to have a full head of downy white hair and robust enough that she had no trouble carrying the steel vacuum canister with one hand. The photograph of Johnny Cash on her shirt stopped at the singer's chin and the high elastic waist of her jeans. She peered at me through thick glasses.

"Store's closed," she said. "Owner's dead."

"I know."

"So whaddya want?"

"Erle's next of kin. Is that you?"

She snickered. "I weren't Erle's type of woman."

"What's the joke?" I said.

"Bein' broke is its own joke. Why you want to bother the family?"

"To see if we can help." I gave the tough old badger what I hoped passed for a winning smile. "I'm with the Rally."

"I knew *that*. You got that I-chewed-bullets-for-breakfast stance all those boys have. Tea and sympathy, is that the idea? You wanna help somebody, c'mon in here and help me scrub the floor." She glanced back at the room, and her shoulders jerked in what was almost a shudder. "Worse than a damn horror movie."

"Tell you what. I'll trade you fifteen minutes of mop work for everything you can tell me about Erle Sharples."

She goggled at me like I'd brought her flowers and chocolate. "You mean that?"

"Blood doesn't bother me much."

"Well, damn." She gave out a smile that was startlingly sweet on her craggy face. "All right, then."

I followed her inside and got my first look at the gun shop in the daylight. The windowless space wasn't much more inviting than it had been at midnight. The brightest bits of color were the occasional orange hunting vest, and the wine-dark stains on the floor and lower walls. My new friend made sure to give that corner of the room a wide berth.

"I'm Paulette," the woman said.

"Van."

She had already filled rolling buckets full of water and set them off to one side, the floor mop leaning against a rack of wading boots. I pushed the first bucket over to the edge of the stain and took the industrial-sized can of Bon Ami cleaning powder Paulette handed to me.

"Who hired you for this fun?" I said as I scattered the coarse granules over the floor.

"Lieutenant Yerby. He claimed it'd be light work."

"Sounds like him."

"You met the man. Then you know." Paulette took a spray bottle and a stack of rags from her pile of supplies and began wiping fingerprint dust from the glass counter.

"Are all the cops around here like Yerby?"

"Naw. Most of the deputies are marking time until he's gone. He'll run for sheriff next election and lose, you watch. Larry Yerby will be tossed like yesterday's fish."

I pushed the wet mop through the powder, which turned an instant vibrant pink. The blood smeared thickly across the sealed concrete floor. Half a dozen swipes, and I rinsed it in the bucket, getting into a rhythm. "What about the town cop? The constable."

"Wayne? He's making do. Can't be a regular deputy." She waved a hand, knowing I was about to ask. "Wayne Beacham was supposed to be in the NFL. Or at least get hisself a full ride through U of O. Best quarterback this county ever produced."

"Injury?"

"Both knees, sophomore year. He can walk okay now but that's about all."

"And the constable job is what the town can do for him."

"The boy's lucky to have it. He raised some serious hell around here after he lost his scholarship. Like a dog that'll bite before it even growls. But he straightened up, got married. Showed he could walk the line." She tapped her Cash shirt and snickered again.

"So who inherits all this now that Erle's gone?"

"He's got no family here. There's an elderly cousin over in Grant County. Henry would know for sure."

Gillespie. The town's lawyer. Of course he might be Erle's executor, either from their friendship or because the town had appointed him. I kicked myself for not thinking of it earlier.

"Henry have an office in town?" I said.

"On Tyne Street." She motioned westward. "Why you so interested in Erle's stuff?"

"It's a nice town. Nice shop." I grinned at her. "Maybe I can buy it and settle down here."

Paulette whooped with laughter. "All right, then, don't tell me." She shook her head bemusedly as she returned her attention to the countertop. Without the fingerprint dust, the room was a touch brighter from the reflection off the glass.

"Erle did have money," Paulette said, scrubbing with a brush at a stubborn spot. "Hated to spend it, but he had it."

My mind flickered to the vials of pharmaceutical heroin.

"From the gun shop?" I said.

For the first time, Paulette wavered. "It's just talk. Small-town nonsense."

"So keep talking, and I'll keep mopping."

She snorted. "I suppose speaking ill of the dead isn't the worst thing I've done. Erle hadn't had this shop forever. He built it 'bout ten years ago, with some of the money he got when Cecily Rae died."

"His wife?"

"Only just. She caught the cancer—ovarian, worst kind, you can fight me on that—and there was Erle, ready to help with any little thing. I'm not saying it weren't a good thing for Cecily. But I also wasn't the only person who noticed how Erle quickly bought hisself new shirts and saw the barber every two weeks. He weren't a bad-looking man when he tried."

"And Cecily had money."

"Couple a million, I 'spect. From her career and her late husband's. He was a bone surgeon down in Bend, making money off all those sports nuts down there. They had houses. Mercy River was more where they came on vacation, even though Cecily grew up here. She were never the strongest gal, even before the sickness. You know what I'm saying?"

"I think so."

"Truth told? I don't expect it was Cecily Rae's idea to make a new will. But she was close to the end and her mind gummed up with all kinds of medicine for the pain, and Erle convinced her they should marry and to let him handle things. He was good at that."

I understood. Not swindling, exactly. Coercion was closer to the mark.

"But they're both dead now," Paulette said. "So I suppose if you really want Erle's shop, it'll be up for sale. Mercy River's a decent place. We make sure of it."

"A deputy at the station said something similar. That the town used to have some kind of bad element."

"You could say."

The water in my bucket was as red as cheap fruit punch. It reeked of rot. I set it out on the porch and retrieved a second pail. Another ten swipes of the mop, and Paulette's urge to chat overcame her hesitancy.

"Mebbe five years ago, we'd get drifters," she said. "They'd camp their trailers out by the forest and come into town for beer and food and giving the coupla Mexican families we have here the evil eye. Men, mostly, but some trashy women, too. Spouting about white people bein' God's chosen and all other races bein' made of mud. That sort of turd talk. Pardon me. But they'd always move on. Then a few of them squatted or rented houses, and it got so they thought of Mercy River as kind of their home base, you know?"

"Yeah."

"Their kind was easy to spot. Tattoos on their hands and necks and all. But it were still a free country. Long as they didn't pee on the sidewalk, weren't much the sheriff could do. After a year there was a bunch more of them, and they got organized. A leader. Meetings. They made bids to buy land right in town, and wanted to start a church so they could hang their flags out in the open and call it religion."

"They give themselves a name?"

"The First Riders." She snorted. "I guess after the Ku Klux Klan, galloping on horses. Mel Blodgett wrote to the county paper when one of the Riders got arrested for parole violation, complaining that the government should give alerts to citizens about ex-convicts so we'd know if they were consorting. Somebody firebombed Mel's car the very next day. I saw it. The baby seat in the back was melted down to jelly. Henry Gillespie, he talked about filing lawsuits on property rights, but other folks didn't see the point after what happened to Mel. People whispered"— Paulette shrugged like whispers were all the proof required—"how

Mercy River was gonna become like them compounds or little mountain towns where nothin' moves without the Riders' say-so."

"This was about three years ago?" I said.

"That's right."

"Before General Macomber formed the Rally. But not long before."

Paulette kept her focus on clearing dust from the plywood worktables. "I suppose the general came to town around then."

"And he saw what was going on. What happened to the Riders?"

"What goes 'round comes 'round. One night a couple of weeks after Mel's car, we had some arsonists come through. Burned everything those First Riders had. Trailers, cars, motorcycles. Even houses they'd rented. Five different places around town. And the Riders in those trailers and houses, most of 'em were tied up with plastic handcuffs or duct tape and left in ditches nearby, with hoods over their heads."

"By arsonists."

"Must have taken them all night. The Riders were mad as ants on a stomped hill, yelling about how a gang in masks had broken in and yanked them all right out of their beds. Of course the sheriff investigated."

"Let me guess. No clues."

"Nope. Sheriff figured it was an insurance scam, that the Riders set it all up themselves. Nobody would rent to them after that. The folks who lost their houses—the general found a way to get them situated again."

"I bet."

"Weren't long after that the First Riders were gone from Mercy River. I heard a lot of them were frightened enough by what happened that night that they left the bunch entirely. Put the fear of God into 'em."

I was sure it did. Waking from a dead sleep, bound and hooded within seconds. I knew exactly how that was done. My platoon in Afghanistan could have filled a bus with the high-value targets we'd taken in the Rangers.

"But that's all done now," Paulette said. "So are you, looks like."

"Just about." The floor was clean, and the wall was at least less likely to terrify anyone. I took another minute to scrub the groove at the top of the baseboard. A bit of flesh was stuck there, wiped white by the mop. I plucked it out and threw it in the bucket.

Paulette made a noise. "You weren't joshing, about blood not bothering you."

"No."

"You been to the war, then. Like most of these boys in town now."

"Yes."

"Suppose saying thank you don't quite cut the mustard for that."

"I don't mind. Thanks is better than most vets get." I picked up the second bucket. "I'll dump these outside."

"Appreciate it. You remember where to find Henry?"

"Tyne Street. Got it."

"If you say any prayers, forget about Erle and say 'em for poor Cecily Rae Desidra. That woman never did have luck."

I stopped, nearly slopping the bloody water out of the bucket and back onto the floor.

"Desidra," I said.

"That's right."

"Did Cecily have a daughter?"

Paulette's eyebrows arched, adding another stratum of lines to her forehead. "Now, how did you know that? Susan. She still lives here in town."

Dez, Leo's girl had said. *Short for my last name.*

I'd just found someone with a motive.

FOURTEEN

DEZ WORKED FOR THE Rally, which meant she could be damn near anywhere around Mercy River right then. I recalled overhearing another Redcap tell someone that the Rally had business offices off the town hall. Maybe someone there could tell me where Dez was assigned today.

The rain had stopped while I'd been talking to Paulette. Pavement and cars shone as if the world were brand-new. I stashed my new collection of Trumorpha vials in the hidden compartment of the truck, pocketing one vial on the chance I could suss out a way to read its bar code, and set out to find the Rally offices.

My path took me across Main Street. Booths had been erected along the sidewalks, each touting a different aspect of the Rally's efforts and stumping for volunteers. It was a dizzying range of effort. Recruiting former medics for home care and hospice work. Online tutoring for children of deployed soldiers. Even retirement planning. I had to give credit to General Macomber's ambition. And his marketing savvy. The booths with the pretty Redcaps had the most success in attracting candidates.

I'd spent an extra second looking at a booth that offered counseling for families of Rangers with mental health needs—MENTAL CHALLENGES ARE NOT MORAL CHALLENGES, the tagline read—and my hesitation was enough to draw the attention of the guy running the booth.

"Hey, there," he said, his friendly smile widening. An active, or maybe fresh out of uniform. He had the same haircut that I'd sported about a year earlier, only a week or two's growth off regulation. "Where'd you grow up?"

"Third Bat," I said, "but I'm passing by."

"Hang for a minute." His eyes were on my scars. "You got family? Because they need someone to talk to just like we do. If you've got people, the Rally can set you guys up with a therapist who takes VA."

"No family. And I already see a shrink."

"Then you're the kind of guy we need," he said, expertly changing tack. "Another Ranger can be a huge help. What's your name?"

"Later," I said. "I have work to do."

He didn't let the smile waver much. "You say 'later,' I'll hold you to it. Come back and let's talk. We got a mom and dad in Sacramento, their son—our brother—is going through a bad patch. They need you."

I nodded and moved on.

The Rally's heart seemed to be in the right place, even if its approach was all over the map. My own charitable work was a lot more localized. I had a Ranger brother right here with his own bad situation, and I was determined to help him first. Even if he didn't want it.

"Shaw," a voice called. Booker, jogging toward me with a rain jacket in his hand and a pair of cleats slung over his cannonball shoulder. He wore a long-sleeved T-shirt and running tights under shorts. His biceps tested the limits of the stretch fabric. Booker was too short to be the man who'd tried to strangle me last night, but I would bet my attacker had the same monster build. "You headed to the football field?" He pointed up the street toward the high school.

"I'm walking that direction."

"Come on." He bounced back into his easy jog, and I lengthened my stride to keep up. "I already missed the start, and I'm playing the second half."

"Only the half?"

"So many guys wanted to play this year, they drew lots to assign teams and times around the rifle competitions. Three games today, twelve different teams. There's even organized betting."

"All profits to the Rally."

"Would the general miss that opportunity? Uh-uh, jack."

At our accelerated pace, we made it to the school in under five minutes. I followed Booker down the stairs onto the sidelines to get a closer view of the mayhem.

Predictably, the heavy rain had turned the field into a mud pit. The clock on the scoreboard told us the game was still in the first quarter. If the players were wearing anything to tell the teams apart, it was lost under a layer of muck. Even the referees were splattered head to toe. Booker and I watched as the quarterback fumbled the ball and a horde of linemen dove for it, throwing up waves of brown water and grass chunks. Just as obviously, the multitude of locals and Rangers packing the bleachers loved it.

"Oh, my crap, this is going to be bad," Booker said.

"Maybe they're playing touch." It was a joke, but Booker looked at me like he wished it were true. We'd both noticed the first-aid station the Rally had erected behind the scoreboard.

Booker started to untie his cleat laces. "If I die, tell Moulson fuck you for me. This was his idea."

"Good luck."

I was halfway up the stairs to the road when I spotted Dez, in her red hat and black running wear, on the opposite side of the field. Even among the Redcaps, she stood out. The Rally had constructed a large booth by the concession stand, and from the whiteboard and the frenzied activity of the Rangers around it, it had to be the betting HQ.

I reversed course and jogged around the field, my hiking boots squelching on the rubberized track.

The whiteboard listed odds on everything from the outcomes of complete games to spreads for each team during their halves, and more obscure wagers. They had squeezed in one extra line at the bottom that listed a prop bet: NUMBER OF QUARTERS TODAY WITHOUT A COMPLETED PASS. The over/under was 4. Somebody was betting on the slick mud to win it all.

"I have to talk with you," I said to Dez.

She finished filling out a betting slip for a corn-fed young Ranger, fifty bucks on his team to dominate during the second game.

Leo? she mouthed silently.

I tilted my head, implying we shouldn't talk here. Whatever got her moving.

Dez turned and handed off her clipboard and money bag to another Redcap. I led her around the side of the bustling concession stand, which smelled of popcorn and buffalo sauce.

"Is he okay?" Dez said the instant we were around the corner, grabbing my jacket sleeve.

"He's safe. But he has to get some things straight in his story. Did you see Leo the morning Erle was shot?" I said.

She looked past me, making sure no one could be listening. "He was asleep when I left at six."

"You punch in early."

"It's our week." She gestured toward the field. "Like April for accountants."

"Working at the Rally office?"

"No, I drove the company truck to Bend that day. Picking up all the food and other supplies for the barbecue."

"What time?"

"What time did I pick them up?"

"What time did you leave town? What time did you get there?"

"I have keys to the Rally office. I opened up and signed out the truck and left." Realization dawned on her heart-shaped face. "You aren't asking for Leo. You're wondering if I have an excuse."

"Driving trucks isn't your usual job."

"My job is whatever the Rally needs doing. Which right now is a lot," she said. "Edwin usually picks up party supplies, but he was sick. Better?"

No. As alibis went, it was looser than a granny knot. Dez might have started the two-hour drive south to Bend immediately. Or she might have parked the truck somewhere quiet and made her way to Erle's. There was no way to tell which was true.

"All right," I said. "Sorry. I'm on edge. The cops are going to ask when you saw Leo, or if you spoke to him that day after Erle was shot. He never called you?"

"No. I thought he was at work, like usual."

"He wasn't. He said he blew off work and went hiking."

"Then that's what happened. You aren't much of a friend if you won't take Leo's word."

Dez walked around me, only to stop and turn when she reached the corner of the stand.

"Thank you for bringing a lawyer," she said, "for Leo's sake. But leave me alone."

I watched her walk away, skirting the field where the mud-covered players tried to run the ball without pitching headfirst into the slime. Leo and Dez were acting nearly as slippery.

Did Leo wonder about Dez, too? She'd left him sleeping that morning. He'd gone to work and found Erle dead, and not told anyone. Protecting Dez could be why Leo was throwing up walls every time I asked him for an explanation.

And the vials of Trumo. Were they a simple coincidence? A relic of Erle's life, but nothing to do with his death?

If Dez stood to inherit, Erle's killing could be a move to regain her mother's lost legacy. Or maybe she had shot him out of simple revenge.

I had one last notion involving Miss Susan Desidra, a theory slinking around the edges. That Dez had convinced Leo to murder Erle for her.

That wasn't true. Despite everything, I wanted to believe in my friend's innocence.

But I wouldn't reject the possibility outright.

BACK ON MAIN STREET, I dodged the volunteers shilling for various causes and headed north and west, where my phone's map told me Tyne Street was located. I'd found the street sign and was walking past a Winnebago RV, searching for Henry Gillespie's office, when a hand about the size and weight of a cinder block fell on my shoulder.

"You." Lester Beacham spun me around to stare up into his bloodshot and furious eyes. "Fuck Face. I know who you are now."

FIFTEEN

Y OU'RE A BUDDY OF that little piece of shit," Lester said, gripping my shoulder and shaking it for emphasis. "The Jap."

"I know you, too," I said. "The sucker puncher."

"What was that shit you were pulling with me and Wayne last night? You fuckin' with us?"

Behind Lester, a Griffon County Sheriff SUV turned the corner and glided up the street. I tamped down my first impulse. Now was not the time to fit the big ape for a body cast.

"Smile, Lester," I said.

He followed my gaze to the hunter-green vehicle. Its passenger window rolled down as it pulled alongside.

"Everything all right here?" It was Deputy Roussa. She leaned slightly over the seat as she gave both of us the X-ray eyes.

"Sunshine and lollipops," I said. "Mr. Beacham here was just telling me how good Leo has it in your jail. He misses getting three squares a day."

Roussa didn't twitch. "I'm sure not for long."

Lester's hand slid off my shoulder. "Later for you," he said with a beery exhalation, and moved off down the sidewalk.

I turned to Roussa.

"We got three empty cells at the station," she said. "Enough room for you and Lester both, if needs be."

The window rolled up, and after another moment, Roussa broke the stare and the SUV cruised away.

I was making a hell of an impression in Mercy River. Another day, and they'd put me in the town stocks. Or set the Rally volunteers to building gallows.

Henry Gillespie's office was his home, and vice versa. A two-story bungalow painted white on gray, with large dormer windows in the front. The kind of picturesque house that raised property values a notch or two on the block. Hanging from a post on the lawn was an honest-to-God shingle. H. H. GILLESPIE, ESQ. LEGAL SERVICES.

I rang the bell. Knocked on the door. No answer. No cars or people on the street, either. I walked around the narrow wraparound porch to the side of the house. The first window looked in on a small and exceedingly cluttered office. Gillespie had skipped the digital revolution. I could have built a sofa out of the stacks of files and folders and binders.

Somewhere in those towers of paper might be a hard copy of Erle Sharples's last will and testament. And if I had a week to spare, I could probably find it. I gave up and moved on down the porch.

Gillespie's bedroom faced the backyard. It had the air of a longtime bachelor. A single dresser, covered with dusty acrylic awards. The closet door stood open to reveal an overburdened hanging rack. He'd made the bed by simply pulling the sheet and down comforter in the direction of the pillow. Everything in deep tones—mahogany furniture, midnight-blue bedsheets. Even the lamp was made of jet-black ceramic. A pile of paperback thrillers waited on the nightstand beside an empty water glass and an ashtray.

It was all a little too familiar. My own place might have held different stuff, but it had the same simplicity, the same depressing ambience.

That wasn't a cigarette lying in the ashtray, I realized. It was a slim syringe.

A used syringe might not mean anything. Zeke Caton had said Henry was old. There were a hundred possible reasons why an old man might be injecting himself, including diabetes. No other obvious indications of a junkie's rig, no burn marks on the nightstand or surgical tubing poking out of the drawers.

Still, it got me wondering if it was really birdshot that Gillespie had intended to buy at Erle's shop early that morning.

I circled the house, aiming to search—very carefully, keeping needles in mind—through the lawyer's trash to see what I could see. Opioid addicts threw away a lot of telltale crap depending on their drug of choice, like bits of burnt aluminum foil or straws for inhaling. Or I might find empty bottles of insulin, and riddle solved. But Gillespie's garbage bins were out at the curb for pickup. The neighbors would notice if I started making like a raccoon.

My phone buzzed. A message from Ganz.

Suit and tie for L.P. delivered to house. Can you drop off at sheriff? Arraignment at 4PM.

Of course Ganz had gotten Leo a suit. He'd probably arranged for hair and makeup, too. I texted him back that I'd take the suit to the jail. It would give me another crack at Leo, now that I had learned about his sweetheart and her grudge against the murder victim.

DEPUTY THATCHER LED ME through the back rooms of the station and unlocked a rear door with one of his many keys. He motioned for me to step out into a small fenced yard, the space for inmates to get their mandated time for outdoor exercise.

"Wait here," he said before closing the door.

The dirt yard obviously doubled as a dog run, maybe for visiting K-9 units, or the deputies' own hounds. A plastic doghouse was set into a concrete slab, too far away from the twelve-foot razor-wire fence to allow anyone to use it as a jumping-off point. A metal water dish for the dogs was similarly secured with one bolt right through the center. The whole area was about fifteen feet by twelve and had a fine view of the stark courthouse wall. All in all, only a fraction less dismal than the jail cells inside.

A second door opened, and Leo came out.

"Five minutes," said Thatcher, and vanished back inside. Talkative.

"How's your head?" I said to Leo.

"Hardly need it at all." He put a palm against the wall and pushed, loosening up his shoulder muscles. "I'm sorry I got pissed before. Just angry at the scene, not at you."

"It can be both."

"I don't need a sergeant to keep me in line, Van. Sometimes you forget that."

"Maybe I'm mad at the situation, too. You shouldn't be in a box."

"The court thing, the arraignment. Ganz coached me." Leo's mouth twitched, whether in discomfort or amusement I couldn't tell.

"Ephraim might still be able to get you bail, if you agree to stay in the county until the trial."

"He seems expensive. You're paying the tab?"

"Yeah."

"Huh." He glanced at the security camera, set high up the wall and covered with protective steel mesh. "Last I knew, you were looking under couch cushions for change."

"I found the right couch."

"You don't sound so happy about it."

I wasn't *un*happy. But the money came with weight. A lot of people had died trying to get their hands on it. I'd found it surprisingly easy to give it away, in big handfuls.

"How did you get the job at the gun shop?" I said.

The abrupt change of subject caused Leo to raise one eyebrow, the other still immobilized by his swollen forehead. "I called the Rally office, asked if anyone in town wanted temporary help. I told them what I could do, so they put me with Erle."

"Dez told you the Rally could do that? Place people?"

"Yeah," he said after a second's pause. I had to walk a careful line. Leo had a blind spot in the shape of a lithe brunette.

"Who'd you talk to at the Rally office?"

"I dunno. Some woman took down my info and called me back like two days later. Why?"

I shrugged like I didn't know. Better to have Leo think about it a while.

"Erle was the town miser," I said. "And he was rich. Robbery could be a motive."

"He didn't get rich off selling duck decoys. Not from the amount of business I saw."

"Maybe another way, then. Did—"

The door swung open. Thatcher stood there, with another deputy as backup. "Time."

Dammit. Our five minutes had turned into three. Thatcher must be sore from the reaming Yerby had given him yesterday.

I jabbed a thumb toward the cells. "Ganz found you a jacket and tie for the hearing. Let's get you out on bail and sort this out."

Leo leaned in close.

"I need you to trust me, Van," he said under his breath. "Leave town. Leave it alone."

He turned and walked into the building.

Thatcher pointed at me. "Stay here."

Left in the dog run, I considered what Leo had said. He was right that he didn't need anyone giving him orders. He wasn't the same half-broken man who'd wandered into Seattle a year ago. He had focus now.

But to what end? Did he know the history between his girlfriend Dez and the murdered man? He wanted me to trust him. I guessed that he must know. Leo would do just about anything to protect the people he cared about. In that, we were alike.

And I couldn't leave until I knew whether he was throwing away his life.

I looked up at the sky. The mist had finally relinquished the valley, and for the first time today I saw breaks in the clouds. A good omen, some would say. I didn't believe in harbingers for good or ill. But I'd take sunlight where I found it.

SIXTEEN

CONSTABLE WAYNE BEACHAM STOOD beside his refurbished police sedan outside the low symmetrical rectangle of the courthouse. He leaned on the car's roof as he talked into his handheld radio. He saw me coming up the sidewalk and straightened abruptly. By the time I passed him he'd closed his conversation and hung the radio back on his belt, next to his service piece.

"Hold up," he said as I angled toward the courthouse door.

"I'm due inside."

"It can wait. You're a friend of Leonard Pak's." The constable's eyes looked hollow, like all the traffic control around the Rally was costing him shut-eye.

"Not a secret," I said.

"Do you work for his lawyer?"

"I work for myself."

"So you aren't a PI," Beacham said, as if he'd caught me in a lie, "but you're harassing people in our town. Trying to kick up shit."

"Which people? Your brother Lester? He's hell at kicking, too, after he gets the first punch in."

"If you keep on with this, I will jail you for intimidation so fast it'll give you windburn. Yerby can add witness tampering to the charges against Pak."

Beacham may have been as penny-ante as a cop could get, but he was still a cop, and on his home turf. He had every advantage. As much as I might enjoy telling him in explicit detail what he could do with his baton, it wouldn't help me or Leo. I held my tongue and walked up the short path between whitewashed ornamental boulders to the courthouse door.

Inside, a sheriff's deputy waited, detector wand at the ready.

"Is this SOP for bail hearings?" I asked as I submitted to a search for the third time in two days.

"Mostly for trials," he said, "but when somebody we all know gets killed . . ." He shrugged, and I took his meaning. People were mad, and pretty much everybody around here owned a gun. No sense in trusting angry people to make smart choices.

"You'll have to surrender the blade," he said. I handed over my multi-tool as an older woman in a floral sweater and pink skirt emerged from a room farther down the hall, wheeling a small cart with a stenograph machine on it. The deputy hurried to assist. I followed their slow train through the double doors into the courtroom.

Like the building that surrounded it, the room was purely functional. Two tables for the lawyers, a bench for the judge, stackable chairs arranged in rows to form a gallery with an aisle down the middle. A dozen townspeople, none of whom I recognized, occupied seats in the gallery. Leo's hearing would be the entertainment that kicked off their weekend.

Ganz had the left-hand table. He was dressed as simply as I'd ever seen him, in a dark blue suit that might have come off the rack, and a flat maroon tie. The papers laid out in front of him were separated into plain manila folders. His thousand-dollar calfskin attaché case was notably absent.

I took the gallery seat directly behind Ganz.

"How are we looking?" I said.

"I'm looking just as I should. You look like what you are. Please sit on the other side of the room, toward the back."

"I'm sure the town constable set his brother on Leo. Maybe to soften Leo up before the arrest. There's something in that."

"Not right here, and not right now. Go."

I went. I was choosing another seat when a woman entered the room from the hall and marched to the table opposite Ganz. They nodded politely to each other. She was dressed as conservatively as he was, in a coral-colored suit jacket and skirt, but on her it wasn't a costume. Both attorneys approached the stenographer, who began to note down some of what they were saying.

Deputy Thatcher emerged from a side door, along with Leo and Deputy Roussa. Lieutenant Yerby brought up the rear. He spotted me in the gallery and gave me a hard glare before taking a seat in the front row.

Roussa waited until Leo was seated next to Ganz, and left through the same door. The blue suit and darker tie that Ganz had brought for Leo fit him well. With his hair pulled back, Leo could have been a bank teller, if it weren't for the vicious bruise still marking his forehead.

"All rise," Thatcher said.

Everyone stood. A matching door on the opposite side swung open to admit the judge in his black robes, followed by a young man who I guessed was a clerk.

"Court now in session, Judge Clave presiding," the deputy intoned.

Judge Clave was somewhere near sixty years old and spare, his thin hands protruding like hawk's talons from the folds of his robe. His close-set eyes gave the impression of a man who not only expected disappointment, but might even crave it.

"Be seated."

We did, as the door to the hallway opened again.

Luce Boylan walked in.

My breath caught at the sight of her. I probably wasn't the only one. The courtroom seemed to hush as she walked quickly to take the same chair I'd recently occupied, behind Leo and Ganz.

What was she doing here? I wanted to follow her to the front of the room, but the clerk was already speaking from his desk in the corner of the courtroom.

"Criminal case for arraignment," he said, his voice as clear as a cantor's.

The judge broke in almost before his clerk was finished. "Counsel has previously stated their appearances for the record, am I right?" The stenographer said yes. "Then let's get to it. Defendant, state your full name."

Ganz nudged Leo, who stood again. "Leonard Tae-Hyun Pak."

"This is an arraignment for you, Mr. Pak. I am going to read the indictment, which is brief. As follows: The state charges, count one, murder in the first degree. On October tenth of this year, the defendant did knowingly and with malice aforethought kill and murder Erle Franklin Sharples."

The gallery audience was silent, waiting. In a town this size, all of them must have known Sharples well enough to make his murder a personal thing.

"Count two, assault of a law enforcement officer. That on or around the same date, the defendant did attack a town officer during the commission of his sworn duty. The prosecution has chosen to forgo the lesser charge of resistance, is that right?"

"Yes, Your Honor," said the DA from her seat.

They weren't tagging Leo with attempting to flee the arrest. Maybe the DA didn't want to distract from the murder charge. Or maybe it was some ploy to nullify a lawsuit against the town for mob violence, or against Constable Beacham for excessive force.

Judge Clave read on. "Mister . . . Ganz. Have you discussed the charges set forth in counts one and two with your client?"

"Yes, I have, Your Honor," said Ganz.

"And does your client wish to enter a plea at this time?"

"Yes. My client has chosen to plead not—"

"Guilty," Leo called out.

"Leo," I said automatically, but nobody heard it over the sudden buzz in the gallery, and from the tables. Thatcher ordered quiet in the court. Within seconds we were all straining to hear.

"Say that again," the judge commanded Leo.

"I'm pleading gui—"

"Your Honor, my client's mental state must be considered here," Ganz broke in. "As you can see, he has been seriously injured and has a hist—"

Leo started to speak again, but Judge Clave made a motion, and this time the call for order was nearly a bellow.

"You first." The judge pointed at Ganz. "Anybody else talks and they are going straight into a cell next door. I won't accept it."

Ganz nodded, his face as solemn as a mortician's. "Your Honor, Mr. Pak's actions are astounding to all of us. He and I had discussed and decided upon a plea of not guilty, and I ask the court to consider his state of mind and physical health at this stressful moment. Additionally, defense has had little time to review discovery, or even to collect—"

"There will be time for all the discovery later, Mr. Ganz. Or before any plea discussions with the district attorney."

"If the court would allow us time, at least, to ensure that Mr. Pak has had medical treatment."

The DA decided to risk the judge's wrath by speaking up. "Mr. Pak has already been examined by a doctor, Your Honor."

"And deemed to have suffered a concussion less than two days ago," Ganz said without pause. "A short checkup is hardly enough to ensure a full recovery."

"Mr. Pak," said the judge, "do you understand the charges against you? And that your guilty plea means forgoing a trial?"

"Yeah," said Leo.

"Has your lawyer discussed the possible sentencing that might result?"

"Sure."

"Yes or no, Mr. Pak."

"Yes."

"And do you feel in your right state of mind today?"

"I do."

"Then that's sufficient for me," Clave said. "I'm resetting this case for sentencing, to be held upon my return in one week." He glanced down at the papers on the bench. "Ten-thirty in the morning, next Friday. If the parties reach a resolution before then, you'll be in touch, Mrs. Lempley?"

"Of course, Your Honor," said the DA, like someone had handed her a bag of rubies.

Ganz was practically vibrating. "Your Honor, time for proper discovery. The lab reports alone—"

"File a motion, Mr. Ganz. Until then, we're done here."

Thatcher ordered the courtroom to rise again, and Judge Clave didn't let the swinging door hit him in the ass. Ganz was talking fiercely to Leo, so low I couldn't hear a syllable. If Leo was paying attention, he didn't show it. Roussa cuffed him and led him out through the side door toward the jail.

Yerby spared a moment to make sure I saw him grinning before he followed.

Delighted with the show, the audience in the gallery chattered as they exited through the door behind me. The DA and Ganz had a short dialogue, during which Ganz gathered his files as briskly as if he were being timed with a stopwatch. As the DA left, Ganz spotted me. His rigid face got a fraction stonier. He walked up the aisle and past me at his usual rapid clip. I hesitated, wanting to go to Luce, who looked stricken.

I finally dashed after Ganz. He was already outside. He didn't say a word until we were into the parking lot, an arrow's flight from anyone who might hear.

"I knew your friend was crazy," he began. "You're crazy. It follows Leo would be the same species. But I didn't think he was stupid."

I didn't say anything.

"He's fucked, Van. At least until after Clave throws him a life sentence with twenty minimum. Then you can appeal, because the judge screwed us on preparation time. I was afraid he might do that. But with a trial, we'd have had a chance to poke holes in the case, maybe even negotiate bail so Leo doesn't beat his brains out on a cell wall in the meantime. Now? Jack with a shit topping. Leo stays right there."

"Why did you think Clave would screw us? Is he fishing for a payoff?"

"You believe everyone's a little crooked, don't you?" Ganz sighed. "Clave is honest. He simply doesn't care about the job anymore. He lost a bid for a federal appointment earlier this year, his third attempt. He's stepping down after December. Why would he give a holy crap if we get his decision reversed on appeal? He won't be around for that trial. And thanks to Leo's samurai suicide today, Clave won't have to spend the last two months of his career commuting every week to fucking Mercy River."

"How'd you get all this on Clave?"

"Because it's my damn profession. Because it always comes down to what people want, Van. Or don't want. God help us, getting a judge without aspirations."

"How long will it take to appeal?"

"A year. Maybe more. But that's not going to be me. I'll come back here for the sentencing, and then I'm finished with this whole nightmare."

"Ephraim—"

"No. When a client refuses all advice, it's a clear signal. His lunacy isn't my problem to solve. There's a Polish expression my grandmother used. *Nie mój cyrk, nie moje małpy.* 'Not my circus, not my monkeys.' You and your Leo, you're the fucking monkeys."

He stalked away, fast enough to create a breeze in his wake.

I'd reason with Ganz later. First I wanted to get to Leo, find out what the hell he'd been thinking. Dez hadn't been at the arraignment. Maybe she was cutting her losses, now that Leo had served his purpose. If he was shielding Dez by taking the fall, he could at least try for acquittal.

Why leap straight into the bottomless pit of a guilty plea? Ganz was right. It was insane.

Then I turned around, and saw Luce in front of the courthouse, blond hair caught on the wind and hovering around her cheekbones, and all my plans went right out the window.

SEVENTEEN

HOW?" I SAID, WHICH seemed enough.

"Ephraim Ganz called me." Luce hugged herself, either against the cold breeze or for solace after what had happened in court. "I left as early as I could, but an accident had us stopped for an hour on the highway."

"Ganz wanted you near Leo."

"He said the judge was amenable to young women. His words. I offered to be a character witness if it might help." She shook her head. "Why did Leo do that?"

"I have half a guess. But only half."

We walked down a side road parallel to Main, which was now teeming with Rangers returning from the rifle competitions. Luce did a double-take at the stream of men with tactical cases and long guns carried openly on their shoulders.

I explained about the Rally, and about Dez and her family history with the man Leo was accused of killing. I even told her about the box of stolen oxymorphone, and how and where I'd found it, which didn't put me in the best light. But Luce knew where I came from. Talking around the truth with her would have felt a lot shadier than breaking into a hundred shops.

By the time I'd gotten to the part about confronting Dez at the football game, Luce and I were halfway across town and crisscrossing narrow streets I hadn't seen before. Mostly homes, but a curio store sold coffee and tea—20 VARITIES, the misspelled sign boasted. I bought a black coffee and a cup of white peony for Luce. Next door to the curio place was a small Baptist church with a playground in its yard. We sat on one of the benches while I finished my story.

"Does Leo love her that much?" Luce said. "So much that he'd go to prison for her?"

"That's what I suspect. That Dez has him dangling."

She frowned. "Not for money. Leo would never protect Dez if she'd killed Erle for the inheritance."

"The woman who was cleaning Erle's shop—Paulette—thinks some old cousin in the next county is Erle's next of kin."

"There you are." Luce nodded. "Leo must know there was bad blood between Erle and Dez. She wouldn't inherit."

"Maybe it's not about money. Erle fleeced Dez's mother. People have killed for less."

"Nope." Luce held the steaming cup in both hands, like a prayer offering. "Leo is worried that Dez killed Erle accidentally, or in self-defense. That's why he didn't call for help, and that's why he wants you"—she extended her finger off the cup to point accusingly—"to stop kicking over rocks looking for suspects. Because you might lead the police right to her."

"Say that's true. Why is Dez letting Leo take the fall?"

"I don't think she killed Erle, either. And she might be terrified that Leo shot Erle for her. *And*, because if Dez went to see Leo in jail to ask him what happened, the whole town would be buzzing about it within half an hour. It would only make the case against Leo worse. You told me how fast everyone connected you with Leo. Add sex into the mix, and imagine how fast that would get around."

"You could have put that better." I smiled.

"You know what I mean. Love is the reason. Neither Leo nor Dez knows what really happened, but they are determined to keep the other one safe any way they can."

Luce had dressed for court, in white turtleneck and soft gray flared pants and a royal-blue Burberry trench that was as much cloak as coat. I was aware of my barn jacket and boots, stained with mud and oil and probably worse. Luce was the only person who could make me feel awkward, and the last person who would want to.

"If Dez isn't the killer, then I'm back to this." I took the vial of Trumorpha out of my pocket. "Erle was murdered for drugs, or some deal related to them."

"Sounds right to me. Much more than Dez picking up a gun and shooting Erle on the spot."

"She's a country girl. She probably started shooting guns younger than I did."

"But not for the same reasons." Luce sipped her tea and looked at me, blue eyes appraising. "I forget how strange your life has been. How— not easy—how *common* violence has been for you. It terrifies most of us, and it should."

"I don't murder people."

"No, you don't. Nor do any of these soldiers in town today, I'd bet. And none of them had Dono Shaw raising them. That's why it's such a reach for me to think Dez could be that cold-blooded."

"Maybe."

"Talk to her again. You and Dez might be on the same side."

It was possible. Whatever theory I followed, I had to do it fast. Leo would be sentenced one week from tomorrow. After that, it would be the penitentiary for him, and convincing the court to re-open his case would take a miracle. Especially without Ganz's help.

"I'll talk to Dez," I agreed.

The sun had slipped below the spire of the church. A long sharp-edged shadow crossed the playground and the bench where we sat, coming to a point in the center of the road. I drank my coffee. Luce held her tea, apparently satisfied to have its warmth in her hands.

"You were going to tell me something," I said, "back in Seattle."

Her eyes flickered to the church, where crimson and gold beams bounced off colored glass running up the edges of the spire. "I was."

"But not anymore?"

"Could we walk back?"

I'd never seen Luce this tentative. Her firm confidence of two minutes ago had evaporated. Maybe, after everything that had happened today—Ganz's summons and her long drive, and Leo's guilty plea as the bitter chaser—maybe Luce felt trapped. Instead of asking why, I made myself smile.

Neither of us spoke, and I'm not sure which of us turned their feet toward Main Street first, but soon we were walking without haste up the gentle grade. Ahead, volunteers raced to break down the booths in the dwindling light. Rangers and townspeople waited outside the handful of restaurants and the saloon, all filled to capacity and beyond for the dinner hour. I wasn't hungry, despite the long day.

More than a few Rangers turned their heads to get a second glance at Luce as we passed. The reactions of men around Luce always gave me a weird and probably Neanderthal mix of emotions ranging from pride to posturing. I walked differently, taking up more space, making eye contact when the stares got too aggressive. Luce never let on that she noticed, them or me.

We walked farther than I'd been on the main drag, passing a long line of lightweight plywood sheets painted white and bolted to a chain-link fence. Ribbons and photographs and even drawings half covered the nearest surfaces, in between names written by hand directly onto the painted wood. It was the Wall of Remembrance that Macomber had mentioned in his speech. The Rally had built a low roof above the Wall to keep it safe from the elements.

I leaned closer. In addition to the names, some Rangers had described where and how their brothers had served. One had stapled an account of the battle in which his fire-team leader had died, multiple pages, single-spaced. A small sign below each sheet noted that after each year's

Rally, the new sections of the Wall would be removed and stored, with the goal of a permanent home to be constructed for its display.

"Do you want to write something?" Luce asked, bringing me out of my reverie.

A donation box hung between each plywood sheet, along with a second box containing staple guns and Sharpie pens in a dozen colors.

I did, I realized. I dropped a fifty in the donation bin, took a pen, and thought for a minute before I started to write.

Alvin Sughrue—Omaha, NE
Juan Davila—San Juan, PR
Lavonte Renz—Lafayette, LA

And after another moment's consideration, I added:

Trev Myers—Denver, CO

Luce leaned in to read the names. "Your friends?"

"There were others. Juan and Al and Lavonte died while I was leading them." I ran my finger down the list. "Al when I was a squad leader. Juan and 'Vonte together, much later, when I was a platoon sergeant."

"And the fourth man?"

"Trev killed himself after he was home." I remembered hearing the news from one of the specialists in our unit. *Myers suck-started his Glock,* he had said. A harsh sentiment to push away the pain.

"You think of them often," Luce said.

"Not as often as I should." Maybe I did have a use for the Rally. Macomber's people might be able to get me in touch with their families.

Luce touched the white plywood sheet next to Trev's name. "It wasn't so long ago we were both worried that Leo might be on this list."

"He's not that guy anymore. He pointed that out to me."

We walked along the Wall. A lot of names. Some Rangers had listed the wives and children their brothers had left behind, along with wishes for God or some unnamed benevolence to watch over them.

In the dirt field past the Suite Mercy Inn, bales of hay had been arranged into a line of pyramids, the smallest of them ten feet tall. Rangers off-loaded more hay from flatbed trucks. A slim guy stood on the back of one truck, pushing a last square bale off with his boot. He slapped the roof of the cab and the truck pulled away and out of the field, the man still surfing the back of it. With the truck gone, a row of tables and beer kegs became visible at the far end of the field, along with a giant pile of scrap wood.

"Bonfires," Luce said.

"You would be right," said a rumbling voice behind us. We turned to see General Macomber. No Redcaps or entourage, just the man himself.

"Sir," I said.

"We haven't met. Charles Macomber." He held out a gloved hand. The general looked more like a pleasant grizzly than ever in a thick suede car coat and woolen cap.

"Van Shaw. Sergeant, Third Bat. And this is Luce Boylan."

"My pleasure," said Macomber, shaking hands with her as well. He waved expansively toward the field. "Mercy River cleared this area to build a new playground and a park beyond it. The Rally asked the selectmen if they might delay construction for a few weeks. The field provides enough space for everyone to gather."

"They obliged," I said.

"It's symbiotic. Not every town would gamble on our men behaving themselves, despite the money we spend here. Where were you deployed?"

"Iraq first. Then nearly everywhere in Afghanistan, over different tours."

He tapped his face, echoing the scars on mine. "Those aren't new mementos."

"No. I was still green."

"Then we have something in common." He smiled and touched his leg. "I climbed back on the horse after my mishap, too. Well done, Sergeant."

"Thank you, sir."

"And you, miss?" Macomber said to Luce. "What brings you to the wilderness of Oregon? Besides Sergeant Shaw."

"A friend in need," she said.

"The best reason of all. Wonderful. Where do you both live?"

"Seattle," we said in unison. Luce smiled at the unexpected harmony.

"I've visited there a few times. Much better weather in your Washington than in D.C. Even with the rains." The general cleared his throat, like a call to attention. "There's a Rally contact who organizes our outreach efforts near McChord. It's a big area. A lot of Rangers and their families. We could use someone who understands what it means to keep fighting."

"Sir," I said, without committing.

"Think on it. We'll talk more, I hope." He nodded to Luce, almost a bow. "A pleasure to meet you. I hope you enjoy your visit."

He walked on, his limp apparent but not slowing him an inch.

"Forceful," Luce said.

"Yeah." And inspiring. And shrewd. I wondered if Macomber's curiosity about me wasn't limited to how I might best contribute to the Rally. John Fain might have filled Macomber in on my connection with Leo, the now-confessed murderer of Erle. As the general had said, Mercy River expected their guests to keep cool. Macomber could be worried I was going to make more trouble for them.

Across the field, figures moved rapidly through the dusk, splashing liquid from gallon cans onto the nearest piles of hay. Luce and I walked closer. Neither of us had corrected the general's assumption that we were a couple. The implications of that hung in the air between us.

"Are you going to follow up on volunteering?" Luce said.

"I don't know. I doubt it. There are—"

"Other ways you can help. Yes."

Luce knew how I'd come into money last summer, and that I'd given most of it away to people who needed it more. Hell, her best friend Elana Coll had been part of the whole scheme. Elana had a lot fewer scruples than Luce did when it came to accumulating wealth.

Somehow Luce had intuited the violence that work must have involved, and how much the memories of that bad time had lingered, like venom under my skin.

A whooping Ranger on the opposite side of the second haystack set it afire, and we watched as the blaze swiftly crested the top and swept down the bales on this side. The gasoline made the flames burn blue-white before flaring into an orange frenzy. Luce and I both blinked, eyes smarting from the heat and shine. I turned my back on the spectacle. I wanted to see her.

"Are you selling the Morgen?" I asked.

Luce took another moment with the bonfire before looking at me.

"I'm getting married," she said.

Behind me, another giant haystack erupted in flames. The rush of light threw Luce's face into bright relief against the field that stretched out behind her.

"When?" I said.

"Over the holidays, I think. We haven't set the date yet."

"A Christmas wedding."

"I didn't want you to hear about it from someone else."

"Sure."

The heat from the bonfire was so oppressive that I felt it as if I wore no coat or shirt. My scalp stung.

"You don't know him," Luce said, as if I had asked. "We'd dated for a while before, and . . . started again last spring."

After we'd broken up, she meant. Not long after.

"Congratulations," I said.

"Thank you." She spoke so softly that it was only her lips moving under the sounds of the fire and my own blood pumping that told me the words.

We watched the bonfires. Or pretended to. A row of miniature suns, each brighter than the last.

"The town's booked up," I said, "but there's room at the house Ganz rented."

"I—I should drive back tonight."

"You can have the place to yourself."

"That's not it. I just wanted to be here for Leo. And so we could talk."

"And now that's done." I nodded. "I'll walk you to your car."

Luce looked startled but said nothing. When I started walking, she did, too.

It was only a handful of blocks to the courthouse. We made one stop, at the corner market, where she bought Luna bars and water for the drive.

"We should have dinner," I said, "before you have another six hours on the road."

"I'm fine."

No hesitation from her this time. We walked the rest of the way in silence. Whatever energy we'd had between us before had grown thorns.

In the courthouse lot, she stopped at a pearl-white Audi. Its parking lights flashed once as she unlocked it.

"New car," I said.

"New for me. I never get to drive it, living in the city. I'm making up for that today."

"You could still get some rest—"

"No. Really."

"All right. Drive safe."

"You be careful, too." She opened the door. "Please."

She got in, started the car, and pulled straight ahead through the empty spaces in front of her, looping out of the lot and out of sight within seconds.

EIGHTEEN

GODDAMN IT.

I mean, *goddamn* it.

Was I supposed to have said something? Asked her something? Had Luce come all the way to Mercy River just to break the news of her engagement? Or to see if I would fight for her?

No. She'd come for Leo. And Luce didn't play games like that. She was a woman who knew her own mind. If she'd told the asshole—I couldn't help but think of her fiancé as a raging asshole—that she'd marry him, it was because she meant it. Felt it.

So who was this son of a bitch she'd reignited this great love with? She hadn't mentioned any old boyfriends in all the time we'd been together.

All the time, like it had been a long relationship. It hadn't. Luce and I had known each other as children, sure, and found one another again when I was on leave from active duty—all while I was dealing with the hell-storm kicked up by Dono's shooting. That had been pretty damn distracting, too. Luce and I hadn't really started dating, if that was the word, until I was finally out of the Army months later. And how long had we lasted? Five or six weeks, tops. Weeks that had flown by in a rush of sex and laughter and me getting my feet underneath me as a civilian. Or trying to.

Then it had ended. The life Luce needed to have wasn't the life I was leading, surrounded by trouble and crime and threat. She'd had more than her share of that as a kid. She'd left, and I'd let her go.

She could feel more than one way. She could want to marry this guy, and want—what else? My blessing? Hard to picture Luce needing that. To make sure we were still friends?

I circled the center of town, walking without concern for direction. By the time my spiraling path connected with Main Street again, the stars were out.

I needed a drink. And I needed to put my questions about Luce in a box while I figured out how to help Leo.

The slim vial of Trumorpha in my pocket felt cool to the touch. If Erle had the drugs, he must have been selling them or buying more, and either way maybe that deal had gotten him killed. He'd turned off his cameras that morning. Expecting someone to join him in the shop. Someone still in town, I was betting.

On the dark stretch of road, the Trading Post Saloon shone as bright and cheery as Easter morning. The buzz of a human hive within grew as I approached the window. Every round table in the main room of the saloon was crowded with cardplayers, ninety percent of them Rangers. A team of Redcaps carried trays back and forth between the tables and the bar. The mustachioed owner, Seebright, had three taps flowing to keep up with demand.

I pulled the ornate door handle, and it thumped against the frame. Locked. At the sound, an obese guy sitting on a tall chair by the coat-rack reached behind him without looking to press the door's push bar and allow me in. The rush of chatter and laughter was visceral. I said thanks to the gatekeeper. He stayed resolutely focused on the football game playing silently on the nearest TV.

Seebright wasn't the only person behind the bar. My new friend Paulette was occupied mixing some sort of Red-Bull-and-vodka concoction at the near end. I took a stool in front of her.

"It's the mop engineer," she said. "What kin I get you?"

"Porter. Thanks."

I surveyed the tables. Seven-card stud was the game of the night. And relaxed was the mood. Some players used poker chips, others tossed cash into the pot. Most of the games had a low enough limit that no one was sweating. A dollar to raise on the first rounds, two bucks after that. A group near the back had made their game more work than play. Stone faces watched one another over a pile of twenty-dollar bills in the center. One of the faces was Rigoberto's, the morose marksman buddy of Zeke Caton's.

"What's the buy-in?" I said.

"As little as you want." Paulette shrugged. "Or as much. It's for charity. You win a hand, you kick ten percent to the kitty." She pointed toward an elfin young woman wearing cat ears in place of a red baseball cap, and carrying a woven basket with a lid. A roar went up from Rigoberto's table. The kitty shimmied over to collect the house's cut.

No cops in the makeshift gambling den, neither the sheriff's deputies nor Constable Wayne Beacham.

"Nice racket," I said.

Paulette chuckled. "If the general wants to throw a party and his guests want to play some cards, that's all right by us."

"Just keep the door locked and the riffraff out," I said.

There was a relaxed lawlessness to the way Mercy River ran their town. I understood it. I might have even liked it, if Leo hadn't been attacked by the mob from this same town, in this same saloon, two nights before.

"Henry, you rat!" a woman exclaimed. I turned my head to see a jowly elder at the same table as Rigoberto, as he reached out with long slim hands to rake in his winnings.

Paulette brought a pint of Black Butte to me.

"Is that Henry Gillespie? The lawyer?" I asked, tilting my head toward the table.

"Sure." Paulette fixed me with an amused eye. "You want to buy some chips?"

It was possible that Henry Gillespie was a junkie. I knew damn well he was near the scene when Erle was killed. My grandfather once told me you could learn more about a man from three hands of cards than three hours of talking.

"I'll take five hundred," I said, laying a handful of fifties on the bar. Paulette raised her eyebrows at the amount before counting out stacks of white, red, and blue plastic chips into a carrying tray. I made a beeline for the last empty chair at the back table, next to Rigo.

"What's the game?" I asked the Ranger shuffling the deck.

"Seven-card," he said, as his eyes passed over my loaded tray. "No limit."

I waved a casual hello to the other players. Rigoberto gave me a slow nod of greeting. Henry Gillespie and the woman seated next to him were the only citizens from Mercy River at the table. Rigo and the current dealer, a blond man with thick stubble and a thicker paunch, were former Rangers like me. The last three players might be actives in the same platoon, fresh off the assembly line. Their shield tattoos might smear if you brushed a thumb over them.

Gillespie was three times the age of any of the younger men. And judging by the mound of chips in front of him, three times the card-player. Rigo wasn't doing badly, either. His carefully arranged stacks totaled somewhere north of three hundred bucks.

I had played a lot of poker, in barracks and off-base apartments and a hundred bars. Enough to know that I was no shark. A true expert could reflexively remember every card that had passed over the table, from every hand, freeing their mind from the work of calculating odds to watch for any hint of pattern in the players opposite them. Comparatively, I was a hack. But I was a determined hack.

The paunchy Ranger who had the deal passed out two cards to each of us, facedown, as everyone tossed in a red five-dollar chip for the ante. He followed with one more card, faceup. He had a three, the lowest card showing, and threw in two ten-dollar chips to get the betting started.

I already knew Henry Gillespie used a needle. The question was for what. He was gaunt enough to have an opioid problem, his clean-shaven jowls the only fleshy part of his spectacled face, but his hands were steady as they counted chips from his stack to match the bet.

I played out the hand, betting a little too high for the cards I was holding each round, and finally folding after the sixth card when it looked like I might be building a strong full house. The blond Ranger to Rigo's right grunted in surprise.

Gillespie folded, too. But he won the next two hands, and Rigo the hand after that. I continued to slip and slide, not committing to one strategy or another. Almost by chance I took the fifth hand with three aces, after one of the actives overplayed his bluff. Belligerent betting had been the default tactic for all three of the younger soldiers. At this rate, Henry and Rigo would own their paychecks through their next enlistment. After every hand, the girl with the cat ears circled around to collect her ten percent from the winner, placing the chips and the cash into her wicker basket.

Ninety minutes later and three hundred dollars in the hole, I thought I had a handle on the others as well. Rigo had a good memory and played a straight game based on the odds. He'd bluff, but only if he had strong enough cards showing to make stealing the pot plausible. He was silent throughout. I had the impression Rigo was always silent, unless forced to be otherwise. The blond guy with the paunch was the worst player. He was slightly toasted, and maybe also prone to distraction. He'd played with increasing fervor, folding if he had nothing at the start and betting large consistently when he held anything worthwhile.

Gillespie was tougher to read. He changed up his level of forcefulness more by reading the mood of the table than from what he might be holding. He never fell for Rigo's traps. I caught him watching me carefully during the second hour, and was sure he'd figured out I was willing to drop hands just to see what would happen. And he kept scratching the inside of his left elbow. More in the past fifteen minutes than before. A nervous tic, or was he craving a fix?

In either case the elderly lawyer played the game without any apparent pleasure. While the actives had joked and pounded back beers, Gillespie had limited himself to a few quiet words with Ivie, the woman seated next to him.

Ivie had touched him on the arm more than once, a gesture more comforting than romantic. A relaxed player, she rarely bet large, apparently prizing the experience over the money. She had dressed for the occasion, in a velvet blouse the shade of pinot noir and silver necklaces that kept snagging in her soft gray curls. In contrast, Gillespie wore a simple black fisherman's sweater over a white collared shirt. Mourning colors.

"I was sorry to hear about your friend," I said to him during the next pause in the game, while the server was passing out a fresh round of lager to the actives and the paunchy blond was outside taking another toke.

He and Ivie both looked up.

"Thank you," Gillespie said. "It was far too early for Erle. Did you know him?" His voice may have once been baritone, but time had allowed tenor notes to creep in.

"I met Paulette yesterday. She told me. A terrible thing."

"Crime is always terrible. Foam-flanked and terrible. Twenty years in the system, but I learned that much in my first month."

"They've arrested the man who did it," Ivie said to me. "He's confessed."

Gillespie snorted. "We'll see how long he serves after the appeal. Bargaining can cut justice off at the knees." He licked his lips and scratched his arm.

I could feel Rigo's eyes on me. The actives shifted in their seats, uncomfortable at the change in mood.

"Do you still practice?" I said to Gillespie.

"I switched my specialty to family law. Never looked back."

"And you benefit the whole town." Ivie placed a reassuring hand on his.

"That must be difficult when it's a friend," I said. "Did Erle have kids? Somebody to take over his shop?"

"None of his own," Gillespie said. His eyes drifted past my shoulder and his mouth snapped shut.

I turned to see Dez by the bar, as the pixieish girl who'd been taking the house's cut handed over her cat ears and basket. Leo's girlfriend would be taking the next shift. Like her predecessor, she wore a short jeans skirt and bright red T-shirt with the familiar double-R symbol on the back.

The blond guy returned to the table, bringing with him the heady scent of kush. "Are we playing or what? I gotta get my money back."

His fool's confidence cheered Gillespie enough for him to shoot me a conspiratorial smile.

Dez passed by the table and pointedly ignored me. Her face, normally the prettiest in town even against the high bar set by the Redcaps, appeared drawn with fatigue. It wasn't hard to guess the reason. Her secret boyfriend had pleaded guilty this afternoon to killing her hated stepfather. Worse, Dez couldn't tell anyone. She had to carry on like nothing was wrong.

Luce had urged me to trust Dez, and share my theory that Leo was taking the rap out of some kind of chivalrous instinct. It looked like Dez could use a friend.

But now wasn't the time. Gillespie's fidgeting could be normal behavior for the old man or the signs of a growing craving. If he left the table to stick a spike in his arm, I'd make some excuse to follow him and maybe find out if Erle had been his supplier.

Rigoberto had the deal. He shuffled and dealt the cards with a smooth rapidity that might have earned an approving nod in any casino. Ivie wound up with the low card showing this time, an eight. I tossed one of my last ten-dollar chips on the table to match her bet. Only then did I peek at my hole cards. Two jacks, to match the one showing. Goddamn. Three of a kind, and just getting started.

Everybody called the bet. Rigo dealt a fourth card faceup to everyone. The eight I received didn't change my standing, but it took one possible match away from Ivie. Rigo had a pair of queens showing. The blond had another queen and a king, both hearts. We were all as quiet as Rigo now. It was shaping up like a whale of a hand. Even Dez had paused in her circuit around the tables to watch.

The following round was clay. No one's fortunes seemed to wax or wane with their fifth card, and even the gung-ho actives were content to call the minimum bet.

On the next round, the last round with the card dealt faceup, I saw my second eight. Full house, jacks over eights. To the other players, I was showing only a pair of eights and what might reasonably become a pair of jacks or sevens to match it. Two pair wasn't going to scare anyone away.

Even better, I hadn't seen another jack cross the table. I had a slim shot at four of a kind. Getting the measure of Gillespie had been my reason for playing, but I couldn't help but feel a tingle at the prospects.

Ivie had been chasing a ten-high straight, at best, and she knew enough to fold. Rigo raised fifty dollars. High, but not the highest he'd kicked. Was he holding three queens and maybe a larger full house than mine? Or bluffing? There were enough possible strong hands on the table that the sharpshooter might be pushing a little, to see what happened.

The blond threw in his last fifty dollars. Did he have the high flush, five hearts, already? Or was he praying to make it on the seventh and final card?

"I raise," he said. We all looked at him. He took a shrink-wrapped spliff out of his pocket, an olive-colored sticky cylinder the size of a basketball player's finger, and dropped it on the pot. "That's coated in hash. Cost me sixty bucks."

He was dead serious. Even Gillespie laughed at the guy's balls.

And it gave me an idea.

"You know we can't smoke that shit, man," said one of the actives in between guffaws.

Rigo tossed in sixty, deciding the matter. "I'll match cash value if one of you guys win."

"Same for this?" I reached into my own pocket for the vial of Trumo and tossed it into the center of the table. It clinked lightly against a stack of red chips, knocking them askew. Everyone stared at it. I watched Gillespie.

"The fuck?" the blond said.

I snapped my fingers. "Trumorpha. Name-brand painkiller."

Gillespie looked quizzical, but no more than that. Dez's attention was on Rigo and the blond to see if they'd accept the bet. Neither of them appeared to recognize the vial in the slightest.

Shit. It had been a reach, but I'd still hoped that the Trumo was more than just Erle's secret stash. If he had been selling drugs to the locals, that might give someone motive.

Rigo shrugged acceptance. "Anybody else?"

The actives called the bet. I put the pot at somewhere around six hundred dollars. We all settled in to receive our final card.

"Move that," Rigo said, frowning at the pint glass obscuring the blond's hand as the cards began to skim from his fingers over the table.

I was seated next to Rigoberto, glancing across him while the blond repositioned his beer, as we all were. So I saw it, barely, as Rigo dealt the last card from the bottom of the deck to land in front of him. He was so quick that the sleight of hand must have been invisible across the table.

Had Rigoberto been cheating all along? His previous turns at the deal hadn't won him those hands. So why now? My eyes turned to the vial of pharmaceutical heroin, presented like a shiny bauble on the colorful pile of poker chips.

I let the farce play out. My final card turned out to be a useless four. Everyone believed I'd clinched the hand when I turned over my full house, and I waited through the groans for Rigo to turn over his cards. Queens over nines. Not that I had to look.

"Close hand," Gillespie said.

Rigo reached out and plucked the vial of Trumorpha from the pot. He read the label, ignoring the people clapping him on the back in congratulations.

He met my eyes.

"Fortune smiles," I said.

Leaving his winnings behind, Rigo stepped into the surge of people, as smoothly as a dolphin diving into an oncoming wave.

NINETEEN

RIGOBERTO HAD RECOGNIZED THE vial of oxymorphone immediately. And had wanted the vial badly enough to risk cheating in front of a crowd of his fellow Rangers. That required ice in the bloodstream. Or desperation.

Rigo was buddies with Zeke Caton. Zeke had been shadowing their captain, Fain, at the saloon. None of them were large enough to be the guy who had attacked me at Erle's shop. That made four men I could connect with one another. Rigo might be headed to meet them now. If I could catch them together it would at least confirm they were all linked to the drugs. But Rigo would be watching to see if I followed.

Zeke said he was staying at the inn. I'd try there first after giving Rigoberto, sharpshooter and card cheat, a head start.

"What's going on?" Dez said, her interest in Rigo's hasty exit apparently overcoming her distaste for me.

"I owe you an apology," I said, "but it'll have to be later." I pointed at the pile of poker chips and bills in the center of the table. "He's donating this to the cause."

"Wait," she said as I started toward the front door after Rigo. Soft enough for the milling crowd not to hear. "Lester is out there."

"Waiting for me?"

"Maybe. He usually has friends with him when he's drunk."

After a day of fate stomping on my toes, I was in a perfect mood for a scrap with the town bully. But I had more important things to do.

"Thanks," I told Dez, and changed course for the back of the bar.

Now, how did Dez know Lester Beacham was gunning for me? She hadn't been around when Lester had braced me on the street. Small town, yet again. Lester had probably been telling anybody within earshot he was going to kick my ass.

The saloon let out onto a large patio, where a haze of cigar and cigarette smoke hovered like dark thoughts around the heads of the people seated at iron tables. Past the patio was a stumpy fence made of cedar slats. The fence separated the saloon from a service alley running behind the shops on Main Street. I stepped through the fence's gate and walked north, toward the inn.

I was nearing the end of the lonely service road when a man wearing a fisherman's cap stepped into view, silhouetted against the light coming from the street beyond. Then a second figure, larger than the first.

"Hello, asshole." Lester, chuckling with delight.

He carried an aluminum baseball bat. I turned, only to see another man twenty yards down the alley behind me, his own bat held with exaggerated casualness in gloved hands. He must have been hiding in some alcove, watching for me to leave the saloon.

"Near got tired of waiting for you," said Lester, "but patience is a fuckin' virtue, ain't it?"

They closed in. I turned, preparing to time my dash at the man with the gloves behind me. Dodge the bat, put his head through the pavement, and run. That was my best and only option.

"Hey," called a voice from the street. All of us turned.

It was John Fain, flanked by Zeke Caton and Rigoberto. They marched into the alley. Zeke and Fain faced off with Lester and the guy wearing the fisherman's hat. Rigo came to stand next to me. He stared placidly at the man with the gloves.

And behind Lester, a last member of Fain's crew appeared at the corner of the building, backlit by the streetlamps beyond. I didn't need a closer view to know this was the brute who'd nearly torn my head off the night before at Erle's gun shop. A handspan over six feet tall, as wide as Lester, and a hell of a lot more imposing.

"Fuck off," Fain said to Lester.

"This ain't your business," said Lester, sounding unconvinced himself.

"Daryll," Fain said. The huge man took one short step and clubbed Lester's cap-wearing buddy on the back of the head with his fist. The cap flew off and the man went down.

Fain opened the left side of his leather sport coat, to show Lester the butt of a gun. "It can get worse."

The man with the gloves faded rapidly away down the service alley. Lester helped his buddy stand and totter away, sparing a second to glare balefully at me. They left the fisherman's cap where it lay.

Wolves frightening jackals away from the kill. Which was me.

"Now what?" I said.

"Now we talk about this." Fain took the vial of Trumo from his chest pocket. "But not here."

"I like here just fine."

I'd gone from being outflanked to outgunned. Rigoberto edged a little into my blind spot and I turned to keep him in sight. He would be harder to take than the guy with the gloves if I had to stick with Plan A, running for it. I steeled myself.

"Take it easy," Fain drawled. "There's a better place. Public enough to suit everybody, without us jawing out in the open. Come on."

He walked away, and Rigo broke off to join him, along with Zeke. Big Daryll stayed where he was. After a moment, I walked past him. The laces of his boat-sized right sneaker were loose. Extra room for his bandaged toes, I guessed. As I followed Fain and the others, Daryll limped carefully toward a GMC Yukon parked at the curb.

Our little group walked up Main Street, through the scattered knots of Rangers still enjoying the night, either on their way to another party or simply sitting on the curb. I could have made a break for it at any time. None of Fain's team seemed concerned that I would flee, which ratcheted my curiosity about them even higher.

Two blocks past the western façades, Fain pointed to a building made of asymmetrical bricks of gray stone, like a short castle wall. Carved into the stone above the archway were the letters B.P.O.E. NO. 1891.

"An Elks lodge?" I said.

"It was once. Now it's a kind of meeting house for the town selectmen. Or a senior center. Opinions vary."

"And it's got a bar," said Zeke.

The door to the lodge had been propped open. Two old men in thick parkas and winter hats wandered out, greeting another duffer as they left.

Fain led us inside, into a bright, cheery room large and tall enough to play half-court basketball. Past an entryway with hooks for coats, the open floor had been divided by folding screens into seating areas, with donated lounge chairs and sofas arranged in rough circles. Well-worn Oriental rugs give a little padding to the parquet floor. A couple of the circles were occupied by older townspeople, mostly wives and husbands.

A pyramid of stacked logs burned in the oversized fireplace, emitting enough warmth to feel from the entrance. The flames reflected softly in the dented birchwood panels that covered the walls. The lodge might have been exactly the same, if a little less ragged, back when the locals were jawing about breaking news on Watergate.

"Safe enough for you?" Fain said, removing his coat. He motioned for me to join him at the fire, as Rigo ambled to a short serving bar that was stocked with well drinks and bottled beer in a glass-fronted refrigerator. The lodge apparently ran on the honor system; Rigo dropped two twenties into a goldfish bowl on the bar.

Zeke Caton dropped onto a couch and unzipped his yellow jacket. Fain picked up a poker, jabbing at the logs to let some air circulate between them. The crackle of the fire would mask our conversation well enough. If any of the locals were bothered by visitors horning in on their club, they held their tongues.

Fain held up the vial of Trumo. "You tossed the morphine into the game to get a reaction. So here we are. Where'd you find it?"

I didn't answer. The logs in the fireplace popped and hissed as sap boiled over. Fain jabbed again at the blaze.

"We searched all through the gun shop," he said. "Sharples's house, too. Nothing there but a lifetime of crappy choices. But you located Erle's hiding place in less than a day. Which either means you're in business with Erle Sharples yourself, or you're very good at finding things."

Rigo brought an open bottle of Johnnie Walker Red from the bar and set it down on the mantle, along with a handful of shot glasses.

Fain poured about two fingers of scotch into the glass with his free hand. "Here's what I think. Your friend, Leo Pak? The Rally got him his job at the gun shop last week. Pak called you in Seattle when he got nailed. So I'm betting you never heard of Erle before a couple of days ago. Which leads me back to how in the hell you found that Trumorpha so damn fast."

I poured myself a drink. The scotch tasted pretty good, combined with the hint of smoke from the fire.

"I ran your name past a friend of mine," Fain said. "Your service record is . . . impressive. More than one officer specifically requested that you be assigned back to their unit when you redeployed. They wanted Donovan Shaw around when shit went down. That's faith."

"The thing about having a face full of Bioglass," I said. "It's hard to blush."

"I'm saying I want you on our side enough to trust you with sensitive intel, Shaw. I need to know you're worth that trust."

In other words, don't tell the cops about the drugs, and we can negotiate.

"I'll go along if it helps Leo," I said.

Fain nodded. "That's fair. Let's start here: I know you found one red box with one hundred and forty-four vials of Trumorpha narcotics. Erle bought that box for us. To make sure that the sellers had exactly what we were looking for." He waved a hand. "We aren't drug pushers. Neither was Erle. But he was our middleman."

"In the middle of what?" I said.

"That box you found was one of two dozen stolen," said Fain. "Re-called stock of injectable oxymorphone pulled from hospitals across the nation. The manufacturers cut their losses before their product created more negative headlines about accidental addicts. The recalled stock was sent to a lab to verify the contents before being destroyed, one of their FDA regulations. But the lab got ripped off. We're trying to re-cover the drugs. Before they hit the streets, and preferably before word gets out that they're gone."

I didn't have to say anything for Fain to read my disbelief.

"The theft was an inside job," he continued. "Somebody knew about the stock of drugs, sitting in a closet until the lab got around to testing it, and they fed the information to a partner. What makes this unusual is that the inside man had a change of heart afterward. Visions of ODs and drug babies plaguing his conscience. He told his boss. The company hired us. Here's a copy of their original shipping record for that specific box."

Fain took a white piece of paper from his coat pocket and unfolded it to show me. Whatever pharma logo or title had been at the top had been blacked out on the copy, along with two or three lines that might have been the address or receiver's name. The readable portions of the page noted the oxymorphone dosages and brand name and quantity of vials contained within one box.

"You understand why I won't reveal the name of our client," Fain said.

The shipping record wasn't what I would call proof. It could be a fake, or even stolen along with the red box of Trumo. Still, if Fain was telling me the truth and Big Pharma truly was hiring private military, I wondered if the company had even bothered to notify the cops.

"Thanks to the inside man, we know who stole the drugs," Fain said. "We offered to buy them back, at better than street value. Erle Sharples was our front man. He bought that specific box on our orders. A down payment. Proof that they had the stuff, and we showed that we were willing to pay."

"Why use Erle at all?" I said.

For the first time, Fain's face was tentative.

"Because the thieves are a bunch of fucking Nazis," said Zeke.

"A white nationalist group," Fain said, recovering. "Not Aryan Brotherhood but bad enough."

Jesus. No wonder the pharma company wanted it hushed up. The media would eat them alive.

And dollars to donuts I could guess which of the hate groups Fain was talking about. The same First Riders who had plagued Mercy River before Macomber had come along.

"There's no way that one of our team could cut a deal with the skinheads," Fain said.

"Especially me," Rigoberto murmured.

"They'd make us for law, or close enough. Erle was . . . not a supremacist like them. But he was known. They'd at least listen to the offer."

"What do you mean, Erle was known?" I said.

"This town used to have a problem with the white power types."

Zeke chuckled. "Not anymore, they don't."

Fain ignored him. "A bunch of the skinheads liked to play soldier and go shooting in the hills. Erle didn't take sides. He'd sell them whatever they could pay for, and maybe not worry about the paperwork."

It jibed. And Fain being up front about the Riders gave his story a little more credibility.

"What was the deal?" I said.

Fain took a slug of his scotch. "Our first priority was making sure the gang still had the drugs. If they'd already found a buyer, or started distribution themselves, we were out of luck. Erle offered the skinheads ten grand for one box. If the box contained the real goods, we'd pay the same price for the rest of the stock."

Zeke agreed. "That's why I went to the gun shop Wednesday morning. Erle told us he had acquired the box. But as I'm walking by, there's the constable and old Henry slinging bullshit to each other. I can't shake Henry from tagging along with me to the shop. We found Erle and his guts on the floor."

So Fain and his team were suddenly left without the first box of Tru-morpha, or their middleman.

As if he were thinking the same thing, Zeke's lip curled. He looked even more like a fox when he snarled. "Now we're up shit creek. If the Nazi fuckers killed Erle, it was because they smelled a rat. Even if they didn't kill Erle, we don't have a backup for him. They're probably hunt-ing for another buyer already."

"We have to find the man Erle was in contact with. Quickly," said Fain. "And you, Shaw, have a knack for finding things."

"When I want to."

"What if I could give you solid evidence that Leo Pak didn't kill Erle? Would that be enough incentive?"

I stared at Fain. What could he be holding? I had a moment to think about the implications of his offer, as Daryll limped ponderously through the door of the lodge. He attracted attention. In addition to his size, his mop of russet hair was striped with black dye, and he wore two earrings in his left ear. His nose had been squashed and knocked crooked by old untended breaks. To the senior citizens of Mercy River, he might as well be a space alien.

Zeke made room on the couch and Daryll eased himself down.

"That was you," Daryll said, glaring at me, "last night at the gun store, yeah?"

"Yeah."

"You broke my toes, man."

"I could have stabbed your neck instead."

He grunted, still not mollified. Ingrate.

"Sorry for that," Fain said to me. "We figured anyone breaking into Erle's must be with the skinhead gang."

"Do you know who killed Erle?" I said.

Fain shook his head. "No details without something in return. I need to find the guy who sold the drugs to Erle."

"Then what? One of you will suddenly claim to have seen Leo across town when Erle died?" Perjury wasn't going to help our case. "Forget it."

"I don't mean another witness. Zeke being interviewed by the cops has already put us closer to this whole mess than I like." Fain frowned past me at Zeke. "No. I'm offering you physical evidence pointing to a different killer. Reasonable doubt, right in your hands."

"And if I don't play, you'll let Leo burn."

Fain crossed his arms and leaned back against the black bricks of the fireplace. "Desperate times, Shaw."

I thought about it. The story about the pharma company hiring them could be pure fiction. Fain's team might be aiming to score the Trumo for themselves. And I wondered how they knew Erle's shady background, to use him as their go-between. What other deals had they made, before this problem had come along?

But if Fain's story was all horseshit, it was awfully ornate horseshit. I'd been hunting for someone with motive to murder Erle. If Fain and his men had been using Erle Sharples as a pawn to reacquire the drugs, then maybe all of us were trying to find the same person. Fain believed I could be his bloodhound to find Erle's contact. There was no reason to talk him out of it.

I pointed to Fain. "The man Erle was dealing with, the one who stole the drugs in the first place. The lab's inside man must have known his name."

"You'll take the job?"

"We're still talking."

"Jaeger. That's the name that the inside man knew him by. The leader of the skinhead group. Jaeger might be a gang handle. No first name, no address."

"Did the inside man meet Jaeger in person?"

"Fifty years old," Fain answered immediately. "Medium size, medium build. With a mustache. Not much to go on, I know. And scary. That was the main thing. The pharma guy said Jaeger was scary."

Daryll snorted at that.

I stood up. "I'll find him. The box of Trumo stays with me until Leo's free. If this is a scam, you'll have bigger problems than some missing dope."

Zeke grinned in amusement. Fain returned my look without blinking. Then he handed me a business card with a phone number written on it.

"And if you pull any tricks," he said, "if you give us information that doesn't lead anywhere, we'll have to create some problems for you in return."

I nodded.

As I left, I saw Rigoberto out of the corner of my eye, looking at Fain and shrugging. *Worth a shot*, he seemed to say. *We can always bury Shaw if it doesn't work out.*

At least we'd reached an understanding.

THE SMALL TOWN HAD quieted enough that I could hear the recorded chimes of the Methodist church from a quarter mile off as they tolled two o'clock in the morning. During the past hour, there had been only four people on the side street that fronted the Suite Mercy Inn. One had been a drunken local, shuffling through and mumbling grievances to himself. The other had been a pair of active-duty Rangers, equally soused but a lot happier. They had propped their asses on the window-sill of the post office until their beers were empty and their heads full of plans for the future.

None of them had noticed the last person, me, standing in a sliver of an alley behind a row of compost bins, ignoring the reek of rotting cabbage and moldy bread while I watched the inn. When the street was empty, I took out my phone and scrolled through some old emails. I didn't have a current number for the person I needed to contact. Armando Ochoa.

I owed Fain one thing. He'd said the word *intel*, and that got me wondering how I might dredge up a little inside information for myself.

Ochoa and I had survived the sixty-one hellish days of Ranger School together. Despite its name, the school was a leadership course open to all comers in the armed forces, not just those of us in the 75th Regiment. Anyone serious about an Army career aimed to graduate from the school and earn the two-and-a-half-inch tab that simply read RANGER. Ochoa was serious about his career.

Both of us were still shy of twenty years old, me a mere private first class, Ochoa fresh out of OCS wearing the shiny butter bar of a newly minted second lieutenant. Our service launched in different directions. I went to Iraq and eventually into the path of the rock shrapnel that tore my face apart for a while. He returned to the Intelligence Corps and on up the ranks.

Last I knew, Ochoa was a captain looking hard at major, and working smack in the middle of the Department of Defense. Fine hunting grounds for a political animal like Armando. And a prime position to help me out.

That was if Ochoa was still in the Army, and still assigned where he had some access, and most of all was willing to use that access to help me. A lot of hurdles. I found the right email and sent a request to call me ASAP.

No sooner had I switched off my phone when Big Daryll's GMC Yukon glided up the street until it found an open space. Fain and Daryll and Rigoberto and Zeke all got out and made their way into the hotel. A couple of minutes later, lights began to illuminate windows. One on the second floor. One, two, and three on the third. In one of the third-floor rooms, I saw Daryll's unmistakably huge shape limp to the window to close the curtains.

You never could tell what information might be useful. Captain Fain understood that. He'd somehow pulled my Army service history—highly classified information—mere hours after meeting me. That had been surprising, and a little unsettling. I felt marginally better now that I knew where Fain and his crew slept.

TWENTY

I WAS WAITING OUTSIDE THE Rally office with two coffees in hand when Dez arrived to start her morning shift, along with the elfin young woman I recognized from the card game.

"You said something about an apology," she said.

"Yeah." I handed her one of the coffee cups.

Dez promptly handed off the cup to her friend, along with a ring of keys. "Jaye, would you open up? I'll be back in five minutes. No more." She eyed me to make sure I'd gotten the message before walking away. I strode to catch up.

"Did Leo know about your mother and Erle Sharples?" I said.

"I still don't hear the word *sorry* coming out of your mouth. Just more accusations."

"Do you think Leo killed Erle? For you?"

Her mouth parted, maybe halfway into telling me to stuff it, and then shut again.

"Because Leo fears the same thing about you," I said. "That you're the one who shot Erle. You two are a matched set."

She stopped. "He—No, that's not right."

"It explains some things. Why Leo's so damned uncooperative with his lawyer. Why he pled guilty. He's trying to keep the police from tagging you as a suspect. And it's working."

Dez took that in, staring in my direction but not really seeing me. Her hand gripped the hitching post outside a small tack and feed store, as if she were afraid the post or she might suddenly float away.

"Oh, Leo," she said at last.

"I had you wrong," I said. "I learned that Erle cheated you out of your inheritance. Leo let slip that you needed money before you could get free of Mercy River. I couldn't figure out why he wouldn't go immediately to the cops when he found Erle's body—unless he thought he was protecting you."

"No, I never went to Erle's shop at all," said Dez. "I had planned to, when I got off work that afternoon. I even told Leo I would. We'd argued about it the night before. He was upset. He didn't think I should be alone."

"Alone with Erle?"

"I couldn't leave Mercy River without confronting him. I'd been avoiding it for too long. And having Leo with me would have—It wouldn't be me standing up for myself. Not with Leo there menacing Erle at the same time."

"Then somebody shot Erle early that morning. You were gone. Leo found the body and thought you'd changed your mind and gone to confront Erle on your own."

"I didn't learn what had happened until after I returned from picking up the Rally supplies down in Bend," she said. "Late that evening. I was probably the last person to hear the news in the whole town. I thought of Leo immediately. I worried what he might have done. But he didn't answer his phone. Why didn't he call me?"

Because Leo was smart enough not to talk about what had happened over an open line. He'd wiped the murder weapon after finding Erle's body, in case Dez's fingerprints were on it. Then he had lain low for the day, unaware that he was already a prime suspect thanks to Henry Gillespie spotting him entering the gun shop. When evening came, he went to the saloon to wait until Dez returned from her trip to Bend, and found himself facing mob justice.

"Jaye went to Leo's arraignment for me," Dez said. "My spy. When I heard that Leo had pled guilty I thought he was throwing himself on the court for leniency. God."

"Your town is fucked up," I said.

"That's why I'm leavin'." Dez said it as a joke, but her voice wavered a little.

"I mean it. I've been in hot zones that didn't feel as tightly wound as Mercy River. When I first arrived I thought it was from the Rally, parading like Ringling Brothers with rifles. But everyone I've met here has a grudge."

"You're a city kid, huh?" Her mouth twisted wryly. "After we leave, this town will be what it was before. Isolated. Rigid. People using their secrets and prejudices to chew one another to pieces."

"So I'm learning. Who's got their fangs out for you?"

"Just my ex. But you already know that."

I shook my head. "An ex-boyfriend?"

Dez looked perplexed. "Wayne, of course. He's my husband. Leo didn't tell you?"

The immediate rush I got wasn't fueled by caffeine.

"You're married to Constable Beacham?" I said.

"Technically. We've lived apart for more than a year now. That's why Leo and I have been keeping our relationship so secret. God, if Wayne knew . . ."

But he did know. I had no real proof of that fact. Except that Beacham had been right up front in the rush to capture Leo, and he'd made damn quick use of his baton. Like it was personal.

"Wayne wants you back," I said, sure enough to make it a statement.

She inhaled. "He used to. I don't know anymore."

"Why's that?"

"I told Wayne last week I was filing the divorce papers. And moving away. He took it a lot better than I'd imagined. Isn't that strange?"

"What?"

"Breaking the news to Wayne went so well, it gave me the courage to confront Erle. I decided it was time to close out all my unfinished business."

Except somebody finished it for her. "Erle wouldn't simply hand over the money."

"No. But I wasn't going to give the creep a choice. He could pay me half the money that my mother left him, or I would contest the will on grounds of fraud. Try to prove Mom was too far gone to fully understand what she was doing and I was too young to raise hell about it." She grimaced ruefully. "Erle was vain. He cared a lot for his reputation."

"That might have worked," I said.

"I'll never know now."

We started back toward the Rally offices. Fain had nearly convinced me that Erle was killed by Jaeger when the deal to buy back the stolen drugs went shitways. It made sense. But there were a lot of weird overlaps that Wednesday morning. The timing of Leo showing up, and Constable Beacham—Dez's goddamn husband—standing right up the road being the weirdest.

Zeke Caton had been there. He'd talked to Beacham, and Gillespie. Maybe he could shed some light.

"I know things are bad for Leo," I said to Dez, "but there's hope."

"That's what I keep telling myself. While things get worse and worse." She halted, right before we reached the Rally office, and touched fingers to her eyes. "I wish I hadn't given away that coffee." She tried to laugh.

I handed her the rest of mine. "I'll get word to Leo. Tell him you're still on his side."

"Thank you. Leo was right. You're a good guy."

I believed she meant that. But then, I couldn't hold on to Luce, so what did I know?

TWENTY-ONE

I COUNTED DOWN TO THE right room, third door off the Suite Mercy Inn's single stairwell, and thumped on it. No answer. I repeated the process on the next room over. After a crash of movement and a muffled curse, the maple-wood door flew inward, replaced by Daryll, who was no less solid.

"Where's Zeke?" I said.

He glared balefully at me over his crooked nose. "Next door."

"Not at home. Where else?"

"Try the pistol competition."

"I'll do that. Tell me the timeline of the deal you guys made with Erle. When you got in touch, when you gave him the money, all of it."

"You're supposed to be finding Jaeger."

"And I'm doing it fast. You want to talk about it out here?"

He glanced down the empty hallway. Maybe checking whether anyone was listening, or judging whether he could clock me one without witnesses. After another quick glower he stepped aside and let me in.

It was a small room, further reduced by Daryll and two packed four-foot-long duffel bags that took up most of the tatty carpet. He hefted one out of the way and tossed it onto the rumpled bed, which groaned under the sudden weight.

"Zeke grew up here. Erle knew him." Daryll limped three steps to the dresser, plucking a can of tomato juice from stacked six-packs and two-pound canisters of protein powder. Half the drawers in the dresser were open and stuffed full of clothes. The closet rack was equally packed with loaded hangers. Either Daryll traveled with a full wardrobe, or he'd moved into the inn for a long stay.

He downed the juice in between sentences. "So we let Zeke handle the liaison shit. He gave the money to Erle on Tuesday morning. Then Erle calls back late that night. He tells us it's already done, he's got the box, and Zeke goes to meet him at the shop first thing Wednesday to confirm it. But Erle's dead. No box, no money."

It had taken Erle less than a full day to go out of town, meet Jaeger, and come back. And, I reminded myself, to hide the box of opiates in his hiding place in the woods. That wasn't a nighttime kind of job, driving the ATV up into the forest. I guessed that Erle had made it back to Mercy River before sundown on Tuesday, stashing the box and calling Zeke Caton to say mission accomplished.

"What about the rest of the deal?" I said. "If the box confirmed the drugs were legit, when would you give Erle the two hundred thirty thousand to buy the whole score?"

I must have needed more coffee. The words came out of my mouth before I connected them with the duffel bags. I reached out and un-zipped the one on the bed.

"Hey," Daryll said, too late.

Christ. FN riot guns with drum magazines. CS tear gas canisters. A case of 40mm sponge grenades and a big Milkor launcher that looked like a huge-bored tommy gun to go with them. And if all of those less-lethal options didn't work out, two M4 carbines.

"Paying off Jaeger wasn't the plan," I said. "You were going to take the drugs."

Daryll folded his huge arms and leaned against the dresser, making it creak dangerously.

"Did Erle know, or was he just your stalking horse to get to the skin-heads?"

"Nobody trusted Erle," Daryll said.

"Guess not."

I didn't have to wonder how far Fain and his men were willing to go to retrieve the drugs. If the white supremacists wanted to push back, no one was going to shed any tears about what happened next.

"Same question applies," I said. "How soon was the deal going down?"

"No point wasting time. If we confirmed they had the right shit, we were going to make Erle set up a meet for the next day."

"Thursday."

"Thursday follows Wednesday, don't it?"

It was Saturday morning now. Had the First Riders already given up waiting and gone home?

"If that's all, get out," said Daryll, shifting his stance. "I've been up all damn night, thanks to you."

"Painkillers not helping the foot?"

"I don't take 'em. Not anymore."

"In between jobs for Big Pharma"—I nodded at the duffel bags— "how do you make your money? All four of you musketeers."

"Out."

I grinned. "Keep those toes elevated."

Outside, I pieced together what I knew about Erle and his movements on the day before he died. He'd collected the ten grand and returned before nightfall to hide the red box full of Trumo. Sundown came early in October, full dark by eight o'clock or so. Say Erle had eleven hours, tops. That was still enough time for a round trip to Portland or Yakima or even across the Idaho border and back if you were pushing it.

But I didn't think the buy would have been set that far away. There was no reason for it. Jaeger and his skinheads knew who Erle was, where he lived. They would choose someplace a short drive from Mercy River, where they could crash unobtrusively for a couple of days before completing the deal and going home with nearly a quarter million in cash.

Instead, they had sold Erle one lonely box and were still sitting on twenty-three, as well as their own thumbs.

How had Jaeger been in contact with Erle? The police report listing Erle's belongings hadn't mentioned them finding a cell phone with the body, either a burner or Erle's personal phone. That was odd. It was possible that Jaeger had taken it, covering his tracks after shooting Erle. Or maybe Erle had hidden the burner in his home, although Fain and his men hadn't found it there.

Erle's home address had been dutifully listed in the police reports. I'd have to see the place for myself. Tossing Erle's house had a slim chance of success, but better odds than throwing a dart at a map of Oregon to find where the skinheads might be holed up.

ERLE SHARPLES'S HOUSE ECHOED the man's penchant for privacy. Set high on one of the hills overlooking the town, the ranch home with its fake log-cabin siding was large enough to let everyone know the owner had some money, and cheap enough to make it obvious that he hated spending it.

A county sheriff's SUV was parked in Erle's driveway. Maybe Lieutenant Yerby had had the same notion about giving Sharples's home a second look. I pulled my cap low and kept driving. I'd have to circle back later in the day.

As I passed, I saw that one windowless side of the house had been adorned with two dozen pairs of antlers. Six- and eight-point bucks, mostly, with a couple of the pairs large enough that they might have been taken from elk. There were deer skulls as well. All of the antlers had been bleached dirty-white by the elements, until their color matched the bone of the skulls. Dez had said Erle was vain. He certainly believed in showing off his trophies.

I stopped for a light. A teenage Redcap was crossing the street in front of the truck.

"Hi," I called out the window. "Can you tell me where the pistol shooting is today?"

"Pronghorn," she said, apparently proud to answer so quickly.

"What's that?"

"The ghost town. Up in the hills?" At my baffled expression she pointed. "You can take a shuttle over there at the hall."

I thanked her and turned right from the left-hand lane to change direction. A ghost town. I shouldn't be surprised. Ganz and I had passed enough abandoned barns and corrals on the drive into central Oregon to house a herd of spectral cattle.

Sure enough, a chalkboard sign in front of the town hall announced shuttles leaving for Pronghorn and the pistol competitions every ten minutes. Smaller writing underneath noted the start times for each round: Target Range, Moving Range, Stress Drill, and something called Special Games. The point leader from each round won a year's worth of ammunition at the firing range of their choice. The overall leader would be awarded an engraved Beretta, an idea filched from the Army's own Ranger contests.

The prizes wouldn't lack for contenders. Twenty men milled around the sidewalk, most of them toting cases for guns and gear.

"Are you shooting today?" A Redcap, complete with clipboard.

"Just watching. Is Zeke Caton on your list there? He's a buddy of mine."

"Um." She scanned the pages, tapping the last one. "Yes! He went up early this morning. He signed up for all of the rounds. Oh, here come the shuttles."

Two Ford Expeditions pulled up to the curb. Rangers rushed to fill their seats to capacity and beyond. I got into my truck when Moulson and Booker knocked on the window.

"You driving to Pronghorn?" Moulson said.

"Hop in."

Booker climbed carefully into the front seat as Moulson tossed their bags into the back and clambered after.

"How was the football?" I said.

"They won. Barely," Moulson answered as Booker scowled.

"Think I pulled a groin muscle," he said, "trying to run in that frigging mud. I was supposed to have Abernathy blocking for me, but the fool busted his foot."

I pulled away from the curb, following the second shuttle. "*Daryll Abernathy?*"

"You heard of him? He was All-American offensive line for Iowa. Skipped the draft to enlist."

I'd really wrecked Big Daryll's weekend. His own damn fault for jumping me.

The shuttles turned east, following the side streets out of town and onto a road I hadn't driven on before. It ran alongside a lazily flowing river, the water equal parts blue and deep green with silt from the bottom. The current swirled in eddies and splashed over the rocks in the shallows.

"Damn, I might move out here someday," Moulson said, "for the fishing alone."

"No calzone places in town," Booker said, scrolling through his phone, "and the cell reception sucks in the boonies."

He was right. My own phone flickered between NO SERVICE and one lonesome signal bar. And we weren't more than ten miles out of Mercy River yet.

We were also climbing, slowly but surely. I guessed the elevation at around half a mile. The terrain had evolved from the thick clumps of evergreen and juniper trees near town to something more arid, while the rolling hills had been replaced by rocky, reddish buttes and peaks. We passed another sign warning drivers to watch for falling rocks. The pavement ended in packed dirt as the road became steeper. My Dodge's engine strained a little to keep up with the newer SUVs.

"You guys been to Pronghorn before?" I said.

Booker gave a thumbs-up. "Last year. They gave a talk on it."

"And Ken here actually paid attention," Moulson jibed.

"Pronghorn was a mining town," Booker said, ignoring his friend like usual, "named for the antelope that used to be thick around here. The railroad at the time went through the town. Then the mines dried up and everybody left, including the train."

In another two miles, I saw the ghost town for myself. The dirt road led us through a tight collection of deteriorating wooden structures, ranging in size from sheds to stables. Most of them had lost their roofs, and all of them sagged sideways by at least a few degrees.

We passed what might have been the railway station, back when trains had run on wood and coal. Whatever track hadn't been torn up for scrap a century ago had long since been buried by the elements, rails and ties alike. The piled stone foundation survived as an incongruous rectangle in the grass.

But Pronghorn's remnants weren't the first thing that caught the eye. A massive orange-red butte towered above the town like a second sky. Eons of weather had formed the huge rock into a roughly cylindrical shape. By late afternoon, all of Pronghorn would be completely in its shadow.

The butte was marked by more than just the elements. A steep narrow road had been hacked and dynamited into its face. The road started at the far end of the ghost town and disappeared up and around the opposite side of the colossal rock.

"A mining road?" I said, pointing to it.

"Yeah," said Moulson. "We hiked up there last year after the shooting. Hell of a view."

"But hold on to your ass with both hands if you try driving," Booker broke in. "There's a deep ravine below the butte on the other side. Right where the road gets narrow."

"The express elevator to hell," Moulson said, sounding elated by the notion. "Hardly know what hit ya."

"Not fast enough for me," Booker mused. "Give me an aneurysm, maybe while I'm sleeping. Like switching off a light."

There was something to be said for that. I'd spent a lot of years accepting the probability of my own demise while training like a demon to prevent it. Japanese samurai supposedly had that same attitude. Readiness for the moment. My only hope had been that if death came in battle, it would come as a head shot. I wouldn't see it coming and probably wouldn't feel a thing. The combat equivalent of Booker's ruptured cranial artery. Full dark. Instantly.

TWENTY-TWO

PAST THE GHOST TOWN, we found the first of the shooting ranges. I understood why the Rally had set the contests here. Aside from the novelty of Pronghorn itself, the desolate town was bordered by broad, flat fields, perfect for short-range shooting, with the steep first edges of the huge butte serving as natural backstops.

We parked and Moulson and Booker thanked me as they hurried off to the competition. The crackle of small-arms fire signaled that one of the rounds was already under way. I walked along the fields, looking for Zeke Caton. Contestants stood in short lines, shooting at targets placed at five, ten, and twenty-five meters. In the distance, I saw a circular target fly through the air on a zip line. That would be the Moving Range. It wasn't tough to guess what the Stress Range would consist of. A whole lot of push-ups and shuttle runs to get the blood pounding, before racing to the firing line and lighting up multiple targets, maybe with a hot reload—one round left in the chamber as the shooter drops the magazine and replaces it in a single movement before firing again. We'd done plenty of stress exercises in Army training, some of it while wearing seventy-plus pounds of battle rattle and ruck.

I hadn't found Zeke among the competitors, and was about to ask someone when I spotted his familiar yellow hiking jacket at the farthest field, where the mining road curved and climbed out of sight above the town. I jogged to meet him.

"Zeke," I said. He turned from the table where he was plugging AA batteries into a palm-sized black plastic gadget. Two spare devices of the same type waited on the table, along with extra batteries and colored light bulbs, and a miscellaneous collection of other electronic bits and pieces. The device had a toggle switch on its top side.

"Hey, man," he said, with a glance toward the range. Half a dozen Rangers were working to get it ready, none of them within earshot. "I figured you'd be out playing Nazi hunter."

"That's why I'm here, to figure out the timing. If Jaeger and his men shot Erle that morning, you and Henry and the constable must have just missed them. Maybe somebody else saw them when they arrived. Run through what happened with me."

He frowned. "Not much to it. We knew Erle had the box. I met Fain at the coffeehouse on Main Street when it opened. We waited there for Erle to send the all-clear."

"Send it to you?"

"I grew up around here. And Erle wasn't a trusting type."

"But your team did some business with Sharples before this, right?"

"Shit." Zeke checked the range again. "That isn't what I'd call relevant, Shaw."

"It might be, if Erle's sideline got him killed. Fain said the skinheads could check his bona fides. What was Erle into?"

"Uh-uh. I can't get into that. Fain would tell Daryll to twist my spine like licorice."

Zeke wasn't budging. I'd have to try a different approach.

"Okay," I said. "We'll stick with what happened that morning. Time-stamp it. When did you and Fain meet? When did Erle tell you it was clear?"

"The coffeehouse opened at seven. Erle gave us the signal at ten past the hour. He sent me a text."

The police report had said Erle turned off the cameras at 6:40 A.M. I still didn't know what he had been doing for half an hour before signaling Zeke. "What did you do after you got Erle's message?"

"Problem was, from where we sat with our coffee, Fain and I had been watching Wayne Beacham dicking around at the top of the dead-end road. Having a cop around wasn't part of the plan. We decided I should still go to the gun shop, so Erle wouldn't panic. I walked up Main to the intersection. By then Henry Gillespie was there, too, talking to Wayne. Kinda screwed the idea of me strolling down to the shop without being noticed. Not that it mattered. Erle was dead already."

Barely. Erle had signaled Zeke that the cameras were off and had been murdered almost immediately thereafter. Leo might have crossed paths with the killer when he arrived at twenty past seven. Why had security-conscious Erle Sharples arranged to hand off the box of stolen drugs when Leo was due to show up for work?

"And you and Fain both saw Beacham the whole time, since seven in the morning," I said.

"Yeah. You think he's a suspect?" Zeke shook his head. "Wayne, shit. I've known Wayne since high school football. He didn't kill Erle. And Henry can barely kill pheasants."

"Just shooting down theories," I said.

"If you want to shoot shit, you're in the right place. Check this out."

He motioned to the range. There were only two firing positions in this field, set a few meters apart and marked by wooden sawhorses. Downfield from each position, four-foot wooden posts had been placed at varying distances on the range, in a pattern identical for both shooters. Each post was topped with a pie-plate-sized steel target with a number painted on it, ranging from 1 to 9. The closest target to each firing position was numbered 5, the farthest 7. As I watched, a guy with his hair shaved into a floppy Mohawk tapped one of the targets with his fist, and it fell backward on a hinge.

"I call it Nine-Ball," Zeke said. "The shooter gets only nine rounds.

Frangible, so they won't ricochet off the target. Draw and shoot all nine targets, in order. First one to knock down all nine of their targets, or highest target hit, wins."

"Not bad."

"It gets better." He smiled wickedly. "For the final eight shooters, it becomes a quick-draw contest. You have to holster and slap the saw-horse between each shot."

"Without blowing your foot off."

"That's why we have these maniacs sign release forms."

"And you invented the game. How many times have you won it?"

"Every time, dude. I'm un-fucking-beatable."

The guy with the Mohawk waved from the rear of the range, near a taller post without a target on it. "Gimme one of the bulbs," he hollered, "and bring the switch."

Zeke picked up a green light bulb and the toggle switch he'd loaded with batteries and jogged downrange. I examined the assortment of spare parts on the table, an idea forming in my head.

By the time Zeke reached him, Mohawk had set up a ladder by the tall post. Zeke handed off the green bulb. Mohawk screwed the bulb into a socket on the post and took the toggle switch from Zeke. He clicked the switch a couple of times and the green bulb obediently flashed on and off.

"Ready for a test," Mohawk said once the two men returned to the firing position.

"Let's do it." Zeke stripped off his yellow jacket and tossed it aside to adjust his hard-shell holster. It was high on the thigh, standard Army placement for the pistol to be within reach but under where body armor would lie. He stepped to the firing position. Mohawk and I moved back behind him.

"Clear," called Mohawk, pointing the little switch downrange. Two men on either side of the small range shouted the same. Zeke was completely still, his hand hovering over his pistol.

A hush had fallen. The light bulb blazed green. Before I'd fully registered the fact, Zeke drew and began firing in one liquid motion, his shots coming so quick that the clangs on the steel targets sounded like a finger riff on a piano. Nine shots, nine separate targets downed, all in barely five seconds including the draw.

There was a scattering of applause and whistles. Zeke holstered his pistol—a compact Glock 19 with an extended magazine—and bounced on his toes.

"S'all right," Mohawk pronounced, pocketing the toggle switch in his baggy fleece coat. "But we need a starting whistle along with the light." He walked to the jumbled collection of electronics at the table. Zeke and I joined him. The ground was less even here, and I nearly twisted my ankle on a hole, stumbling against Mohawk.

"Sorry," I said, dusting him off.

"Lay off the morning beers, friend," he said.

"That's a pretty good draw," I said to Zeke, without a lot of enthusiasm.

"You can do better?"

"Not for free."

"Hundred bucks," he said, as Mohawk went to install the starting whistle at the bulb. "And I'll make it easier. One shot, first target, winner takes all."

"Make it a thousand. Against telling me what kind of work Erle handled for Fain."

"Fuck." He made the word two syllables. "We back to that? Come on."

"You have to bet big to win big, champ."

Zeke peered downrange, then at me. "Deal. But you better have that grand on you."

He grabbed a gym bag from under the table and brought out a metal lockbox for a pistol, and a frayed soft holster. "I'm gonna guess that you're still a Beretta guy, yeah? Standard-issue?"

"It's what I know."

"I like my Glock. Faster action." He handed me the box, its lid open to show a Beretta M9, new enough that it still smelled of factory oil.

"If this is a hustle, you picked the wrong mark," Zeke said, holding out a loaded magazine.

I'd just seen Zeke draw. His gun had cleared the holster at least as fast as I'd ever managed when I was in uniform. And I wasn't sure he had even been trying.

"Set it up," I said, taking the magazine.

He grinned and went to join Mohawk. I went about threading my belt through the holster clips.

By the time they returned, I had taken my place at the second firing position, to Zeke's right.

"You want a warm-up shot?" he asked, toeing the line behind the first sawhorse.

"Nope."

"Confidence. I like that. Ollie here can judge which of us hits his target first, if there's any question. We'll shoot at number nine. All right?" Halfway down the range. Eleven meters.

"Ready?" Mohawk said, moving behind us.

"Yeah," Zeke said around his grin. I nodded.

I exhaled the tension from my body. My feet were already planted, knees bent, left side angled toward the target. Left hand resting against my thigh.

Mohawk shouted, "Clear," and the answer came back.

My right hand floated an inch above the grip of the gun.

I watched the center of the pie-plate target, not the bulb.

A second passed, then another.

The bulb stayed dark.

"Ain't working," Mohawk said. Zeke turned to look at him, and with my left hand I pressed the toggle switch in my pocket, the one I'd lifted when I'd stumbled against Mohawk and substituted a different switch into his fleece jacket with its batteries in backward.

The bulb blazed green and a high whistle sounded. I drew and aimed and fired. The target banged down, as Zeke wheeled around to see for himself.

"Goddammit," Zeke said. "Ollie, you fucking idiot."

"Must be faulty," said Mohawk, unperturbed. "I'll get a new switch."

Laughter rippled through the small crowd of spectators.

"Well," Zeke said, holstering his Glock. "That don't count."

"Hell it don't," said one of the spectators. "My man kept his focus." There were murmurs of support. No one seemed to mind seeing the champion taken down a peg.

"He hit the target first, Z," called Mohawk as he walked downrange to check the light.

Zeke swore again.

"So spill," I said.

He puffed out his cheeks. "Two out of three."

"Think of it this way. I'm going to be kicking over every rock in Erle's life. If I know what he did for your crew, there's a chance I can keep that information quiet."

Zeke spat into the arid dirt. "I tell you, you don't say shit about it to Fain. Okay?"

"I wasn't even here."

"There's a guy like Erle in every county. The kind who goes to swap meets and shows all over America. Fifteen, twenty years of swapping beers and bullshit with dickheads like him from Kentucky or Montana or wherever. Yeah? Birds of the same feather. A network of buddies like that can come by any matériel a man might ask for. Even if he's a picky shopper."

And who knew ordnance better than Spec Ops soldiers? I thought back to the duffel full of grenade launchers in Daryll's room.

"So Erle was your arms supplier. That's not so unusual, a few guns falling off a truck," I said, "even if they are Army-issue."

"It's who those guns came from, dude," Zeke said.

I put his hints together. Erle dealt in guns. Erle was known among the white power groups. When Fain's team had needed arms, they had turned a blind eye to how and from whom Erle had acquired the weapons. Even if it was from the same First Riders that Macomber—and probably Fain and his crew—had kicked out of Mercy River.

"Jaeger knew Erle before this," I said. "You think he figured out that Erle was fronting for your team?"

"Don't know. Don't care. Erle fucked up somehow, and they blew him away. You're wasting our time with this shit, Shaw. Just find Jaeger. We'll handle the hard stuff."

He hitched his belt and walked away, swagger back in place. Let Zeke have his games. I might not be the fastest gun in the West, but I was in the running for the slyest.

BEFORE I LEFT PRONGHORN, I drove up the mining road that spiraled around and up the giant butte. A series of signs at the bottom illustrated falling rocks and warned SINGLE LANE ROAD—NO PASSING—NO TURN OUTS—USE AT OWN RISK. I kept the truck in second gear as it climbed the grade.

Booker hadn't been kidding about the ravine on the butte's opposite side. I became extremely aware of the lack of any guardrail between the truck and the drop, only five or six short feet away. I stopped the truck and got out to take a closer look.

While the road had only climbed halfway up the butte, about two hundred feet from the floor of the ghost town, the ravine fell another hundred feet or more below that. Its bottom was not the flat pastureland that Pronghorn had been built upon, but a jagged reach of black volcanic rock, its sharp pillars and mounds like rotted teeth in a primeval maw. I wondered how many wagons and horses and miners had been lost to the chasm over the decades that the mine had been operating. If I poked around down there, I might find rusted bits of barrels and old horseshoes. And likely some bones to go with them.

Moulson had joked about the suddenness of that brand of death. Not fast enough, Booker had insisted.

I had to side with Booker on that one. Spare me that horrible moment of realization, before the end.

I'd kept very busy since last night. Since Luce. Staying in motion had spared me from having to think much about her engagement, and what if anything I was supposed to do about it. I couldn't shake the feeling that Luce had wanted me to say something, share something, more than simple congratulations. Because despite our breaking up, there was still chemistry. I wasn't imagining that. Had she wondered if I was changing my ways? Or was she proving to herself that she'd made the right choice?

I took the toggle switch I'd pickpocketed from Mohawk and tossed it into the ravine, like a coin into a well. Make a wish. Luce and me. Maybe a quick and final end was best for our relationship, too.

TWENTY-THREE

MY PHONE BEEPED AS I neared Mercy River. I'd missed a call while the phone had been out of range, from a Northern Virginia area code. I grinned as I tapped the number to call back.

"Shaw?" Armando Ochoa answered.

"Hey, Armando. Are you one of the Joint Chiefs yet?"

"How the hell are you?" he said. "Scratch that, where the hell are you?"

"Right now I'm in a town called Mercy River. Oregon."

"The Rally."

I should have expected Ochoa would be clued in.

"Armando, I have to call in my marker."

He paused. "What's so serious?"

I didn't want to tell Ochoa the whole story. Besides incriminating myself, it would make him an accessory after the fact, and maybe worse, if things in Mercy River escalated. And while I trusted Armando, our friendship had been a long time ago.

"I'm trying to help a brother out of a jam," I said. "I need background checks on some former Rangers. Service records, VA, whatever the regiment can provide."

"You're joking, I know."

"Plus color commentary, if anyone is willing to talk off the record. I need to know the story on these guys."

"Uh-huh. Sure. You know I can't call up SOC and ask nicely for the files, right?"

"It's important."

Another pause. Ochoa sighed. "And I gave you a promise. Dammit."

In the sixty-one days of Ranger School, food had been nearly as scarce as sleep. We ate once or twice each day, wolfing down a meal in seconds. It wasn't nearly enough. Constant stress and exercise burned four times the calories we ravenously consumed. Already-fit soldiers would lose twenty or thirty pounds. It was all part of the Army's gauntlet, pushing us past our assumed limits, mentally, physically, and emotionally. The drop rate was staggering. Our class had started with three hundred and twenty men. One hundred and nine remained by the third and final phase. It came down to who wanted it badly enough to keep moving forward when everything you had was spent.

As a big kid pumped up from my initial cycles of training, I at least had some muscle to spare. Ochoa did not. He was small and lean and one of the fastest runners over long distances I'd ever seen outside watching the Olympics. He could beat thirty minutes in our five-mile tests like he was strolling on the beach. But in the middle of our final phase, Ochoa's reserves of endurance finally found their limit.

We were in the swamp, outside of Elgin Air Force Base in Florida, our unit wading hip-deep in brackish water, when Ochoa stopped dead in front of me. It was two hours before dawn would even start to paint the horizon. Only the glow of his cat eyes—the reflective tabs on his helmet—kept me from knocking him over. Thinking he was stuck in the mud, I started to give him a pull, then felt his arm shaking under my hand.

"Mando?" I'd said.

"Can't catch my breath." He leaned, and I tightened my grip to keep him from keeling face-first into the icy water.

"Move your asses," I heard Whitlock say behind us. Whitlock had the platoon leader role for this exercise, and he was enough of a dick-weed even before the pressure got to him.

"Mudhole. We'll catch up," I said. Whitlock moved on without offer-ing to help, as I'd known he would.

I scrabbled at my arm pouch. I had sugar packs and a few bites of jerky that I'd been holding on to, watertight in a Ziploc.

"Eat these," I said, practically stuffing the food into Ochoa's mouth. "No time to wait."

"I can't—"

"We have to move. Move or die. Come on."

I hauled at him, practically lifting the skinny cat and his forty pounds of gear into something resembling forward motion. He stepped, stum-bled, stepped again.

"Less than a mile to the extraction," I said. I wasn't positive of that. They sometimes moved the finish line on us. But Ochoa didn't need to be reminded of the truth right that minute. I poured a packet of sugar into his hand so he could wash it down with sips from his canteen.

Switching arms every hundred yards or so, I pushed and threatened and half carried Ochoa to the inflatable Zodiac. My shoulders felt like they were made of molten lava. Whitlock was mad enough to scream, our team was so far behind the pace. By the time we reached the camp and the blessed three-hour nap that awaited, I'd badgered a powdered sport drink and a precious hoarded candy bar off a buddy and gotten a few bites of it down Ochoa's throat. He told me later that he didn't remember hiking from the boat to the camp.

Three weeks later, on the day before graduation, Ochoa walked up and crashed down next to me on the couch in the lounge. I had my leg propped on ice packs, nursing swollen ligaments in my knee. The back of my neck was coated in ointment. Something in the swamp had given me dermatitis harsh enough to blister my skin.

A reality show had been playing on the TV, Jersey meatheads sharing a house with Malibu blondes. Watching television after two months of torture was a surreal experience. Even the dumbest shows were enter-taining in their insanity.

"I owe you," Ochoa had said.

"For what?" I'd muttered, still looped from the unfamiliar full night of sleep, and a natural epinephrine high that came and went at odd times, like jet lag without ever boarding a plane. My brain found the right groove a second later, and the memory of the swamp came back. "That's the job. Forget it."

"I was going to give up. I would have been dropped, or at least recy-cled." Recycling meant a Ranger candidate was sent to the purgatory of the Gulag, to do crap work like post beautification or shaking out parachutes while waiting for a chance to start the phase all over again with the next class. "You'd be there right along with me, if we'd fucked the mission."

"So buy me a Baby Ruth. And a beer. Two beers—I'll pour one on my neck."

"You aren't that stupid." Ochoa's expression belonged on someone a lot older than nineteen. "The world runs on favors. Take it."

I grinned at his grave face. "Fine. You owe me. When they name you Don Corleone, I want the New York sports book."

Ochoa had shaken his head and bounced off. I hadn't given the in-cident another thought. But years after, when I learned Armando had been assigned to the Defense Department, I mentally filed that favor under *Someday*.

"Can you help?" I said to him over the phone.

"Gimme the names," Ochoa said.

"John Fain, captain. Zeke Caton, I don't know what Zeke is short for. And two others that probably served in Fain's platoon. Daryll Ab-ernathy, and Rigoberto. I don't have a last name on him yet, but I'll get that."

"No, don't, it'll make this too easy for me," Ochoa said, as dry as parchment.

"One more. General Charles Macomber."

"Oh, come on."

"You know him?"

"God, do you live with horse blinders on? Did you pay any attention to the regiment news during your enlistment? Or did you spend all your time learning new ways to rappel onto your head?"

I didn't bother interrupting.

"Macomber was talked up to run the regiment after Kosovo, when he was a colonel. But he chose a political track into the Department of Defense. I assume he was gunning for higher command in SOCOM. He made brigadier general and then MG. He worked on the Hill for a few years. By the end he was a regular fixture in front of Congress, arguing the Army's case for better equipment, better benefits."

"So far he sounds ready-made for a statue in the park. What happened?"

"If I remember right, it was more about his method than the motive. He got religion. He singed the ass of more than one ally by pushing instead of compromising. I think finally there was some sort of scandal or fight behind closed doors. Before the dust settled they had put him out to pasture."

Literally. There was no shortage of fields here in central Oregon.

"Why the hell are you looking into General Macomber?" asked Ochoa.

"Because someone with a lot of influence pressured the local sheriff into letting Fain walk right into the jail and talk to my buddy. A prime suspect in a murder case. And Fain claimed he called a friend and got the complete file on me. Unless Fain's got somebody with connections owing him a favor—"

"Like me," Ochoa broke in.

"Like you. I don't buy it. I think the general made that call."

"He could get your record in a heartbeat," Ochoa agreed. "Probably arrange to have you drafted and both of us posted to Antarctica, too."

"Too much?" I asked.

There was a pause.

"I know someone who might get us records for the enlisted men on the quiet," he said. "I can say it's some sort of private background check, job placement or something. Fain will be tougher. And Macomber . . ."

"We can't pretend like we're recruiting a former general," I said.

"Yeah. And you know I can't go poking into mission specs, right? Not if we want to stay out of Leavenworth."

"Not needed. Just the personal records. Thanks, Armando."

"Hey, you know how much I miss lapping you on the track at Benning."

THE DEPUTY MANNING THE front desk at the sheriff's station laid it out for me: Leo would be allowed no visitors other than his attorney, and no communication except through same. By orders of Lieutenant Yerby. If I wanted to leave a message at the desk, Ganz could pick it up later. I declined.

Shit. Leo would be isolated until his sentencing, and undoubtedly shipped out to the pen in Deer Ridge or Salem immediately after. I couldn't even set his mind at ease by telling him Dez was innocent of Erle's murder.

The county SUV was gone from Erle Sharples's house. I peered through the fence that bordered the backyard, under the BEWARE OF DOG sign, and pounded hard enough to rattle the gate on its hinges. There was no eruption of furious barking. Maybe the cops had taken the dogs away. Good. I didn't know what kind of mutts Erle had owned, but I doubted they were Pomeranians. I let myself in through the gate, and through the locked back door.

I was the third interested party to examine the house. Slim pickings left. Anything that might have offered a clue to Erle's recent activity had been removed—no cell phones old or new, no address books or desk calendars. There was a clean rectangle on the coffee-spotted desk where his computer had been. The cops had left the monitor and mouse and keyboard, like borders of a puzzle with the center missing.

I searched anyway. Under drawers, behind headboards. All I found were enough dust bunnies to fill a country mile, and a lot of crap that wouldn't fetch ten cents at a garage sale. After an hour I gave up hunting for hollow places in the cabinets and unlocked the kitchen door that led to the attached garage.

A two-car garage, complete with two cars. Or one car, hidden under a tarp, and one canopied Ford pickup truck, not much newer than my Dodge. The truck was obviously Erle's day ride. The interior was as messy as his house, although he'd made a half-hearted attempt to keep it under control by stuffing trash into an overflowing plastic grocery sack. I went through the sack. Food wrappers from the handful of restaurants in town, mainly. A couple of gas receipts from the town's Shell station.

And a crumpled piece of baby-blue paper that held a big wad of chewed gum. Spearmint, by the smell. The paper was a flyer advertising a pawnshop called Monarch Loan in Prairie City, Oregon. It had a dirty black streak from where it had been tucked under Erle's windshield wiper. I checked a map online. Prairie City was in the next county, a couple of hours of serpentine driving south and then east out of Mercy River.

The wad of gum still had enough elasticity to stretch when I'd unfolded the flyer. So it was new, if nauseating. The flyer might be new as well, or it may have been floating around the trash pile inside Erle's shabby truck for weeks. Still, it was the closest thing I had to a clue, and after peeling off the last of the gum, I pocketed the flyer.

Before I left the garage, I surrendered to curiosity and drew back the canvas concealing the car. I let out a low whistle, and pulled the tarp the rest of the way off to admire the whole machine. A Plymouth Barracuda. Early 1970s, I guessed. The color of a polished penny with a black vinyl top. The 'Cuda wasn't in display shape, carrying a few dents on the body and alligator mottling of the copper paint job. It didn't matter. The car radiated malevolent intent, from the slanted air intakes on the hood to the broad Goodrich tires.

I wasn't a gearhead, normally. But I couldn't help but wonder how the Barracuda would handle the corners, out on the winding highway toward home.

Back in the heart of town, the volunteer booths were buzzing on Main Street. A final recruitment push on the Rally's last full day. A Redcap handed me a printed card that ran down the events for the grand finale. To accommodate the crowd, the bonfire field would serve as the central location. There would be a DogEx—hot dog cookout—following the conclusion of the combatives competition in late afternoon. An awards ceremony hosted by General Macomber would close things out. At least for the official program. It was a fair bet that the carousing would continue far into Sunday, or at least until Mercy River ran out of booze.

I'd have to miss the festivities. If Jaeger and his skinheads were still in Oregon, they wouldn't stay forever. The pawnshop flyer was my best lead, and I needed every hour before nightfall to chase it down.

TWENTY-FOUR

PRAIRIE CITY APPEARED AS wholesome as its name. On my circles through town, I passed a schoolhouse that had been converted to a bed-and-breakfast, and a barn-red railway depot that the sign lauded as being on the national register. The picturesque little town didn't strike me as an easy place for a white power gang to go unnoticed. I'd had time on the drive to put myself in the skinheads' place, as sickening as that sounded.

Fain had refused to tell me any details about the lab from where the Trumo had been stolen, including the location. How far away had it been? I had to guess that the Riders had driven their cargo at least across state, maybe even across the country. Twenty-three boxes like the one I'd found wouldn't fit in a regular car. Jaeger would also want safety in numbers, some muscle around for the deal. An RV would be large enough. Or a pickup truck with a camper. Two vehicles, maybe. One car to haul the goods and one to haul the gorillas.

And I doubted the skinheads were roughing it in the Northwest wilderness for days on end. They'd want a motel or an RV park, something out of the way where they could keep an eye on the cargo and not have to worry about the management getting curious. I pulled over to hunt for likely prospects on my phone.

Prairie City had a couple of motels, in addition to the schoolhouse B&B. Plenty of Best Westerns and Super 8s and KOA campgrounds in the surrounding area served tourists hiking the Umatilla and Malheur forests. I crossed anything too quaint or too public off the list, leaving a dozen possibilities. There was nothing for it but to keep driving.

FOUR HOURS LATER, I'D seen enough trailer parks and motels that they had begun to blur together. None of the vehicles in the lots had looked right. I'd eaten lunch on the run, downed a half gallon of orange juice for the sugar rush, and watered enough of the roadside with recycled coffee to grow a garden. Maybe I was too late, and the skinheads had given up.

The sun was going down. I decided to go a little farther north and check places at this edge of the forest before calling it a lost day.

My phone flashed an incoming call with Ochoa's area code. I had to unplug it from the charger with one hand, and got it to my ear on the fifth ring.

"Yeah, I'm here," I said before he hung up.

"Hey. I've got some papers for you. Is this phone secure?"

"It is. But I'm on the road. Can you run through the headlines?"

"You gave me four names. Or parts of names. I had to dig up the rest. John Fain, captain. Rigoberto Rivas. Daryll Abernathy. Zeke Caton. That's Caton's full name, by the way, not short for Ezekiel. All four of them knew each other in the regiment."

"I guessed that much."

"Abernathy and Caton were in the same Ranger class, and the same company for their first three rotations. Rivas was a year ahead of them. He was a platoon leader under Captain Fain in Afghanistan. Caton took some family leave to care for a sick relative, and when he came back he was posted to a different company. Fain's."

I heard Ochoa banging away on a keyboard.

"Solid records for the three enlisted men. All made staff sergeant within five years. Not that they earned themselves shiny medals like you did."

I scratched my scars reflexively. "Nobody wants to earn medals like I did."

"That I believe. But they are your kind of ass-kicker. Take a gander at Rivas's shooting qualifiers. I'm surprised the Army team didn't nab him."

"What do they do now?"

"Hold on, I haven't gotten to the really interesting part. After six years, Caton and Rivas were both discharged OTH."

Other than honorable. A strange result, for soldiers capable of upholding the regiment's exacting standards.

"What happened?" I said.

"Assault on a superior. Specifically, they were accused of aiming their sidearms at the head of a lieutenant in the regiment, as intimidation. The lieutenant had recently filed a report of bad conduct against Abernathy. Apparently Caton and Rivas decided to demonstrate just how bad it could get."

"And Abernathy?"

"Slightly better. RFS'd out of the 75th, followed by a general discharge a couple of months later."

Released for standards could cover a wide range of performance problems, from not maintaining the required physical fitness to disciplinary issues. I thought back to Daryll's sleepless night, abstaining from any pain meds despite his busted toes.

"Abernathy spent some time in stateside hospitals before mustering out, too," Ochoa went on. "I don't have his medical records, but my guess?"

"Drugs," I said.

"That sounds right," he confirmed. "Or drying out if he was stateside and hitting the bottle too much."

Practically every combat vet I'd ever known had a history with their favorite painkiller. Even when you're twenty-two years old and indestructible, the human body isn't built to handle what the Army asks of it, all day, every day. Medics were liberal in passing out candy from what they called the morale pouch. Aleve had been my go-to. I would pop the little blue ovals like they were M&M's. Vicodin was even better, but I had known the dangers and weaned myself off before the happy haze started to cook my brain. Not everybody was so lucky. Maybe Daryll Abernathy had become hooked.

"What about Captain Fain?" I said.

"John Fain's a piece of work. I mean that in the good way. ROTC out of Tennessee. Did two rotations with the Hundred and first in Iraq before he applied for Ranger School. The Distinguished Graduate for his class. Three re-ups after his first enlistment."

"A high-flier. Like you."

"You would think. Fain hitched his star to General Macomber early on. Maybe that was a mistake. After Macomber was jettisoned, Captain Fain's career tapered off. He finished out his fourth enlistment and resigned his commission."

"How long ago was that?"

More typing. "Three years," Ochoa said.

A busy time, three years ago. Macomber had formed the foundations of the Rally. Fain had abruptly left the Army and a promising career. And the First Riders and their ilk had been unceremoniously ejected from Mercy River.

"What about now?" I said. "Do you have anything on the four of them since they became civilians?"

Ochoa chuckled. "Civilians like you are? Somehow I don't picture you sitting in a cubicle, hoping to make middle manager."

"That isn't my life," I admitted.

"Not theirs, either. The Army doesn't have many records beyond some mailing addresses. They don't lean on the system. No educational assistance, no applications for VA benefits—not that Caton and Rivas would qualify, with their discharge status. Not even job counseling."

The four men had already found a way to make a living. I wasn't convinced it involved playing janitor for pharma company messes. Even private military contractors didn't need to stay off the grid entirely.

"I appreciate the help, Armando," I said.

"If all my favors were this easy, I'd be rich as well as brilliant. Listen."

Ochoa shifted so that he was closer to the speaker. "It is my professional opinion that you should get your ass away from this bunch. If they're all hanging out together years after the Army decided their services were no longer needed, it's not to throw back a few shots and reminisce. Right?"

"I'll take it under advisement."

"Sure you will. That concludes our broadcast day. Catch you later." He hung up.

Before I resumed my tour of the rural hospitalities, I thought about what Ochoa had told me. There was a common thread running through the fabric of Fain's men. Loyalty. Rigo Rivas and Zeke Caton, hamstringing their own Army careers to help Daryll Abernathy. General Macomber's struggle and eventual exile after pushing too hard for veterans' aid. I understood that kind of allegiance. It had nothing to do with nationality or armies or even regimental pride. It was about the guy standing next to you, the one who could be counted on to watch your blind side while you watched his.

Hell, loyalty could be the sign hung around my neck, too. I was here to help Leo. And I hadn't lost any sleep over my methods, either.

THE SECOND MOTEL ALONG the edge of the forest was named Dixie Hot Springs. It consisted of only eight tiny and sorrowful cabins, set far enough apart for residents to park in between them. Four other lots along the same row had been torn down to their cement foundations. A faded yellow Caterpillar bulldozer sat off to the side, near a huge mound of broken boards and drywall chunks, like it was waiting to be unleashed on the survivors.

The sign glowing VACANCY was an understatement. Halfway down the row, a plain brown panel van with Idaho plates squatted between two cabins. The next door over boasted a rusty blue Camaro, more money in the tires than the body work, also with plates from the Potato State.

Bingo. Those shitheaps looked exactly right.

I cruised past without pausing. Tactically, the motel sucked. It was the sole business on a narrow forest road off the highway. No way I could stake it out unobserved, unless I wanted to climb a giant ponderosa pine tree. At least the other cabins appeared empty. No witnesses around, or potential collateral damage if things went slantways.

Not that I intended any violence. I'd sneak close enough to confirm that the cabins housed a bunch of inbred mooks with shaved heads and narrow suspenders, and get the hell away.

The sun had barely dipped below the horizon, but this close to the thick canopy of the forest, it was already as dark as midnight. Half a mile up the highway, I found a side road and a place to stash the Dodge behind trees. Before I left it, I slipped the Browning into my coat pocket. Be prepared.

Back at the motel's road, I stepped off the highway and began picking a slow path through the brush parallel to the road. Slow, but silent, and invisible from the motel grounds.

By the time I reached the cabins, exterior lights had switched on automatically outside each door. The glowing bulbs just served to deepen the darkness behind the tiny buildings. I inched toward the brown panel van, brushing twigs and leaves aside with every step.

The discordant sound of a television commercial came from the near cabin. A door opened, then closed again. I waited. No footsteps, or voices.

The windows on the panel van were smoked. Peering in, I could distinguish a large rectangular shape, like a sarcophagus, concealed under blankets and bedsheets. I did some quick mental arithmetic, comparing the size of the red box I'd seen to the volume of the sarcophagus shape. Twenty-three boxes of the same size could fit under those sheets.

The near cabin had a window on this side. I edged along the splintery wall until a slice of the room came into view. One bed, unmade. The front door, closed but unbolted. A backpack leaning against the wall. The TV shrieked. No other sounds, or movement. I risked leaning a little farther. The room was empty. The unlit bathroom was open, proving the case. Were they out? Or gathered next door?

I backtracked to inch my way around the rear of the place, gently pushing branches aside, moving toward the blue Camaro and the second cabin. It wasn't necessary to get close.

As I watched over the roof of the car, two men in white tank tops and white suspenders passed the window. Both of them were half as thick as they were tall, and their heights were substantial. I only saw them for an instant, but it was enough time to clock their shaven skulls and long scraggly goatees, and the crooked mess of gray and watery blue ink covering their arms and necks. Tattoos of swastikas and axes and crosses and numbers I didn't have to read to recognize as skinhead code—shit like 23 for the letter *W* standing for *white*, 88 for Heil Hitler, 14 for some supremacist credo about a future for white children that I didn't know or care to know.

A third man, much leaner than the two nearly identical hulks, came into view and stood in profile to the window.

He was a different physical type. Leaner, and older, with enough years on him that his buzzed hair and broad horseshoe mustache carried far more gray than brown. He was dressed simply, in a black collared shirt with buttoned sleeves and black work pants. As he listened to whoever was speaking in the room, he stood perfectly straight with his arms at his sides, not moving at all. No reflexive nodding, no expression on his face beyond focused attention.

Jaeger. I was sure of it. Even setting aside his seniority, he looked like someone in command. His strange stillness reminded me of a snake, waiting to see what prey might cross its hiding place. Eerie.

Three men in the cabin, maybe more. I could fade back to the highway and call Fain, and let him deal with Jaeger and the rest.

But that would surrender any leverage I had now. I didn't completely buy Fain's story of being hired to recover the Trumo for the drug company. Maybe he and his team were dealers themselves. I couldn't trust that Fain really held evidence that could clear Leo.

I needed something more to bargain with.

I needed the drugs.

Spike the Camaro. Boost their panel van. Drive off. Simple.

Unless the van didn't start on the first try. It didn't give the impression of a vehicle that enjoyed regular maintenance. Jaeger's men would hear its engine turning over. A few seconds' delay at the wrong moment, and I could catch a bullet right through the windshield.

Okay. So I needed to keep the skinheads occupied for a few moments. What did I have to work with?

My eyes alighted on the Caterpillar bulldozer, sixty yards away at the end of the row of cabins.

Hello, beautiful.

I retreated to unlock the van and strip its wires for a quick jump, before slipping back into the brush and making my way to the mound of demolition debris. Fishing through the pile, I found broken pieces of two-by-four with nails still extruding at weird angles, twisted and bent when the heavy tractor had torn one of the cabins apart. I took the boards to the Camaro and jammed them up into the car's rear wheel wells, wedging the shiny sixteen-penny nails into the treads of the tires.

At the bulldozer, I picked the simple lock on the battery box above the broad mud-encrusted treads. I'd driven tractors before. Small ones first, as a teenager while working construction with Dono. Years later, bored during days off rotation at Fort Benning or on base while in theater, I would wheedle or bribe the Army equipment operators to show me how the bigger machines worked. I had enough experience to get the Cat moving, which was all I needed now.

The dozer's fuse box was in with the battery. I tore out the fuses for the horn and running lights before unlocking the driver's compartment. The operator had been kind enough to leave the key for the engine, attached by a string to the dash.

I checked the cabins again. No one had emerged. This would be the tricky part. I had to hope I was far enough away that the sound of the Cat starting would be lost in their conversation and the racket of the TV.

I turned the key. The engine caught with a low rumble as the gauges on the dash swept to full, but no horn sounded or lights blazed. I let out the breath I'd been holding.

Still no movement at the cabins. A thumbwheel on the Cat's controls set the speed of the machine. I dialed the wheel to a single mile an hour, pulled the right-hand stick to bring the blade up a few feet, and pushed the left stick forward. The tractor eased into motion. I angled the stick, and the treads responded by turning a few degrees, straight toward the cabin with Jaeger and his crew.

I thumbed the speed to its maximum and jumped out the open door, as the engine roared and the Cat lurched forward.

At a little under four miles an hour, the bulldozer wouldn't win many races, but it ate up the distance with startling haste. I sprinted to the van, yanking open the door and leaning in to touch the stripped wires together. The alternator clicked rapidly. *Come on, dammit.*

Someone shouted from Jaeger's cabin. I tried again, and the engine stuttered and roared to life.

An almighty crash and ripping sound echoed through the forest, like a tree being torn out by the roots. I was in the driver's seat and popping the brake in a hot second, the van rolling even before I floored the gas. I swung hard right, driving over the tracks ground into the soil by the bulldozer as it pushed the entire cabin off its cement foundation. The shattered one-room box sagged to one side while the machine lumbered into the thicket beyond. One of the beefy thugs fell clumsily out of the hole that had been a window.

Jaeger was already outside, picking himself off the ground, caught in the light spilling from the next cabin over. Our eyes met. His were a very pale green. Almost more clear than colored.

He didn't look furious, or even perturbed by the destruction of the cabin. It was as if something behind his intense gaze clicked at that moment, capturing an X-ray of me as the van rushed past him. Marking me with cold detachment.

His stare stayed with me as I sped down the road and out of sight.

TWENTY-FIVE

TWO MILES UP THE road, I risked pulling over for a minute to verify my cargo. I climbed into the back of the van and yanked the bedsheets aside.

Red boxes, identical to the one I'd found at Erle's, their stacks held together with bungee cords and thin rope. I counted. Twenty-three boxes, as expected. Splitting the tape seal on the nearest lid with my knife, I popped it open to find trays of Trumorpha neatly arranged inside.

I laughed, releasing tension I hadn't even realized I'd been holding. At least I hadn't gone to all that risk to steal someone's old furniture.

I couldn't drive around in a stolen van carrying thousands of vials of first-degree-felony narcotics for long. Step one was to transfer the cargo to my truck. Step two would be tricky. I didn't want to bring the Trumo into Mercy River. Too many eyes, some of them familiar with the red boxes. I briefly considered using Erle's hiding place in the woods, but I couldn't be sure that was a secret known only to me. Ideally, I could arrange to send the drugs far away, quickly and quietly, without getting my ass busted.

I had a friend who knew something about that line of work. Hollis Brant.

Hollis had been my grandfather's closest confidant for half their lives. Dono thought up the plans, and Hollis was the guy who could deliver when it came to smuggling and all manner of transpo. Somehow I'd fallen into that same role when it became void after Dono's death. I suspected that Hollis confused the two of us occasionally, Dono and me. Not that Hollis was senile. But my grandfather and I were alike in many ways.

ONCE WHEN I WAS about eight years old, Hollis had come to our home for a late dinner and to plan something with Dono. I'd been living with Dono for two years by then. Long enough that the memories of my dead mother had started to fade, but not so long that I was comfortable being around my granddad. I never became completely comfortable, to be honest. It wasn't in Dono's nature to put people at ease.

After our dinner of beef potpie I was sent upstairs to bed. Sleep was out of the question, full belly or not. Besides my fascination with whatever the two men might be talking about down in the front room—this was well before Dono would allow me a hint of his true profession and begin teaching me the tools of his trade—I was too scared to close my eyes.

Earlier that day I'd been poking around my grandfather's books. He liked history and books on home construction, and I could usually find something in the tales of pirates to interest me. Granddad encouraged it. A few of his books were in the Irish language, which we regularly spoke at home. I liked practicing. It made me feel closer to my mother, who'd sung Gaelic lullabies to me about blackbirds and robins. Knowing words that none of my schoolmates or teachers would understand felt like a secret I shared with my granddad.

But that afternoon I'd found a different book. Bound in green cloth, it felt very old, with thin crinkling pages that threatened to split each time I touched them. It smelled even older, like when Granddad had cleaned the dust out of the attic vents. A book of Irish legends and folk stories.

And it was illustrated. I realized that when I opened it and was struck by a drawing of a ragged woman flying through the air, her eyes wide and staring and her impossibly elongated mouth open in a horrible scream. I'd closed the pages immediately, only to be drawn back, frightened to see it again, but knowing she was still there.

Finally I screwed up my courage to open the book and quickly cover that page and its ghastly picture with a comfortingly thick volume on plumbing repair. From the facing page, I read about the ghost. The *bean sí*, it was called. She wailed mournful songs to foretell the death of a family member. The evil wraith was often seen washing the garments of the soon-to-be-dead in the waters of the river. Each family had a *bean sí* of its own, the book said.

The weather had been high that night. Most parts of our home were over a hundred years old. The house moved with the strong wind, adding its groans to the whistling outside my window. Foretelling.

I got up. Rules or no, I had to go downstairs.

"What are you doing?" Granddad said, before I'd made it halfway. He was out of sight around the wide entrance to the front room. I could hear the fire in the fireplace snapping and hissing. My hand edged down the bannister.

"I need—I need my comics," I answered, daring to take another two steps.

"It's lights-out. Y'know that."

"Not for reading. Just so . . ." I wasn't sure what to say. But I was close enough now to lean forward and peer around the molding of the entrance. Granddad was seated in his red leather chair, a coffee mug in his hand. Hollis sat by the fire, an empty glass next to him. The room was warmer than upstairs and both men wore T-shirts. Hollis wore shorts, too, but he did that even when it was winter and raining.

"You drift off fine every night without comics. Get upstairs," Granddad said. He meant right now. He always meant right now.

"I do know that feeling." Hollis thumped his broad fist on the hearth. "Having your treasures around you. Makes you feel right in the world."

His face was pinker than usual, maybe from the fire. "S'why everything I own is on my boat. Take it all with me anywhere I sail."

I nodded. I didn't really understand but nodded anyway because Hollis seemed to be on my side.

"Can I sleep down here?" I said.

Granddad angled his head at the couch, the only logical place to bed down on the ground floor. No way I would be allowed to stay on the couch, not while they were talking here.

"I can stay in the kitchen," I said hurriedly.

His dark brow furrowed. "On the floor? What's the matter with you?" Then his eyes widened in realization and shifted from me to the fireplace mantel.

The green book. It was there. Like it had followed me downstairs.

"Ah," Granddad said.

Hollis reached out a long arm and took the book down to read its cover. "*Béaloideas Eireann.* Folklore, eh? My."

"I found that where you left it," said Granddad. "In the hall."

Another strike against me. I remembered now that I hadn't wanted to touch the book after I'd read about the wailing ghost, in case I might accidentally see the picture again. I'd intended to come back to it soon. But I'd forgotten.

"Which of these caught your eye, lad?" Hollis said, leafing through the brittle pages.

"*Bean sí,*" I said. Pronouncing it a little like *bean sigh.*

"Banshee," Granddad corrected. "Reading spook stories makes for long nights, Van."

The wind, as if agreeing, rattled the shutters.

"Go on, now," said Granddad.

I looked at the staircase, and the shadows at the top. My feet stayed frozen.

"*Leaba,*" Granddad said. *Bed.* A command in Irish left no room for further negotiations.

"I've a cure for the nighttime haunts," said Hollis, rising swiftly to walk over to his coat, which he'd draped over the back of the couch. "Somewhere here . . ."

Granddad exhaled like a bull. I wouldn't meet his eye.

"This," Hollis said, holding up a bright blue stone. "Banishes all evil, bad dreams, and wickedness."

He handed it to me. The stone was a translucent azure, with flecks of gold. Pretty, but more or less the same as crystals I'd seen in weird stores on Broadway, places that sold crocheted purses and offered to clean your aura for ten dollars.

Hollis may have read my face. "Ancient, that little rock is. My grandmother had it from hers, and now down to me. Works every time. You borrow it. I've got other charms and wards back on the boat."

Hollis turned to Granddad. So did I. Was it real?

Granddad finally sighed.

"You look after that, now," he said to me. "Magic that powerful is rare."

"Okay."

"Get."

I got.

Back under the covers—all the way under—I used my tiny key-chain flashlight to examine the stone. I supposed it could be old. It had cracks in it. I held it tightly in my hand and turned off the light before Granddad caught me with it on.

From downstairs I heard Hollis and Granddad, their words muffled but loud enough for me to make out the happy spirit in their talk. I closed my eyes.

No banshee tonight. I'd lost my mother. But Granddad would be safe, no matter what I thought I heard on the wind.

"HELLO, VAN," HOLLIS ANSWERED my call. "Your ears must have been burning. Do people say that, if it's only thinking about someone and not talking about them?"

"You're having a good night." I pictured Hollis at home on his boat in

Shilshole Marina in Seattle, lounging in the untidy cabin with a double shot glass of whiskey held in his thick paw.

"I'm a little in my cups, it's true. I've just now put Gloria in one of those taxis that regular people drive now, off to home. A fine woman."

Gloria was Hollis's girlfriend of three months. It must be serious, with that kind of longevity.

"Hollis," I said, "I need your expertise."

"A professional matter, then. All right."

"I have to move some items. And hide them, for at least a few days."

"Dimensions?" he said.

"Twenty-three boxes, about twelve-by-twelve-by-ten. Four to five pounds each. Inside each box are one hundred and forty-four vials about three inches long. They're fragile."

"Vials? Not dangerous, I hope. Biohazards and whatnot."

"No. But they are very hot."

"Huh," he said.

"I'm not selling the junk. Just keeping it out of circulation."

"Never imagined anything else, lad. Is it only the vials you care about? Or the boxes, too?"

I thought about it. "I can sacrifice the boxes so long as I remove any papers from each one first."

"Time frame?"

I gave Hollis the coordinates of my location in Oregon, just west of nowhere, and told him about the panel van I'd stolen from the First Riders. "So I can't sit around for too long, and I can't drive it into a town," I concluded.

"Right." There was a pause while he considered the problem and took a sip of whatever he was drinking. Irish whiskey, almost certainly. Hollis stuck to his roots. I could have used a belt myself.

"You've got a problem, boyo," he said finally.

"You sound happy about that."

"I should. By good chance, I think I've got a solution for you, if you don't mind my taking a hand in it myself."

"From all the way in Seattle?"

"Not so far, if you know the right people. Give me ten minutes and I'll ring you back." He hung up.

I'd known Hollis my whole life, minus the ten years I'd been soldiering. He could still surprise me. The phone buzzed in less than five minutes.

"Right," Hollis said without preamble. "You're a few miles south of the county line, I see. Can you find Quillmark Ranch?"

"Let's say yes."

"Good. Be there in about three hours."

Three hours? Impossible, unless . . . "Hollis, I only wanted your opinion. The vials might burst at altitude."

"We'll see about that. I have to move quickly now. Call me if anything goes amiss."

I was about to say the same, but Hollis had hung up again.

Quillmark Ranch was on the map, in the middle of the county, and only twenty miles' drive from where I sat. A big spread. Large enough for a landing strip.

I hoped Hollis wasn't exaggerating about our prospects. He was an optimist by nature, and practically boisterous on the sauce.

On the other hand, Hollis had been smuggling things since before I was born, and had never been arrested. Maybe I should have a little more faith.

I LEFT THE TRUCK with its stolen payload in the hills above the ranch, wanting to recon Quillmark's grounds without announcing my arrival. The ranch was an unfenced expanse of at least a mile square, all of it so unvaryingly flat the acreage had to have been graded by a small army of surveyors.

It was also as dark as the deepest Amazon jungle. Only the moon allowed me to discern one long stripe on the flat earth, where the texture differed from its surroundings. The landing strip. Two single-story buildings sat offset from the strip, black boxes on a dark gray field. I watched the ranch. Nothing changed. After an hour I was satisfied, and returned to the truck.

With time to kill, I decided to have a closer look at the Trumo. I brought the box I'd opened to the passenger's seat. Inside, tucked next to the stack of plastic trays, I found a single page—the box's shipping invoice.

The invoice was identical to the one that Fain had shown me, his supposed proof that they'd been hired to find these same boxes. Except that on this copy, I could read the parts that had been carefully blacked out on Fain's.

Two names. A company logo proudly emblazoned in blue and black at the top of the sheet. *HAVERCORP NATIONAL*. And on the same line. *Last Updated By: AARON CONLEE.*

HaverCorp was a security company. Professional guards, armed transport. I'd seen their armored trucks on the streets of Seattle. For some reason Fain hadn't wanted me to read HaverCorp's name on the page he'd shown me. Or to see Aaron Conlee's.

In ten minutes I had the rest of the boxes open and had leafed through the rest of the invoices. All of them identical. HaverCorp, and Conlee, every time.

I could see a pharma lab hiring HaverCorp to safely convey a few hundred grand of legal heroin across state lines. So why would Fain hide that fact? Why not just tell me the drugs had been stolen from the armored car company? Perhaps HaverCorp was the client he was truly protecting, and the lab story was a smokescreen.

Another half hour until I expected Hollis. Time enough for some online research.

HaverCorp had made headlines during the past year, but not in any way they would want. An armored truck robbery in New Orleans, another three months later in Michigan, and a third four months after that in Ohio. The robbers had evaded all cameras. They'd left the Haver-Corp guards bound and blindfolded. Reports varied on whether there had been three or four or five in the gang, even at the same score.

There were other similarities. All three of those jobs had been at night, after the armored car had finished collecting cash from businesses and banks in their daily route. The company and the Feds were silent on the amounts stolen—which probably meant the hauls had been sizable enough to cause HaverCorp serious embarrassment. In each case, no one had been hurt, no shots fired.

Jaeger and his First Riders had had a busy year, at HaverCorp's expense and embarrassment. I had a better understanding now why Fain had concealed the company's name.

Things had gone very wrong on their fourth score. Not an armored truck that time, but an unmarked HaverCorp van in Henderson, Nevada. A mere thirteen days ago. Both guards dead by GSW. The driver and the hopper, who completed each pickup while the driver remained in the truck, watching for trouble. Not closely enough this time.

One of the crime blogs had photographs. Full color, and too graphic for the news services. Police at the scene. The blanket-draped corpse of the hopper lying on the sidewalk, one foot hanging off the curb. Blood obscuring the driver's-side window in pink whorls and streaks. The hopper had been gunned down as he stepped out of the van, the driver behind the wheel. Almost as an afterthought, the final paragraph noted that the van had been carrying pharmaceuticals. HaverCorp declined to comment on the type and amount.

The change in MO was ruthless. Maybe the guards had seen the face of Jaeger or one of his men, or maybe the white power leader had simply decided that killing guards was more efficient than tying them up.

Two dead. And I'd let Jaeger go, in favor of jacking his drugs out from under him. Goddamn.

I couldn't help that now. If Fain had been straight with me yesterday, I might have acted differently tonight. Hindsight bought me nothing good. I pushed the mental image of the shrouded corpse on the sidewalk away.

The Feds were getting nowhere in solving the robberies, and Haver-Corp had decided to give the private sector a try and hire Fain and his team to stop Jaeger before he hit another one of their trucks. I could buy that.

Aaron Conlee was the piece that didn't fit. A quick search found a few men and one or two women with that name. The closest was a man. Very close, living in Portland. His online life was heavy on Instagrams of restaurant dinners with a woman I guessed was his wife, and retweets of baseball news and jokes. The selfies he'd posted showed a white guy about thirty, thickening and balding before his time, with thick-framed retro eyeglasses. He had a LinkedIn profile, too. Employed two years as a senior system administrator for HaverCorp National, in Hillsboro, west of Portland proper.

Conlee was a system administrator. I knew enough about IT jobs to know sys admins handled the care and feeding of big data centers, big networks. Everything that passed through the company's computers might be available. Confidential email, proprietary documents, even financial transactions. A guy with the right security clearance, in a company like HaverCorp, could have an all-access pass to all kinds of potentially lucrative information. Especially if he knew how to cover his tracks.

Hell, the possibilities made my fingertips tingle, and I wasn't even in that line of work anymore.

So if Aaron Conlee had been Jaeger's inside man at HaverCorp, and the company and Fain knew it, Conlee was already caught dead to rights, an accessory to murder one and a lot more. Why keep that such a secret? And why hadn't the Feds used Conlee to take down Jaeger's crew?

I couldn't shake the feeling that I was being played. It was something deeper than Fain protecting his client's name.

But that didn't matter. What counted was getting Leo out of jail. And the Trumo vials added up to nearly thirty-five hundred little bargaining chips.

Time to meet Hollis. I started the truck and let it coast at a walking pace down the black hill toward the airstrip.

Twenty minutes later, my engine idling near an access road onto the ranch, I saw the first hint of the plane. Its running lights glimmered like a star that had lost its way. A mere two thousand feet up and dropping fast. With a dark runway and an unreliable moon, the pilot must be trusting the instruments more than his eyes.

The single-prop craft came in straight and low. Its wheels touched the tarmac. A newer model of Cessna, I guessed. In the moonlight, the plane was a sleek dart, in spotless white over a maroon underbelly. I let the truck ease forward to meet it.

The propeller was still spinning when I saw the familiar shape of Hollis Brant emerge from the passenger's side and practically slide off the wing to meet the ground. There was no mistaking those long arms and bowed legs, even if he lacked any hint of his usual simian grace in his first unsteady steps away from the plane.

"You good, Hollis?" I said through the truck's open window. The plane continued forward, circling to face the open runway, ready for a quick takeoff.

"My Lord," he said, inhaling great gulps of air.

"Okay, then."

I got out of the van. The interior lights of the Cessna came on. The pilot was a woman, dressed for the cold at high altitude, in a light blue quilted coat and leather gloves and knit cap. Her broad face carried a few deep character lines and a deeper disapproving frown.

"You should be unloaded already," she said to me as she stepped out of the plane. She had a slight accent. Quebecois? "We have to be back in the air in twenty-five minutes."

Hollis nodded like he'd heard it before. I went to the back of the van and opened the doors to remove the first of the boxes. The pilot began walking around her aircraft, feeling the fasteners.

"What's the plan, Hollis?" I said. No way all twenty-three boxes would fit inside that puddle-jumper.

"To never allow myself to do that again," he said.

"I didn't place you as a nervous flyer."

"I love flying, but not with a big head. My mistake was forgetting a flask. Help me with these."

He moved the passenger's seat forward to reach inside and heft out a large metal drum, setting it on the ground with a clank. The drum shone bright silver under the plane's lights. At the center of its rounded top was a small gauge. I leaned forward to see that it measured PSI.

"A pressure cooker?" I guessed. The drum must hold five gallons. That would make a lot of stew.

"Close. It's for industrial adhesive, originally. But much the same idea."

He lifted out a second drum and handed it to me. Its substantial weight reminded me that despite being near sixty years old, Hollis was still a strong son of a bitch. I set the drum aside while Hollis brought out an oxygen tank and, finally, a bright yellow five-gallon jerry jug, its contents sloshing.

"Salt water," Hollis said, slapping the jug. "Straight out of the Sound. We'll suspend your fragile little bottles in this, keep the pressure in the drums at sea level, and everybody's happy."

"Brilliant," I said.

"Yes, I am. Now we'd best get to it, before Veronique there leaves us behind."

I began unloading the red boxes, setting them into a line and flipping each one open for quick unpacking.

Hollis popped one of the vials out of its plastic tray. "Mind if I inquire?" he said, holding it between his thick fingers.

"Pharmaceutical heroin," I said. "Hide it well."

Hollis blinked. "I will certainly do that. And speaking of hazards, you owe Veronique thirty thousand dollars."

I stopped in the middle of lifting four boxes out of the truck bed. "Really."

"Not right this minute. I told her you were good for it."

The fact that I could afford thirty grand made me happier, but only slightly.

Hollis filled the drums halfway with water from the jerry jug, while I began removing the thin plastic trays from the boxes, upending them over the drums to pop out the vials. Each glass tube fell into the water with a tiny splash, sinking quickly to the bottom. It became a rhythm, emptying the trays, replacing them in the box, throwing the box into the truck. Hollis joined me. Veronique continued her preflight check.

"Time to leave," Veronique called as the last vials sank to join their fellows. We closed the drums, screwing each wing nut into place.

"I can handle this in the air," Hollis said, holding up the oxygen tank he would use to pressure the containers.

"I'm not joking," Veronique said, already climbing into the pilot's seat. "If this plane isn't back before dawn . . ."

Hollis and I ducked under the wing to load the tanks into the back.

"No chance you'll get inspected when you land?" I asked.

"The lovely V there is simply picking up her passenger and dropping him off at Friday Harbor, as per the flight plans filed a week ago."

"Quite a coincidence."

"You're all right, then?" he said. "You don't seem yourself."

I handed him the empty jerry can. "Luce is getting married." The words were out of my mouth before I knew it.

"Oh." He set the jug gently in the plane. "I am sorry to hear that."

"Yeah."

"When you get home we'll raise some hell," he said, clambering into his seat. "Drink and cards and enough food to make the *Francesca* list to one side. How much longer will you be down here?"

"If it's more than a week, you'll hear my scream from all the way in Seattle."

He laughed.

"Thanks for the help," I said to Veronique.

"Just have my money ready."

Hollis shrugged—*What can you do?*—and shut the door. I backed off and watched as the little Cessna revved, picked up speed, and floated into the sky as easily as a feather caught by the wind.

TWENTY-SIX

THUNDER GROANED IN THE distance as the Dodge crossed the line back into Griffon County. I stopped to toss my collection of empty boxes into a Future Farmers of America donation bin. Maybe the red containers would make good chicken roosts.

By the time I hit Mercy River, rain was pelting down. The surprise storm had driven the Rally's final hours of celebration indoors but hadn't put a damper on the party. The Trading Post Saloon and the diner across the street were both standing-room-only. Revelers who couldn't squeeze their way inside crowded the boardwalk planks, huddling under the saloon's awning or standing in the rain with heads under hoods and hands cupped over their pint glasses, not letting the downpour interrupt their conversations. For many of them, the Rally was their last chance to cut loose for many months.

Moulson stood with a knot of men outside the diner, wearing a slouch hat with a brim so stiff I guessed he'd bought it at the mercantile this same weekend. He spotted the Dodge, and quickly and emphatically motioned for me to join the party.

I was tired. Too tired to stand around and throw back beers, and too tired to chase down Fain and his soldiers right this minute. I waved to Moulson and kept moving.

Two blocks later I changed my mind. I coasted to stop at the curb, my tires splashing a long wave of rainwater up onto the sidewalk.

"Where you been, dude?" Moulson said as I joined him. "You missed one hell of a party. Well, mostly." He waved an enthusiastic arm at the packed diner, nearly knocking another man onto his ass.

"I've seen some fireworks already," I said. Rain trickled off the brim of my cap. "But I didn't want to miss saying good luck. You and Booker headed back to Lewis tomorrow?"

"Tonight," he said. "Ken's drivin', he lost the coin toss. Hey!" he shouted through the diner window. Booker turned at the sound, along with half a dozen others. He nodded assent and began to squeeze his way through the throng to the door.

"When do you roll out?" I said, meaning when would their battalion deploy.

"We start workup next week. Figure we're on the ground at Bagram sometime after Thanksgiving."

Booker finished fighting his way to the sidewalk and pulled his collar tighter. "Thought you were in the wind, Shaw."

"Not yet. Moulson was telling me about your rotation. Your first time?"

"As a Ranger, yeah."

I took out my phone. "Give me your numbers."

They did and I texted them mine. "Call me when you get back to the world. We'll grab a beer."

Booker, the sober one of the pair, glommed on first and smiled. "You making sure we reassimilate okay? A lifeline outside the regiment?"

"Never hurts to talk."

"Damn. Guess the Rally's mission statement sank in with somebody."

I stayed for a round and talked with the two specialists about their assignments, their excitement at finally putting their training to use, and their plans for after they came home. Moulson was going to find an apartment off base with his girlfriend. Booker's parents were moving up from Oakland to be closer, now that he'd be with the Second Bat for a while. Tomorrow the two men would be back on base, readying themselves. But not tonight. Tonight was the drink before the war.

WHEN I WOKE, IT was to the sound of water splashing and spilling over the sides of the house's gutters. The room seemed out of focus, daylight shimmering through heavy rain outside the windows.

No dreams this time. And no pill to help me sleep, either, I realized.

I checked my watch, which meant pulling back the sleeve of the shirt I was still wearing from the day before. At least I'd taken my shoes off before falling onto the bed.

Ten-fifteen. Sunday morning. Okay. At least I had my bearings.

The house was cold. Maybe Ganz had turned the heat off before he'd left for Seattle. I dredged up the memory of a note on the kitchen counter, Ganz saying that he'd be back for Leo's sentencing, and something about the house being paid up through Monday. No valediction or signature. Politeness apparently wasn't worth Ephraim's expensive time. Or I wasn't, after the fiasco in court. I wondered how Leo was holding up. Five days until his sentencing.

After an icy shower, the room felt warmer and my head felt like it was screwed on right. With fresh clothes and a clean rain jacket, I might be presentable. The twenty-three pages of folded HaverCorp invoices made a thick paper brick in my pocket. I stuck my baseball cap—still damp from the night before—on my head and the Browning on a belt clip and walked out the door to find John Fain.

GENERAL MACOMBER MUST HAVE ordered the rainstorm to help Mercy River clean up after the Rally. Except for the odd red Solo cup in the gutter and some torn banners still touting active military discounts, the town looked clean and ready for Sunday services. For once the citizens on the street outnumbered the Rangers. While quick-marching to the inn, I was assailed by the heavy scent of frying meat.

The food won out. I hadn't eaten since before I'd demolished Jaeger's cabin the night before, and my stomach urged me to make up for lost time. The aroma carried me down the street to the diner, where I had the kitchen throw pancakes and bacon and sausage into a paper container. I ate the meal with my fingers as I walked up the boardwalk.

Two blocks on, I spotted Fain. He was leaning against a lamppost, smoking as he watched the people hurrying through the rain on the main drag with an expression like he was ready to cut the weaker civilians from the herd.

"Where the hell have you been?" he said when I was ten yards away.

"Working."

"The men had bets going that you'd skipped town."

"Not while Leo's here." I pulled the invoices from my pocket and unfolded them to show Fain. His eyes widened as he took in the Haver-Corp company logo, and below that, Aaron Conlee's name.

"Where did you—" he began.

"I'll be outside the town hall in twenty minutes. Bring the evidence to clear Leo. If you're not there, or your hands are empty, I'm gone for good."

"Shaw."

I walked away, down the block and around the corner, to watch the reflection of the road in a sports store window. Would Fain follow? No, he had turned and was striding in the opposite direction, likely to the inn. Three blocks north and on the other side of Main Street. I circled the block at a run, determined to beat Fain there.

Big Daryll's GMC Yukon was parked at the curb in front of the inn. I waited behind the same row of compost bins that had been my cover two nights ago. A more conspicuous hiding place now that it was daylight, but I would only need a moment.

Fain appeared on the street. He went into the inn. Five minutes later, Rigoberto and Zeke Caton came out and half ran to a bright orange Challenger. Rigo jumped behind the wheel and they raced off. Another minute, and Fain emerged as well, carrying a paper grocery sack. Daryll followed, walking carefully on his broken toes. The Yukon's parking lights flashed as Daryll unlocked the car and crossed in front of the vehicle to get into the driver's seat. Fain was already inside, as eager to roll as a Labrador.

I jogged across the street, opened the back door of the Yukon, and jumped inside.

"Easy," I said, putting a warning palm on Fain's shoulder as his own hand dipped into his jacket. "Let's play nice." I sat right behind him. If Daryll had a weapon, it had to be in an ankle holster; out of quick reach now.

"We're the good guys," said Fain.

"Jury's still out on that," I said, reaching into the front and taking the grocery sack. "Put your hands on the dash."

He complied. "Where is Jaeger?"

I ignored him, glancing in the sack. Inside was a large sealed freezer bag, holding folded clothes. Gray coveralls or work pants. And paper boots, the kind with elastic to slip over regular shoes, so you didn't track dirt into the house that a real estate agent was showing, or get spatters on them during a paint job.

No paint on these. But plenty of flaking, rust-colored drops.

"Start talking," I said to Fain.

He took that as permission to turn a fraction, so he could see me out of the corner of his eye. "That night you broke into the gun shop. Daryll was covering the back. I covered the front, watching from the vacant store next door."

I'd seen the renovated store, awaiting tenants. "Go on."

"It was a prime vantage point. The upstairs windows let me see the entire street." Fain started to twist around and I moved another foot to stay in his blind spot. "Somebody had already forced the lock on the door. I went through the place to make sure no one was camped there. Squatters wouldn't surprise me in a town like this. I found the coveralls and the shoes, up on a high shelf."

"Just sitting there."

"Not for long. I could still smell the blood on them. The shooter must have worn the coveralls over his civvies to keep himself clean, and set them there right after. I don't know why he didn't trash them. But they can't be Leo Pak's. The coveralls are size XL. Your guy would be swimming in those."

Not exactly exculpatory evidence, wearing baggy clothes. But it did undercut the police theory that Erle's shooting had been a crime of opportunity. The killer had brought gear to keep blood off of him.

"And"—Fain tapped his forefinger on the dashboard—"the marks inside the paper boots are from a big flat tread. Street shoes."

"Leo wears desert boots," I said, finishing the thought.

"Yes, he does. Pak's innocent. Those clothes prove it."

"If I believe you."

"Come on. That would be a pretty elaborate lie."

"I've heard weirder. But let's go with it. You found the bloody clothes. Then what?"

"Then you and Daryll start beating the shit out of each other and I left the clothes where they were to go and find out what the hell was happening."

"John had to help me walk back to the inn," Daryll said, speaking up for the first time. "Humiliating."

"It gave me a chance to think on the situation," said Fain. "The shooter might come back to get his clothes. But I couldn't stake out the vacant store around the clock. I didn't tell anybody about the clothes, not even the men. I came back an hour later and sealed them up in plastic and hid them."

"You should have trusted us," Daryll said to his boss.

"Trust is at a premium right now," I said.

"We delivered," said Fain. "Where is Jaeger?"

"Probably running back to Idaho with his tail between his legs," I said. "You'll get the Trumorpha when Leo's free."

"Our deal was you lead us to Jaeger." Fain's voice rose, startling an elderly woman passing by on the sidewalk. I smiled and nodded to her. Boys being boys.

"Your objective was to acquire the Trumo," I said. "Keep it off the street, you told me. Or was that bullshit?"

Fain and Daryll were silent.

"Thought so," I said.

"Those freaks butchered people," Daryll said through his teeth. His eyes in the mirror told me it was eating him up, not being able to turn around and get his hands on my neck.

"I found that out," I said, "too late to do any good. Whose damn fault is that?"

I popped the lock to open the door. Fain took his hands off the dash, more frustration than conscious choice, and thought better of it. My Browning's muzzle made a circular indent behind his ear.

"At least hand over the drugs," he said. "Maybe they'll give us a lead on Jaeger."

"The Trumo stays where it is. If anything happens to me, a package with three thousand vials will show up in the nearest FBI office, along with a letter explaining everything. My insurance that you and your boys behave."

I slipped out of the Yukon. As I walked away, I kept an eye peeled in case Zeke and Rigo circled back, wondering what had happened to their boss. Bad enemies to have. I'd have to step very lightly around Mercy River until Leo was a free man.

But that wasn't the problem at the front of my mind.

Leo wears desert boots, I had said.

Yes, he does, Fain had answered.

Leo had only worn socks when Fain had visited him in the jail. His boots had been bagged and tagged in an evidence locker.

Did Fain's reach extend to every corner of the sheriff's station? Or was there more to this than I was seeing?

TWENTY-SEVEN

Ganz PICKED UP ON the fourth ring, at the instant I had resigned myself to leaving a voice mail.

"Surprised you answered," I said.

"I thought about ignoring it," Ganz said, "and decided that not talking now would lead to unwanted visitors at my home in the middle of the night again. I will give you two minutes."

"Okay. A hypothetical situation. If I came across evidence that pointed to someone other than Leo being the shooter, but that evidence had been removed from the scene, what are my options?"

Ganz's pause ate up a good five seconds of my allotted one hundred and twenty. "You have quite an imagination, with a hypothesis like that."

"If I dropped it on the sheriff's doorstep, what would happen?"

"I'm assuming the supposed evidence is forensic."

"Good assumption."

"Then the situation might—*might*—lead to that evidence being brought into the chain, and examined, and proven to be linked to the case. But that's a long step away from having it admitted in court. The prosecution can throw up all kinds of arguments, especially involving the mystery of where the evidence was all this time. Convincing a judge that a piece of evidence might be compromised is a lot easier than proving its purity, in these circumstances. Judges such as Clave don't like it when the defense's Exhibit A magically falls out of the sky. Plus, lest we forget, your guy has already confessed to the damn crime. None of this even comes into play until Leo's appeal."

"Which you're not spearheading."

"Don't put this on me, Van."

I exhaled. "You're right. Sorry."

"If the police found the evidence during the normal course of their investigation, that would be one thing," Ganz said, maybe to soften the blow. "We could push for a reevaluation of the plea based on Leo's mental history, et cetera. But the case is closed. So are our options, for now."

"I almost forgot. Lieutenant Yerby has clamped down on Leo's visitors since the plea. Can you get a message to him? Tell him that Dez is on the side of the angels."

"Am I supposed to understand that jargon?"

"You've gone over two minutes," I said.

"I'll bill you." He hung up.

Dammit. I'd held out hope that the bloodstained clothes—if they were legit—would allow Ganz to get a crowbar into the case against Leo. But Leo's kamikaze choice to plead guilty may have sealed his fate.

And I'd let Jaeger walk. The likeliest suspect in Erle Sharples's death, and the certain killer of at least two other innocent people.

Two so far, I reminded myself. Jaeger would undoubtedly keep robbing HaverCorp trucks, and more guards would die. Thanks partly to me.

I had the drugs and the blood evidence and none of it did me or Leo any good. Holding all the cards. Still losing the damn game.

If the cops had Jaeger in their sights, they might have the resources to place him in Mercy River when Erle Sharples was killed. Maybe there was DNA on the coveralls that could link Jaeger or one of his skinhead goons to the shooting. An outside chance, but one I'd miss if I didn't try.

I might not know where Jaeger was now, but I did know where to find his inside man at HaverCorp. Aaron Conlee. I looked at the system admin's online profile again. Conlee didn't fit with the Hitler-worshippers I'd seen at the cabins. Just a regular guy with a wife and a life. His face was familiar, and I wondered if I'd seen it before. Take off his old-school glasses and change his hair, and he'd be another person entirely.

Portland was less than three hours away. Worth the drive to find out if Aaron Conlee, possible skinhead, probable accessory to murder and armed robbery, was as unassuming in person. Fain might want to keep Conlee and HaverCorp under wraps, but I had no such concerns if it could lead the cops to Erle's real killer.

CONLEE'S HOME ADDRESS HAD been easy to find through the public records. He'd applied for a build permit on his property in University Park on the north side of Portland. Nice house, nice neighborhood. I wondered how much systems administrators made, and whether it would cover the mortgage on the sleekly modern three-level townhouse I was assessing from across the suburban street.

I'd rung the doorbell of the townhouse when I'd first arrived, pizza box in hand. The house had remained silent. Nobody home. Or maybe the Conlees weren't answering the door on a lazy Sunday. Or they might be in their backyard, if the row of townhouses had outside patios. No way to tell without watching the place for a while.

A dog park occupied a chunk of the public space across from their home. I claimed a bench at the far side of it.

The townhouse looked like a soft nut. Security wasn't high on the block. No cameras placed anywhere around the front of Conlee's home. Any people meandering around the dog park would be nicely shielded by a crop of slim trees. The townhouse bumped right up against its neighbors, so there was no chance anyone might glance out a window and see me. On the downside, there would be no going around back, either. If I went in, I'd have to take the direct approach.

So I watched, and ate slices of thin-crust pepperoni, and stayed alert in case any of the dogs jumped the fence in an attempt to steal my food.

I was so focused on the Conlee place, I missed the blue Camaro until the car was past the townhouse and most of the way down the block.

Holy shit.

It disappeared around the corner. For a full minute I wondered if I'd been mistaken; that this Camaro had been a different rust-spotted muscle car than the one I'd seen at the Dixie Hot Springs cabins. Then it glided back into view. Two men squashed shoulder to shoulder tested the capacity of the Camaro's front seats. Men with long goatees and neck tattoos peeking out of their collars.

The car stopped at the curb opposite the snug garage that took up the first story of Conlee's townhouse. The two hulks stayed in their seats. Moments later, a Chevy Tahoe with a wide red stripe down the side of its white paint job turned onto the street. It parked a few cars behind the Camaro. The hulks heaved themselves out of their car. Its shocks eased up half a foot in relief. The doors of the Tahoe opened. I saw the driver first, a disheveled weed with peroxided hair and gray tattoos snaking out of the sleeves of his white T-shirt.

The final man was Jaeger. He waited as the rest came to him. He wore the same black business shirt and work pants that I'd seen before, with a short brown shearling coat and black scarf to ward off the cold.

I'd come to Portland to see if I could confirm Aaron Conlee's connection to the skinheads, and here they were, all but posing for a photograph. Could I somehow nail them here? Fain was three hours away. And I didn't have a bone to throw the cops to get them onto Jaeger's trail. The skinhead leader might be scum, but he wasn't a person of interest. Not yet.

Jaeger's group walked quickly across the street and up the stoop to the Conlees' door, the peroxided prick in the lead. There was a pause. My view of the door was blocked by the broad backs of the two hulks. They were enough alike that they might be cousins, from their shaven heads and goatees to the same olive surplus work jackets and jeans tucked into black leather boots.

I kept my head down. It wasn't likely that Jaeger would spot and recognize me from across the park, but I'd left the Browning in the truck, not wanting to have a weapon on me when I broke into the Conlee home. A rookie mistake like that turns an easily plea-bargained misdemeanor into mandatory penitentiary time, if I were to be caught somehow. With Jaeger now on the scene, I was second-guessing my decision.

The door opened. As the hulks moved aside I saw Peroxide extract a pick gun from the lock and put it in his pocket. They went inside and shut the door.

Damn. Was Jaeger here for the same reason I was, to toss the house? What could he be looking for? Conlee was already feeding him Haver-Corp's secrets.

The neighborhood continued its day. Kids shrieked as they rode bicycles over the sidewalk curb. A minivan waited at the stop sign, the sound of Billy Preston on an oldies station drifting out its window. I knew the song from Dono's record collection. "Nothing from Nothing." The townhouse door remained closed.

A worse possibility occurred to me. The skinheads might be waiting for the Conlees to return to their picture-perfect home. Probably not to have a pleasant coffee while they selected the next armored car on their hit list.

I didn't know Aaron Conlee, or owe the man anything. He might be as big a piece of shit as the white power thugs that broke into his home. But letting him and maybe his wife walk right into a nightmare wasn't something I could let happen.

I'd made up my mind to head Conlee off and warn him of the danger if he showed, when the door to the townhouse cracked open. One of the two beefy hulks stuck his bald head out, peered around, retreated back inside. The door swung wide and the bruiser walked down the stoop, followed by Jaeger, and a man I immediately recognized by his glasses as Aaron Conlee. The second hulk and the peroxided guy brought up the rear of their little parade.

Jaeger's men stuck close to Conlee's side, almost herding him as the group walked to the red-striped Tahoe. Behind the glasses, Conlee's high forehead and cheeks were pale.

All five of them got into the Tahoe and drove off.

Had I just witnessed a kidnapping? I wasn't sure. More certain was the fact that the townhouse was a safer target for a quick search now.

The block was clear. I went straight to Conlee's garage door. If the peroxided guy had known his stuff, he wouldn't have risked a full two minutes standing out in the open, struggling to beat the chrome-plated dead bolt Conlee had on his front entrance. Locks on the twist-handles of garage doors are cheap, and easy. I might as well have had a key.

As I lifted the door waist-high, its hinges gave out a soft shudder-ing groan. I slipped underneath, and the door creaked in a higher pitch as I closed it again. Visible even in the darkness, past a worn-out little Mazda Miata, was the bright white outline of an interior door. I listened. No footsteps running to investigate the sound of the garage opening. I turned the knob and went in.

The garage opened onto the kitchen. Like the exterior of the house, the kitchen's appliances and countertops had a glossy tasteful moder-nity. But beyond that the room was a pit. A sour smell hit me before the details sank in. Every countertop was loaded with crusty dishes in precarious stacks. Food in half a dozen colors had dripped on the stove and the floor and even the refrigerator.

Making my way through the attached living room and a spare bed-room revealed a little more of the couple's lifestyle. The furniture was decent, but a step or two down from the house itself. What art and electronics they owned wouldn't be worth a thief's time. Maybe the Conlees had sunk all of their money into buying the house.

Jeans and long-sleeved tees and crumpled boxers garlanded the couch, and soft piles of old socks and shirts lay under the coffee table.

Men's clothes. No similarly discarded yoga pants or bras or anything else obviously feminine.

And those stacks of dirty dishes in the kitchen held a lot of single plates and forks. Maybe Aaron was kicking it solo these days.

I didn't find any cell phones or computers on the first floor. No obvious signs of neo-Nazi sympathies, either. Not for the first time, I wondered how a computer tech in liberal Portland got connected with ultra-right-wing supremacists.

Ten minutes gone. I'd give myself another ten to hunt through the upstairs before pulling out.

Halfway up, the stairwell made a ninety-degree turn at a small landing, leading to the upper hallway at the top. The master bedroom was the first door on the right. It wasn't quite as sloppy as the kitchen. At least the tangle of bedsheets wasn't covered in dried food.

I started going through the nightstand. Started, and stopped, my hand frozen on the drawer pull. I had heard a thump.

Had it come from outside? A squirrel or pine cone landing on the roof? I stood, my breath as motionless as my body.

Thump.

Inside. Definitely inside.

From the bedroom closet.

My heart was choosing a bass beat over treble. I stepped backward, away from the front of the closet. Had someone heard me come in, and hidden there? If he were armed and nervous, a bullet could fly right through that stylish white oak.

Thump.

I reached out and turned the knob and yanked the closet open.

It was a woman, bound with wide strips of filament tape and lying on the floor of the walk-in space. From her dark bobbed hair, I recognized her as Aaron Conlee's wife.

More tape covered the bottom half of her head, like a mockery of a bandit's mask. Her eyes were wide and terrified. She thrashed, making another thump.

Holy fuck, what had I walked into?

"Hold on," I said to her. "I'll help you."

She thrashed again. Her hair was matted to her skull with sweat.

I could drag her out, but that might make a horrible situation even worse. And I would need my knife to cut the thick loops of tape off her arms and legs. I did *not* want her to see the knife right now.

Instead, I backed off and sat down on the carpeted floor of the bedroom and tried to project harmlessness. It didn't feel natural.

"I'm going to untie you," I said, "and we're going to call the police. I'll give you a phone. Can you hold still while I let you loose?"

She nodded, hesitantly at first, then as if she couldn't stop.

"Okay," I said. "Turn on your side and we'll free your hands first."

After another moment she rolled to let me reach her wrists and held perfectly still while I sliced through the sheaf of sticky tape between her forearms. The tape around her wrists was tighter. Her hands had turned the color of lavender soap, her fingers swollen. A simple silver ring on her wedding finger was half embedded in puffy skin.

When the last of the tape parted, I tensed, half expecting her to lash out or at least yank at the gag. But she stayed on her side, arms still behind her, as I quickly cut the thick loops binding her thighs and calves and ankles.

"Do you want to take the rest off yourself?" I asked. She didn't respond. I knelt by her head and very carefully parted the tape with the point of the knife behind her ear, where there was at least a fraction of space between the mask and her skin. I was nearly through when I saw that she was weeping. I gently peeled the tape from her face. It pulled at her skin, reluctant to let go. She finally moved, a small turn of the head to let me strip the last of it off.

I backed away again and sat on the carpet.

"What's your name?" I said.

"Schuyler," she said, her voice sounding parched.

I held out my phone for her to make the call. A lousy break, but I could always tell the cops that I somehow heard Schuyler banging around from outside, and that the door was unlocked. That story would at least be a hair's breadth more plausible than claiming I was walking by and got a psychic flash of danger.

"No," she said. "Don't call the police."

"We need the cops. Maybe you need an ambulance, too." She wasn't physically hurt that I could see. And she was fully dressed, from a Nordic-patterned turtleneck down to Keds sneakers. That didn't mean she hadn't been touched.

She shook her head as violently as she'd been nodding it before. "They'll kill Aaron."

"Why did they take him?"

"I can't tell you. Please, just let me go."

"You can go. Or I'll leave," I corrected. "But without answers I'm calling the cops and telling them what happened here."

"No!" Schuyler was hastily on her feet, unsteady as a fawn, and tottering into the hanging rack of clothes. Only by striking the rail with her forearm did she catch herself before falling back down again. I stayed seated.

"Is it about Aaron's work? The information he can get at Haver-Corp?" I said.

She froze. "How did you know that?"

"What is it that Jaeger wants?"

"Jaeger," she said, as if testing the name.

"The older guy with the white mustache and black clothes."

"He's insane. He showed up here—" Schuyler trembled and moved past me into the master bathroom. She turned the tap and held her hands underneath the faucet, letting the water run over her reddened fingers. "He said if Aaron didn't go along quietly, his men would murder me while Aaron watched. That they would use knives, but that I would be alive for a long time to feel it. He said it like he was telling us the weather. Who does that?"

"If you won't call the cops, then let me help," I said. "I can protect you."

Her laugh was a harsh cough. "They'll kill you."

I was pretty sure that Jaeger planned to kill the Conlees, too, but I kept that to myself.

"They left you tied up here so Aaron would cooperate. Where are they going?" I said.

"To HaverCorp's offices, I think. That man—Jaeger—he told Aaron to give him all the deliveries scheduled for next month. He was furious. I could tell that, even if he never did much more than whisper. He has a strange voice. Frightening."

Schuyler took a long inhale of the steam rising from the sink. A tiny gold cross dangled from around her neck, collecting droplets of mist.

"Jaeger wanted more armored car routes?" I said.

"Everything. Something about losing junk from the last time. I don't know what he meant."

"How far away is Aaron's office?"

"Forty minutes. Why?"

Count on at least seventy round-trip, plus time to pull whatever delivery routes Conlee could dredge out of the databases. That left another hour before Jaeger would return here. I just hoped that Conlee was still walking around by then.

She washed her face in the bathroom mirror. Her shaking had stopped. With her square bones and a prominent nose, she might never have been conventionally pretty, but she carried a frank attractiveness that went beyond that.

"Who are you?" she said. "You're not with Jaeger."

"Do I look like a skinhead?"

"I suppose not. But you . . ." She leaned away, perhaps unconsciously.

"Yeah." I sat down on the counter to give her some space. It wasn't difficult. The master bathroom had two sinks and a full shower and Jacuzzi tub. "This isn't Aaron's first time, right? Handing over intel."

Schuyler gave me a slow once-over, eyes sharp even through her pinkened corneas.

"That's what you are." She cupped a handful of water into her mouth and spat it back out. "One of the general's."

The general. Son of a bitch.

"Charles sent you here. I should have realized," Schuyler said, dashing the water from her fingertips like she wanted to fling me away with it.

"How do you and Aaron know General Macomber?"

She stopped, towel clutched in her hands.

"You really don't know, do you?" She stared at me in astonishment. "Charles is Aaron's father."

"HIS FATHER," I SAID. "Aaron changed his name?"

"His mother changed it for him, when she and Charles were divorced. Aaron grew up here on the West Coast, while his dad was God-knows-where with the Army. But Aaron has never stopped trying to win the great man's approval," she said, as bitter as reheated coffee. "He even joined the Army himself right out of high school, desperate to become like you people."

"It wasn't enough," I said.

"He didn't make it through. Didn't earn the banner or whatever you call it."

The scroll, not that Schuyler truly cared.

"That experience nearly destroyed him." She walked out to the bedroom. "When he and I met, Aaron was out of the Army and out of work. He told me once that he'd rather have been killed in combat than to have failed. I was dumb enough at that age to find those kinds of emotional wounds intriguing." She folded her arms. "Toxic machismo. He grew out of it, I thought. We both went back to college and got real jobs. We made it work. For a time."

I'd been right about Conlee's slovenly housekeeping signaling deeper troubles at home. But I'd been wrong about a whole lot more.

Three armored car robberies of cash. One security van heist, to score drugs.

Three scores with no witnesses, no casualties, the guards neatly trussed and blindfolded. A fourth that ended with two guards slaughtered.

Christ, I'd been dense. Not seeing the trees for the forest. Method was everything.

The last job had borne all the signs of rabid, panicky amateurs. The first three? Executed with absolute precision. Military precision.

"When did you move out of this house?" I said to Schuyler.

"A month ago. I only came by this afternoon to pack up some clothes. I left after—" she stopped herself.

"After you learned Aaron was feeding HaverCorp's secrets to the general."

Schuyler looked as though she had sipped vinegar. "And how do you know about that, if you're not one of Charles's attack dogs?"

"I'm piecing it together," I said. "My friend is in trouble because he got caught in the middle of the general's business."

"He's not the only fool. I actually bought Aaron's lie that HaverCorp wanted to hire him badly enough to give him a signing bonus up front. Enough for the down payment on this place." She waved an arm toward the ten-foot ceiling. "But it was Charles, of course. Playing with people's lives like toys."

"How did you find out?"

"Little things. Noticing how much Aaron and Charles had been talking during the past year or two. I thought they'd finally mended fences. But around the times of every call, Aaron would have to go in to work at strange hours. He said it was to monitor some nighttime jobs. HaverCorp keeps their backup data center here, in case anything disastrous happens at their central location in Illinois."

She sat on the rumpled bed. "And then right after my birthday last month I found a stack of cash Aaron had hidden in the garage. He tried to tell me it was old, or that he'd won it gambling and forgotten about it. Stupid. Him this time, not me."

Conlee had been giving his father the armored car routes, and Macomber had issued marching orders to Fain and his crew. They had been careful. One job every few months, in different parts of the country. Still, the Feds must have guessed the first three HaverCorp robberies had been the work of one crew, based on the MO. Jaeger's sticking his nose in and killing those guards may have upended a few official theories.

"And you never heard of Jaeger until today?" I asked Schuyler.

"No. Damn Aaron. What has he done?"

I had to shoulder some of the blame, too. I stole the drugs from Jaeger, kicking the ever-living shit out of the hornet's nest. Then Jaeger and his goons came here to terrorize Schuyler and force Conlee to give them more targets. Goddamn it.

"At least let me get you somewhere safe," I said.

"I can't turn Aaron in. I can't. If he'll only stand up to Charles . . ."

"Later. Now we've got to—"

We were interrupted by the sound of a door opening downstairs.

Schuyler gasped. I edged toward the bedroom door to listen.

Footsteps on ceramic tile. Too many to judge the number of people.

"Sit down," a man ordered.

"You have what you want," another man said. Schuyler put her hands to her mouth. The speaker must be Aaron Conlee. Still alive, at least for the moment. How were they back from his office so soon? "I can get you more, later. Much more."

"You can," said the first man. "You will." His voice sounded like a whisper delivered by an actor onstage, loud enough to hear but strangely hushed, almost painful. Schuyler had described his voice as frightening. Echoing through the house, it made my skin prickle.

Jaeger.

"Please," Conlee said, "let her go. I'll do whatever you want."

There was the sound of a grunt, and the impact of someone falling. The staircase to the upper floor started at the living room. Jaeger and his men were directly below us.

"Do you have a pistol?" I murmured in Schuyler's ear. "Anything?"

Her expression was enough to tell me no. I hastily scanned the room. Nothing here that might serve as a weapon. No exit.

"Go cut the bitch loose," Jaeger said in that calm, echoing rasp, "and bring her down here. We need to get some thoughts right in their heads."

Heavy steps dutifully began marching toward the stairs. Schuyler nearly screamed, a whimper that was fortunately lost to the sounds from below.

We were out of options. The enemy was coming to us.

TWENTY-EIGHT

STAY BEHIND ME," I said to Schuyler. There wasn't time for more.

When I judged the man in front was near the top of the stairwell, I took two fast steps out of the bedroom and had a second to catch the shock on the hulk's fleshy face before I kicked him full force in his broad chest. He toppled backward, into the peroxided guy behind him, both of them crashing into a pile on the stairway landing halfway down.

I raced after them. Peroxide was nearly upright, pinned between his burly buddy and the wall, his face in profile. I punched him and his head snapped sideways as he slumped. From the floor, the big man hauled at my leg. I fell onto the stairs leading upward. Someone shouted from the living room. Tucked into the waistband of the stunned Peroxide's jeans was a small automatic. I grabbed it and pointed the muzzle right in the center of the big man's goatee.

"Let go," I said. He released my leg. When he moved, his blond buddy slid unconscious to the floor of the landing.

"Reese?" someone yelled from downstairs.

"Up," I said, hauling the hulk's shoulder so that he stood and walked ponderously down the stairs ahead of us, my new little S&W pressed against the back of his neck. Behind me, I felt Schuyler close at my heels.

Jaeger and the hulk's cousin waited in the living room. Jaeger had left his shearling coat and scarf on the entryway table, so that he wore only black from head to toe. Aaron Conlee rose from the couch at the sight of me and Schuyler.

Cousin Number Two held a revolver large enough to be substantial even in his plump hand. He brandished it uncertainly, not sure whether to aim it at us.

"You," Jaeger said when he saw me. He stood as I'd seen him before, with his hands relaxed at his sides. Motionless. His eyes were such a pale green I could see their glitter from across the room. The skinhead leader might have been examining a curious species of insect, for all of the concern he showed.

"Schuyler?" Conlee said to his wife

"Aaron, go outside," I ordered. I had a gun. The cousin had a gun. Maybe Jaeger did, too, but even if he didn't, it was at least three against me. Best to vamoose before they started thinking hard about their chances.

"Don't you move," Jaeger said to Aaron. In person, his whispery voice was even more eerie.

"Aaron, go," said Schuyler. Conlee hesitated.

"If you leave now there will be no forgiveness," Jaeger said. "Only retribution."

There was a cough and movement from the landing. The peroxided skinhead was waking up.

"Aaron," Schuyler pleaded.

That did it. Conlee walked robotically toward the double doors. The cousin tensed and raised his revolver another fraction. The hulk I was holding started to turn, and I screwed the S&W into his ear canal to tell him how I felt about that.

"Lose the gun," I said to the cousin. "Behind the sofa."

He didn't move, though his eyes moved to Jaeger. I cocked the S&W. The hulk I was holding winced at the sound.

Without turning his gaze from me, Jaeger nodded. As detached as if we were all acting out a play for his benefit.

The cousin licked his lips and reached out to drop his revolver between the couch and the wall.

Schuyler opened the left-hand door. They stepped out.

I smacked my forearm across the back of the hulk's bullet head. He dropped to his knees. I pointed the gun warningly at Jaeger as I patted his coat on the entry table. No weapon, but his wallet and other things were in the pockets. I took the coat. And his scarf.

"Running won't save you," Jaeger rasped as I walked backward into the sunlight.

"Another time," I said, and shut the door. I took Jaeger's black scarf and knotted it quickly around the twin door handles. It wouldn't slow them down for long, but we'd only need a minute to get out of sight.

Schuyler was already leading her husband in a fast walk across the park on the other side of the street. I ran to catch up. A collie in the off-leash area barked at us. Its owner called it, but it continued to dash in circles, up to the fence near us and back again, elated by its temporary freedom.

You and me both, dog.

TWENTY-NINE

WILL WE BE SAFE?" Schuyler said, not for the first time.

We were racing down Highway 206 out of Wasco. On each side of the two-lane road, a seemingly endless array of towering wind turbines stretched toward the far horizon. Each turbine was over four hundred feet tall, if you counted the rotating blades, but between the vast expanses of sky and the smooth land the enormous machines appeared almost delicate. Perspective. Our current troubles were minuscule when compared with the war Moulson and Booker were headed toward.

Still, trouble was trouble. Nothing from nothing leaves nothing. That song had been playing on repeat in my head since Portland.

Schuyler had taken the front seat while Conlee sat stiffly in back. He'd been silent during the two hours we'd been driving. His wife's question roused him out of his shock.

"Jaeger," he said.

I looked at him in the rearview. "When did he first show up?"

"It was . . . about two weeks ago. I went to the grocery store after work. He and his men were waiting at my car when I came out. They knew my name." He turned to Schuyler. "Yours, too."

"And they knew where you worked," I said.

"Jaeger said . . . he said this would be just once. That if I gave him an easy delivery to rob with good stuff, he'd leave us alone."

Until the next time. Then the skinhead would be back, and bolder.

"He asked for drugstore deliveries. Something they could sell quickly. He didn't want a big truck. I couldn't find anything like what he wanted, but the oxy stuff—"

"Oxymorphone. Go on."

"That was due to be picked up in a week. Jaeger wanted it sooner. He made me change the date, so that he would have it the next day."

Which put Conlee's name on the shipping records I'd seen.

"You should have gone to the police," said Schuyler, reaching back to touch his leg.

"They knew all about you," Conlee said to her. "Where you worked, and even that you were living with Doug and Francine right now. Jaeger said if I told anyone, he would know, and he'd find you and—"

"They're animals," said Schuyler.

Conlee didn't have to finish the thought. Maybe Jaeger had left it to his imagination. What a husband could imagine would be much worse.

"How did they find us?" he said.

I had some guesses on that. Jaeger led the supremacist First Riders. Erle Sharples had sold guns to the Riders, and to John Fain as well. Erle had to wonder what Fain had planned for all those rubber bullets and grenade launchers. And General Macomber had shown up in Mercy River around the time that Jaeger and his supporters were very efficiently rousted from town.

If I could connect the dots, Erle could, too. The HaverCorp robberies had made the news. Three robberies, and Macomber's kid working for that same company.

Very cute, Erle. Tell Jaeger about Aaron Conlee, and the access Conlee had to all that lucrative HaverCorp data. Collect a finder's fee. Then when Fain needs a middleman to buy the stolen drugs back, you deal yourself in for a slice there, too. Except that overreaching got you dead.

"Does Jaeger know who your father is?" I asked Conlee.

"I don't think so. He never said his name."

I didn't think so, either. That little fact was valuable, too much so for Erle to share it with Jaeger for nothing.

"But you told your father about Jaeger," I said to Conlee, "and the general said he'd take care of that little problem."

Conlee sighed his assent.

It fit. Macomber would want to protect his son and Schuyler, of course, but he would also want to be sure that the trail didn't lead through Aaron back to the Rally. Being a major general with highly trained and motivated former Rangers ready to run through concrete walls for him, I was sure Macomber had had no hesitation giving Fain the order. Had they planned to kill Jaeger and his men outright? Or to shock-and-awe the shit out of the skinheads, and ensure the bastards wet their pants if they ever thought of coming near the general's family again?

Having met Jaeger in person, I wouldn't have bet on intimidation working. The man was scary enough himself. I knew from scary, having grown up with Dono Shaw.

"We have to tell Charles you're finished doing his bidding, Aaron," Schuyler said. "No more." Conlee didn't reply.

I had been driving with one hand and fishing through the pockets of Jaeger's coat with the other, while being careful not to leave any prints. Three hundred dollars or so in small denominations. An Idaho driver's license in the name of Arlen Fisher. The license hologram and ghost image could be legit, but I suspected Fisher was a false identity. Regular people recycle their license photographs with each renewal, until the state forces them to update it. The photograph of Jaeger staring expressionless at the camera might have been taken this morning. The issue date was from last month. So new that there wasn't even a scratch on the card's magnetic strip yet.

In Jaeger's left-hand button pocket I found a thumb drive.

"That's it," Conlee said, pointing. "Jaeger made me download all of the car routes that HaverCorp has scheduled during the next month. Everything within our northwestern region."

He held out his hand for the thumb drive from the backseat. I ignored him.

The Riders didn't want to ride too far for their next score. Or scores. They could be aiming to hit a bunch of the HaverCorp trucks in quick succession and make a killing. Literally, if Jaeger stuck to his pattern of eliminating every potential witness.

"Jaeger took you to your corporate office today," I said. "Any chance he or his men were caught on camera?"

"We didn't go there. I work remote a lot. He made me log into work from a FedEx shop, using their computers and Wi-Fi. He didn't trust me using my laptop or my home network. Thought I might have some way to silently call for help. Then he sent all the info on the armored trucks to himself using a temporary email."

That explained how the skinheads had made it back to Conlee's townhouse so fast.

"So this is a backup," I said, holding up the thumb drive.

Conlee nodded. "He didn't trust that I wouldn't corrupt the data somehow."

"Won't your company know somehow? Don't they have safeguards?" said Schuyler, sounding as frustrated with HaverCorp as she was with Aaron.

"I wiped the audit trails. The records of who's seen what data. They can't find me. They aren't even aware I can do that." Conlee couldn't keep an edge of pride out of his voice. His wife went silent.

Despite Schuyler's description of Jaeger as a maniac, the white power leader was cunning. Conlee was a loose end. Jaeger had forced him to hand over every scrap of information on the HaverCorp routes, likely planning to kill the married couple immediately rather than count on fear keeping them silent.

And now I was on Jaeger's hit list as well. Hunting us down wouldn't be his first priority, but he would get around to it once he'd made his fortune. He'd said there would be retribution, and he had meant it.

I'D BEEN IN MERCY River half a week, with Macomber's Rally swirling all around me, and it had never occurred to me to wonder where the general lived.

Conlee knew. His father had purchased a home in the town, to use when planning and executing his annual hoopla and all of the local charity work that went with it. Like Erle Sharples's house, the general's home was set above the town, a surprisingly simple one-story abode of gray stone and red shingles. A small cave for the old bear.

Macomber answered the doorbell himself. He wore a blue plaid shirt tucked into woolen trousers, and soft leather slip-on shoes, one covering his prosthetic foot. The general hadn't waited for sunset to start winding down after the big weekend. Ice in his glass of scotch clinked as he waved a confused hand in greeting.

"Aaron. Schuyler. Hello." He stepped aside and we walked past him into the entry hall, floored with gray flagstones to match the exterior of the house.

"Dad," Conlee said.

"It's Shaw, isn't it?" Macomber said to me.

John Fain stepped through the sliding glass door off the patio, where he and Macomber must have been sitting when we rang the doorbell. His eyes widened at the sight of Conlee. Fain would have fared poorly at the saloon poker tables.

"It would save time if we cut the bullshit, General," I said. "You know who I am."

Macomber's face clouded. Enlisted men didn't talk back to senior brass.

"Aaron. Are you all right?" he said.

"Yes. Because of Shaw. He saved me and Schuyler."

Fain crossed through the square living area. "What happened?"

Schuyler's jaw clenched. "What happened was that those madmen came to our home. They were going to kill us, Charles. All because of you. You talking Aaron into your damn cause."

Macomber and Fain both stiffened.

"Yeah, she knows about the robberies," I said. "I do, too. You've got bigger things to worry about. Like how to keep both of them safe."

"I should have anticipated this," Macomber said to his son, "and sent John and his men to protect you."

"Too late now." Schuyler stalked past Fain and into the living room. It was a warm space, dominated by a red brick fireplace and a well-padded beige sofa set made more for comfort than appearance. She sat in the chair and took off her shoes, rubbing her feet with the same ferocity she had shown to Macomber.

But the general was staring at me. "How did you find Aaron and Schuyler?"

"Off the shipping records in the boxes of Trumorpha." If Fain hadn't made the mistake of crossing Conlee's name off on the copy he'd shown me, I wouldn't have thought twice about it. The Feds would tighten the net before long. Fain and his team were expert soldiers but leaning hard on beginner's luck as criminals.

"Has that been rectified, Aaron?" Macomber asked. "Can the records be traced to you?"

"I changed the name on the route approval after Jaeger left. Too late to change their printouts, I guess."

The general turned to me. "I owe you a great debt, Mr. Shaw."

"Reward me," I said. "Tell me how a bunch of regiment vets turned into armed robbers."

Macomber exchanged a look with Fain.

The captain shrugged. "I told you Shaw was a wild card," he said. "We might as well fill him in."

Macomber grunted assent and walked over to place his scotch on the mantel of the dark fireplace. He sat, slowly bending his artificial leg, on an ottoman by the hearth.

"You know all of the activity and none of the intention," he said to me, smoothing his trouser leg in a reflex motion over the artificial limb underneath.

"Four years ago, I was in Washington," he said. "That was an entirely different kind of fighting than I was used to. Even the Army's politics have nothing on the Pentagon. But I was making a difference, I thought. There was a bill proposed to the House, as damned near bipartisan as one can get these days. Expanded medical care for all veterans. More autonomy for doctors to order tests without administrators shutting them down. Vouchers for services better covered outside the VA network. Even transportation for those needing care outside their home cities. Expensive, but we had momentum."

His charisma was palpable. Even knowing what I did about Macomber, I was half ready to charge right out and taxi a carload of vets myself.

"What happened?" I said.

Macomber didn't stir but managed to puff up regardless. "Much of that momentum could be traced to corporate backers. They made promises to match a percentage of the government's funds. A publicity gambit, but a worthy one. The corporations trumpeted their involvement, which gained public support. If the House passed the bill, the companies would match five percent. Senate passage gained another five. When it became law, a full twenty percent would be covered by donations. Almost eighty million dollars, spread out over a decade."

"HaverCorp's donations," I said.

"Philip Havering, yes. The company is privately owned by the Havering family."

"What went wrong?"

"Not coincidentally, HaverCorp was up for a large government contract at the time. All of that positive media was effective. Havering got his approval."

"And he dropped his support."

"Oh, not that obviously. But two of our key congressmen challenged the bill. Another demanded riders on it, such expensive additions that they hobbled debate. I can't prove corruption, but those legislators had no lack of funds in their next reelection campaigns. Smart business on

Philip Havering's part. Four or five million to save twenty times that amount."

It was sort of amazing, Macomber's ability to project raw fury without moving or changing his voice at all.

"So you think Havering owes you," I said.

"He owes them, the way I see it. The men he cheated. Don't you?"

I didn't answer.

"Of course, I'm aware that HaverCorp's money isn't Philip Havering's personal fortune." Macomber waved a hand as though that were inconsequential. "This isn't about payback."

"Nonsense," Schuyler said. "You wanted to sting Philip Havering any way you could. Because you can't stand his ducking out on a deal that you believed would have been your legacy. I know you, Charles."

Her words rolled off the general like water from waxed paper. "What I can't stand is the waste, Schuyler. Havering had a chance to help tens of thousands of people. Instead he chose to slink away."

"It was my idea to go to work for the prick," Conlee spoke up. "I saw the announcement of HaverCorp opening their data center in Portland. I had the experience. It's always the boots on the ground who have the real knowledge." He glanced at his father and was rewarded with a nod.

"Aaron," Schuyler said, "don't you see? You've helped them point their guns at people. Innocent people."

"Nonlethal measures only," Fain said. "Rubber bullets and tear gas."

Schuyler scowled at Fain as she replaced her heels. If she could have used them to step on his face, I was sure she would have.

"We weren't sure at first how to use the information Aaron retrieved," Macomber continued. "After the House bill collapsed, I had been toying with the notion of starting a fund specifically for the regiment. An organization with the flexibility to care for men during their first few years out of the service, especially. Those are usually the hardest."

He glanced at me. I was sure Fain had shared my Ranger history with the general. Macomber might have conjectured what I'd been up to in the time since I'd mustered out.

"John was a friend," said Macomber, with a slight smile in Fain's direction. "He shared my opinion that Havering owed his country. Eighty million dollars. We couldn't possibly recover that much, but we could take enough, safely enough, to get the Rally off the ground. With capital, and an effective track record, other companies would get on board. Success breeds success."

"Men have risked a lot more for a lot less," Fain said.

And honor would be satisfied. I couldn't decide if the general was overly confident or actually nuts. My grandfather, working alone, could have done more damage to Philip Havering's wallet with one score targeting the man's art collection, or whatever the rich SOB owned.

"You sound like a true believer," I said to Fain. "What's in it for your happy little band, Zeke and Daryll and Rigo? Are they willing to die for the cause, too?"

Fain's eyes flickered at that. It was Macomber who answered me.

"John's men understood. They stepped up. A few missions, carefully planned and executed. Minimal risk. Then we would be finished."

"Does Jaeger know about us?" Fain asked Conlee. "About the Rally?"

"I don't know," Conlee said.

"I think Erle Sharples figured out Aaron was piping you HaverCorp's intel," I said to Macomber. "He was the one who pointed Jaeger toward Aaron, so the skinheads could draw water from that same well. If Erle was that crafty, my guess is that he wouldn't say anything to Jaeger about the Rally, or about Aaron Conlee being the son of General Charles Macomber. Those were his aces in the hole. Maybe he had the notion to blackmail you later, or he could barter the information to the cops if he ever got busted for trafficking in stolen arms."

"That piece of shit," Fain said.

Schuyler stood up. "None of this should matter. A madman threatened my life and your son's life, Charles. If you think you're still in control of this situation, then you're just as crazy. Aaron."

Conlee looked up at his wife from the couch without lifting his head.

"I'm leaving here tonight," Schuyler said. "I want you to come with me, Aaron. If you choose not to, I won't argue. But it will be the end. Mr. Shaw, thank you for saving us. Truly. You've put yourself in a terrible situation to help complete strangers. I'll always be grateful. And I'll pray for you."

She walked to the sliding glass door and went outside and closed it behind her.

"She'll calm down, Aaron," said Macomber. "You two will talk it out."

"You need me here," Conlee said.

"I need you safe. On that Schuyler and I agree. Our team can deal with Jaeger."

"How?" said Conlee. "Jaeger's got the next month all laid out for him. Hundreds of truck routes. The same information we copied onto the thumb drive." He gestured at me, and the general followed his gaze.

Fain folded his arms. "Once he robs one or two, that information will be worthless." He turned to me. "After we took down the first two armored cars, HaverCorp changed all their schedules, nationwide, in case someone in their dispatch department had leaked the regular cash pickup times. They didn't consider that it might be a breach at the database level."

"They will," I said. "The Feds may already have their cyber people on it. They'll find anyone poking around in there."

"They won't find me," Aaron said.

"You're not listening," I said. "It's over. Jaeger's going to hit another truck. More guards will die, and maybe bystanders, too. Call the cops. Call Philip Havering. Head this off before it happens."

"There's another option," Macomber said, almost under his breath.

I was ahead of him. "I politely hand over the information to you, and you use it to intercept Jaeger and his men."

Fain smiled tightly at Macomber. "Told you he was smart."

"And then what? You kill them?"

The general's mouth twisted, like he was tasting the idea. "Jaeger has murdered two people that we know of. A court might reach the same conclusion."

"So much for nonlethal measures."

"I don't like the idea of killing, either," said Fain, "but what choice do we have? Even if we prevent Jaeger from robbing a truck now, he'll come after Aaron and his wife. Let us handle this. Give us the drive."

"Forget it," I said.

"It doesn't matter, Dad," said Conlee. "I can run the same search."

Macomber leaned forward, still focused on me. "Jaeger is scum. The worst mankind has to offer."

I agreed, completely. But it didn't change my decision. The general wanted total victory, to eliminate the threat of Jaeger and retain his golden goose at HaverCorp. Money for the cause. I stood up and walked to the door of the little stone house.

"Sergeant Shaw," the general said, "your file revealed more about you than your accomplishments. Were you aware that you nearly peered out during selection?"

I wasn't. Ranger classes, near the end of assessment, rate and rank their fellow candidates. Who they would most like to serve with, and why. Those who peer low may be dropped entirely, no matter what else they've done to earn their way. If you don't have the confidence of your brothers, you don't have anything.

"Your performance ratings were excellent," Macomber continued, "as was your combat record later. But you were lucky to be there at all. Your classmates found you arrogant, and more than willing to game the rules for your own gain."

"Right on both counts," I said. "Get to the point, General."

"You're a man who needs a purpose, I think. And I also suspect you haven't found it since you left. You can make a difference. Help us."

I left. Before the son of a bitch actually convinced me.

THIRTY

I NEEDED A DRINK. BUT first I made a phone call.

"You know how time zones work, right?" Ochoa said.

"Hello, Armando. This will be quick."

"Damn right it will. I've got a date. I'm hanging up."

"One question. You probably already have the answer somewhere in the service records you got before."

I told him what it was. He cursed, but spared three minutes to find what I needed to know, and then a woman's voice called in the background and Ochoa ended our conversation without another word.

Minutes passed while I sat in the driver's seat of my truck and considered the implications of what Ochoa had told me. One domino clicking into the next, until everything around me fell down.

Maybe I needed six or seven drinks.

I DROVE THE DODGE down Main Street. Past the chain-link fence where the Wall of Remembrance boards had been. The boards were stored away now. Unless that was bullshit, too, like the Rally's corporate sponsors. Who gave a crap where the money came from? In its scattershot way the Rally managed to help a lot of vets. I wasn't blind to that.

But it still felt like Macomber had soiled something honorable with his personal grudge. Brightly colored wallpaper hung over dry rot.

With the Rally over, I had my pick of parking spaces, and the saloon was nearly empty. Jim Seebright stood behind the counter, serving a glass of red wine to the lawyer Henry Gillespie.

"This seat taken?" I said to Gillespie.

He allowed his head to tilt half an inch. I sat down and ordered an ale and a shot of Black Bush.

"You neglected to mention over our game of poker that you're a friend of the man who killed Erle," Gillespie said, focused on his wine glass.

"I am. But he's innocent."

Gillespie didn't bother to reply to that.

"The jamboree's over. Shouldn't you be gone?" Seebright said.

"You guys don't think much of the Rally," I said.

Seebright's mouth pursed. "I don't bite the hand."

"But it's curdling," said Gillespie, as much to the bartender as to me. "Whatever the high-and-mighty general asks for, this town salutes and bends right over. This horror with Erle . . ." He waved a hand. "It's the expected outcome of inviting gunmen here."

"Gunmen who saved your town from becoming Skinhead Central," I said, downing the shot. "As long as we're being honest."

Gillespie looked stunned.

Seebright actually laughed. "That's darned honest, all right," he said.

"Tough day. I'm pissed off at the world."

"We were on our way to solving the problem of the supremacists ourselves," Gillespie said.

"Sure. Fifteen or twenty years of writs and injunctions, and you'd have the First Riders by their tattooed balls."

"You're unusually well-informed, fella," Seebright said.

Gillespie grimaced. "What are you arguing for? Vigilante justice?"

"No," I said. "I'm working hard to find the good in the bad. Speaking of . . ." I took a pull on the beer. It tasted like the first of many to come. "Why were you friends with Erle Sharples? Everybody I've talked to says he was the local shit-stirrer."

"I am aware," Gillespie said, unkempt brows meeting in the middle, "that Erle could be argumentative at times. And that many didn't like him, and thought him shady. But he was also sharply intelligent, and funny as all hell when he chose to be. I suppose I was Erle's friend because he let me be, which was a rare thing for him."

"That's fair," I admitted, and ordered another shot.

"Why are you friends with a man who's confessed to murder?" Gillespie asked.

"Because no matter what the fuck Leo claimed in court, he didn't kill Erle," I said, my voice louder than I'd intended. "Because he stood with me when I needed it most. And because he let me help him right back. Which was a rare thing, too."

"Cheers to that," Gillespie said. He held up his wine glass and we tapped rims.

The door opened and Dez came in. The men greeted her as she walked to the bar. Gillespie actually stood up, which prompted me to do the same. Dez was wearing jeans and a shiny gold zip-front running jacket. Her cheeks were flushed.

"I saw you through the window," she said to me.

"A drink?" I said.

"God, yes. The Rally is over, and I can go home. What's that?" She pointed at the shot glass.

"Bushmills." I held up two fingers for Seebright, who was giving me side-eye, saying, *Way to go.* Or maybe, *Watch out, she's the constable's girl.*

"Susan, I looked into what you asked me," Gillespie said to Dez. "The answer is no. And I'm sorry."

"Don't be," she said. "It was just a thought. I'm better off."

"Catch me up," I said.

"You're the one who gave me the idea," said Dez, "about contesting wills. Whether I might have any claim to Erle's estate, given his marriage to my mother."

"I'm afraid too much time has elapsed since Cecily's death," Gillespie said. "You *were* legally Erle's daughter, but—"

"But I don't like to think of myself that way. Which is proof enough for me that Erle's house is tainted. I can make my own money and feel a whole lot better." She sipped the whiskey, and Gillespie and I followed suit.

"I'll be signing the remainder of the estate over to Bob Bell tomorrow morning," said Gillespie.

"Erle's last relative?" I asked.

"For now. Poor Bob is not long for the world himself."

"Oof," Dez said, setting the shot glass down. "I'm wiped. Can you drive me out to my house? I've been staying with Jaye all weekend, since she lives right here in town."

"I'll drop you," I said.

I said good night to Gillespie and Seebright, both of whom had their eyebrows hovering up around their hairlines. We left them to their gossip.

"Leo?" Dez said when we were alone in the truck. His name packed with enough emotion for a sonnet.

"I don't know," I said. "There's some evidence that might point to someone else, but Leo's lawyer says that's no good to us until the appeal."

She was silent for the time it took us to get off the paved streets of town and onto the gravel back roads.

"He'll be free," she said finally. "I can't accept anything else."

I nodded, appreciating the sentiment if not the logic.

We turned onto Piccolo Road and neared the house. Dez stiffened.

"It's Wayne," she said.

Constable Beacham's silver police cruiser was parked on the concrete slab of driveway. The only electric light in a quarter mile shone from a side window near the rear of the house. The bedroom.

I killed the headlights and let the truck roll to a stop at the edge of the dirt road.

"Wayne still has keys to your place?" I said.

"Yes."

"Does he ever do this? Just drop by?"

"I told him not to. Months ago."

When I opened the truck door—slowly enough that it wouldn't creak—Dez mimicked my movements. I didn't bother trying to convince her to stay put. We walked on the slope of the ditch toward her place. Nothing moved at the house.

Wayne was a cop. Cops lurking around at night made me even more wary than if it were a stranger. Walking through the front door felt like a bad move.

I stepped over the mud and rotting grass at the bottom of the ditch, and Dez jumped to follow me. We crossed the plowed rises and troughs of the fallow field that surrounded the house. Crickets silenced their whirring at our approach, a silent wave preceding us. We stopped to listen at two hundred feet out. The house remained quiet. With the moon hidden behind the clouds, the single lamp in the bedroom seemed as bright as a searchlight. I took a long curving path to come up on the window's blind side.

Through the heat-warped pane I saw the foot of Dez's bed, and the very ends of two legs on it, legs in blue trousers with a gray stripe down the side and thick-soled black oxfords. As if Constable Wayne had lain down on the bed and fallen asleep.

Dez peered over my shoulder. I heard her teeth click as she stifled a sound in her throat.

We circled around to the back door. I tried the knob. Locked. I put out my hand, and Dez silently placed her key in it. I let the lock guide me, not so different than using picks, letting each pin lift and release its hold separately. The key turned with a faint click, and the doorknob with it. I held it there with two fingers and motioned for Dez to stay where she was, out of the line of sight from the doorway.

The rear door opened on the little house's only hallway. Light spilled from the bedroom onto the hallway's runner rug, trapping scarab beetles woven into its pattern. The rug padded my footsteps as I walked to the bedroom door.

Wayne Beacham sat upright on the made bed. He was dressed in his full town constable uniform, service belt and all. His long legs stretched straight out in front of him as if to show off the precise creases in his trousers. His chin rested on his chest, the tone of his skin a close match for the white of his dress shirt.

I turned in time to catch Dez by the upper arms as she came toward the bedroom.

"Don't," I said.

She pulled herself gently free and went to see for herself. Her body sagged against the wall, cheek against the sunshine-yellow molding.

"Oh," she said. "Wayne."

His uniform jacket had been hung neatly over the back of a wicker chair by the tiny feminine desk next to the bed. A spiral pocket notepad was left open on the desk, with a ballpoint pen placed precisely beside it. I risked walking into the scene to see what had been written.

> Sue
> I'm sorry for Erle. I thougth it would help us
> I love you
> *Wayne*

The words were small and tightly formed, including the misspelled one, in an odd mix of cursive and printing.

Jesus. Constable Beacham. Not Leo or Dez or even Jaeger and his men.

Beacham must have shot Erle before heading up the dead-end street to the dress shop and its broken window. Before Fain and Zeke and Gillespie had seen him working there. Which meant Erle had been dead longer than anyone had assumed. At least half an hour before Leo had arrived on the scene.

Spit had dribbled from Beacham's lips onto his shirtfront, the stains dry now. I leaned down to see. His mouth was coated with drool and maybe salt. The room didn't yet have the low reek of death. Instead, the constable gave off a dry whiff of old sweat.

Running parallel with the salt tang was another sharp scent. Whiskey. Enough booze that once I caught it in my nostrils, it was all I could smell.

"I'm going to check the house," I said to Dez. "You okay here?" She said yes, but I wasn't sure she'd really heard me.

A bottle of Jameson's waited on the yard-wide circle that passed for a dining table. The liquor left at the bottom wouldn't cover the handspan of a child. Next to the whiskey, an empty prescription bottle. I squatted down to read its label. It was Beacham's own prescription, filled a few weeks before, twenty 0.25-milligram pills of Halcion for treatment of insomnia. Take as needed, no more than one pill every twenty-four hours. No telling how many he'd taken, or how much of the whiskey he had downed. It had had the intended effect. Somnolence. Respiratory depression. Death.

Dez was still looking at her husband.

"He . . . Did he." A statement asking a lot.

"Yes. There's an empty bottle of sleeping pills on the table."

She shook her head. "He was so angry. All the time."

There was something I had to know. I walked back inside the room and picked up the notepad with a tissue from a box on the desk and brought it to Dez. When she reached for it, I drew it back.

"Better not to touch," I said. Her eyes moved over the note, backed up as she read it again, over and over while its terrible meaning sank in.

"Erle?" she said. "Oh, God. Wayne, what did you do?"

"Is this Wayne's handwriting?"

"Yes. He has some dyslexia. He sometimes still made mistakes like that. But Erle." She stared at the note. "Why?"

"Maybe Wayne thought you'd get the money back. That it would change your mind about leaving him."

Or if it didn't, at least Beacham would wind up with half of her inheritance in the divorce. He'd win either way.

But now wasn't the time to talk that through with Dez. She still had her eyes fixed on the paper, as though willing it to speak truth to her.

When I returned the notepad to the desk, I spared a moment to examine Beacham's shoes. On the right sole of the size-twelves, the outer rim of rubber was missing a deep notch. Regular use had worn the shallow tread flat. It had been a long time since the shoe leather had seen polish.

"I'm going to go get the truck," I told Dez once we were back outside on the porch. "Do you want to stay here or come with me?"

She chose to walk. We took a different path, around the house to the road and straight to the Dodge. Instead of turning around, I drove us to the packed earthen driveway and stopped next to the police cruiser.

"Hang tight," I said, grabbing my pack.

Back inside the bedroom, I removed the bloodstained coveralls and paper boots from the freezer bag Fain had given me—careful not to touch them directly—and placed the folded bundle on the wicker chair where the constable's jacket hung.

I compared the tread marks inside the paper boots to Beacham's shoes. Same flat tread, same notch. No question, at least not to my unscientific eyes. They matched.

The note might be enough to spring Leo. The clothes should clinch it.

I left the house and closed the door before calling 911.

THIRTY-ONE

THE REST OF THE night passed in a blur of questions. First from Deputies Thatcher and Roussa, who were first on the scene, and then Lieutenant Yerby at the sheriff's station, after he'd separated Dez and me. Our story was ninety-eight percent true and thus hard to screw up: we'd driven to the house, seen Constable Beacham's cruiser, Dez unlocked the door, and we found the body and called for help.

Still, Yerby seemed determined to find a hole in our tale, until Roussa confirmed that Henry Gillespie and Jim Seebright had seen Dez and me off at the saloon only thirty minutes before my call to 911.

Around one o'clock in the morning, Yerby let us walk. Roussa drove Dez back to her friend Jaye's house. I let the Dodge coast down the deserted road toward the rental house while I had one last conversation over the phone with Ganz.

Ephraim was not pleased to be woken yet again. He was halfway through a complex string of epithets before I managed to interrupt and explain what had happened. I claimed that I'd seen the suicide note while checking Beacham for signs of life. The bloodstained coveralls and boots I pretended not to have noticed. The cops would bring those to light soon enough.

Ganz promised to rustle the bushes at Judge Clave's office once they opened. For now, he told me, don't do anything. The *else* on the end of that command was implied.

I lay in bed in the rental house, counting stains on the popcorn ceiling. Waiting between rounds of interrogation with Yerby and the deputies had given me plenty of time to think. I'd normally feel some regret at a suicide, even the suicide of a fuckup like Wayne Beacham. But I could guess why Dez's estranged husband had chosen to use a gun from Leo's workbench to kill Erle. And why he'd hung around the scene after the murder.

Leo came to work when the gun shop opened every morning. Beacham made early morning rounds through the town, checking locks, looking for vandalism like that conveniently broken window at the dress shop. It wasn't a stretch to say that the constable knew Leo's schedule and counted on it.

I could piece together most of Beacham's probable actions that morning. He had slipped away from the dress store and thrown the coveralls and boots over his uniform before murdering Erle. Then he had forced the lock on the shop next door to quickly stash the bloody clothes and hightail it back before he was missed.

The rest of his intended plan was simple. The constable would wait for Leo to arrive for work, and then kill him, too, staging it as a justifiable shooting. Beacham could have pretended that he had overheard the shot that killed Erle and had run to investigate. The town would probably give him a medal. For killing his wife's lover.

Except that Henry Gillespie and Zeke Caton had shown up, allowing Leo to escape out the back of the gun shop. Bad luck for Beacham. He'd have had to be content with Leo getting busted for Erle's murder.

Maybe the constable's overzealous application of the baton to Leo's head had been a last-ditch effort at killing him, or at least getting one good shot in before the arrest.

The facts weren't a perfect fit. I couldn't figure out how Beacham had known Erle's security cameras were turned off. How he'd known it was the right moment to enter the gun shop. He must have moved very quickly. Fain and Zeke had seen him at the broken window at seven o'clock, within twenty minutes after Erle must have been killed. And I also couldn't reason why the constable had taken Erle's cell phone. Had Erle called him? Was that how he'd learned the cameras were turned off? But why would Erle have told Beacham that?

I thought back to how strained Beacham had looked when he had braced me in front of the courthouse. How hollow. Hard to live with killing someone. Even if you have a lot to gain by it. Even in war. The number of Rally booths dedicated to stress management and mental health were proof of that.

The constable was dead now. His only reward would be a full-dress funeral, if the town permitted it. A few words from a book, a folded flag, and then Mercy River would do its best to forget the whole fucking mess.

WITH THE MORNING SUN high above the horizon, I set the kettle on to make instant Sanka. Ganz had left behind a can of the granules. Maybe I'd caught a taste for it from him, like a virus.

A computer had come with the rental house, a desktop tower so old that I doubted the owners worried much about theft or damage. I booted it up and plugged in the thumb drive I had liberated from Jaeger. I wasn't certain what I was searching for—though I could admit to some professional curiosity about the cash trucks—but a little knowledge about Jaeger's potential targets could be useful.

The thumb drive held a lone Excel spreadsheet. I scrolled down the sheet for a quick count. More than five hundred rows, each detailing a single truck's daily schedule. The column at the left told me the type of truck—*Full-Armored*, the big tank-like monsters, *Protection Transit*, a smaller version for chauffeuring clients, or what HaverCorp called a *Road Truck*, which must be one of the lighter unmarked vans for less obvious deliveries. Jaeger and his gang had stolen the drugs from a road truck in Nevada. No one had expected trouble.

I read through a few rows, getting a feel for the information. Every truck had target times for hitting each stop. Another series of columns specified the coordinates of the required route. If HaverCorp ran a tight ship, the truck's GPS tracker would signal any deviation from the route, and alert the dispatcher that something was wrong.

A few of the truck routes were pickup-only, stopping at stores and banks to take the day's cash receipts. Those routes didn't attempt to predict how much the drivers might be taking on; a column labeled *$ COLLECT* next to each stop was left blank.

The big money was in cash deliveries. The truck—always a full-armored—would leave the dispatch, pick up preloaded ATM cassettes from a central bank, and distribute those little boxes of twenty-dollar bills to area banks throughout the day. One Portland truck was scheduled to carry more than seven hundred grand.

A good haul, but maybe not worth the risk when that score had to be shared with multiple accomplices. One full-armored would be a tough enough target on its own. If Jaeger's goal was to hit as many armored cars as he could, as fast as he could, before HaverCorp took precautions, he was even more insane than Schuyler Conlee claimed.

I toyed with the spreadsheet menu, figuring out how to filter and sort the data. Cash deliveries only, highest dollar value at the top.

At first I thought what I was seeing was an error, or a row of junk data somehow mixed in with the others. The first space under the column labeled *$ DISPATCH* read *11,200,000*.

Eleven million dollars. In cash. It must be wrong. No bank would require—

Not one bank, I saw. Multiple banks on the route, all branches of Prime Bank National, each one of them receiving somewhere between half and three-quarters of a million dollars. From where?

I'd missed seeing columns at the very far right, past all of the drop points on the route. The columns were blank for most trucks. For this one, under *ORIGIN* it read *FRBSF-RNWA*. Under *TYPE* it read *RECIRC-50*.

The Federal Reserve Bank of San Francisco's local branch was in

Renton, Washington. I knew that, the way that a mountain climber knows what nearby peak is the highest and most dangerous.

Holy shit.

The kettle's whistling had become a shriek. I got up and poured the frothing water into a mug, where it melted the granules instantly. My mind was churning at about the same rate.

RECIRC-50 must mean recirculated bills, in fifty-dollar denominations. Each Federal Reserve branch takes in billions from banks and other vendors across the nation. Currency still in halfway decent shape is sent right back out to other banks. Moving cash where it's needed is part of the Reserve's mandate. Macomber had told me HaverCorp had won a big government contract. Maybe making deliveries for the Reserve was part of that package.

I had stumbled upon one of Prime Bank's major deliveries for the year. Sixteen Seattle branches. Enough money to keep their ATMs stocked until Thanksgiving.

It wasn't a perfect target for theft. Every bill through the Fed is scanned, the serial number recorded. If stolen money turned up at another bank after a theft, the FBI would be on that trail like coyotes after a housecat.

But there were a thousand ways to launder cash, including selling it for a percentage or spending it overseas where the FBI had no jurisdiction. And eleven million was eleven damn million.

Jaeger would go for the big money. I was certain of it, just as I was sure that he would immediately murder the guards to eliminate witnesses, as he had in Nevada.

A column on the list told me how many potential victims. Two. A driver and a hopper, to make the dash into each Prime branch. Plus any civilians who were unlucky enough to be within range.

I wasn't responsible for whatever that freak and his damned First Riders did. I could remind myself of that truth as often as I liked. Maybe it would help to while away the winter nights to come.

The Federal Reserve route was scheduled for Thursday morning, three days from right now. If Jaeger was as smart as I thought, he wouldn't risk hitting another truck first. HaverCorp might start swapping routes around.

I could call HaverCorp myself. Read them their own truck route details, shock the crap out of them, and the Reserve truck would be out of danger. Which would only kick the problem downfield. Jaeger would shift his attention elsewhere, and other people would be in line for a bullet. Including me and the Conlees. I hadn't forgotten Jaeger's promise.

Or I could call the FBI. Convince them I wasn't a crank somehow, without giving them enough details to hang Conlee and the general and Fain's team along with Jaeger. Maybe they would be able to nail Jaeger in the act.

It was the "in the act" part of that idea that worried me. The FBI would wait until they had Jaeger dead to rights, to where a robbery charge would be undeniable. Confronted by a tactical team closing in, it was easy to picture Jaeger's men turning that scene into a charnel house.

Three days. Eleven million dollars. I had a lot of thinking to do.

THIRTY-TWO

WHEN LEO AND GANZ walked out of the sheriff's station, I was sitting on one of the two white-painted ornamental boulders that doubled as vehicle barriers for the walkway. Leo had on a clean black T-shirt and the same jeans as when he'd been busted. And a battered pair of Nikes, which Dez had brought from Leo's room at the inn. The deputies had kept his boots. Those were still evidence.

"That was trippy," Leo said to me. "From talking sentencing over the weekend to full release by Monday night. How'd you swing it?"

"He swung nothing," Ganz said. "Judge Clave realized that accepting the guilty plea of a man with—you'll excuse me—a documented history of psychiatric concerns would be extremely actionable, now that there's another suspect with more substantial evidence against him and no chance of challenging the case."

"Wayne's dead," said Leo. "I still can't believe it."

"Very dead. Very tidy as far as the authorities are concerned. Suicide confessions, now, those swing some weight." Ganz looked at me on that, a question in his eyes. But instead of voicing it, he handed a manila folder to Leo. "Here's the paperwork. Hang on to that. You are released on your own recognizance, pending a formal decision on dropping the charges."

"I can leave town?" Leo said.

"You can and you should, until the court summons you back. I guarantee that plenty of these good people don't give a flying fart about evidence or the court. They'll think you're guilty. One of them will get himself drunk and angry and this carousel will start all over again."

"Beacham's death has already got the town on edge," I said. "Two people asked me about it on my way here." I had also spied Wayne's brother Lester, sitting on one of the painted logs that made a sidewalk barrier for the grocery store parking lot. Holding a large can concealed in a paper bag, but not showing much interest in it. All of the fight wrung out of him.

Ganz fixed me again with that curious look. "It was remarkable luck, Constable Beacham deciding to end things, and leaving conclusive proof of his guilt."

"And me finding him. Is that it?" I said. I knew what Ganz was implying, and I didn't like it.

"Truth can be stranger than art. Ah, good."

A Cadillac livery pulled up in front of the station. Before the driver could step out, Ganz opened the rear door for himself.

"I am taking my own advice and returning to Seattle in time for a late dinner," he said. "If you should get into trouble again—"

"—call anybody else," I said.

"Perfectly phrased."

He shut the door and the Cadillac sped away.

Leo stared at me. "You didn't really . . ."

"What?"

"Kill Wayne Beacham. Set him up to take the blame."

"I'm not a murderer."

"Sorry. Sorry, man. I'm just fried." Leo stretched toward the heavens, like the ceiling in his cell had been four feet tall. "Where's Dez?"

"Talking to the coroner and the cops about her husband's body." I motioned for him to follow me, and we walked toward the courthouse parking lot. It was the end of the day and the lot was nearly empty.

"She's been a rock. All this shit, and now Wayne's dead. I need to see her."

I stopped behind the Dodge. Abruptly enough that Leo nearly ran into me.

"We're going to talk first," I said. "About John Fain. And HaverCorp."

His face dropped. He sat on the Dodge's bumper.

"You've had a hell of a year, Leo," I said.

"It's not what you think."

"That's funny. When I tell people you've got a sense of humor, they never believe me."

"Van."

"There were too many overlaps. Too much weird voodoo. The Rally giving you a job with Erle, right when he was playing double agent for Fain's crew. Then Fain getting in a twist about your welfare. Fain is Macomber's boy. I doubt he gets a vitamin shot without the general initialing his ass first. But suddenly he's granted approval to visit a murder suspect in jail. That got me wondering why Macomber would give a damn."

Leo wouldn't meet my eye.

"A buddy of mine in Army Intelligence clued me to your first assignment after you rotated out of our unit," I said.

"Captain Fain's company."

"That may be the first true thing out of your mouth since I got to town. How much does Dez know about your side hustle?"

"We talked it over before I agreed to join Fain's crew," Leo said. "She supported it. Dez and I don't have secrets like that."

So Dez had been playing me, too. A laugh leapt unbidden out of my throat. "Right."

"Telling you would make you an accessory, man. And I knew how you felt about—about shit like bank robberies."

"That it's for morons."

"Fain and his fire team, they were already rolling when I came on board," he said, standing up. "They'd done the first job, smooth as anything. I know these guys. They're solid. And General Macomber, he's committed to keeping civilians safe. He and Fain drill us on it every time."

A knot of muscle in my neck jolted. "It wasn't Dez you were worried about. You didn't want the cops looking hard at Erle, because that might lead them back to your gang."

"Not at first," Leo said. "I really thought it could have been Dez who killed Erle. She was planning to see him that day anyway. If he'd attacked her . . ."

"What about after? Did Fain order you to take the fall? Promise you an extra share of the cash if you wound up doing time?"

"I'm not a fucking stooge, Van. Staying in jail was my idea. If I acted like my head was on loose, I could keep the heat off the team until they caught up with Jaeger. Then Fain would spring me. He said he had evidence that could prove it."

"Christ, Leo."

"Don't spit on what the Rally's doing. We gave two hundred grand to a burn unit last month. You've seen that kind of horrible shit."

"Whatever serves the cause, right?" I said.

"It means something."

"More than either of us. Fain had me dancing like a puppet. He said he'd only hand over the evidence to clear you if I helped them find Jaeger."

Leo froze.

"Well, the captain must have been bluffing," Leo said. "Fain would have cleared me anyway if you refused."

"We'll never know."

"Fuck. *Fuck.*" He paced up the length of the truck and back. "I wasn't told. I swear. When Fain came to see me at the jail, he asked how I knew you from the 75th. He didn't mention your name again."

"They couldn't be sure you'd go free, evidence or not. They used us both. How good is your Rally if they're willing to sacrifice you, Leo?"

"The guys wouldn't let that happen."

"But they wouldn't care if Jaeger burned me, if it got them what they wanted."

"I never knew they were using you. I would have kicked at it."

"You could have trusted me."

"I wanted you to go back to Seattle, remember?"

"Another manipulation."

"I told you to stay out of it—"

I hit him. One solid straight left. He dropped to one knee.

"Go to hell," I said.

He didn't move to get up, just stayed down and scowled. I left him there. My truck, too. Walking away, feeling like I could hike all the way back to Seattle if it would put Leo and the whole damn town in my dust.

THIRTY-THREE

I HAD TO TALK TO someone. Luce was out of the question, for all kinds of reasons. My old neighbor Addy Proctor would give the smartest advice. I imagined calling her and telling her about Mercy River and everything that went with it, and finally balked. Addy could handle tough news, but I wanted to keep at least one of my friendships unsullied by my bad choices.

Someone who knew my grandfather would be the next best thing. I was near the empty field where the bonfires had been lit three nights before. The Rally's cleaning crews hadn't yet hauled away the piles of charred wood and ash that remained. Someone had left behind a folding camp chair, fallen on its side. I righted it and sat down with my phone.

"Hollis?" I said when the line opened.

". . . hear me?" he said, voice shouting over the low unbroken howl of diesel engines churning. "I'm just off the marina."

"If you're headed out . . ." Hollis's own line of work was usually done at night, meeting ships far offshore and swapping all manner of valuable contraband. He drew the line at smuggling anything the DEA or ATF would take an interest in. Mostly. Twelve-bottle cases of A and cigar boxes of T sometimes found a temporary home in the hidden compartments of his fifty-foot Carver.

"I'm headed into port," he said. "Are you still wandering the wilderness?"

"I am," I said. "And I need—I guess I need to figure some shit out. If you've got time."

Hollis eased the throttle back until the diesels settled into a slow thud. I imagined the *Francesca* bobbing on the waves of the Sound.

"All right, then," Hollis said. "What kind of manure are we talking about?"

I rewound to my first arrival in Oregon and gave Hollis a blow-by-blow account of everything that had happened since. He had to stop me twice, explaining he didn't want to miss anything, as he corrected the *Francesca*'s course to keep it from drifting in to shore. The sun had set in Mercy River by the time I finished. On the night breeze, I smelled the ash of the dowsed firepits.

"I'll tell you this," Hollis said. "If a man's judged by his enemies, you're a mean bastard."

"Yeah. Having a team of Rangers assessing me as a threat doesn't put me at ease."

"Them, too, but I meant this Nazi of yours. Jaeger. He's the real problem."

"I'm less worried for me than for the guards he's going to kill, the next chance he gets."

"That's because you're you, Van. Don't take this for an insult, but self-preservation isn't your strongest suit. Jaeger wants to kill you. I've not been in that situation much myself, but I hope I would treat a zealot out for my blood a little more seriously." Hollis grunted. "Or maybe it's a confidence thing. An overabundance on your part."

"So, what? I hide in a hole until the cops bust him?"

"Maybe you do. That would be a sane response. If he goes to prison for long enough, you wouldn't have to look behind you every time you turned a corner."

There was the seed of an idea there, but it wasn't sprouting yet. I set it aside.

"Plus," Hollis said, "if your fellow Rangers are anything like you, they'll do a fine job of defending the general's son and his wife all on their own."

"Fain's team will protect Aaron and Schuyler," I said. "And Leo's a grown-ass man. If he wants to run with that crew, that's his fool choice."

"Until the FBI finds them."

"It will happen. Fain and his crew are thinking of armed robbery like a raid, like the mission is over after they get away with the money. Understanding how the cops run down evidence isn't part of Ranger School. They'll leave a trail eventually, if they haven't already. But that's not the worst possible outcome."

"Worse than arrest?"

"If they're confronted, they won't run. They'll fight. It's hardwired into us: turn and burn until the threat is eliminated. People could die."

"You said they use rubber grenades and such."

"They have assault rifles, too. The cops will be firing real bullets. I'm not convinced Fain's team won't dial it up if shit gets real."

"Might as well try to weigh their souls," Hollis agreed. "Speaking of. This Federal Reserve truck. I notice you didn't mention a number."

"Eleven million."

Hollis inhaled, audible even over the engines. "That doesn't come along every day, does it?"

"No. Jaeger will make a run at it. So will the general, once he has his son pull the same information and realizes what he's sitting on. It'll be a slaughterhouse if they both converge at the same time."

Hollis was humming tunelessly. "A shame we can't steal the money ourselves first. What I could do with eleven million."

"Never mind."

"I was listening, truly. Merely dreaming over the possibilities."

I was, too, I realized. Not about pirating the cash. About getting there first.

"Hollis," I said, "can you clear your calendar for a couple of days to run some errands? A shopping trip?"

"Wait, now. I was joking.' This sort of job really isn't my trade. Your grandfather in his youth, his wild days before I knew him, he was supposedly something to see. But he smartened up."

"You'd be in a support role, away from the action. Very low-risk for you."

"And for you? Or are we back to talking about overconfidence?"

I didn't reply.

Hollis sighed. "I suppose I could tear myself away."

"Thanks. I'll call you later tonight."

"Just remember what I said about your grandfather living long enough to get wiser." He hung up.

Tales grew taller over time, but even accounting for exaggeration, young Dono Shaw had cut a swath across Northern Ireland, New England, and parts of the contiguous U.S. before a federal rap earned him a stretch on McNeil Island. He'd settled nearby in Seattle afterward, and gradually changed his MO to become the cautious professional thief and burglar who had raised me.

Still, maybe direct action was in the blood. The more I thought about my idea, the more it turned into a plan. And the more it became a plan, the more it quickened my pulse.

HOURS LATER, AFTER I'D read through the armored car schedules taken from Conlee and considered every option for the tenth time, I reached a decision. John Fain's business card was still in my pocket.

"I want to talk to you and the general," I said when he answered.

Fain grunted. "He's here now."

A moment passed. The basso voice of Macomber came through from a distance; Fain had put me on speaker.

"Shaw?"

"You said you owed me a great debt. Is it enough to buy a place on the team?"

"I thought you didn't approve of our methods. Or did you see a number in those armored car deliveries large enough to change your mind?"

At least Macomber wasn't going to play dumb. He'd wasted no time in having his son pull the truck routes again, and he'd zeroed in on the same eleven-million-dollar prize that I had.

"Jaeger's my priority, General. What's yours?"

"Jaeger is a danger to my family. Everything else comes second."

"Does that mean you aim to go all the way?"

He was silent for a moment. Asking Macomber if he planned to order another man's death must have given him pause, no matter what euphemisms I used on the open line.

"Do you have an alternative?" he said finally.

"I do. But it's high-risk."

"So is living. What do you propose?"

"Meet me at the town hall in an hour. Bring the team if you want. They'll have to get on board with the plan."

"Why the hall?" Fain said.

"Seems like a suitable place to call a cease-fire with each other," I said, "and declare war on someone else."

THIRTY-FOUR

LATE AT NIGHT AND with the Rally over, the town hall looked forlorn. Both glass-fronted bulletin boards outside had been emptied of notices, and a padlocked chain connected the twin ten-foot doors. I leaned against the wooden rail that bordered the hall's veranda. Soon I saw the headlights of Daryll's GMC Yukon approaching. It double-parked in the angled spaces on the far side of the lawn. Daryll and Rigoberto got out and made their way along the flagstone path. Daryll's limp had improved. He wore layers of flannel shirts over jeans, and heavy work boots with steel caps to protect his toes.

Rigo was more streamlined in Nike gel-soles and running gear, a black compression shirt, and shorts, as if it weren't fifty degrees out. His short sleeves revealed a mural of tattoos, including a faded blue one on his forearm. The outline of a badge. He also wore a wedding ring, which hadn't been on his hand at the card game.

"You two the advance guard?" I said.

"We're early," Rigo said, stopping at the bottom of the veranda stairs. "Captain Fain told us you let the skinheads get away."

"Captain Fain needs to get his head clear. He said he wanted the drugs secured. They're secured."

"So you say." Daryll crossed the veranda to sit on the railing opposite me. "How do we know you won't sell them yourself?"

"You don't. Just like I don't know whether all the money you guys rip off from HaverCorp ends up with the Rally or in your own pockets."

"Check that," said Rigoberto, raising his chin. "You damn near accusing us of stealing from brothers. That'll get your ass kicked all over this yard."

"A crusader." I turned to Daryll. "You, too?"

"You know it. The general's righteous."

The righteous fight. Protect the Ranger at your side, defend those who can't defend themselves. An ethos founded far more on the people you loved than on abstract concepts like patriotism or democracy. That attitude made the job—the direct and calculated killing of the enemy— possible. Believe in it, and you stood a better chance of returning home mentally and morally intact. I had believed.

Rigo and Daryll and maybe the rest of them bought into that same philosophy for the Rally. If it served the mission and the men, their actions were justified.

I pointed at Rigo's badge tattoo. "Cop?"

"I was, before the Army. Maybe again someday." He cocked his head to one side. "What's your job?"

"Still figuring that out," I said.

"Don't throw in with us expecting to get rich," Daryll said. "The general gives us a cut to pay our bills, but that ain't what this game's about."

"So what's in it for you, besides charity? Do you miss the action?"

"Some," Rigoberto said. "How can you not miss what you're the best at?"

I almost laughed. *Way to turn the question around, Rigo.* I'd been wrestling with that same question ever since I'd returned to Seattle, even if it was a different kind of action that tempted me.

A Lincoln Town Car pulled in next to the parked Yukon. Fain was driving, Leo and Zeke Caton and General Macomber along for the ride. I didn't think their team had any hostile inclinations. But my skin prickled at the potential danger anyway.

"Shaw," Fain said. He took a set of keys from his pocket to remove the padlock and chain, opening the doors into the cavernous space. Leo's lip was swollen. Damage I'd inflicted, even as his older bruises were finally healing up. I felt a twinge at the sight of the new scab hiding the corner of his mouth.

"I assumed we wouldn't require Aaron," the general said to me as our group entered. "I've sent him and Schuyler to stay with relatives until we can be assured they're safe." He flipped the row of light switches with one hand. The chandeliers high above our heads sparked to dim life, energy-saving bulbs brightening slowly.

"Pulling more information from HaverCorp's databases won't change things," I said, crossing to one of the large tables that had been pushed against the wall. "Help me move this."

Rigo acted first. He and I carried the table to the center of the floor. The men gathered around it.

"Let's talk objectives, General," I said. "Jaeger's seen me. He knows your son and his wife, and he can probably trace Aaron's relation to you, given time. We know he's killed before and he's promised to do so again."

Macomber frowned. "I've already told you stopping Jaeger is my concern. Or don't you believe me, Shaw?"

"I believe you. But I also think eleven million dollars is enough to dazzle anybody. Enough to prop up your Rally for years."

"Go on."

"I don't give a shit if you get the money or not. My priority is stopping Jaeger before he murders the guards or anyone else. I think we can do that. Maybe the Rally gets rich, too. But if you want my help you'll have to put Jaeger first, even if it means losing a chance at the cash."

Macomber met my gaze for a long moment, then looked around the table at Fain and the others. "I want your opinions, men. Jaeger's a threat, but Aaron and Schuyler are safe from him now. Don't let that influence you."

"Eleven million could do a lot of good, sir," Fain said.

"My thought exactly," Zeke Caton said. "Can't we hit the truck and track Jaeger down after?"

Rigo was already shaking his head. "Then the Nazi fucks will pick another cash truck from the list. We can't guess which. Those guards will be just as dead."

"That could work for us, too," Daryll said. "Picking another truck, I mean, not killing guards. We nail Jaeger. If we miss out on the money this time, we've got a lot of other trucks on that list."

"Not carrying millions," said Fain, "but it's a good option. I can get behind it. Pak, we haven't heard from you."

Leo spared me a glance before he answered.

"We go for Jaeger," Leo said, "and I won't vote on the other. This is my last jump with the Rally."

Every one of them had an immediate response. Daryll and Zeke swore, and Rigo folded his arms. Macomber took a deep inhalation that communicated a similarly fathomless disappointment. Fain simply stared.

"What's that shit about?" said Zeke.

"Pak. We need you," Fain said.

Daryll bumped Leo's shoulder with a ham-sized fist. "Come on, man."

"This may be our last such mission, regardless," said Macomber, defusing the unexpected tension. "Let's make it count. Shaw, we're agreed that Jaeger is our primary target. What do you have in mind?"

I took a map from my pocket, unfolded it, and spread it out on the table. The map had been in one of the seat pockets of the Dodge since Dono's time, long before mobile apps had made it a relic. Some of the streets it listed were years out of date. Still, it would illustrate my idea.

"Fuckin' *Antiques Roadshow*," Daryll said, touching a crease where the paper had split.

"Seattle," the general said, reviewing it. "And those lines you've drawn . . . the route of the bank truck."

I nodded, pointing to the far edge of the map. "The Federal Reserve branch is all the way down here in Renton. But the Prime Banks on its route are all in Seattle proper. Starting on Rainier Ave, working northward through the city, and then back south for the second half."

"You want to throw in with us?" Zeke said. "'Cause we can handle things just fine without some cherry getting in our way."

I gestured to the inked lines of the route. The lines forming a closed and randomly spiky shape like a piece of abstract art. "Tell me where you'd hit the truck."

"First stop," Zeke said without hesitation, tapping the first dot on Rainier. "When all the money's still in the truck."

"Okay," I said. "Let's run the numbers. The armored truck is scheduled to roll up on its first stop at eight-fifty in the morning, right before the bank opens. That's rush hour on a five-lane thoroughfare. Not quite bumper-to-bumper, not on Rainier, but plenty of movement. Lots of eyes on you. Cops cruise the central district arteries about every thirteen minutes, on average. Traffic cameras at many intersections, too. Eleven million dollars in fifty-dollar bills weighs about four hundred and fifty pounds, in sixteen different bags if we assume one bag for each bank branch that day. So a rough guess is that you'll be exposed between four and five minutes while you ride up, secure the guards, open the truck, unload, and exfil. Meanwhile, everybody on the street with a cell phone will be live-streaming the show."

They were silent, and staring. I caught the hint of a smirk on Leo's face.

"How the hell do you know all that?" Fain said.

Zeke recovered enough to sneer. "He's bullshitting us."

Leo scratched his head bemusedly. "If Van says it, it's solid."

"You suddenly on his side now?" Zeke said.

"Always was," Leo said. Fain frowned.

"Shit, I'm convinced," Rigoberto said. "Forget the Rainier branch."

"You've made your point, Shaw," said Macomber. "We haven't done the recon. Not yet."

"There's more," I said. "You don't know where Jaeger is going to make his play, either. If he gets to the armored truck before you, you're screwed and the guards are dead. If you get the money first, Jaeger misses his chance but he's still running around free."

"Not acceptable," said Macomber.

"And if you both try for the truck at the same time . . ." I shook my head. "Bloodbath."

"Do *you* know where he's gonna be?" Rigo said. Honestly asking, without the sarcastic tone of Zeke's.

"Forget predicting the future," I said, "or taking the money before Jaeger is neutralized. We should hijack the armored truck instead. Two of us will replace the guards. We deliver any drops ourselves. And when Jaeger makes his move, we catch that son of a bitch right in between us."

"You're including yourself in this plan?" Macomber said, breaking the stunned silence.

"I am."

"How do you intend to take over the truck without anyone noticing?" he said. "Much less stand in for the guards."

"Pretending to be the hopper is the easy part. I know enough about the procedure for making money drops to fake it. No bank will think twice about a guard delivering the expected amount of cash. But I won't have to play that game for long, if at all. Jaeger will have the same bright idea as Zeke, to hit the truck early in the day. More money for him. As for how to boost the truck, let me worry about that."

"That move might protect the guards," Leo said. "It won't protect you if Jaeger shoots first."

"I'll be ready for him."

"And maybe I should cover your six, Sarge."

I looked at Leo. "Thanks."

"It would be better if we could figure where Jaeger will strike," Fain said, following the inked lines of the route with his finger, "and be waiting there."

"He'll have to hit the truck when its doors are open," I said. "That's the only time the truck is vulnerable. Stopping it on the street between the banks would leave him with a giant safe he can't crack. I'll case the banks on the route tomorrow and pick the likeliest branches."

"I hope you have as much experience as you imply," Macomber said. "We're risking a lot on your word."

"I wasn't always a soldier." I turned to Fain. "I can show you a picture of Jaeger from his fake license. If your team is rolling just ahead of the truck, you might be able to spot and intercept him before the truck even comes close."

The general smoothed a crease in the map as he mused. "Jaeger had three of his men at the house, Aaron said. John will have five with him, counting Shaw."

"Four who are mobile," said Fain.

"I can still drive," Daryll said, shifting on his broken foot.

"Those aren't odds I like," Macomber said, "not with nonlethal weapons. Jaeger might enlist more men."

"A compromise, sir," Fain said. "We go with M4 carbines with under-barrel grenade launchers attached. The guns give us the intimidation factor and live rounds in case we need them. The launchers will have sponge grenades if we have to take Jaeger's men down hard."

Hard was the right word. A sponge grenade wasn't nearly as benign as it sounded, a foam-rubber bullet the size of a plum that could rupture a spleen or shatter a jaw at fifty yards. At closer range, it could kill.

The general grimaced. "That's a single-shot weapon."

"Ideally we won't need to use even that," said Fain. "And we'll also have the bigger launchers, the Milkors."

"These are city streets," I said. "How will you hide the guns?"

Fain raised an eyebrow. "You worry about the truck. I'll deal with the arms."

I didn't love the idea of Fain's team rolling into Seattle with assault weapons and 5.56mm rounds. But it would be pointless to argue against it, not to mention hypocritical. Against Jaeger and his pack of rabid dogs, I would have lethal measures as my backup, too.

"What about the money?" Zeke said to me.

"Once Jaeger's bagged and tagged? I walk away. The rest is up to you."

"Really. You don't want any part of eleven million bucks."

Fain came around the table to stand in front of me. "Our team's down one man, Shaw. We need you to help cover us. Four minutes in the open, you said."

"Which is why I'm telling you to nail Jaeger and get the hell out. Forget the cash."

"You'd leave brothers in the field?"

"It isn't the field," I said, "it's a crime scene. And that's my specialty."

"Enough," said Macomber. "Stop Jaeger. Acquire as much of the cash as you can manage, with the men you have." He frowned in my direction. "We have arrangements to make and not much time. John, we'll regroup in the morning."

"I'm headed to Seattle tonight," I said. "My arrangements are there."

"One thing I don't get," Rigoberto said as I started folding the map. "We hogtie Jaeger like a Christmas present for the cops. So what? He can just claim he's an innocent bystander."

"We'll leave enough evidence at the scene to send him away for life."

"Life for robbery?" Rigo frowned.

"For the murder of the HaverCorp guards in Nevada. I've got Jaeger's stolen drugs. And his jacket, and a few items with his fingerprints, including the fake license with his photo on it. One hundred percent chance that asshole is already in the system." I walked toward the door. "We're going to frame him for his own crime."

THIRTY-FIVE

DEZ AND LEO PULLED into the driveway on Dez's Suzuki as I was tossing my rucksack into the truck. Strapped to the seat behind Leo were bags of their own, a black leather weekender and a large roller case that might have been through more wars than I had. Two people and luggage made a precarious load for the little two-stroke machine. Its brakes squealed with the strain of halting the bike's momentum.

"Fain told us all to saddle up," Leo said.

"So you came here."

"He came here," said Dez, removing her helmet. "I came with him." Her heart-shaped face was drawn tight with fatigue. The last time I'd seen Dez in person, she was half buried under the shock of finding Wayne Beacham's body. Since then she'd been yanked between police interviews and funeral arrangements and Leo's release from jail.

"How are you holding up?" I said.

"Hour by hour." Dez ran her fingers through her hair to rearrange the mess made by the helmet into a more attractive dishevelment. She seemed to do so unconsciously, habit and expertise gained from every time she rode the bike.

"We're both leaving this damn town," said Leo, "without further fucking ado."

"What about Daryll and Rigo and the rest of them?" I said.

He stopped in the middle of unhooking the bungee cords from around the bags. "I told you I'd watch your back. As long as those skinhead freaks are running loose, I figure I'm on the clock."

"Besides, the general doesn't want me around," Dez said. "No girls allowed in the tree house."

Shortsighted, given that Dez and Leo had risked and deceived and suffered more than any of Macomber's followers to protect the Rally.

"Leo told me you supported him, when he joined up with Fain's team," I said. Making it a question. How had she been okay with her man becoming an armed robber?

She looked at Leo, then back to me. "I spent the last two years driving between Mercy River and hospitals and clinics and support organizations all over the western states. And I will tell you straight out: the vets' health-care system is a huge impersonal clusterfuck. Any condition not directly related to a soldier's service—that's ninety percent of the problems they face, with the burden of proof on the soldier—and aid will be denied, or postponed, or plain stop after the doctor who pokes his head into the room for the five minutes he's got in his schedule for each case prescribes a fistful of medications. Meds that threaten to turn half of the patients into addicts and tempt the other half into selling their pills to pay for better care, or just to buy groceries. I know that's not every soldier's experience. Especially not every Ranger's, since you guys tend to be hard chargers in your civilian lives, too. More of you wind up landing on your feet. But Jesus."

Dez's exhaustion had stripped her to a white-hot core. "These government programs take months to implement any change, and years to find out whether the change had any positive results. At least the Rally provided immediate help when it had the funds. Jobs or loans or paying for a twenty-year-old's physical therapy after his knees develop inflammatory arthritis from running with sixty pounds on his back every day. *Anything* to get these peoples' lives rolling in the right direction. Leo wanted to do something. *I* wanted to do something, more than holding their wives' hands and hoping I could bring them some Walmart gift cards next time so their kids would have school clothes. I didn't like the risks Leo was taking, but I sure as hell understood why. He would join Fain's gang, and he would stop when I left Mercy River. Leo and I agreed on it."

"We trusted each other," Leo said, putting his arm around Dez. She leaned her head against his. "But not you, man. That was wrong."

"I'm sorry, too," I said. "Faith has been in short supply. You wouldn't tell me you were part of Fain's crew. I didn't believe you had your head on straight. Bad choices built on wrong guesses."

"Just promise me no more lies," Dez said to both of us. She walked to the motorcycle and began unstrapping the bags herself. Her roller bag was held more or less in one piece with stickers for REI and Volkl and Burton. Leo would have to stay in shape to keep up with Dez.

"No more secrets," I agreed. "We deal with Jaeger, and we're done."

Leo hefted the roller bag, which took both hands. "You might want these for the job. Toys straight from Big Daryll's duffel."

"Did Fain give you shit after I left?"

"Yeah. Captain Fain's big on unit cohesion. As much as if we were still in the regiment. He asked me at the town hall in front of everyone whether I would accept him as tactical command in Seattle. His exact words. That if I had a problem I should voice it right there."

"What did you say?"

"I voiced the fuck out of it." Leo spat. "Asshole. I told Fain what I thought of him using my freedom as a bargaining piece, forcing you to work for him. He hadn't informed *me* of that little maneuver because he wasn't sure I'd fall in line. Would I put the mission ahead of a brother? I said I'd follow the plan in Seattle, but I wasn't ever taking his orders again. That he'd forgotten what Rangers were about."

"Bet that was received well."

"Fain looked like he hadn't taken a shit in a month. And Rigo and Daryll and Zeke, they read the room and kept their mouths zipped. Macomber is seriously pissed at his number-one boy tonight."

"And at you, too, I'm guessing."

"Screw the general and his stars." Leo grinned so wide that his cut lip split again. "Let's move."

"God," said Dez. "You're like children sometimes."

"Roger that," I said. "Get in the truck."

THIRTY-SIX

AT FIVE O'CLOCK IN the morning we emerged from the I-90 tunnel and rounded the bend to see the lights of downtown. Dez leaned forward between the front seats.

"First time here?" I said.

She nodded. "Where's the Space Needle?"

"Hang on." We merged onto Interstate 5—maybe the only time of day when traffic wouldn't slow us to a crawl—and continued north to Mercer Street. In another moment, the glowing disk of the Needle appeared like a UFO on the horizon.

"It's different than I thought," she said, craning her neck to look through the windshield.

"It just got a face-lift."

"Space-lift," Leo said drowsily. Dez elbowed him.

"I mean, it's . . . delicate," she said.

"Hope you got a place we can crash," Leo said. "Jail got me used to a free bed."

I'd let the happy couple have my apartment. I would grab a nap in the cabin of the small speedboat I owned, moored down near Hollis's slip at Shilshole. There was a lot to do, and only fifty hours left on the clock.

LATE THAT AFTERNOON, LEO met me at a teahouse called Baek's Finest in the International District. I'd snagged a window seat with a good view of 6th Ave outside.

"Hope you didn't pick this place for me," he said. "I hate kimchi."

"Try the roasted green." I motioned to the steaming pot at the center of the table.

He poured and scanned the street as he waited for the tea to cool. The bold royal blue of the Prime Bank logo stood out among the hot pot restaurants and print shops, at the top of a T made by a three-way intersection of 6th and Lane. Underneath the illuminated sign, the bank's name was echoed in Chinese. The tea shop was a couple of blocks south of the Chinatown Gate, the district's main tourist attraction. Too far away for any cheesy souvenir stores selling kung-fu slippers or stuffed pandas.

"I drove the armored car's route," I said, "and then the first half of it again. This branch is the clear winner."

"Why this one?" Leo said, eyes on the bank.

"It's only the second drop of the day. A hell of a lot better choice than the first bank on Rainier," I said. "There's a pay parking lot right across the street from the bank. Makes a good spot to watch the intersection."

We both shut up while the server, a woman with ice-white hair and skin as delicately crackled as ceramic glaze, came to ask if we'd like something to eat. Leo spoke to her in Korean. A long enough conversation that I assumed he was ordering food. She smiled and moved away.

Seeing the old woman reminded me that I hadn't spoken to Addy Proctor in a week. I hadn't even asked Luce how she was doing. I was a little ashamed at that.

I pointed. "See that courtyard next door? The one with the metal sculpture?" Leo turned around to look at the paved triangle of public space, with a giant cylinder of bronze adorning the center.

"Thing's like a pencil holder," he said. Kids skateboarded in a loop around the sculpture, off the curb and back again.

"There are stairs under it leading down into a parking garage. You could hang out there for an hour and nobody would notice. Plus another lot in that direction for Uwajimaya." The Asian grocery's flagship prompted a constant stream of shoppers between the lot and the store, on the far side of the courtyard.

"Lots of exits, too. The freeways are right over there."

"And the train station." I nodded in the opposite direction. "But the biggest reason I like this branch is that when the armored car rolls up Thursday morning, most of these shops will still be closed. Including this one." I glanced at the old lady as she bustled about behind the serving counter, clinking plates. "Fewer bystanders."

"That's why *you* like it. Will Jaeger care if the street is quiet?"

I shrugged. "We can hope."

"Like they say, hope ain't a plan," Leo said.

"Yeah. I'd stake out this branch all day tomorrow if we had the time, on the slim chance I could catch sight of Jaeger or one of his grunts and confirm my guess. But there's too much to do."

"I see somebody else," Leo said, and I glanced behind me as the familiar apelike figure of Hollis Brant hurried across the street, waving an apologetic hand at a car who'd stopped for him.

He arrived at our table at the same time as the venerable server, who set down a tureen full of what looked like darkly refried beans, garnished with pine nuts, and a plate of golf-ball-sized spheres of rice.

"Timing is everything," Hollis said, beaming at the server.

Leo spoke to her, and she quickly fetched a third bowl as Hollis settled in. "Pat jook," Leo told us. "Red bean porridge."

"Thank the gods," Hollis said. "Your man here has had me running all over town since the cock crowed."

"Which you've heard when?" I said.

"I've not spent my entire life on city streets, you know," Hollis said, as we tucked into the porridge. It was surprisingly sweet, less like curd than like sugared oats. "The Brant family home near Cullybackey was a long stroll from anything resembling civilization. We kept animals."

"I take it back. You're a man of the soil. Did you find the clothes we need?"

"After three stops"—he frowned—"and after spending all morning drying the . . ." He spared a glance for the server, who was at the other end of the shop talking on the phone. "The salt water off three thousand tubes of glass."

"What about the detour signs?"

"Curse it, man, I just sat down. I've a fellow to see about the signs later tonight."

"Detours?" Leo asked.

"I'll explain later," I said. "Right now I have to call Fain and schedule a dry run for us tomorrow morning. We'll drive the same route, at the same time of day, and see what that tells us."

"Thorough."

"No rest for the wicked." I stood up and put two twenties on the table. "Leo, I'll be by the apartment tonight. I've got a couple of tasks for you and Dez to handle tomorrow."

"You know, your grandfather was like this before a job," Hollis said, in no seeming hurry. "Out-and-out churlish. You would have thought he was angry at the whole world."

"But it was when he was happiest. I remember."

"Of course you do."

I walked outside, sunglasses on despite the overcast day, the brim of my Mariners cap pulled low. I knew what Hollis was getting at. That, like Dono, I was more focused, more myself, when working a score. He wasn't wrong.

But I knew something that Hollis didn't. I'd felt the same precision of thought and action while leading fire teams and entire platoons on missions. It wasn't committing a crime that brought on that feeling. It was the degree of difficulty. The highest possible stakes. That more than anything made me sharper. Better.

The idea made me wonder if it might have been the same for my grandfather, if our lives had been reversed. But then Dono could never stomach authority. One of his earliest arrests, at fourteen, was for punching a garda who was giving him shit for loitering outside a pub in Belfast during school hours.

I was so amused by imagining Dono suffering through basic training that I nearly missed catching a yellow flash of badly peroxided hair, as its owner disappeared into the Prime branch.

I jaywalked across the street and pretended to browse a selection of Zen garden manuals in the window display of a Japanese bookstore. The block was clear of rusty blue Camaros or two-toned Chevy Tahoes. No burly hulks with goatees, either. And no Jaeger. Had it been someone else with a tragic dye job? I watched the bank at the end of the block out of the corner of my eye. I didn't want to risk getting closer. They'd seen my face, and they would sure as hell remember it.

A blond head attached to a tall skinny frame came out of the bank branch and jogged through the crosswalk to the pay parking lot. Gotcha. Even with his jacket zipped up to hide the neck tattoos, it was undeniably the asshole from Jaeger's crew. He got into a mud-spattered silver Jeep Cherokee and the car pulled out of the lot and up Lane Street before I had a prayer of reading the license plate. The person driving cut a big enough shape that I guessed him for one of the two hulking cousins. Maybe the one with a bruise on his gut from when I'd kicked him down the stairs at Conlee's townhouse.

I grinned. Jaeger and I were on parallel tracks. While I'd been scoping out the Prime branch from the comfort of the teahouse, his boys were doing the same from the parking lot. Peroxide had probably gone inside to check out the camera and the guard on duty.

They were picking their target, and I was willing to bet heavy that Jaeger liked the look of this branch as much as I did.

Welcome to Seattle, you son of a bitch. I'll throw you a party you won't forget.

THIRTY-SEVEN

DAWN BEGAN TO WARM the back of my neck through my apartment window as Leo and I laid out items on the dining table. Our PCI—pre-combat inspection. Most of the objects and equipment in front of me would be packed into my ruck.

The largest item by far was a zippered green nylon travel bag, stuffed so full that its seams showed with the strain. It held Jaeger's shearling coat, wrapped around a mass of Trumorpha vials. I'd buttoned Jaeger's fake driver's license and other personal effects safely in the pocket of the coat. Ready for the cops and their fingerprint analysis, if all went to plan.

I didn't have much more to carry, but what I had was ominous. A multi-tool with a three-inch blade. A stun gun about the size of a large remote control. Cable ties. Two black hoods, made by sewing the eye holes shut on ski masks.

And one of the weapons Leo had liberated from Big Daryll's arsenal. A Serbu mini-shotgun. Seventeen inches long and loaded with twelve-gauge rubber rounds. The Serbu only held three shots, but I could carry it inside my coat in a makeshift sling without being obvious. My tiny Beretta Nano would be my emergency piece, tucked into an ankle holster.

Leo's ruck would hold something more intimidating. He'd opened Dez's battered roller bag to reveal one of Daryll's Milkor grenade launchers—insisting with a shrug that the team had a spare—and loaded its six chambers with forty-mil sponge grenades. He'd carry his own small shotgun as well, not that he was likely to need a backup to the giant-bored launcher.

"The HaverCorp trucks have gun ports," Leo said with a mean smile. "If one of those shitheads gets within twenty yards, I can put him on his ass."

If all went to plan, there wouldn't be a shot fired. Fain and Daryll would be our advance guard, reconnoitering the streets and banks ahead on our specific route. Rigo and Zeke Caton would tail us. The Chinatown branch of Prime was the likeliest point of engagement, but we couldn't rule out the possibility that Jaeger would hit us elsewhere, maybe even between banks if he had the means to blow the armored truck open. I didn't want to be inside that big steel box if Jaeger detonated shape charges on the doors. Fain and his team would close in the instant that the skinhead leader raised his head.

But before all that, Leo and I had a truck to hijack. Hollis would pick us up in half an hour. By then, we'd have eaten and gone over the contingency plans one last time. Leo had spent part of Wednesday arranging our backup plans.

He finished his packing, and sat down on the floor to stretch his legs while I filled skillets with eggs and bacon.

"Did you throw in with Fain for the action?" I said.

He looked at me.

"I'm serious," I said. "I know you've missed this. Doing what we do."

"Kinda. It's more about having purpose. That's the real thing, man. It's not like we're thrill-seeking. Well, Rigo, maybe. He ain't happy unless he's in motion. Daryll, he's a team player, wherever Fain goes he goes. And Zeke . . ."

"Zeke likes money."

"Yeah. Most of the cash goes to the Rally, but the general gives us a cut from each job if we want it. Zeke always wants it." Leo leaned to one side, popping his shoulder. "For me, it's what I can do to give back. If you hadn't helped me a year ago, I might be dead now. Sure as hell I wouldn't have found Dez."

"I'm glad you did." Dez had gotten even less sleep than either Leo or me the night before. She'd excused herself before sunrise, saying there was too much energy in the apartment and she would be better burning some of it off. I gave her directions to Top Pot a few blocks away, which would be the day's first batch of donuts out of the fryers.

"Damn," Leo said. "Luce. I saw Luce in the courtroom before they pulled me back to the jail. All this shit happened and I forgot."

"Ganz thought having her there might help your case. That was before you went batshit."

"Yeah, well. I have to thank her. Are you and she—"

"No."

He grunted. "Okay. Least you're sure."

I dished up the eggs and put the bacon on paper towels to soak up the grease. I put the pan in the sink and filled it with water. Drops hissed and popped into instant steam as they hit the hot metal.

"She's getting married," I said.

Leo was silent as I wrapped up the bacon, pressed it, unwrapped it again to put the strips on the plates. We ate the food quickly. Our eyes roamed over the gear and weapons, checking and double-checking. The preparations distracted me just fine.

"Maybe Luce didn't come to Mercy River only for me," Leo said at last.

I'd chased that same thought a dozen times in the past few days. Chased it, batted it around, and finally let it run free. It might be true. It wasn't going to change anything.

"Time to go," I said.

RAINIER AVENUE SOUTH BECAME a sluggish tributary at a quarter to nine in the morning. I'd heard once that the stoplights were timed to let the north- and southbound vehicles flow at a steady speed, all the way from the valley to Beacon Hill. It never worked out. Too many bus stops that took extra time, too many illegal left turns.

And occasionally, an armored car about to park where the right-lane traffic had no choice but to go around it.

Leo and Hollis and I watched the dark blue hulk of the HaverCorp truck wait at the stoplight, a long block south of the Rainier branch of Prime Bank. We waited until it had passed us. Leo and I got out of the Nissan SUV that Hollis was driving. He popped the trunk for us to retrieve our rucks.

"All set," Hollis said, mostly to himself.

"See you soon," I said as I clicked my ruck into place and tightened its straps. Ready to move very quickly.

We left him. Leo and I were dressed the same, thanks to Hollis's shopping trips. Thick navy-blue trousers with matching blue baseball caps and black rubber-soled work shoes and long-sleeved button-down shirts in a neutral brown. Not a precise match for HaverCorp colors, but close enough. If anyone examined us that closely, we had bigger problems than our fashion sense.

Over the shirts we wore plain coyote-brown windbreakers which Hollis had acquired at a military surplus store. The windbreakers concealed the little shotguns, slung under our left arms for a right-hand draw. I'd taped the stun gun to my belt on the other side. Our clear latex gloves were the only visible giveaway of bad intentions, but those couldn't be helped.

Leo had clippered his hair, short enough that his scalp showed pale on the sides of his head. He wore wraparound sunglasses to hide the obvious cast of his eyes. I had glasses as well, but mine weren't nearly as cool. The overlarge horn-rims would distract from my facial scars. Just two guys off to work.

Except today's work required us to assault two security guards who were doing their jobs. Even if our actions would put them out of harm's way, this was the part of our plan I liked least. The part Dono would have despised.

We stepped around the long metal sidewalk barrier. Hollis had placed it there before the sun had risen, and another far at the opposite end of the block. The barriers redirected pedestrians to the other side of the five-lane thoroughfare. Not that there were many people walking on these streets, but every edge helped.

The HaverCorp truck had parked in front of the Prime branch. A line of cars was already jammed up behind it and slowly working their way around. Roughly half the size of a railroad boxcar, the massive truck was too wide for drivers stuck behind it to easily see what might be happening around the sides.

"Remember the cameras," Leo said.

I had. The trucks had exterior cameras that allowed the driver to watch the blind spots to the sides and rear. While the cameras didn't record what they saw, it would be better not to be spotted approaching. We edged to the right, strolling along the metal-gated windows of a cash-for-jewelry outfit.

We had covered more than half of the long block between us and the truck. No sign of the hopper, who should be returning to the truck after dropping off half a million in fifties from his first heavy satchel of the day. Where was he? Was there some bureaucratic mix-up? Or was the first drop of the day always this slow?

"We can't dawdle," Leo said, reading my mind.

"I know."

A husky young guard in his HaverCorp blue zip-front emerged from the branch with an empty black satchel gripped in one hand. Thirty paces from us. He glanced our way and saw two blue-collar guys engrossed in conversation, the one in ugly glasses apparently texting away. Keys tapped glass as the bank employee relocked the branch door.

I saw the rest as if it were in slow motion. The hopper moved to the truck. He reached up and paused while his partner inside pressed a button to unlock the passenger door. He pulled the latch to swing the high door open. We tracked his progress out of the corner of our eyes. Fifteen paces. I pressed send on a text message to Hollis I'd prepped. The hopper lifted the satchel up, and the driver reached across to pull it inside.

Leo and I pulled the surgical masks from under our baseball caps down over our faces. The hopper was too busy climbing into the truck to notice, turning sideways to awkwardly shuffle his bulk onto his seat.

The high blare of an air horn from a block away pierced the air like a lance. So loud it verged on painful even at this distance.

Leo moved. Three lightning steps, leaping up and into the cab of the armored truck through the open door, right over the legs of the hopper and onto the driver. I was right on Leo's heels, shoving the startled hopper with every ounce of strength I had. He tumbled and fell heavily between the seats with a grunt of surprise. I forced my way inside and lunged to grab the passenger door and shut it behind us. Outside, the air horn was still blaring.

Leo was practically in the lap of the driver, the muzzle of his mini-shotgun pressed into the man's neck.

"Keep your hand off the fucking button," he said.

The driver seemed too stunned to even blink. The hopper was less cooperative. He fought to rise from his awkward place, on the floor between the seats, unable to reach his sidearm.

I planted my knee between his shoulder blades and held the stun gun in front of his face. A tap of the button, and sparks arced across the prongs with a nasty ripping sound.

"Stay down," I said.

He opened his hands wide and eased all the way to the floor. Stun guns were crappy choices for personal defense. But they were fantastic for making people compliant.

I stripped him of his gun and reached over to do the same to the driver. Then I stuck the piece of duct tape that had attached the stun gun to my belt over the watchful eye of the truck's interior camera.

Less than thirty seconds had passed. I scanned the outside. Our sidewalk was clear. Nobody on the opposite side of the road was taking any interest in our newly acquired truck. Hollis's symphony on the air horn had drawn their attention long enough for us to get this far.

Four bodies crammed into the front of the truck's cab was about the closest that close quarters could get. I left Leo to keep the driver immobile while I climbed over the prone hopper into the back of the truck.

Open compartments along each side were stuffed full of black canvas satchels, each tagged with the name of the receiving bank. Over ten million in recirculated fifty-dollar bills.

I grabbed the hopper by his collar and hauled him into the back. He didn't protest this time. I unzipped his HaverCorp uniform jacket and rolled him onto his face to finish stripping it off. I kept one foot on his neck while I unstrapped my rucksack.

"Stay cool," I told the hopper.

I quickly zip-tied his wrists behind his back, and his ankles, and his legs above his knees. Rangers got a lot of practice in capturing and detaining targets. The hood would be last. People tend to panic when their vision is obscured, and a panicky person is harder to secure. Sure enough, the hopper twisted his head around, trying to evade the black ski mask.

"Run for it. You can still get away," he sputtered.

"Another word and I'll gag you," I said, pulling the makeshift hood into place.

Leo had forced the driver down between the front seats. He was a slimmer build than the hopper. It was easy work to drag him into the back. While I secured him next to his partner, Leo hastily unstrapped his own rucksack.

"Time?" I said, tossing him the driver's HaverCorp jacket and cap. He'd already removed his surgical mask.

"Three minutes behind."

"Go." We had to count on three extra minutes not being enough variance from the route to catch anyone's attention back at HaverCorp's central office. The two guards might not be fully informed of the millions they were carrying, but sure as hell management was. Somebody would be watching.

Leo shifted into drive and accelerated fast enough that I rocked to one side as I pulled on the hopper's uniform jacket. I was sweating from more than the layers of clothes on a warm day. Missions were like lengthy boxing matches, rapid bursts of intense activity that jacked the heart rate, followed by abrupt drops. Over and over.

I found the satchel tagged for the Chinatown branch of Prime Bank. A heavy one, twenty-five pounds of hard currency. I threw it toward the front.

It might have been imagination, but I could swear I felt a kind of heat coming off of the hoard of cash that filled both sides of the armored car. Like the sheer mass of all that money created its own energy. I pocketed my surgical mask and wiped my face on my sleeve.

Leo juiced the gas to beat a yellow light. I climbed into the passenger's seat with my rucksack.

It would take at least nine minutes to reach the International District branch. I pulled out two comm headsets and handed one to Leo. He waited until the next light, doffed his HaverCorp cap, and slipped the headband on to adjust the earpiece. I was already radioing Fain.

"We're in motion," I said.

"Crossing Holgate Street now," Fain said. "Clear on Alpha, Bravo, Charlie."

Holgate was five blocks ahead of our current position. No sign of any trouble. Alpha was Jaeger, our primary objective. Bravo was any sighting of Jaeger's men or the skinhead vehicles I'd described. Charlie was police. Romeo and Sierra Teams were the respective call signs for Fain's car and for Zeke and Rigo, whose car was coming behind us.

"ETA seven," I said.

"Seven," he repeated back. "We'll be ready."

This plan counted on Jaeger showing up in person for the score. And four enemies, or more, was tough odds, even if we had the advantage of surprise. I unpacked Leo's grenade launcher and set it within his reach.

Corps Fourteen, radio check, the truck's speaker intoned.

Leo looked at me. "Should we answer?"

I spared a glance at the interior camera. The blacked-out lens might have alerted HaverCorp to something off, if headquarters could tap into that feed. We'd known it was a risk.

I exhaled and grabbed the mike. "Corp Fourteen, copy."

A few seconds passed. Leo changed lanes quickly to merge onto Dearborn.

Corps Fourteen, proceed, said the dispatcher.

Was that all? Proceed to next stop? Or did *proceed* mean to repeat a code word that meant the situation was normal? I cursed not having time to fully prepare. Cowboy work, Dono would have derisively called it. Yelling yee-haw and racing in with guns blazing.

I hung the mike back up. If it was wrong, it was wrong. Nothing for us to do but keep rolling.

From my ruck I removed the green nylon bag with Jaeger's shearling coat and the drugs wrapped snuggly inside it. I wedged it between the seats.

My mind was rerunning our game plan once the armored car touched the curb. The strong bet was that Jaeger wouldn't delay until the cash was dropped off inside the branch, sacrificing a second half-million dollars after letting the first drop go at Rainier. His team would aim to hit the truck the moment that our door opened.

Or, more accurately, the moment that I opened the door. I would be front and center when it went down.

"Take a right on Maynard and circle around," I said to Leo.

"Already there," he said, as cool as if he were running errands on a Sunday afternoon.

Jaeger's two hulks would be the muscle, taking down the guards and unloading four hundred pounds of cash. I'd have to contend with them first. Either Jaeger or the peroxided guy would be the driver. That meant at least three men on the truck—the hulks unloading the heavy satchels, with a third acting as lookout.

All of that conjecture depended on Jaeger only bringing the three men I'd seen at the cabins and at Aaron Conlee's. He could have more. We didn't know how many skinheads the First Riders still counted in their ranks, or how many Jaeger would trust with a job like this. Would he keep the score and its millions for his inner circle? Or would he want safety in numbers? I hoped he was greedy.

I pinged Fain. "Any change?"

"No. Alpha may not be here."

Too many unknowns. And our primary target still missing. I could hear Dono's teeth grinding in my mind.

Corps Fourteen, hold and await instructions, said the radio.

Bad on bad. No stopping now. Our truck was barely half a block from the bank.

We turned, drifting slowly past the Japanese bookstore, past an empty lot on the other side of the street.

In the dirt lot, two painters wielded rollers on ten-foot extension poles, putting a fresh coat of taupe on a cinder-block wall. White overalls and caps and masks swathed their nearly identical brawny shapes. They'd shaved the distinctive long goatees, but it was unmistakably them. Tweedledee and Tweedledum.

"Made them," Leo said without glancing toward the cousins.

I got on the comm to Fain. "I got eyes on two Bravo. White painter's clothes. Across and three doors north from the bank. Where are you?"

"Past the bank at the courtyard," said Fain. "No sign of Alpha."

Where the hell was Jaeger? And what was Fain doing, that he hadn't ID'd the two cousins? They were right out in the open.

"Silver Cherokee directly across," I said to Leo and Fain, nodding toward the parking lot. The same Jeep I'd seen the peroxided skinhead get into while casing the bank. The Cherokee was already out of its spot and pointed toward the lot exit. With the glare off the glass, I couldn't tell who the driver was. "Acknowledge."

"Roger that," Fain said. "We're on it. Sierra Team has the two Bravo in sight."

Corps Fourteen, hold position where you are. Come back, said the radio.

The cars in front of us moved. Leo pulled up in front of the bank, filling the short stretch of curb before the stop sign.

To our left and across the avenue, the parking lot with the waiting Jeep. Behind us, four stores down from the parking lot, the two cousins in their painter outfits.

We watched the mirrors. The cousins didn't appear.

I pinged Fain. "Any change?"

"No," he said. "Alpha may not be here."

"Are they waiting for us to crack the door?" Leo said.

Jaeger might have another lookout, watching this side and signaling them when to move. We couldn't wait. I grabbed the satchel containing the cash for this drop and cut the security strap holding the zipper closed. My mini-shotgun fit well enough atop the stacked, plastic-wrapped bricks of fifty-dollar bills.

I gave the street one last check. None of the people on the sidewalk looked remotely like a white power thug. I couldn't see Fain or Zeke or Rigo, either.

Corps Fourteen, do you copy? the radio insisted.

Shit. We'd have to be satisfied with leaving Jaeger's prints at the scene with his soldiers. Maybe one of them would give him up for a reduced sentence.

"Ready?" I said to Leo. He was focused on our left side, watching the Jeep Cherokee, waiting to see if the painters appeared in his mirrors.

"Go," he said.

"Romeo and Sierra, we're rolling," I said, signaling Fain's teams that it was time to take down the targets in sight. My left hand held the satchel containing half a million dollars. I popped the door latch, readied the shotgun, kicked the door open, and jumped out.

THIRTY-EIGHT

N O ONE APPROACHED ME. Nothing happened. Jaeger's team must be waiting until I made the drop.

As I turned to close the truck door, a tire shrieked on pavement in front of the armored truck.

"Contact, on your three," Leo said, his voice over the headset even as I spun right and crouched low behind the truck's fender. A man with a chin-strap beard came running onto the sidewalk from the street, the pistol in his hand seeking a target. I shot him dead center from ten feet away with the shotgun still partly in the satchel, the rubber slug rebounding in a barely visible flash of orange off his chest. The muzzle blast threw green confetti into the air. Shredded bits of fifty-dollar bills. He crumpled to his hands and knees, his pistol skidding away, and I kicked him in the head.

He wasn't one of the skinheads I'd seen before. Jaeger had brought reinforcements.

I shouted to the handful of people on the sidewalk to run.

Goddammit, where was Fain?

From down the block, there was a chatter of an automatic weapon, and throaty booms of grenade launchers. A voice on the headset—

Rigo or Daryll—called out, *Contact-Eyesontwo-IntersectionSixthandLane.* Where I'd seen the silver Jeep.

Leo's grenade launcher banged, firing out of one of the armored truck's gun ports, and I heard the snap of small-arms fire on the other side of the truck. I slammed the passenger door closed. At least Leo and the guards would be safe.

The hulks were coming, thundering up the sidewalk in their painter whites and masks. I dropped prone, rolling off the curb and halfway under the truck. A shot whanged off the side of the truck where I'd been standing. I aimed and fired from the gutter. The round took the first hulk between the eyes, snapping his head back like a heavyweight punch. He collapsed on his face. His cousin dodged left to take cover behind the armored truck. I aimed under the chassis and shot him in his thick ankle with my last round. It may have been illusion that I heard bone snap. His scream wasn't imaginary. He fell, and I crawled quickly under the truck toward his writhing form.

More sounds of fire from Fain's team, and the snaps of small arms, too. I couldn't worry about that now. I reached the burly cousin. He was howling through the pain of his shattered ankle but reached to claw at my face. I clubbed him into unconsciousness.

I was exposed here. I fished the surgical mask out of my pocket and scrambled to put it on. My fake eyeglasses had fallen off when I rolled under the truck.

Movement to my right, across the street. I was cold meat. I dropped the empty shotgun and scrambled to reach the Beretta in my ankle holster. A skinhead with a black overcoat and facial tattoos running up the street spotted me, and I ducked back behind the truck. He raised his pistol and Leo popped out from the driver's door and shot the skinhead like some deadly jack-in-the-box.

Jaeger. There he was, jumping up from where he'd taken cover, sprinting between parked cars, a pistol in his hand. He had shaved his head and mustache since Portland, but it was him.

"Shaw, position." Fain, on the headset.

"Eyes on Alpha, middle of the block. Where the fuck are you?"

"Contact to the north. Hold."

A sedan coming from the far side of Lane Street screeched to a halt, blocked by vehicles abandoned in the chaos. I saw Peroxide at the wheel.

Jaeger yanked a teenage girl lying on the sidewalk to her feet, curling his arm around her and shoving the pistol up under her chin. He hauled her toward Peroxide and the sedan, a clumsy four-legged creature scrambling sideways across the intersection. Getting away.

Leo tossed me his grenade launcher as I ran past him to try for a clear line of fire. Halfway to the waiting sedan, the girl tripped and fell. Jaeger left her in the middle of the street and sprinted away. I was forty yards from the sedan. My first shot cracked the windshield. The hard rubber projectile bounced high into the air, even as my second grenade caught Jaeger in the shoulder, knocking him partway onto the hood of the sedan. The launcher clicked on an empty chamber.

A thick-muscled skinhead leaned out of the passenger window of the sedan and I dove behind the nearest car as his pistol snapped twice. Jaeger pushed himself upright and off the hood. The girl was still lying in the middle of the intersection, completely exposed to fire.

Zeke and Rigo came running from the north, low and fast behind the parked cars toward the armored truck, carbines with their under-barrel launchers at the ready. In their black body armor with full-face motocross masks and goggles, they looked like giant poisonous insects.

"There," I shouted, pointing out Jaeger. The skinheads' leader almost fell into the open rear door of the sedan as his men continued to shoot wildly, Peroxide joining the fight by firing from the driver's seat. I was pinned halfway between the armored truck and Jaeger. Who was escaping even as I watched.

Rigo aimed but was forced to move as a Toyota pickup with Daryll behind the wheel sped past them. Daryll swung the pickup ninety degrees to the left and reversed with a screech of rubber into the gap behind the HaverCorp truck. The muscled skinhead's pistol cracked again. Glass from a car window over my head rained to the pavement.

"Pop the back door," Zeke called to Leo, motioning to the armored car. His voice hollowed by the hard plastic mask. Leo had retrieved one of the guards' pistols and ignored Zeke to begin laying down suppressive fire at the sedan.

"Go after Alpha," I said over the headset, as the sedan's engine roared into reverse.

"I'm set," Daryll fairly screamed. Not to me. The men converged on the HaverCorp truck.

Fain appeared from behind the pickup, the second big grenade launcher in his hands. "Jaeger's gone." He reached into the driver's side to press the release button. The door's lock made a vibrating clunk as it surrendered its hold. Zeke scrambled up onto the bed of the pickup and disappeared into the back of the HaverCorp truck.

Past where Jaeger's sedan had fled, I saw the silver Cherokee, front bumper crumpled against a lamppost and a skinhead in surplus Vietnam-era fatigues lying on the ground next to it, one leg still inside the vehicle. The small-arms fire had quieted. I risked running into the open, past the block to where the teenage girl lay.

She was in shock, her face more blank than distressed. I didn't see any signs of injury. It was only the fear keeping her frozen in place.

"Let's get you safe," I said to her. She shrank from my touch. My appearance—masked and intense—wasn't any comfort.

No time to argue. I scooped her up with both arms and carried her at a near-run back toward the parked cars opposite the armored truck. The closest cover. Sheltered from Fain's team in case the bullets started flying again. Leo covered me from the opposite side of the avenue.

Sirens now, echoing from the canyons of downtown to the north. More from the east. Zeke threw one of the cash-heavy satchels out of the armored car onto the bed to land with a boom.

"Time to leave," I said. Leo raced across the street to join me.

"No," Fain said. "Help unload."

He raised the launcher and laid down three shots in rapid succession to land thirty yards up the road. White smoke burst and bloomed from each impact. The grenades continued to jet thick streams into the air that obscured any view of the street to the north.

Fain turned and fired another three smoke rounds in the direction of the bank, shouting between the shots. His eyes behind the motocross mask were wide and unblinking. "Three, cover the south sector." Using Rigo's call sign. He spun to face Leo. "You, work with Two to unload the bags."

"I'm with him," Leo said, nodding to me.

"Get the fucking bags," Daryll shouted.

"No time," I said. I put the sirens at six blocks away, closing fast. "The cops will have us trapped in thirty seconds." Another bystander, a middle-aged man, stumbled dazedly off the curb. Behind him, the skinhead with the facial tattoos that Leo had knocked cold with the sponge grenade stirred, got one knee underneath him. His pistol lay within reach. I ran toward them.

"Shaw," Fain shouted, abandoning call signs as he reloaded the launcher with expert speed. "Goddammit, we need you."

"Take the bike," I said to Leo as I grabbed the skinhead's pistol off the pavement. "I'm right behind you."

He hauled ass south through the oncoming tendrils of smoke, toward the bronze sculpture and its stairs leading into the belowground level of the Uwajimaya parking lot. We had left two motorcycles on the far side of the upper lot the night before, as our contingency. The underground level would allow Leo to sprint directly across and resurface near the bikes.

I punched the rising skinhead so hard that my own teeth rattled. He collapsed.

"Pak," Fain shouted after Leo. I grabbed the bystander and hauled him to sit near the stunned teenager. Thick white clouds billowed over the entire block. Fain shouting for Leo, for me. Darryl and Zeke arguing as I left the civilians and hurried across to the armored truck.

The sirens howled, not just north and east now but all around. Any control of the situation we'd had was gone. I turned to urge Fain one last time to get his men the fuck out of there.

THIRTY-NINE

SHARP AND FAMILIAR CRACKLING sounds popped me back to the planet, like a bubble surfacing in water.

M4 carbines. Two- and three-round taps. Multiple weapons. All this I knew before my thoughts had coalesced. The sound of the gunfire moved farther away.

I looked toward it, still without any conscious brain activity that might command my head to turn. Half a block from where I lay, Zeke and Rigo were moving in the opposite direction in a bounding assault between parked cars, covering each other and firing bursts in practiced synchronization.

Firing bullets, not rubber grenades. At a cop car, barely visible behind the curtain of white smoke that had only begun to dissipate.

Immediate aggressive response. Hammered into us until it was instinctual. Eliminate the threat.

My chest hurt. A lot. The white light threatened to come shining back, but seemed to change its mind as my next breath sharpened the hurt into a fleeting glimpse of agony.

The Toyota pickup was gone. Daryll and Fain with it. I was lying next to the unconscious mass of the cousin I'd shot in the ankle, half un-

Fain shot me.

The impact was an ax, swung full force into the center of my chest. I fell to the pavement.

Somewhere Rigo shouted and was answered by more voices. Light flooded into me. A brightness so all-encompassing that it banished everything else in the world, even color, even sound.

I felt as peaceful as I'd been in a long time.

A long time.

der the back bumper of the armored car. The white light wasn't entirely my imagination. Ivory smoke swamped the road. I caught a faint but terrible acrid whiff of CS gas in the still air. Fain must have laid down every grenade in their arsenal.

In the reflections of store windows—where the glass wasn't broken—I caught flashes of red and blue behind the wall of smoke and noxious gas to the south. Maybe they'd cordoned off the block. More bursts of carbine fire echoed off the building. No answering fire from the police in that direction. No visibility, no clear targets.

Cops in either direction on 6th. Rigo and Zeke in the middle of the block, raining hell. And me, stuck right here. Feeling like a rhinoceros had stepped on my thorax.

Could I escape into the bank? No exit there. The grocery was fifty yards away, which might as well be a hundred miles. I couldn't run. I didn't even have to try standing up to know that.

The volume of fire from Zeke and Rigo slowed, stopped. Out of ammo, or reloading?

I got my answer as a car engine thundered. Lifting my head to see over the rounded gut of the unconscious hulk as a Ford Mustang peeled out from the curb and raced north, toward the police who had been the targets of their suppressive fire. Christ, I hoped it had been suppressive fire. The alternative would be massacre.

Think, Shaw. Cops would be closing in from the cordon at any moment. Bluff my way out? No. Even if my HaverCorp disguise bought me an extra minute, I couldn't just fade away, not with dozens of police around. As soon as they found the guards hogtied in the back of the armored car, I would become the focus of all kinds of mean attention.

The motorcycles. Leo and I had left the bikes in the grocery lot next to a collection rack for shopping carts. Easy to find in a rush. Like now. He'd chosen two older Kawasakis, common enough not to stand out but with enough horsepower to kick a pig halfway to Canada. I hoped Leo had made it to the bikes and escaped. If he'd tried to come back for me, the cops would have nailed him.

But that salvation was even farther away than the grocery itself, and on the other side of the police cordon. Impossible.

Impossible without getting crazy.

Shit. A bad idea beats no idea.

I reached up, grabbed the bumper of the armored car, and hauled myself to stand before I had time to realize the pain. An iron vise squeezed my rib cage as I climbed through the open back door. My legs buckled, held, and I managed to turn around and pull the thick steel door shut with a clang.

The guards still lay in their hoods on the floor of the truck. In the side compartments, nine or ten satchels of cash remained. Fain and his team had run out of time, and then some.

"Get us out of here," one of the guards yelled. Thinking I was a cop, maybe.

I stumbled to the driver's seat, stepping over the green nylon duffel with Jaeger's coat and drugs. The truck's engine was still running. Through the windshield and the smoke I saw the roadblock two hundred feet away. Three cruisers set at angles with six or seven uniformed cops crouched behind them. One edged out along the engine side of his vehicle, risking fire to get a look at the street. And me.

I put the armored truck in drive and floored it.

The six-cylinder diesel punched us forward and the transmission screeched as it tried to keep up. I prayed the truck wouldn't stall. Beyond the fading columns of smoke and the flashing red and blue light show, cops fanned out, pointing in my direction. No one risked shooting. Not yet.

I'd had courses in mobility training on the Army's twenty-ton Stryker personnel carrier. The HaverCorp truck was smaller, but the attitude still applied. If something's in your way, make it regret that choice.

I barreled toward the blocking cruisers. Twenty miles an hour. Thirty. The truck roared through the artificial fog of smoke and stinging gas. I heard the simultaneous blast of a gun and the smack of buckshot striking the front tire's hub, which had about as much effect as spitballs on a window. I veered left, aiming the corner of the truck's enormous front bumper at the grille of the first police cruiser in line. My eyes blurred from gas vapor leaking through the ceiling vents.

The armored truck smashed into the cruiser's grille, swatting it backward into its mates with a crash like dropped china plates. One of the bound guards screamed in terror. The truck shuddered but barely slowed. I straightened the wheel, leaning forward, willing the huge machine to go faster. Smashed cars or not, the cops would be on my tail within seconds.

The Uwajimaya lot was directly to my right now. I timed the spaces between trees and swung hard around. The truck bounded up the curb and over the sidewalk, crashing through the short fence of the parking lot like it was made of cardboard. People fled from the truck as if from a monster. I kept the accelerator floored and looked for the motorcycle—There. Closer than I'd thought. I swerved and hit the brakes almost immediately, the truck shuddering to a stop. The bound guards were both yelling now. I jumped out, landed, and collapsed to my hands and knees.

Get up, Shaw. For fuck's sake, move. You're not hurt. The bike is right there. Move.

Leo had taped the key under the front fender. I found it, peeled it away, half fell onto the seat, and got the key into the ignition. My fingers shook. The armored car shielded me from the roadblock I'd hammered through, but there would be other cops.

Shouts, and more sirens. When the engine caught, I barely heard it. I found myself popping the brake and goosing the throttle, and the bike lunged ahead. The air rushing at my face filled my lungs and revived me. I leaned low—a smaller target—and flew out of the parking lot exit.

The cops had emptied the road of civilians. I had a clear path into the complex intersection of boulevards and avenues on Dearborn. SPD cruisers had blocked the Dearborn side from traffic but the intersection was too wide for an effective barricade. Cops ran between the cruisers, readying for pursuit. I gunned the cycle across the broad expanse and onto the overpass for the Metro line. If there was a shot fired, I lost the sound in the wind.

Now I was soaring. Following the emergency route that Leo and I had arranged. Going the wrong way on a one-way bus lane. Clocking a mile a minute and more, with no traffic in my way and the city streets far below.

As perfect as it seemed, this was the dangerous part of the route. While I raced along the overpass for miles until the bus lane merged onto I-90, the cops had every chance to radio ahead. If I stayed on the freeway too long I would be trapped in the traffic flowing into the tunnel and onto the bridge over Lake Washington. Cooked and quickly eaten. They'd have every SWAT hard-case on both sides of the water waiting for my ass.

I aimed to be long gone before then.

A bus loomed ahead, rushing at me like an angry beast. I hugged the outer barrier, my handlebars only inches from scraping the cement wall. Willing the bus driver not to panic and drift the wrong way. He leaned hard on the horn, holding its single blaring note until I was far past him and seeing Beacon Hill flash by my peripheral vision.

The front tire wobbled. Not the bike, me. I inhaled as much as my chest allowed and tried to use the stab of pain that came with the breath. Seeking adrenaline any way I could get it.

One mile. Two. The bus lane rejoined the express lanes running down the center of the freeway. I was flying head-on into the morning crush.

Another bus came at me, closing the distance at our combined speed of one hundred twenty. I swung left this time, feeling the heavy drag as the leviathan rushed past, threatening to tip me and the bike over. I caught a glimpse of one passenger, her face stretched in an O of shock.

Then I was through, at the edge of the barrier dividing the express lanes from the main freeway. I screeched to a near-stop, waiting for a gap in the hissing river of oncoming cars, then kicked it and sailed across five lanes and a shoulder, hearing the stutters and songs of furious horns, onto the exit ramp that made a full circle and shot me out onto Rainier.

Nearly back to where the morning had started, one hour and a full century ago.

Three minutes later, I stopped the bike on a block of one-story houses with muddy yards and missing roof shingles. I left the key in the ignition. Maybe I'd get lucky and somebody would steal it.

Peeling off the HaverCorp jacket was embarrassingly slow. I had the shakes, and not just from the cold sweat on my face. Finally I freed myself and stuffed the jacket and mask and comm headset deep into one of a dozen trash cans waiting for pickup.

I walked the last blocks to where I'd left the Dodge, slowly, shakily. At one point I stopped and leaned against a rusted-out Hyundai like we were two drunks reliant on one another to stay upright.

There was something wrong in my chest. Something more than the obvious and expected contusion from taking a sponge round at ten paces. The whole cavity felt squeezed. My heart rate was still somewhere north of ninety. I could feel it, an animal battering itself against the bars of its tight cage.

Gingerly, I pressed three fingertips where the round had hit. Steel needles mixed with the oxygen on my next inhale, and my vision blurred at the edges. Fuck. I didn't need to attempt that again.

Get to the truck. One step at a time. That seemed more in the realm of possibility.

Turned out it was. I even unlocked the door and crawled into the cab and closed the door again.

And that was all.

FORTY

HEY," A VOICE SAID. "You're alive."

The voice was masculine and scratchy and high-toned. With a touch of an Ulster accent. Yes. Hollis. I felt proud at my powers of recognition.

And confused. The face in front of me was female, strong of bone, and undeniably beautiful. I liked the eyes especially. Ocean gray and blue.

Hey, Luce. Why are you talking like Hollis?

Hollis stepped to the side, the better to peer at me around Luce, who was seated next to wherever I was lying. A high black ceiling, and high-set windows with bits of stained glass around the edges. I knew those, too.

"Why are we in the Morgen?" I said to Luce.

She leaned back a fraction, assessing. "You don't remember?"

"Easiest place," Hollis jumped in. "She had to bring you somewhere."

"You called me," Luce said, "and told me where you were, and then the line cut off. That was scary enough. When I got down to Rainier you were unconscious in the front seat of your pickup, and that was even worse."

"Sorry," I said.

"You woke up when I opened the door. You even moved over to the passenger side and told me . . ."

She hesitated.

"You told me to call Hollis," she finished. "By the time I did, you had faded out again."

I looked around. The sun was high enough that it caught the windows, which meant it must be sometime around noon. Any later and the alley outside would be submerged in its customary shade. I was lying on one of the long built-in benches that lined the walls of the bar. The four-top tables had been pulled away to make space. The Morgen's main room was a long, uniform rectangle. Luce had painted the walls and ceiling and permanent furnishings a flat utilitarian black, the better to show off the hints of color—the window glass, the bottles, and the big tapestry behind the bar with the nude woman on horseback in the roiling surf, from which the bar got its name.

"I was running errands," Hollis said, "when Lucille got hold of me." His way of cluing me in that he hadn't given Luce the whole story. That would be my decision. "We talked over where to take you. The Morgen here was closer than the marina and my boat."

"And my place has too many stairs," I finished.

"I don't know where you live now," Luce reminded me.

"Right," I said.

"You're just lucky I know how to drive a stick."

Her joke covered the awkward moment well enough. I tried sitting up, and found it easier to slide my legs off the bench and let the weight tilt me skyward.

"Easy, boyo," Hollis said.

But my head felt better, even if my chest was still in the grip of a python. "I remember using you like a crutch to walk in here," I said to Hollis.

"What happened with Leo?" Luce asked. "Can they appeal his plea?"

"Leo's free," I said. "The real killer committed suicide and left a note."

She stared. "You didn't tell me."

"I didn't. It's been . . ." I wiped a palm over my hot forehead. "There's no real excuse."

Someone outside knocked on the dark green door that was the Morgen's main entrance.

"I'll get that," Luce said, standing up before either Hollis or I had moved. She strode away.

I turned to Hollis. "Where's Leo?"

"I don't know. No word from the man. From either of you. Christ, when the sirens started . . ." He blinked hard and shook his head emphatically. "I thought Leo might have holed up at your place. I was about to drive there when Luce got hold of me. What the hell happened?"

"Fain chose the money over catching Jaeger." That was all I had time to say before the sunlight through the opened door cast the customarily dim bar from charcoal-gray into cool silver.

Luce stepped aside to allow a man to walk in. Six-foot-four at least, not counting the cowboy boots. With a mane of sun-streaked brown hair sweeping back from his forehead, and crisply dressed in a white button-down shirt and midnight-blue jeans. He carried a teal backpack by its top strap. Luce touched him on the upper arm and guided him toward Hollis and me.

Her touch lingered long enough for me to understand their relationship. The tall guy was Luce's fiancé.

"Van, this is Carter," Luce said.

"Hey," Carter said, and knelt down without offering his hand. "How are you feeling?"

"You're a doctor," I said.

"Not yet I'm not. Just an intern at U-Dub Med." He unzipped a side pocket of the backpack—which I took for an EMT kit—and uncoiled a blood pressure cuff. "Lucy didn't tell me what happened."

Lucy?

"Batting cage," I said. "I took a fastball to the chest."

"Any trouble breathing?" He extracted a stethoscope from the pack.

"Yeah."

"All right. Take your shirt off and let's see where you got hit."

I was still wearing the generic brown shirt and blue pants that formed part of my HaverCorp disguise. Luce would have noticed my odd choice of clothes. They had probably clued her not to take me straight to an emergency room. I unbuttoned the shirt and rolled my shoulders back to cautiously peel it off.

"Damn," Carter said. Luce inhaled.

I looked. A violent purple blotch with red outlines sat on my breast-bone like some sea anemone, a finger's-breadth to the right of the center of my chest. It had swollen at least half an inch above the surface of the undamaged skin around it.

"Well. Hematoma like nobody's biz," Carter said. "Let me feel it. This might be uncomfortable."

I'd always hated that phrase, and his probing the bruise didn't im-prove my opinion. By the time he pressed the third time, prickles of sweat had erupted on my scalp.

"Sharp pain?" he said.

"Sharp enough."

"No fracture," he said, "or you'd know for sure. But you might have tears in those intercostal muscles between the ribs. It's the breathing that worries me. Inhale." He touched the stethoscope to my chest.

I took a breath.

"Can you inhale deeper?" he said.

"I can. I don't."

"That's what I mean. You might have a pulmonary contusion. That means a—"

"Bruise on my lungs."

"Yes. Well." He checked my blood pressure, which was normal. My pulse was around seventy, a lot higher than my usual resting rate sub-sixty.

Carter nodded. "You need to go to the hospital, no question. For X-rays and maybe a stay. Something like this could turn into pneumonia, or ARDS. That's—" Carter caught himself. "You might need oxygen. And a doctor needs to cross-check any pain medication you take. So no self-prescribing."

"But no surgery, either," I said.

"If it's what I think, there's not much to do except rest and monitor progress and let it heal," he said with some reluctance.

"Right."

"But there could be internal hemorrhaging. That builds up over time, and it can become very bad, very, very fast."

"He blacked out," Luce said.

"That true?" said Carter to me. "When you got hit?"

"For a few seconds. I figured it was just shock."

"I meant in your truck," Luce folded her arms. "You didn't mention it was your second time."

Carter checked my skull. "No sore spots to indicate a blow? Falling on something?"

"No."

"Could be shock," he said. "It's also possible that your heart stopped for a moment."

Hollis spoke for the first time. "Jesus, Mary."

"Like a defibrillator," said Carter. "One big thump can make the ticker stop or start. You got lucky."

"Yes," said Luce, her light skin all the way into pale.

"Go to the hospital. Seriously."

"It's a serious day," I said.

Carter didn't seem sure how to take that. "Okay, then." He stood up, all six-four-plus-boots, and zipped up his kit. "No more Hernandez heaters in the batting cage for a while. Okay?"

"Thank you," Luce said.

"Thanks," I echoed.

"No problem."

Luce walked Carter to the door. I occupied myself by standing up. It went better than expected.

"D'you want Harborview or Swedish?" Hollis said. "Or do you use the Army hospital?"

"Not yet. We have to find Leo. You're right, he'd go to my place. That's where Dez is."

"Should have known." He sighed. "No Jaeger, no millions. And you nearly dead."

"Like I said, not yet."

Luce shut the door. She didn't walk back to us immediately. I went to the bar and grabbed the soda gun and filled a pint glass with water, downed it, filled another. Swallowing hurt, but everything hurt.

"Thanks for calling Carter," I said.

"Doesn't make a difference if you won't follow his advice," she said. She hadn't overheard me and Hollis talking. She didn't need to have. Luce knew me well enough.

"Still." I finished the second glass. "Good of you."

"He knows who you are. Who we were. He came anyway."

"Good of him, then."

I moved around the bar and walked past her to open the door. Hollis moved so quickly to leave it was as if he'd dropped a lit match in his back pocket.

"Cowboy boots?" I said to Luce.

"He's from Oklahoma. Cut him some slack. You'd like him."

I didn't think so. Neither did Luce, probably. But we could pretend.

"See you," I said.

"Yes."

I closed the green door behind me. As I walked up the alley, I heard a click as Luce slid the dead bolt home.

FORTY-ONE

OUT ON THE STREET, Hollis had his ancient beast of an Eldorado warming up, and the canvas top down.

"In October," I said, looking at the open-air seats.

"I live dangerously. To your place?"

I tried Leo's phone. No answer.

"Cross your fingers that he's there," I said. I didn't like thinking about the alternatives.

I lived in a third-floor walk-up studio off Broadway and across from the light rail, which was a fresh enough addition to Capitol Hill that longtime residents still called it the new station. The apartment wasn't much, and I paid through the nose for it. I also dropped heavy coin each month for a reserved parking place in a lot nearby. Location, location. Hollis pulled into my space, and we walked back to my building.

"You all right?" Hollis said.

"I just had a physical an hour ago."

"Not quite what I meant."

I let it lie. We walked up the flights to my floor—the minor exertion making my chest ping like alarmed radar—and down the hall to 3C. I gently pushed Hollis to one side of the door before knocking. Safety first.

"Who is it?" Dez.

"It's Van."

She yanked the door open. "Thank God."

"Leo?" I said.

"He's here," she said, even as Leo came out from the bathroom, holding the same thick Taurus revolver he'd taken from the HaverCorp guard.

"Shit, Leo," I said.

"I know. Sorry, man." He reached into his pocket and held up his burner phone. The screen was spiderwebbed with cracks. "Happened when I dove to the ground during the fight. I've been checking voice mail every ten minutes, in case you got in touch."

And of course I wasn't about to leave my voice on a recording. "Forget it. I'm just glad you made it."

"I didn't think you got out. The cops came in like a fucking invasion right as I reached the motorcycle. I couldn't get back to you."

"It was smart not to try. You wouldn't have made it past the roadblock."

Dez wrapped her arms around him and squeezed. "No more."

"No," Leo said. "That's it for me. Goddamn, what a day."

"Dez, this is Hollis. Our friend."

"Delighted," said Hollis, "and glad you're both home safe."

Dez beamed. Hollis had that gift. Instant likability. "Have you seen the news?" she said.

They led us to the living room. Dez sat in front of her laptop, clicking between multiple windows.

We had our choice of a dozen video clips, plus live streaming. It was the story of the year, a gun battle in the heart of Seattle. Every local station had arrived within minutes. Some quick-acting KOMO producers had already obtained blurry coverage from bystander phones taken from blocks away, or out of the windows of nearby businesses.

I had Dez show me every clip, turning off the sound to concentrate on the images. I was looking for myself, and for Leo. None of the professional cameramen had caught us in action. One clip taken from a third-floor office showed a brief fuzzy image of me, lying supine near the armored car. Another from street level revealed what might have been Leo as he dashed off-camera. I backed up the clips and checked again, to be sure. We weren't remotely identifiable. The clips mostly caught smoke and the barest glimpses of black figures who I knew to be Zeke and Rigo laying down fire, their muzzle flashes visible through the clouds. They were the focus, which took attention off us.

There could be other video, of course. Something more revealing that the cops hadn't released. Nothing we could do about that now.

I refreshed the search and discovered one more uploaded video, over half a minute in length, recorded by a shopper in the Uwajimaya parking lot. It was the best of the bunch, and I imagined that the local CBS affiliate had paid handsomely for the rights. The shopper had had a ringside seat as the HaverCorp truck—with me at the wheel, invisible behind the glare and the shaky motion—crashed through the fence and onto the lot. There was a pause in the action and anxious talking from the civilians after the truck stopped. Then the image jumped as they re-pointed the phone in a rush, catching a glimpse of me on the Kawasaki speeding out of the lot and up the street.

"Holy shit, Van," Leo said.

"You do keep it interesting," said Hollis.

I backed up the video to watch it again. With the surgical mask on, my dark hair was my only identifiable feature.

Dez tapped one of the two intact burners lying on the table. "There's no word yet from John Fain."

"There won't be," I said. "Fain ran a game on us. He must have spotted Jaeger before Leo and I even reached the Chinatown bank. But he laid back and waited for us to roll up with the money. Probably worried that Leo and I would abandon the truck as soon as they had Jaeger secured. But he waited too long. Jaeger brought too many men. Fain's team couldn't deal with them and unload the cash before the cops rolled in. Jaeger escaped. Then Fain compounded the mistake by waiting too long to exfil. His elite team's precious cohesion unraveled. When Leo and I bugged out on him, Fain lost it completely."

Hollis's mouth twisted. I had filled him in on the day's fiasco during our short drive to the apartment. "More than that," he said. "The damned traitor shot you."

"He *shot* you?" Dez said in alarm.

"'S'okay. I'm bulletproof," I said.

"That motherfucker," Dez said.

Leo's hands gripped the chair like he was ready to throw it out the window. "I'll kill him."

"I figured Fain would go for the money," I said. "That many millions was too much to pass up. But I also believed he would follow Macomber's orders and make Jaeger his first priority."

"Even over you." Hollis's face was cold, an uncommon expression for the man.

"We were still outnumbered. Leo and I took out four of Jaeger's thugs. Plus Jaeger and his bleached-blond getaway driver and a muscle-head in the sedan. That's at least seven, and I heard gunfire from the north, so Rigo or someone else must have engaged with more of the enemy there." I shook my head. "Jaeger wasn't fucking around."

We turned our attention back to the news clips. Reports varied on how many robbers had been arrested. Some had the estimate as high as eight. None listed as killed in the firefight. Every station noted that no police or civilians had been wounded, but that some witnesses were being treated for shock and minor injuries.

KING TV brought on a former SWAT commander to speculate on the nature of the firefight. He proposed that the video had captured a falling-out between members of the same gang in the midst of an attempted heist. He was also privy to an inside source in SPD who shared off the record that all of the suspects in custody bore the unmistakable tattoos of white nationalist groups. The SWAT guy noted the violence of such organizations and gave thanks that, thus far, no one appeared to have been killed in the onslaught.

I joined in that sentiment. Fain hadn't crossed the line all the way into killing cops.

We watched the news feeds until the talking heads started to repeat themselves, and then gave each video one more view before I felt reassured that my easily identifiable face hadn't been caught on camera.

"Maybe all of Fain's crew made it out," Leo said.

Hollis growled. "We know Jaeger did."

"So it was for nothing," Dez said. "All that fear and worry and risk."

I smiled grimly. "Not quite. Not with our little gift for the police."

I closed the laptop. Tired and wired all at once. Sleep was probably the smart choice. Or at least sitting down. My breath made a wheezing sound that I usually associated with the flu.

"It would have been a lot cleaner if Jaeger had been captured at the bank." I settled onto my bed and leaned back against the wall. It felt as good as any plush easy chair. "But I'll settle for his grunts in custody and every cop and FBI agent in the Northwest having Jaeger's photo taped to their dashboards."

"That puts paid to that maniac," Hollis said with satisfaction. "What about Fain?"

Leo folded his arms on the table to rest his forehead. Maybe he was as tired as I was. Didn't seem possible.

"If I never see Mercy River again, I'll die happy," Leo said, his voice muffled by the table.

"I have to go back once more," Dez said. "For Wayne's funeral."

In all of the planning and chaos of the past day, I had nearly forgotten that Dez had to bury her husband.

"That town might be bad news for us," Leo said to her. "Everybody knows you're with me now."

"Give it a day," I said. "Tonight we rest and keep one eye on the news."

"There was talk of a hospital," Hollis said, eyeing me.

"Only as a last resort. After this morning, the Feds will have every ER in the state watching for any unusual injuries. Including contusions that might have been caused by rubber bullets."

"Then I'm staying here," said Hollis. "I heard what Carter said. Some-one needs to watch your breathing."

Dez stretched. "We'll take that on. One night on Van's floor won't kill us."

I didn't argue. There was toughing it out, and then there was stupid, and going to sleep alone and possibly letting my lungs fill with fluid would be the latter.

My burner phone on the table buzzed to life, rattling and moving like a windup toy. We all stared at it.

"Who had that number?" Hollis said.

Only one person not standing in front of me. I rose with some effort, and picked up the phone to open the line and listen.

"You there? It's me." Fain's voice. Sounding strained.

I didn't say anything.

"We have to talk."

Which was something close to funny. He was the one who felt the need to reach out. I was doing fine as it was.

"It's not secure. The situation." There was another pause, different than before. I heard Fain take a long breath and swallow.

"We're not safe," he said, and hung up.

Dez raised her pierced eyebrow. "What was that about?"

"He said we're in trouble."

"That's an officer. Steps in shit and looks around for someone to blame it on," said Leo.

"It wasn't a threat. He wants to talk."

"Let him rot," said Dez.

Hollis and Leo echoed that opinion.

While I felt the same, I had to wonder where Fain was coming from. Did he somehow think we'd wound up with the cash? The bulk of the satchels had been left behind in the armored truck. If Daryll had made it out in the pickup, I didn't think Fain's team had managed to grab much more than two or three million.

Not that any number followed by six zeros was chump change. But after licking his chops over many times that amount, Fain might feel cheated. He'd practically let Jaeger skip away to get a shot at it.

I didn't owe Fain anything, not even hatred. The only people I needed to worry about right now were in this room. And they deserved some peace. For however long it lasted.

FORTY-TWO

REST WAS HARD TO come by. I was used to insomnia. Tired body, active mind. I had done some of my best thinking—and my craziest, which often amounted to the same thing—during hours when even bats were coming home to roost.

Tonight was different. My brain felt sluggish. My body couldn't find comfort enough to relax. Any way I lay, my ribs and chest complained about it. Sitting up helped. I finally convinced Leo and Dez that the bed was wasted on me, injury or no, and I dozed fitfully in the one tall chair that I owned. A leather wingback that was a little too large and way too outlandish for the rest of my tiny apartment. I'd spotted the chair in a shop window while walking on the east side of Capitol Hill a month before. It had instantly reminded me of my grandfather's favorite chair, an ancient piece, even though Dono's chair had been the color of merlot wine instead of café au lait. I didn't even haggle over the price.

At four past four in the morning, the burner hummed again. I didn't have to get up to answer it. It had been in my chest pocket since Fain's first call.

"We have to talk," he said again, "not over this line."

I agreed with at least half that statement.

"I figure if this is the cops listening, it's too late to matter. And if it's you, then you got no reason to say word one to me, am I right?"

That strain I had heard earlier was still in Fain's voice. Along with something else. Resignation? Regret?

"I will be—*we* will be, don't fade away if you see the others—at the corner of First and Yesler at nine o'clock tomorrow morning. That's a public square, right? A busy place. If that's safe enough ground for you, be there. This is the only chance we'll get."

The line went dead.

"Fain called back?" Dez, whispering from the bed. She and Leo had fallen asleep right after a midnight snack of pot stickers and chow mein left over from dinner. Open take-out containers still rested beside the bed, grains of sticky rice scattered like a trail leading to the sheets. I could hear Leo's long heavy breaths. When he slept, he slept all the way.

"Yeah," I whispered back. "Fain wants to meet."

"I don't know Army stuff, but that sounds like a dumb trap to me."

"Me, too. Except that he wants it in Pioneer Square during morning rush hour." I knew the place back to front. It wouldn't be difficult to see them coming, not with a few extra eyes helping me.

"Leo and I talked, while we were downstairs waiting for the Chinese food. I decided to ask the Seebrights to handle the funeral arrangements for Wayne. Jim will do a good job."

"If you're worried about being safe there . . ."

"No. Thank you. It's not a question of feeling safe. It's about being free."

She sat up and pulled one of the layered blankets to cover herself, even though she wore a white EL VY band T-shirt long enough to come down to her knees.

"Wayne had a grip on me for a long time. I was his girlfriend when he had everything, and his wife when he had nothing. It didn't change how he behaved. Always making sure I would do whatever he wanted. Give up whatever he asked. Even if Mom hadn't left her money to Erle,

Wayne would have thought of it as his inheritance, because he had me. And I would have believed it, too. Does that make sense?"

"I think so."

"Him killing Erle, killing himself, and blaming it all on our relationship. That's his last turn of the screw. Trying to make me feel how he wants me to feel, even after I'd left him. Even after he's dead." She hugged her knees to her chest. "No more. I'm not going to stand over Wayne's grave and pretend to be sad in front of everybody. I am sad, but for the lost time. Not for him."

"That I get."

"I'm going to Utah to meet Leo's family. And then I'm going east, just to drive around for a while. Leo wants to join me."

"He'd be a fool not to."

I heard the smile in her voice. "Thanks."

She rolled over and began to curl up to Leo's back, and then turned her head toward me again.

"Are you upset about Luce getting married?"

Leo had told her the joyous news. "You don't beat around the bush."

"Are you?"

I shifted in the antique chair. It creaked. My chest creaked some with it.

"Yeah," I said. "I am."

"Sorry."

"But I'm trying to be happy for her."

"Tryin' beats Dyin'. That was on a tin sign in our garage when I was little." Dez's words were beginning to slur.

"It's true, mostly."

"That sign spooked me. The word *Dyin'*, right there in big bold red."

"Big bold idea for a kid," I said, but Dez was asleep, matching Leo's slow inhalations with her own.

I sat and concentrated on my own breathing, which still sounded like a busted accordion, and let myself think about other topics than Mercy River, or Fain's guys, or anything about this hellish day. Including Luce. Instead I considered why people felt the need to put vintage signs in their houses, and what it might have been like to be a child way back when those signs were shiny new on the wall of the penny arcade, and soon I slipped into something next door to sleep.

An hour or two later, I woke as lightly.

The only chance we'll get, Fain had said. What had he meant? That if I didn't show, he was giving up? Or that if I wouldn't make whatever deal he wanted, he would come after us?

I'd had more than enough of dealing with John Fain. And General Kiss-My-Ass Macomber. I wouldn't put it past the general to have ordered Fain to sacrifice Leo and me if it gained the Rally millions of HaverCorp's money. Macomber had that kind of single-mindedness.

So where was Captain Fain's mind now? And why had he sounded almost desperate?

I realized I had decided, sometime during my short nap, to meet him in Pioneer Square like he asked. Time for us to conclude our business. All markers called in, all accounts paid. I didn't want Fain's unknown motives hanging over us, like a sword dangling from a single slim thread.

FORTY-THREE

PIONEER SQUARE CLAIMED THE oldest buildings in the city, accommodating a constantly rotating lineup of the newest businesses. Tech ventures and gig economy start-ups, attracted by the allure of funky office space among the red bricks and cobblestones. Their companies either succeeded, moving somewhere bigger and less prone to crumbling, or they crumbled themselves.

The chamber of commerce kept pressure on the city to clean the square up, keeping it safe for tourists to join the underground tour or to stroll along First Ave's art galleries and Persian carpet showrooms. Still, homeless people drowsed under the arches of the Victorian-era pergola, and the local missions never lacked for lines at mealtimes. The square refused to take the coat of whitewash, to be modernized, homogenized.

I watched from the shadows of a huge arched stone doorway, across the square from the Yesler intersection. Leo was across First Ave., watching from the inside of a café. Hollis waited with his Cadillac in a pay lot, three doors down from Leo. My chest throbbed, both on the surface and deep within. I couldn't walk at much more than a stroll without my lungs pricking me with masonry nails. But I was still moving.

At ten minutes to nine, Zeke Caton walked up First from the direction of downtown and stood at the corner, leaning against one of the pergola's posts. I continued to scan the streets. No sign of Fain or Rigoberto or Big Daryll. Or of the cars their team had used at the armored car job. Zeke wore jeans, a white Trail Blazers sweatshirt, and a black rain jacket, unzipped. Enough room under the baggy jacket for a half a dozen pistols, if he chose.

I could wait Zeke out, and follow him. Chancy. They'd be watching for a tail.

At five minutes past the hour, I texted Leo and Hollis that I was on the move, and abandoned the cover of the stone archway to walk around the fenced triangle of ornamental green space and its sixty-foot-tall totem pole, coming up on Zeke's five. He didn't turn around. That didn't mean he hadn't spotted me.

I stopped halfway between the totem pole and Zeke. A moment later he glanced my way, and derisively held up his empty hands as he walked toward me.

"Where are the others?" I said.

"Hey. We thought you'd been busted." He made a show of looking around him. "Or maybe you were."

"If you or I were wired, we wouldn't be strapped. The Feds don't arm informants."

"Guess not."

"So whatever this is, let's get to it."

Zeke showed his teeth. "No shoot-outs today."

He tilted his head toward the cobblestoned edge of Yesler thirty feet away, where a black Chrysler minivan pulled up to the curb. The side door popped out and began to slide open. I stepped to put Zeke between me and the minivan.

"Take it easy," Zeke said.

Through the minivan's open door I saw Fain, seated in the first row behind the passenger's seat. Rigoberto was driving, both hands visible on the wheel. Daryll was not in the vehicle, and I scanned the square again for his huge form.

Fain raised his hand slightly in greeting.

"Move," I said to Zeke.

He did. I walked two arms' lengths behind him to the Chrysler.

There was something off with Fain. His tanned face carried a tallow-white undertone, even as his cheeks flushed pink. As we drew closer, I could see that his car seat was padded behind and underneath with folded beach towels. His legs had been propped up on a stack of pillows.

"Shaw," he said. I kept walking, to where I stood a little behind the door, in Rigo's blind spot. Fain would have to turn if he wanted to see me. He stayed put.

"We just want to communicate," he said.

"I got your last message fine. Straight to the heart." I pointed at Zeke. "Get in the car."

He glanced at Fain, who nodded curtly. Zeke shot me one last mocking grin and climbed into the passenger's seat and closed the door. With the three of them facing the other direction, I felt a micron safer. We waited as a knot of pedestrians hurried past, absorbed in their morning routines.

"I'm grateful you made it out," Fain said. "When you came toward us, you raised your weapon. Everything at that moment seemed like a threat. I overreacted."

"Tell it like it is, boss," Rigo said flatly. "You fucked up."

I kept checking the streets. Leo was watching from across the avenue, but one man couldn't cover me from every direction on a busy thoroughfare.

Zeke knew what I was doing. "Daryll's dead, dude."

I looked at him. "The cops?"

Fain paused, and for an instant I thought it was emotion choking him up. Then he exhaled long and low, as some kind of agony released its grip on him.

"Jaeger's killed him," he said. "After Chinatown, Daryll and I got away in the pickup while Zeke and Rigo covered us."

"I caught that part of the show from my floor seat."

"Jaeger and two of his animals spotted us a few minutes later. Pure chance. We were blocks away from the bank, trying to reach Rigo on the comm. They carjacked us. Pistol-whipped Daryll and took him, along with the pickup and the few bags of cash in back."

"And Jaeger left you there."

"He shot me. One round missed the armor and hit my gut. More bad luck." He clenched in pain again. Somebody behind the stopped van honked. None of us acknowledged it. "I'm patched up for now. The general has a doctor waiting in Mercy River. He'll keep it quiet."

I wasn't positive Fain would survive the six-hour drive, but nobody would profit from hearing me say it out loud.

"You're sure they aced Daryll?" I said.

"Jaeger called me last night, using Daryll's phone. He knows who you are now. Who all of us are. That's why you and I had to talk."

Fain didn't have to spell it out. Jaeger had made Daryll talk. Daryll Abernathy, former All-American, had suffered through a long day and a bad death.

"Jaeger said he'd let us live, if we handed over the rest of the cash," Fain said. "I told him to cram it."

"Pretty much your only option."

Jaeger, our target, had wound up with the only money anyone had managed to lift from the armored car. Outcomes like that made you question what sort of people Lady Luck favors.

Fain indicated his remaining men. "My team can watch each other's backs in Oregon. I have to assume Jaeger forced Daryll to tell him about the Rally, and the general. He'll be coming for us. We have time to prepare. You deserve the same. I figured I owed you that."

A bright blue Interceptor SUV glided through the intersection. The city cops had bigger concerns than a minivan holding up the morning commute. We watched it go.

"You saw Jaeger's men?" I said. "They might be his last survivors."

Fain grunted. "A skinny turd with bleached white hair. The other was an iron freak. Too many muscles to move. I didn't have time to see more than that."

He exhaled another long release of pain.

"We should have taken Jaeger when we had the chance," he said.

I didn't reply. Fain didn't mean it as an apology.

"Next time," he said, closing his eyes. "Next time we won't hesitate."

He pressed a button and the minivan's door began to slide closed. Rigo put the van in motion. They drove straight down Yesler toward the waterfront and out of sight.

I stood on the corner, letting foot traffic swirl around me, allowing myself a long moment to assess exactly how screwed the situation was. I had to assume Jaeger now knew everything Daryll had known. The names of Fain's crew, including Leo. My name and background, too. Aaron Conlee's relation to Macomber. Every detail of the Rally's robberies, down to the cash taken. And more. How Macomber was the man who had forced Jaeger's First Riders out of Mercy River. Dez and her relationship with Leo. Maybe even details about Leo's family in Utah.

And Luce. Macomber had met Luce, knew her name. Had he mentioned her to Fain's team? She could be vulnerable now, too. I cursed myself for introducing them, and then set my recriminations aside.

Fain was right about one thing. No percentage in second-guessing our past decisions now. They hadn't worked out well for any of us. Especially Big Daryll. All we could do now was prepare for the fallout.

FORTY-FOUR

LEO AND I MET Hollis at the Cadillac. Hollis rolled down his window, and Leo sat on the hood while he and I kept wary eyes on the street.

"What did those bastards want?" Hollis said.

"To offer an olive branch." I told them about Daryll's death, and Jaeger learning about the Rally and where its money came from.

"Damn, Daryll," said Leo. "He's got parents in Iowa. Who's gonna tell them?"

"We'll have to leave that for the cops," I said. "Jaeger's still out there. He's aiming to settle scores with the general before he goes underground."

Leo stayed seated on the hood, leaning back on his palms like he was enjoying the uncommon day of sun. His posture didn't match the tension in his face.

"Hey, I know Daryll wasn't one of your guys, Van," Leo said. "But he was one of us. Still is."

I swallowed the first reply that came to mind, that I didn't owe dead Daryll shit after he and the rest of Fain's crew had left me for the wolves. That might be true. But Leo was equally right.

"Okay," I said. "I shouldn't breeze on past it. Daryll was a brother. We can help his family once we're clear of this. Fair?"

"For now, yeah."

"Fain's headed to intercept Jaeger in Mercy River."

Leo grunted. "Hard for me to see from across the street, but Fain didn't look right."

"He's dying. Gutshot."

"Sounds more than right to me," said Hollis, surprising me with his vehemence.

"Daryll dead and Fain down," Leo said. "Bad odds, if Jaeger has many men left."

I didn't say anything at first. I'd promised Leo and Dez no more secrets. We'd had enough evasions and half-truths and outright lies between us to fill a lifetime. But I was wrestling with that promise now.

"Should we back Fain up?" Leo pressed.

"I need a favor," I said. "A tough one."

He shifted uncertainly. "Guess I owe you that."

"No. It can't be about *owe*. If you do it, it's because I'm asking, not because you're forced."

"No second thoughts after. Is that what you mean, lad?" Hollis said.

"That's what I mean."

"All right," said Leo. "Shoot."

I handed Leo my apartment key. "I want you and Dez to head out for Utah. Take your family on a short vacation. The kitchen cabinet across from my stove has a false top. You'll find cash. Take what you need to stay on the road awhile."

He frowned. "What are you going to do?"

"I'm going to Mercy River."

"Not a chance. Not without me."

"It's what I want."

"Come on, man. Don't ask this."

I waited. After holding my stare for another moment, Leo slid off the hood.

"I thought you were done with that protecting-me bullshit," he said.

"It's not to defend you from Jaeger. You can handle yourself."

"Then what?"

"This is going to get worse, Leo. Jaeger's hunted by the Feds, Fain's team is a wounded animal. Insanity and desperation. When it goes down, every one of them is likely to be dead or headed to prison for halfway to forever. I don't want that for you. I don't want Dez to lose you just when you're free again."

"Nobody wants that. It's better odds that you live through a fight with me around."

"I'm not going in guns blazing. I'm looking for the angle, like I always do. You said as much."

"So I should let you go alone?"

"That's what I'm asking."

He swore again and turned to Hollis for support. Hollis shrugged.

"Van's grandfather was as much a bastard," he said. "I gave up trying."

Leo clenched a fist.

"I'll do it," he said, "if you can swear to me this isn't some suicide run. I'm not standing aside for that crap. And I won't be the one who tells the old woman, Addy, or Luce, that I let you get dead."

"I'm planning to survive this one. Promise."

He walked around and got into the passenger's seat of the Caddy. "Then good luck, brother."

Hollis put the Eldorado in forward and let it ease into the street. Leo didn't meet my gaze all the way out.

He would forgive me. If I lived.

I walked to the opposite side of the lot, through an alley and down to Western where I'd left the Dodge. My chest burned with the effort of quick movement. I ignored it, gunning the truck's engine into a snarl to catch a gap in the traffic.

Fain's team would probably stick to I-90 and the fastest route for their wounded captain. If I pushed it, I could reach Mercy River before them. If I was lucky, I would beat Jaeger there, too.

Jaeger didn't give a shit about the Rally's money. It was blood he was after.

I couldn't clearly express how I was so certain of Jaeger's resolve. But I'd seen the man in person, and recognized what he was. An emptiness. Other humans didn't count. Not the HaverCorp guards he'd murdered, or even his own men whom he'd abandoned at the bank. Only Jaeger mattered to Jaeger. He was singular and untouchable. And I'd shaken that certainty.

He had a couple of million in ready cash now. Properly laundered, enough money to keep himself invisible from the FBI manhunt until he chose to strike. Sooner or later, he would appear.

Sooner would be better. If the skinheads were headed to Mercy River, I would be ready. That small town was drawing the remaining enemies together, as if it exerted some sort of evil gravity. As if it wanted to see who would be left standing in the end.

FORTY-FIVE

DRIVING WAS HARDER THAN I had imagined. I had chosen to roll down I-5 and the slightly longer route on Highway 26 out of Portland, counting on speed to make up the difference in time. Taking a more direct route was almost certain to cross paths with Fain and Zeke and Rigo. I didn't want them to know I was coming. Not yet.

Following the relatively straight line of the interstate had been no problem, but the state highway's curves meant moving my arms and shoulders to turn the wheel. Within an hour, the Vicodin I'd taken couldn't keep pace with the throbbing in my chest. I realized I was sweating when the blowing AC made me shiver. As if taking pity, the next highway sign promised a rest stop in six miles.

I parked the Dodge between two moving vans and waited in line as a family with sugar-crazed young children finished at the restroom sinks. A red cross painted on the side denoted the rest stop pulling double duty for the gentle ski slopes above its parking lot. Too early in the season for snow now, but the way station was still busy with commercial truckers and people getting a jump on the weekend.

I washed my face and felt better. I'd be in Mercy River before night-fall. One more pill, one more cup of coffee, and I'd go the distance.

As I exited the restroom, a white-and-red Chevy Tahoe pulled off the eastbound highway into the rest stop.

I reversed direction, walking around the long A-frame of the building and into the trees nearby. Concealment. Evasion. I was in no shape for a fight.

The Tahoe parked twenty yards off. Peroxide and another goon with an oily black ponytail and denim jacket clambered eagerly from the back. The muscle-bound skinhead who'd shot at me in Chinatown rolled himself out from behind the driver's seat. A moment later, Jaeger stepped out of the passenger's side.

Had they followed me? Doubtful. I'd hit the rest stop at least ten miles ahead of them, and had kept a close watch when I'd filled the truck's gas tank near Longview. They weren't looking around the rest stop parking lot like they expected to find me.

There were only so many roads into central Oregon, fewer as you drew closer. My bad luck to pick the same route and time as the men who wanted to kill me.

The three thugs began walking toward the building with the restrooms. Jaeger stayed where he was, by the open door of their car, apparently gazing up at the dry slopes of the ski area.

My Dodge was still out of sight between the moving vans. I made my way through the evergreens, and when I was as close as the forest allowed, I stepped from the tree line and walked quickly to the truck, keeping my face averted. The thugs were still inside the men's room. Jaeger still standing by the Tahoe. As motionless as ever.

I could be out of the lot before he spotted me.

But there was a question I wanted to put to the white power leader. Now might be my only chance.

I brought the Dodge around in a big curve—my chest twinging only a little—and flirted briefly with the idea of running the son of a bitch over, witnesses or no witnesses. Instead I pulled up parallel to the Tahoe, only twenty feet away from Jaeger himself.

He turned his head. I was fairly sure he was surprised to see me. It was hard to tell with Jaeger.

"You're even uglier without the mustache," I said.

"Shaw," he said. His eyes flicked in the direction of the building. His thugs weren't in sight, but two carloads of teenagers had descended on the restrooms. "You won't shoot me here." His whispery voice managed to carry over the mountain wind.

"We won't shoot each other. And you'll probably get away before the Feds arrive, if you haul ass."

He glanced at the highway without apparent anxiety. "They can't save you, either. You're already dead. All of you. That fat general and his tainted brood, sneaking away to hide. Perhaps my men will skin them like rabbits."

"You're a fierce bunch, all right. Are those three rejects all that's left of your army?"

The madman actually smiled. A calm lift of the lips, like a teacher being patient with his slowest student. The closest thing to emotion I'd seen from Jaeger.

"We are reborn," he said. "The money we took from you means victory. Land, church, guns. Those who have strayed will return to the fold. Every warrior sent to prison finds a dozen more seeking direction. Incarceration makes fertile soil for our truth. Within a year the First Riders will be ten times as strong as we ever were. Mercy River shall know us again. They must understand the cost of their deceit."

"Understand like Erle? What tipped you off to him?"

Jaeger's smile slid away as quickly as it had arrived. My grin took up the slack.

"You never figured out old Erle was playing both sides, did you?" I said.

"It doesn't matter. The scum was struck down. Just as you will be."

Over his shoulder, I saw the First Riders exit the rest stop. Within seconds they were running toward us across the lot, desperate to protect their leader. Jaeger noticed my divided attention.

"I'll be coming for you, Shaw."

"You won't like what you find," I said, and let my foot fall on the accelerator.

FORTY-SIX

JAEGER HADN'T SUSPECTED ERLE, or killed him. That theory had been superficially confirmed with Constable Wayne Beacham's suicide note, but now that I'd heard it directly from Jaeger himself, other guesses and facts started arranging themselves into a neater order. The picture they formed had me rethinking Beacham's role in Erle's death.

Those notions kept me occupied for the rest of the drive, and even kept my mind off my bruised chest cavity. At least Jaeger would be similarly distracted. The possibility that I'd called in an anonymous sighting on a wanted fugitive at a rest stop on Highway 26 would force the son of a bitch to backtrack and seek another road into Griffon County.

My body wasn't the only thing ailing. The Dodge had begun making a rattling sound on each acceleration. Maybe ignition timing, maybe a valve problem. My truck had over two hundred thousand miles on the odometer, a number I'd added a fair chunk to over the past week.

Mercy River had subsided to its normal drowsy rhythms. Happy hour on a Friday night added only a few more cars cruising the streets. The reader board at the school touted BINGO 5:30, and townspeople were already drifting into the gym.

The inn was even more abandoned than the roads. Most of the room lights were extinguished, including those behind one specific window on the third floor. I made my way around the building and picked the lock of the rear door to walk quietly up the back stairwell.

I didn't know for certain that Daryll had kept his room. But the big man seemed to live at the inn, and I doubted he'd found new accommodations. I stepped lightly down the hall and unlocked the door.

Still his. Tomato juice and protein powder waiting in vain on the dresser, closet full of triple-XL clothes.

No huge duffels full of weapons, however. Damn. I had hoped that Fain's team hadn't taken everything for the score in Seattle. If it came down to a fight with Jaeger and his men, I wanted an M4 or at least a combat shotgun, something with more range than the Browning on my hip.

I checked under the bed. No weapons, but I found plastic storage bins full of a granular powder, and boxes of clay pigeons. I realized the powder must be the phosphorescent explosive they'd made for their shotgun targets. Volatile stuff. It might come in handy. I washed a canister of protein powder down Daryll's sink and filled the canister full of the sand-like mix.

Behind the dead man's hanging clothes, I found a leather carrying case with what was certainly a rifle inside and unzipped it eagerly. I nearly laughed out loud with disappointment. The rifle was a bolt-action Remington with mossy camouflage finish. Not even a scope. The Remington would be great for plinking cans at long distance or hunting for venison, but unsuited for modern warfare.

Beggars and choosers. The rifle was empty. I zipped the case closed and searched the room for .30-06 rounds, only to be let down again. Nothing.

At least I knew where to find plenty of ammunition. Erle's Gun Shop. I slipped out the back of the inn with my new rifle and the canister of flash-bang.

I'D EXPECTED THE GUN shop to be as quiet as the rest of the dead-end road, but as the Dodge rattled to a stop, the door opened and the lean form of Henry Gillespie, Esquire, stepped out of the windowless store. Crap. He motioned to me, and I joined him.

"Would have thought you'd left town," he said, shaking my hand.

"I did. Events brought me back."

"Ah. Wayne's funeral, I expect." His jowly face clouded. "A terrible thing. I still can't understand it. How is Susan?"

I figured Dez would want me to give a publicly acceptable response to her husband's death. "She's holding up."

"Of course."

He stepped aside and ushered me into the shop. With all the lights on—and the bloodstains gone—it was close to welcoming inside.

Paulette stood near the worktables, removing items from the pegboard and adding them to orderly piles in front of her. She wore a white-and-gold sweatshirt with the image of Dolly Parton today instead of the Man in Black. She laughed at the sight of me.

"Look who it is," she said.

Gillespie's head pivoted between us. "You two know one another?"

"He's my protégé in the custodial arts."

An elderly man sat in Erle's office chair. His wizened frame made Gillespie's seem robust by comparison. The clear plastic tube of an oxygen tank looped under his nose and led down to a shoulder bag beside him on the chair. There was room for both the tank and his narrow butt on the chair, with inches to spare.

"Van Shaw, this is Bob Bell," said Gillespie.

"Erle's cousin?" I asked.

"Yes," he said. "Pleasure to meet you."

"Bob and I are trying to determine what to do with all this," Gillespie said, sweeping an arm around the room. "To hold a sale or take a job lot offer from another dealer."

"That's why I came by, to see if the shop was open," I said, lying only a fraction. "I need some ammunition."

Bob Bell's shrug was as light as the flutter of a butterfly. "Whatever you like."

I found a box of .30-06 on the shelves behind the counter and brought it forward.

"Don't mind selling any and all of it, if you've a mind," Bell said to me.

"You're not keeping the shop?"

He gave a wheezing laugh. "Can't run things myself. Henry here doesn't care for guns."

"Maybe you found yourself a buyer, Bob," said Paulette, nudging me. "Go on. Bidding starts at a dollar."

"What about family?" I said. "They could run it for you."

"Hardly any left. Just my boy—my foster son. He's a busy fellow, working with his Army friends here and everything."

A son with the Rally. A local, and a Ranger too, I could assume.

Oh boy.

I was suddenly gaining a new perspective on recent events in Mercy River.

"Your son looks after you," I said to Bell, "over in Grant County?"

Paulette nodded. "I told you Erle's cousin lived there."

"My boy makes the time somehow," said Bell.

"And I'll bet he came to see you while he was on leave from the Rangers, too," I fished.

Gillespie was back to gazing at me oddly.

"That's right," Bell said. "I'm proud of him. Served his country and he volunteers here to boot. Better to help young Army families than my old carcass."

I placed a fifty on the counter. Bell waved, barely removing his hand from the armrest.

"Take the bullets. I meant what I said. Everything must go."

My private tour of Erle's garage popped into my head.

"I need a car," I said. "My truck out there is about down for the count." I couldn't have the Dodge giving out on me at a bad moment.

"Erle did have a couple of vehicles," Bell said. "I'll beat Blue Book price on 'em."

Paulette encompassed every sly thing in the world in her grin.

"I expect I know which vehicle our friend here would like," she said.

I expected I knew, too.

FORTY-SEVEN

TWILIGHT EDGED THE SKY toward its tipping point. Dark enough that, from my vantage on the crest of the long hill two hundred yards above General Macomber's house, I could make out the shapes of amber lampshades behind drawn curtains. But still light enough that fingers of smoke drifting from the chimney of his little cave-like dwelling showed white against the black asphalt of the road beyond.

No shadows passed the windows. Macomber wasn't fool enough to expose himself. The more I considered the house, the more its inviting glow seemed like just that—an invitation.

I switched my focus to the hillside itself. Judging which outcroppings of rock and clumps of scrubby trees might offer the best cover, the best angles.

One spot stood out, about halfway down the slope. A squat boulder had rolled down the hill on some long-ago day and been trapped in a copse of pine trees, which had grown around and over the rock. Not only did the boulder and trees offer a good line of sight to the rear and side of Macomber's house, it was a few quick steps from another rocky prominence with better coverage of the front of the house and the road. That would be my choice, if I aimed to keep watch.

I retreated behind the hill and made my careful way along its crest, until I'd gone far enough to risk another look. The boulder was below me now, off to the right. No longer visible in the growing dark and with the thick scrub in the way. But the pine trees above it marked the spot. I tightened the strap of the rifle case over my back and crawled over the crest of the hill.

The surface was more dirt than loose rock, which helped to silence my movements as I moved slowly down the slope. Thickets of brush made good cover. Belly-flat and face-first down the hill, like a spider. The angle actually eased the constant throb in my chest a little, encouraging new blood flow into the clotted bruise. I stopped every few feet to listen.

Perhaps half an hour had elapsed since I'd started my descent. Slow enough progress that the chirrup of crickets around me never ceased. No hurry at all. If I was right about my guess, and too hasty to confirm it, I might catch a bullet in the head as a prize.

Twenty yards from the boulder, I heard a shift of boot on sand. Someone adjusting their position for comfort. I waited, the minutes stretching out. The sound didn't reoccur. Whoever it was, they were good at keeping silent. But not as good as me.

I inched forward. Ten feet away now. I lay in a short ditch. A worm's-eye view. Close enough that the shapes of the trees and the boulder were distinct against the night sky. And the man. I clocked him as he turned, a skull-crusher harness on his head holding his night vision in place, the goggle of the NOD like a stunted horn.

It wouldn't be Macomber or the wounded Fain taking watch, and this guy didn't have enough hair to be Zeke Caton.

"Rigo," I whispered.

A scrape and a thump, as he hit the deck. He didn't speak.

"Hold your fire," I said. "It's Shaw."

"The fuck?" his harsh whisper came back. "Show yourself."

I raised my hands above the ditch. "Peace." A soft click as Rigo adjusted his opticals to get a look at me in the darkness. He spat out a string of impassioned and impressive curses.

"You've got a damn death wish, Shaw. I could have blown your head off."

The reverse was also true, and we both knew it.

"I want to talk to you," I said.

"You snuck up on me for a conversation? You're warped."

"Watching the house for Jaeger was my original plan, but you got here first."

Rigo hummed assent. "The enemy of my enemy is a friend, that it?"

"That depends on who you think the bad guys are."

He shifted his position to watch the house. His whispered answer, when it came, was all the softer from him being turned away. "Not you. The captain shouldn't have burned you, Shaw. It was wrong."

Rigoberto wasn't his usual taciturn self. Maybe it was being away from the group, or being in the dark. Or he was keyed up for the coming fight.

"I gave Fain hell about it," he said. "Never yelled at an officer before. But that doesn't make up for leaving you there. Is Pak okay?"

"Yeah. I cut him loose, him and his girl."

"Jesus." He said it like he was giving thanks. "I been checking the news. We didn't get anybody killed in Seattle."

"I know."

"I've been holding on tight to that fact. I was a cop. Once. And now I'm the guy shooting at cops. Not to take them down, but how the fuck would they have known that? Daryll's dead. Fain damn near. He won't go to the hospital. And we left brothers behind. Worst day of my life, Shaw. Worse than Nangarhar or even Tangi Valley. No damn question."

"But you haven't left."

A moment passed. "You're here, too, man. Is that just to save your own skin?"

"No."

"What, then? Not to back us up."

"Is the plan to kill Jaeger when he approaches the house?"

"Snake rears its head, you have to cut it off." Rigo said it so fast, I wondered if he had been repeating the thought like a mantra. "Right?"

I didn't have an answer for that, either. The former police officer, trying to stay on the side of the good guys any way he could. Talking himself into crossing a point of no return.

"Are Fain and the others in the house?" I said.

"Ready to light it up. Macomber, too, if it comes to it."

"When you change shifts, I'll go down with you."

He finally turned away from the road. "You're not killing Fain. No matter what he did to you, we will stop that shit cold."

"I'm not here for Fain, either. I have to talk to your team about something else. And I need your help."

I laid it out for him. The swearing Rigo had done before was nothing compared to what came out of his mouth now. But he listened.

FORTY-EIGHT

GENERAL MACOMBER LET RIGO and me in through the sliding glass door.

"Sergeant," he said, flat-footed at the sight of me. "Unpredictable as always."

We walked into the dining room of the house, where an assortment of shotguns and pistols were laid out on bath towels on the oval table. The metal barrels glinted under the teardrop lights of the hanging chandelier.

Zeke carried a CamelBak filled with water, ready for his watch on the hill.

"What the fuck is Shaw doing here?" he said.

"An alliance, I hope," Fain said from his seat in the overstuffed easy chair, his words hardly audible over the spruce logs crackling softly in the fire next to him.

"We could use good news," Macomber agreed. The old bear moved a little more slowly than usual. The fringe of hair around his ears was unkempt.

"I ran into Jaeger and three of his men on the highway," I said. "He'll assume I called the FBI on him."

Fain hummed thoughtfully. "Then he'll be forced to take back roads to get here. And he'll be even more cautious." If the general was tired, Fain appeared six long steps past that. The waxy tone of his skin had jaundiced.

"You let Jaeger go? Again?" Zeke looked at the general. "We don't need this pussy."

"Yeah, we do," Rigo said, handing his carbine with its night scope to Zeke. "It could be days before Jaeger makes a move. We can't cover the house in two shifts and stay sharp."

"That's Daryll's deer rifle," Fain said as I set the leather carrying case on the table. "Where did you get that?"

"From his room. I didn't think he'd mind my aiming it at Jaeger."

"A good choice if you're defending covered wagons." At death's door, Fain had acquired a sense of humor. Their team was full of new tricks tonight.

"Jaeger might decide Mercy River is too hot and change his destination," I said. "He's also after your family, General. Are they still with relatives?"

"Yes. But not at their home."

"You can't assume that's enough. Jaeger has time and plenty of money. If he can't find your family himself, he can bribe someone who can. Or hire people to track them, if they're on the move and using credit cards or bank machines. It's not difficult."

"I'll call them," Macomber said. "Make sure they know what to do. In the meantime, our best chance to take Jaeger is here, on home ground. I appreciate your coming here to warn us."

"I also wanted to ask you some questions."

"I got to get into position," Zeke said, headed for the back door.

"Hold up. You'll want to be here for this." I turned to Fain. "That morning Erle was shot. You and Zeke met at the coffeehouse when it opened. You saw Constable Wayne up at the top of the dead-end road."

"Those aren't questions," Fain said.

"Then Erle texted to say the coast was clear."

"Yes, dammit."

"Did you read the text?"

He started to answer, then stopped and thought again. "No. But I was there when Zeke's phone beeped."

"Okay. So Zeke received a text, and walked up to the road, but by then Henry Gillespie was bending Wayne's ear. Yeah?" I prompted Zeke.

"That's right," he said.

Fain nodded. "I saw the old man there, too."

"So when did Wayne shoot Erle?" I said.

They looked at one another.

"I don't follow you," Macomber said.

"If Erle sent Zeke that text, and the constable was in sight the whole time, then Wayne couldn't have been the killer."

"But Wayne Beacham confessed," the general said, "in his suicide note."

"If it *was* a suicide note," I said. "Let's put it together. Erle turned off the security cameras when he arrived at the gun shop. He'd stashed the box of Trumo in his personal bunker, up in the forest behind his shop."

"Damn. No wonder we didn't find it," said Rigo.

"I expect Erle planned to take his ATV up the hill and retrieve the box. He wouldn't want that captured on camera and sent into the cloud. It could be used against him someday. But he was murdered before he could leave."

"By Beacham," said Fain.

"No. Constable Wayne was already up at the top of the road with the owner of the dress store. They saw Erle pass them on his way. It's in his report. Then forty minutes later, Zeke gets that text. Gillespie arrives. Erle wasn't shot after that, not by Wayne or anyone else. Gillespie didn't hear any gunshot. The lawyer's old, but he's sharp, and his hearing is fine."

Macomber frowned. "Perhaps the constable simply lied on his report, and managed to slip away from the dress store long enough to shoot Erle before Gillespie arrived."

"Then who sent Zeke the text," I said, "if Erle was already dead?"

I waited. The surviving members of Macomber's crew exchanged uncertain glances.

"There's only one answer," I said. "Wayne sent Zeke the message. Zeke killed Erle Sharples, with Wayne's help. They were working together."

"FUCK OFF," ZEKE SAID to me. "I didn't shoot anybody. Wayne did it."

"No," I said. "You were Erle's guy. He turned off his cameras that morning, as expected. You were behind the gun shop, watching the electrical feed to the rear camera. I found the stripped wire, and the impressions left by the alligator clips from a meter. When the power dimmed, you knew it was safe. You went in through the back door in coveralls and paper boots and you killed Erle with the gun from Leo's workbench. You took the burner phone Erle had been using to communicate with you. You hid the bloody clothes next door and ran to meet Fain at the coffeehouse at seven o'clock. Wayne was already parked up at the top of the dead-end street. My guess is that Wayne had vandalized that window himself the night before, to give himself a reason for being there. Wayne was your lookout. And you were going to be his. Fair trade."

I crossed the living room to Fain. "The text Zeke got when you were at the coffeehouse wasn't from Erle. It was from Wayne. The go signal. You can see a long way south on Main Street from the dress store. Once Wayne saw Leo coming, he texted Zeke. Zeke would join him on Larimer Road. Wayne would follow Leo into the shop and kill him. Both Wayne and Zeke would swear they heard the shot that killed Erle. But then Gillespie wandered onto the scene and screwed their plan. They couldn't pretend Leo had killed Erle anymore. Erle was dead, but they never got their crack at Leo."

"This is bullshit," Zeke said. "I got no reason to do any of that. Pak's my boy."

"Leo was a sacrifice," I said, "to Wayne. Wayne wanted his wife back, or at least wanted her lover dead. He probably hoped to get a slice of Erle's fortune in the bargain, if he could stave off the divorce. But he was wrong about getting the money. Maybe you misled him, Zeke."

"Erle was working for us, Shaw," Macomber said. He stepped from the dining table to Zeke, a show of solidarity. "The Rally. Caton wouldn't jeopardize that."

Zeke held the carbine in the crook of his elbow, the butt of the stock under his arm. As relaxed as a cat in sunshine. "Wayne killed Erle. Anything else is a fairy tale."

"I met Bob Bell today," I said.

Zeke's stubbled face drew tight.

"Bob Bell?" Macomber asked.

"He's Erle's cousin, over in Grant County. The man who just inherited everything Erle owns. The gun shop, a couple of million that Erle snaked by marrying Cecily Desidra, and whatever other money he might have squirreled away from dealing arms to Nazi shitheads. Bell gets it all, for however long his health holds out, which might be counted in weeks." I folded my arms. "Bob Bell is also Zeke's foster father."

Everyone had turned to Zeke. Zeke was focused on me.

"So what?" he said.

"Everybody knows everybody here," I said. "You told me that yourself, Zeke. You're Bob Bell's kid. You played football with star quarterback Wayne Beacham. You were friends, or at least you knew him well enough to bond over your shared problem, Erle Sharples. Wayne would be rich if Erle hadn't swiped Dez's inheritance. You'd be rich soon if Erle was dead. I'm guessing Wayne got enough drinks in him one night to sob on your shoulder about Leo screwing his wife, and you started thinking how you and the town constable could help each other. Alibi each other."

"Wayne confessed, dickhead."

"He died. He didn't confess. I think Wayne's death was inevitable. You weren't going to trust him to keep quiet about Erle's murder, especially once he missed the chance to kill Leo in return. You weren't going to share Erle's money, either, no matter what you might have told him. Wayne was always going to be your fall guy."

I pointed to Fain. "The bloody clothes were left where they would be found eventually. You stumbled on them first."

"It was odd, the clothes dumped in plain sight like that," Fain mused. "I said that to you at the time."

"Hey, I heard what the cops found, too," Zeke said. "Wayne's fucking footprints in the boots. That's conclusive."

"Prints from a worn pair of dress shoes," I said. "Not the spit-and-polish pride that the constable usually showed. That was the second thing, after Erle's missing cell phone, that seemed out of place to me. Wayne's body had dirty shoes on a sharp dress uniform. You'd been thinking about framing Wayne for a while, but you didn't think hard enough.

"It's not tough to guess the rest. When the time came, you gave Wayne a drink with a couple of his prescription Halcion ground up into it. The rest of the pills washed down his throat after. Drive him out to Dez's house and set him up there with the note. It couldn't have been hard to get copies of his unusual handwriting. Who would check that close? Any shakiness could be chalked up to the drugs and booze."

"You guys aren't buying this crap." Zeke looked around.

"But you *are* gonna be rich," Rigo said to Zeke from his place by the fire. "Right? I keep getting stuck on why you didn't tell us about this family connection with Erle before."

"Who had the idea for Leo to be your plant at Erle's Gun Shop?" I said.

"Zeke," said Rigo.

I turned to Fain. "Who suggested that you and Zeke meet that morning at the coffeehouse, where Wayne would be in plain sight?"

Fain kept his eyes on Zeke. Same answer.

"None of that means anything," Zeke snarled.

"Leo means something," Rigo said. "Daryll did, too. Maybe none of this last week would have gone down like it did without you."

Fain hissed, not entirely from pain.

"If Shaw is right, you used me to set up Leo," he said. "Used me to try and murder him. And you've told us a dozen times in the past week how Shaw couldn't be trusted. That he might flip Pak to turn us in. Poison dripped in our ears."

"There's an easy way to clear the air," Macomber said. "Caton, give us your cell phone. The one with the text from Erle, telling you it was safe to go to the gun shop. If that checks out, so do you."

Zeke scoffed. "I destroyed that. After Erle died, it would be stupid to keep it around. Who are you going to believe?"

"It doesn't matter," I said, taking out my phone. "Fain can give me the cell numbers. I've got a friend who will chase down the records. Times and content of every text between Zeke and Erle. We'll check Wayne's messages, too. I'll bet he got a little careless. Maybe even incriminating."

"You're well connected," Fain said.

"I wasn't always a soldier," I reminded him.

Zeke was nearly as pale as Fain. His eyes flicked between me and Rigo. Rigo's hands were empty. Mine, too, except for my phone.

"It's not true," he said.

I started dialing.

"He's lying," Zeke said, turning to the general. "He's a fucking outsider."

"We'll know soon enough," said Macomber, his hands on his hips.

Zeke practically vibrated with frustration and fury. A pine knot popped in the fireplace.

With that same fluid motion as his quick draw, Zeke spun and shouldered the carbine and pointed it at my chest. Metal tap-tapped on metal, his trigger finger reflexively pulling a rapid-fire burst until his mind caught up with a hard fact.

"Empty," Rigo said, patting his pocket where he'd placed the rounds from the carbine.

Zeke stared at him, looking almost hurt.

"You'd have had to kill us all," Fain said to him. "But you knew that."

Zeke's eyes cut to the table, and the line of waiting pistols.

"Fuck it," he said, and dropped the carbine. His hand was halfway to the nearest Glock when General Macomber shot him above the ear with a compact pistol he'd drawn from the small of his back. Zeke's head snapped to the left and he fell to his knees atop the carbine. As if going to sleep, he leaned slowly to one side, falling against the wall and sliding to rest facedown.

FORTY-NINE

RIGO HAD HIS OWN Glock in his hand. My Browning was already leveled. But Macomber had beaten us both to the draw. We all stared at Zeke Caton's prone body. His arms lay at his sides, almost in a posture of standing at attention. Blood dribbled out from his shaggy hair to drip on the gray flagstone floor. The flow was already diminishing.

"I'm sorry, General," Fain said.

"So am I," said Macomber. He placed the little pistol on the table and sat down heavily.

Rigo holstered his weapon. "Goddamn." He looked at me. "When you told me your suspicions up on the hill, I thought you were dog nuts."

"I wasn't sure," I said. "I had to see if Zeke would crack."

Fain hissed again. When the pain subsided, he managed to talk through gasps. "Shaw. Do you truly have a way to check those cell records?"

"No."

He exhaled. "I don't know whether to thank you or curse you."

"Thank him," Macomber said. "If Caton was willing to let Pak die, I don't know what he might have decided about the rest of us. We've committed enough crimes to hang one another. Without trust we are lost."

"If we live," Rigo said. He picked up the dropped carbine, popped its magazine, and withdrew a fistful of rounds from his pocket to begin reloading.

"I won't," said Fain. "I can't even stand. But there's time for the three of you to get away. To make sure Aaron and Schuyler are safe."

"We're not leaving you," Macomber said. Rigo agreed, without looking up from his task.

Fain took a moment to breathe. "Gentlemen, I respect the hell out of each of you. I include you in that, Shaw. I took you for a coward; I'm truly sorry. But I'm done. If I go into the hospital or even turn up in a morgue, there will be questions you can't answer. That the Rally can't answer."

"The Rally is finished, Captain," said Macomber, looking at where Zeke lay. The firelight gave the body the illusion of movement. "I built it on sand. It has to crumble."

"So rebuild. Start it again the right way. Call it my dying wish, if it helps."

"John."

"Go to hell," Fain said through gritted teeth. "Sir."

"This place isn't secure, General," said Rigo, as he moved to check the street from the front window.

"Go," I said to Macomber. "Protect your family. I'll stay with Fain."

"Pointless," Fain started to say, but I shot him a glance that said, *Wait.*

"What do you need?" Rigo said, motioning to the table.

"Hand me one of the shotguns," I said, "and leave the NOD."

Rigo and I went out the back and circled the house in opposite directions, around to the front to make sure the road was clear. I covered him as he started the general's Lincoln and drove it across the arid lawn to the front door.

"Good luck, Sergeant," Macomber said. I shook his proffered hand without taking my eyes off the road. "I don't know how to thank you, or what I can do—"

"Do what Fain said. Rebuild. You've got a whole wall full of guys and their families who need the Rally. It may be tainted now, but it doesn't have to stay that way."

I moved back to the open doorway and waited as the Town Car swung in a circle over the lawn and onto the pavement. Macomber got in. Rigo and I nodded to each other through the windshield.

In a moment the Lincoln was out of sight, heading away from the heart of Mercy River. I watched until I was sure no one was following it, and then slipped back into the little cave of the house.

One dead man on the floor. Another soon to follow in the chair. Fain seemed to have burned the last of his reserves in the excitement. His breath was even, but his head lolled in semiconsciousness.

I bolted the back door and checked that the blinds were closed at every window, and turned out all the lights except one small lamp near Fain. By the time I returned to the living room, he'd come to.

"You're not here to guard me," he said in a whisper.

"No."

"Revenge, then? For Seattle? I don't know what you could do to me—"

"No. Disinformation is what I had in mind."

He looked blank for a moment. Then a sickly grin unfurled on his sallow face. "You'll leave me for Jaeger. So that I'll tell him—what?"

"That I betrayed you all. That I'm on my way to Pronghorn to dig up the armored car money from where you stashed it and drop General Macomber into the mine shaft at the same time." I glanced toward Zeke Caton's corpse. "That should help sell the story."

Fain made a noise. A kind of laughter. "I'm understanding better why your COs wanted you back in their platoons. To keep a close eye on you."

"Can you do it?" I said.

"I'll stay alive for a full month, if it means screwing Jaeger. But get me a piece of paper. I'll write a note that will tell him the money's at the mine. Just in case."

I put a pillow and a large book on his lap, so Fain didn't have to move his hand much to scrawl. In ten minutes, he'd finished, and his head drifted back onto the chair. I collected the shotgun and Daryll's rifle. As an afterthought, I took a hatchet from a bucket of kindling wood on the hearth. The last thing I did before leaving was open the front door wide. Encouraging visitors to come right in.

Fain raised a hand off the chair's armrest as I passed him.

"Go with God, Shaw," he said.

Tomorrow, maybe. Tonight I had too many sins ahead of me.

FIFTY

HOLLIS CALLED ME AT one minute after midnight, just as I reached the stretch of road outside Pronghorn that followed the river. I couldn't see it in the dark, not even by the bright starlight, but I could hear water rushing over rocks and swirling against the tree roots at its shore. The river must be running high and fast for the sound to carry over the Barracuda's throaty engine, and the wind whistling past the open window.

I pulled over to the side of the cracked pavement and killed the lights. It took me an extra second. I wasn't used to the controls in my new car yet.

"Hollis?" I said.

"Van. I'm never sure if this time of night is late or early for you," he said.

"You called it right tonight." I stepped out and took the shotgun with me. "Any later and I wouldn't have a signal."

"You're working, then. Good, good."

"What's wrong?"

"Nothing. Not on this end. Just . . . after all of the bedlam during the past few days, I felt the need to check in. Premonitions, maybe. Are you well?"

I walked down to the river's edge, feeling the grind of rocks shifting under my soles. The water was visible only through the absence of light. A wide dark ribbon that made its speed known by sound and by the smell of clean droplets thrown into the air. I took in a lungful. Breathing hardly hurt at all.

"I'm all right," I said to Hollis. "My chest is healing."

"That's a blessing. Luce asked after you."

"Tell her I've recovered. Scratch that, I'll call her myself." I could apologize—again—for being a jackass.

Hollis chuckled. "It's just as well. I never—"

"Hang on."

I set down the phone and listened closely. The night enveloped a lot of sounds. Splashing water. Frogs in the marshes. The slow tick of the car's engine cooling. Nothing else.

"I'm back," I said.

"And busy, right. I'll leave you to it."

"Hollis."

"Yes?"

"Did Dono ever kill anyone?"

The pause was long enough for me to count five ticks of the engine.

"Why do you ask?" Hollis said. "No, never mind—not the point. And it's over the phone, for heaven's sake." There was another pause. I let him think.

"You don't speak much about your time overseas," he said finally. "Not to me, at any rate. I'm not sure which of us that's meant to shield, but no matter. Your grandfather, now. He was much the same. Close to the vest."

"About when he was young."

"About a lot of things. His family in Belfast. His life during the Troubles. I learned more about those times from your grandmother in the short years I knew her than I did in the decades I was Dono's friend."

"I can see that."

"Most of all, Dono didn't talk about crimes he'd done before I knew him. On the rare occasions that I would ask, he'd sidestep. Or tell me to shut it, depending on the day. But we both know what sorts of jobs he was suspected of. Sometimes convicted of."

Armed robbery. Weapons charges. Assault with intent. Everything short of the big M-One.

All crimes I'd committed myself in the past two days alone.

"Of course, this was back when police were more inclined to grab the collar of the sorry fellow nearest them, or find the same man they'd pinched last week, instead of running down clues and worrying about lawsuits," Hollis said. "So I take rumors with a grain of salt."

"You're stalling, Hollis," I said.

"I know I am. It's a hard thing to say."

The engine had gone silent.

"Yes," he said. "I believe Dono killed someone. More than one. Between his temper and his . . ."

"Savagery."

"*Instincts* was what I was grasping at, but yes. That. Compare those unfortunate traits with the decision he made later in life to avoid guns, and yes. I think your man killed people, maybe innocent people, and it weighed heavy on him. Perhaps more than he ever thought it would. He rejected the Church early on, so he didn't fear any eternal damnation. His suffering was more earthly than that."

"Dreams," I said. "That's where it has teeth."

"I understand."

"Thanks, Hollis."

"You're all right, then? Is there anything I can do?"

"You just did it."

I hung up.

My grandfather and I had last spoken when I was barely eighteen. Still a kid in most ways, even if life had shoved a few lessons down my throat early on. Dono and I had never talked as adults. I wondered if he would have ever shared what made him turn that corner in his life. What he might have said about my dreams, and I about his. Comparing the weight of our souls.

A mosquito buzzed around me. I caught it before it found my neck. After listening again for the sound of any pursuit, I got into the car and made it howl on the road into the rocky hills.

FIFTY-ONE

UNDER THE STARS, THE barren buildings of Pronghorn stood like pieces of sculpture, as if their serrated boards and gaping holes had been deliberately shaped instead of succumbing to time's pitiless gnawing. The Rally had kept its promise to leave the ghost town's fields unscathed. Except for the occasional hard crunch of a brass shell under my foot, there was no indication that any man had walked here in years.

The warning signs at the mouth of the mining road had been stamped on simple steel rectangles. It took me about ten minutes to cake the signs with mud scooped from a nearby ditch. When I'd finished, the signs were unreadable, and virtually camouflaged against the rock wall of the massive cliff behind them.

Driving up the mining road in the dark was, in its way, less nerve-wracking than in daytime. It was easy to see the path, and harder to be distracted by the yawning chasm that awaited any mistake. I made the Barracuda hug the cliff wall, climbing the road up and around the gigantic column of rock at no more than a walking pace.

When I reached the opposite side of the butte, I stopped the car. The driver's door opened less than a foot before it tapped rock. I picked up the hatchet I'd taken from Macomber's house off the passenger's seat, squeezed myself out through the gap, and went for a walk.

The walls of the colossal rock—orange-red in sunlight, chalk-and-charcoal now—had been pockmarked by eons of erosion. I examined the crags in the cliffside above, stopping my walk every few feet to check again. Staring up the rock wall made my head swim. I could feel the waiting drop a few short steps behind me.

When I had gone far enough up the curving road to be out of sight of the car, I spotted an overhang on the cliff wall above. A ledge, no more than a yard wide. Perhaps a hundred feet above where I stood, and less than half that distance below the very top of the butte.

The mining road was especially narrow here on the northern half of the rock. Eleven or twelve feet, no more. Looking west, I could see a clear mile of the dirt road far below, leading up from the valley and the river beyond and winding its way into Pronghorn.

This felt right. Not perfect, but there wasn't time for perfect.

I walked back to the car to get the night-vision goggles and a couple of other things. I gave the cliff face and the ledge above another careful assessment using the NOD, examining its surface in shades of green and making sure it would work. I marked the position, so I could easily find it again from the top of the butte.

Then I used the hatchet to hollow dirt from a pitted hole in the wall, at about eye level. Not a large hole, only about a foot square, but large enough to hold what I placed there.

Five minutes later I was back in the Barracuda and continuing my slow drive to the top.

There were no trees on the broad flat surface of the butte, only the occasional clump of brush hanging on for dear life in the eternal wind. I parked the car close to the mine shaft, or what remained of it. The shaft's entrance was no more than a shallow pit so barred and boarded up that a rat couldn't have found its way deeper inside. Fifty paces past the sealed mine was the cliff's edge. I stepped up to it—carefully—and looked down until I found the ledge. Close enough to see it clearly in the starlight, and far enough that climbing down to it seemed like madness itself.

Like the man said: Let's go crazy. Let's get nuts.

I'd transferred my tools and other possessions from my ailing pickup to the trunk of the Barracuda. From a flat storage bin, I removed a fifty-meter coil of thick nylon rope I kept for towing or for strapping things to the truck's roof, and a pair of leather work gloves. In the toolbox I found a large D-shaped carabiner.

I got back in and drove the car to the right spot, parallel to the cliff's edge, a scant ten feet from the drop. I made very sure to set the parking brake.

The rope went around the Barracuda's bumper. I cut off a length to fashion a sling around my waist and thighs. Not as comfortable as a harness, but it would serve. The carabiner snapped to a small loop I'd made in front.

I threaded the end of the long rope around the bumper through the carabiner and looped it back again, so that the rope circled the metal ring. It took a few moments to pull the full length through the carabiner. I leaned back, testing the tension. The rope stretched taut between the car's bumper and the metal carabiner. It held. If I pulled the rope out to the side with my right hand, I could feed myself slack and move backward in a controlled fall, a few inches at a time.

It was as safe as I could make it. I slung Daryll's rifle in its case over my back and tightened the strap, and then did the same with a small rucksack over the rifle case before putting on the leather gloves.

I left the shotgun lying on the ground, under the front bumper of the car. It wouldn't do me any good down on the ledge. If the situation became so desperate that I needed a shotgun, the Barracuda would offer the only cover up here on the barren roof of the world.

I began to walk backward toward the edge, slowly, keeping heavy tension on the rope.

The cliff's edge wasn't sharp, but a brief slope that swiftly grew steeper until it was vertical. I shuffled backward, bending at the waist.

I didn't spare much thought for the void below me. Falling from this height, I would probably miss the mining road entirely and plummet all the way down into the ravine.

I concentrated on moving in a steady rhythm. Grip the rope in front of me with my left hand, step back with my right foot, feed myself a few inches of rope with my right hand, step with my left foot, move the left hand again. My chest pinged with pain, angry at the sudden exercise. I ignored it. Soon the soles of my hiking boots were touching the upright cliff face, and the rope was touching rock as it curved up and over the edge to the anchoring car.

Hand, foot, hand, foot. The sling dug into my kidneys. My chest throbbed every time my muscles contracted over the bruise. Hard enough that I had to force myself to breathe deeply, against the pain. Hand, foot, hand, foot.

I allowed myself a look. The ledge was another twenty feet down, and slightly to my right. I edged over until I was directly above it, and let my hands relax. The rope hissed through the carabiner as I slid down to safety.

The ledge was bliss. A full yard at its widest and three times that in length. I sat down and knotted the rope around my waist and let my breathing return to normal. It took much longer than usual.

I blinked spots from my eyes to check my watch. The luminescent hands read two-fifteen. Would Jaeger show before daylight? Was Fain still alive? No way to know. No need to worry. I'd done all I could.

I took off the ruck and the rifle case and set them on the ledge. The ruck held two bottles of water and the NOD scope and field glasses and my Browning, along with the box of .30-06 ammo from Erle's shop. I'd considered test-firing the rifle but had discarded the idea. The sound of the shots would carry out here. A warning that might be heard for miles. I drank half a bottle, the water feeling perfect on my throat.

If Rigo had driven through the night with Macomber, they could be out of the state by now. The general's son and daughter-in-law would be safe soon. I hoped Macomber would follow through and make the Rally legit. They did good work.

So had I, with the money I'd stolen last summer. Or acquired, given that I'd taken it from people who'd stolen it themselves, most of them dead by the time the money came into my hands. That was the difference. I wouldn't risk anyone's life but my own. Generals sent their soldiers.

The stars began to fade in the east. I drank more water, and kept a watch on the dirt road, where it slithered across the plain far below. A family of deer picked their delicate way out of the trees alongside the road, almost a single drifting entity at this distance. Something caught the herd's attention and they vanished like mist.

Somewhere far beyond the Blue Mountains the world was warming. It gave encouragement to the wind, which pushed at the strap on the rifle case, as if eager to get started. Each gust of wind wailed faintly as it felt its way around the mountainous rock.

As the first touch of sunlight crested the hills I caught an answering bright dot, a mile to the west. I raised the field glasses. The dot split into headlights, and the lights became bookends to a large flat grille. The new dawn was far enough along to show the pale vehicle's stripe as red instead of merely dark.

They were here.

As I watched through the glasses, the Tahoe wound its way over the plain. Driving fast enough to kick up dust on each turn.

If Fain had lived long enough, he would have told Jaeger that I'd just left. But if he had died before the skinheads reached Macomber's house, Jaeger wouldn't know how much of a head start I'd gotten on the money. Maybe they feared I was already gone. The Tahoe sped out of sight behind the butte, hurtling toward what remained of Pronghorn.

Good.

I unzipped the rifle case and drew out the bolt-action Remington. For covered wagons, Fain had said. Gunfight at the O.K. Corral. I filled its magazine with four rounds and drew back the bolt to load a final round in the chamber. I looped the rifle's strap around my arm and lay down flat on the ledge.

The rock warmed quickly under my body. I inched sideways until the right side of my torso hung half off of the ledge. I wasn't worried about slipping off. The rope knotted around my waist wasn't taut, but it wouldn't let me fall far.

I didn't want to lose the gun, though. That would be bad.

Daryll had equipped his deer rifle with a simple tang sight, a tiny circle on a short column that flipped up on a hinge. I sighted it to zero elevation and windage. Neither should be a concern. I would be shooting straight down at no more than a hundred feet. As easy as anything. But I'd only have time for one shot, firing a weapon I'd never held before.

I lay very still and breathed easily. The rock ledge pressed on my bruised chest, but the slight pain didn't disturb me. In another minute I heard the Tahoe's engine, revving high as it climbed the mining road. A moment later the sounds of its tires chewing dirt joined in.

I didn't turn my head in the direction of the Tahoe. It would come. I didn't need to check if Jaeger was inside it. He would be. I stared down, both eyes open, right eye focused through the sights of the Winchester.

A red and white blur appeared in the corner of my vision, and quickly expanded. Moving fast, despite the treacherous road. Would they glance up? See me? Stop?

The Tahoe's hood came sharply into focus. Almost below me now.

I exhaled.

Squeezed the trigger.

The canister of explosive powder erupted like a second sun from the cliff. White light lanced my eyes and the sonic boom nearly tumbled me from the ledge. The flash receded nearly as fast as it had come, leaving vibrant red spots in my eyes. In my ears, the combined screams of grinding metal, of engine pistons, of human voices. Those clearest of all.

Through the haze in my vision, I watched the Tahoe roll and tumble down the ravine to smash against a giant black tooth of volcanic rock with a sound like a tin can crushed underfoot, its horrible swift momentum spinning the truck up and over the rock and down again, out of sight into the waiting maw.

One more distant muffled drumbeat of metal and glass followed, much farther away. Then silence.

Not quite silence. A steady insect whine persisted in my eardrums, the residue of the blast. I sat up carefully, unsure of my balance. My forehead and arm stung. I brushed away pebbles and dirt embedded in my skin. By the time my hands, operating mostly on their own, had repacked the rucksack and rifle case, and unknotted the rope from around my waist, I felt reattached to the earth.

Climbing back to the top of the cliff was almost easy. A tsunami rush of adrenaline lent me strength and a little too much urgency. My chest burned and I told it to fuck off. I had to force myself not to clamber recklessly up the rope, to stop every few feet and secure the lines around my belt as a safety measure. When I reached the cliff edge I hauled myself over the top in one pull and rolled to stand, already unclipping the metal carabiner.

Throwing the rifle and ruck and rope into the backseat, I started the Barracuda's engine and reversed it into a wide turn, to aim the car back down the mining road.

The explosion of the flash-bang canister had tinted the road and cliff face with waved stripes of yellow powder. If any part of the can had been spared obliteration, I couldn't see it. The next real rain would wash away most of the visible evidence.

I stopped the car at the spot where the Tahoe's fall had torn away a slim chunk of the road's edge, making it that much narrower. Stepping out onto the three feet of remaining earth between the car and the drop, I hung on to the Barracuda's door and looked down into the ravine.

I could make out one fender and a torn flap of roof on the Tahoe, far below. Most of what remained of the devastated vehicle was hidden behind a wall of serrated boulders. Two hundred and fifty feet down from where I stood, but not straight down. Its shattering drop had thrown the truck and the men within it a few degrees to the left.

Pieces—a taillight, a ragged chunk of door, hundreds of glittering bits of glass along with half of the rear window—had been wrenched from the Tahoe when it struck the black tooth of rock on the way down.

And a leg. A human leg, just barely in sight on the steep incline behind the black rock, the sole of its shoe pointed up toward me.

It moved.

I reached into the car for the rope and tied it around the steering column. Before casting the rope down into the chasm, I clipped the Browning to my belt.

The side of the ravine wasn't sheer like the butte above. I could step backward down its slope, digging my feet into the gravel for purchase. The rope reached most of the way to the black volcanic rock. Nearer, I could see where the crashing Tahoe had crumbled the rock's knife edges and slashed its face with white and red paint. I held on to the black pillar as I climbed step by careful step around it.

The leg belonged to Jaeger. He must have been thrown clear. Spared—if that was the right word—the plummet into the bottom of the abyss with his men.

He lay on his back, in a position of repose, as though he were sunning himself in the new morning. His bare skull glowed whiter than usual, framed by his black shirt and black jean jacket, loose gray stones surrounding his head. Being halfway to upside down on the slope hadn't made his face any ruddier. I stepped closer. The other side of Jaeger's head was crimson with blood. His ear was gone, torn away like the bits and pieces off the truck.

My foot crunched on the stones. He turned his bloodied head to look at me.

"Can you hear me?" I said.

"I hear you fine," he said in that loud whisper. "See you, too."

His left hand drifted toward the pocket of his jacket. I dashed forward, nearly plummeting down the slope in my haste, to fall against him. My hand trapped his inside the pocket, and I reached with my right to pluck a snub-nosed revolver out of his yielding grip.

Close. Too close. The snake still had fangs. I stood up—as close to straight as the ravine allowed—and backed away.

"You got the money?" Jaeger rasped.

"There is no money," I said.

"You lie. You came here for it. It's up there."

"I came here for you."

Realization dawned on Jaeger's pallid face.

"I told you that you wouldn't like what you found," I said.

He grunted. His glittery green eyes moved to the gun in my hand.

"Finish it," he said.

I wiped my prints off the revolver and tossed it aside. Against the side of the black rock was a smaller, smoother stone of the same volcanic source. I sat down.

After a moment, Jaeger started to laugh. Sandpaper on soft wood.

"Yeah," he said, still laughing his harsh whispery mirth. "It won't look like no accident if you shoot me."

The sun was fully over the hills now. Despite the cloudless sky, the day would be cool. I sat and looked out over the ravine. Birds had begun to settle on the rocks and brush near the Tahoe. Cautious, but interested. Attracted by the smell.

Jaeger saw me watching.

"My men?" he said.

"No."

As if agreeing, a crow cawed below us, chasing off some of its smaller competitors.

Jaeger moved. Bending his leg first, then his arm. He pushed himself onto his side, and then onto his belly. Inch by inch, he turned so that he was facing up the slope. It took many long minutes. He got to his hands and knees, somehow. Then he began to crawl.

It was not a fast crawl, but it was forward movement. I watched from my place on the stone. He made it around eighteen feet before he stopped for the first time. A racking cough shook his body, and he was still for a long while. A wounded version of his preternatural calm. I thought he was done. There might be all manner of parts broken and hemorrhaging inside of him, getting worse with every motion.

He continued. Ten feet more before he stopped again. Only three on his next try. The sun was much higher in the sky now.

I could end it. Pinch his nose closed and cut his suffering short.

That would be more than he'd given Daryll. Or Fain. Neither of them had been granted a fast trip into the dark. I stayed where I was, and watched.

Around noon, Jaeger sagged sideways. I stood up and slowly climbed the slope to where he lay. Dried blood speckled his lips. The green eyes were dull and half-lidded. Behind me, a wing flapped against the black rock with scrabbling haste.

I pulled myself back up to the road, coiled the rope, and went on my way.

The forsaken town could accept a few more ghosts.

So could I.

FIFTY-TWO

NEUTRAL GROUND AGAIN, JUST barely. The border of Luce's domain, near the Morgen and her apartment above the bar, a stone's throw from Pike Place. I sat on a bench in Steinbrueck Park, my back to the fountain that looked like whale flukes, watching the ship traffic on Elliott Bay.

My cup of coffee and a sack lunch I hadn't gotten around to eating rested next to me, on a weighty stack of *Portland Tribune* and *Seattle Times* editions from the last week. I could have read the same stories online, or similar coverage from a dozen other news sources nationwide, but I liked the tactile sensation of turning the pages of the local papers. There was an implied truth to the new facts uncovered each day, and more thought given to the conjecture. Many facts, and at least as much guesswork.

The bodies of Zeke Caton and John Fain had been discovered in General Macomber's home on Sunday. Macomber, it was reported, had left Mercy River the day before and had been letting Fain use his house. That story broke in the Portland paper as the investigation into the armored car robbery in Seattle was finally pushed off the front page of the *Times* by a burgeoning teacher's strike.

On Tuesday morning, a third bit of news: hikers in central Oregon came across the wreckage of a Chevy Tahoe with four dead men nearby, the apparent result of a tragic accident. Recovery efforts were initially hampered by mud from heavy rains the two days prior. By that evening, however, the Griffon County Sheriff was on the horn to the Portland press, trumpeting that nearly two million dollars in Haver-Corp National delivery satchels had been found in the destroyed Tahoe, and that the FBI would be stepping in.

The three stories combined like wind and clouds and heat forming a tornado. The Feds claimed that the HaverCorp robberies had already been linked to a small but highly militant supremacist organization called the First Riders—Jaeger's coat and fake ID we'd left in the armored truck had undoubtedly helped them reach that conclusion—and that the bodies found in the ravine were members of the same group.

The Bureau's special agent in charge also stated that the FBI had connected the murders of Zeke and Fain to the dead men found at the Tahoe. I had to do some guesswork myself on that. The papers had mentioned that both bodies at Macomber's house had been shot in the head. Maybe Jaeger had finished the job he'd started with Fain, using the same revolver I'd taken from his pocket.

Journalist and police attention shifted to General Macomber, who had not yet made a public statement. One reporter cited an unnamed source in law enforcement, who had theorized that the skinheads had been on the run and desperate after the debacle in Seattle. Addresses near Mercy River had turned up in searches on previous residences for a couple of the busted First Riders. The Riders may have been seeking to add to their Seattle score with the cash donations gleaned from the three-day Ranger Rally.

That theory had some holes in it, I knew. There was no mention of Fain's original gunshot wound or why Jaeger and his men had been driving up a remote butte in central nowhere, or how the skinheads had even known about the Rally—the background and goals of which earned its own sidebar story in the *Tribune*, free and gushingly positive publicity for Macomber's cause. But no one was going on record with a better tale.

I wondered how much leeway the Feds would be allowed to run down those open questions. Internal pressure might be applied to staple Jaeger's file together with the HaverCorp investigation and put the cases to rest. The cash had been recovered and the bad guys neutralized. As much as the cops preferred things tidy, running down every loose end would strain the overtime budget.

At least one person wasn't fully satisfied. Angela Roussa—formerly Deputy Roussa, now the newly promoted detective lieutenant of Griffon County—had let it be known through Ganz that she would appreciate my accompanying Leo when he returned to Mercy River to make his formal statement as part of dismissing the charges against him. She wanted me to clarify a few facts about my movements during the past week.

I didn't have to tell Ganz my answer to that. If I ever laid eyes on Mercy River again, it would be from the window of a jetliner at twenty thousand feet. Just one dark speck in a vast range of hills and fields.

Leo and Dez had called me from the highway somewhere between Leo's family home in West Jordan and Bryce Canyon, where they were leading his parents on an impromptu camping trip. I caught them up on the sorry fates of John Fain and Zeke Caton and Jaeger.

Dez wept at the revelation that her estranged husband hadn't murdered Erle Sharples after all. She said she didn't believe Wayne would have gone through with the plan to kill Leo. Then she hedged her words slightly, saying it would be better if she believed that. We'd never know the truth, so why not have faith? I agreed.

Leo's anger with me had ebbed. We still clashed on whether I should have returned to Mercy River alone. But he'd been keeping an eye on the news, too, and had seen photos taken by locals of the destroyed Tahoe, and of Oregon Search and Rescue extracting the dead men in and around it. I thought I had detected some relief in Leo's voice at having missed their final moments. Maybe he'd heard something different in mine for having been there.

The breeze gusted, lifting the top newspaper pages and threatening to dump my coffee. I rescued the cup and offered the thick stack to a homeless guy in three layers of coats who'd shambled past more than once, as part of what seemed to be his endless patrol of the park. He'd gazed longingly at the papers, maybe for reading material, maybe for insulation. The autumn air carried the first snap of winter. I threw in the sack lunch.

An oil tanker trundled along the bay, headed for the calm waters of the open Sound. It was nearly out of view when Luce stepped off Western Avenue and crossed the park. She wore the same coat of deep red as when I'd seen her at the 5-Spot two weeks ago, with a soft white scarf looped around her neck, its ends tucked tidily into the coat. She angled her face to the left a few degrees so that the breeze swept her loose hair out of her way.

"Thanks for coming," I said when she was close.

"Of course." She sat down on the bench, keeping her hands in her pockets. "Cold today. How does this air feel on your lungs?"

"My chest is fine. It looks like somebody painted it with yellow and green markers, but it's healed inside."

"Good. I—we—were worried."

"That's why I wanted to see you. To apologize. I shouldn't have drawn you into my troubles last week. It was selfish."

"You didn't even know you'd called me, Van."

"Not consciously. But I did, and you helped, and you didn't ask questions. Same for Carter. You both had to make a choice and take a risk for me without knowing what you were signing up for. That's a crappy position to be in. I'm sorry."

Luce hunched her shoulders. Half a shrug, half against the chill.

"Later that night," she said, "when all anyone at the bar could talk about was the armored car and the shoot-out downtown and all of that, I wanted so badly to talk to you. To ask."

It figured that Luce would have immediately linked that day's havoc to me. "You can ask now, if you want."

"No. I didn't need to know what you'd done. Still don't. Whatever it was, I know you had the right reasons. I'd just wanted to make sure that you were safe."

We both sat for a moment. This close, even with the breeze, I could catch a hint of the rose-scented skin cream Luce used each morning. If I cared to try.

"Leo called you for help when he was afraid," Luce said finally, "and you called me."

"If my skull hadn't been full of cotton—"

"When I found you in your truck, I thought you might be dead. You woke up when I opened the door and spoke to me." She wouldn't meet my gaze. "You said something before you told me to call Hollis."

"I told you that I loved you."

Luce looked stricken. "You remember that?"

"No. But it's what I would have said."

"God." She rubbed her fingers over her brow. "This is crazy."

"Carter's a good guy," I said.

"He is. I'm going to marry him."

"You know yourself better than anybody I've ever met, Luce. If you say he's the one, I don't doubt it."

"That's not the question. The question is what I should do about you. I don't want you to be out of my life completely."

"But."

"There will be trouble," she said. "Again."

"That's also not a question." I took a breath of chill air. "I can't lead a regular life. Maybe I might have once, and maybe someday the chance will come around again. But it's not who I am now."

"Well, that's just giving up. You're better than that."

I had a sudden image of Jaeger's dead eyes, those shards of clouded green glass.

"I try to be," I said. "It's not always possible."

"So, what? We cut all ties with each other? Can you do that?"

"My heart already broke once this month."

Luce laughed, even as her own eyes glistened. "That's terrible."

"And true."

I looked out at the bay. A towering anvil of clouds was rolling slowly in off the water, pushing the layer of lighter cumulus ahead.

"I can love you and let you go," I said. "You can care about me and let me go, too."

"Don't pretend you're doing that for me. I don't need some noble gesture."

"No. This is better for me. Safer. Everybody gains more than they lose."

Luce's gaze on me was almost tangible.

"We could choose to see it that way," she said.

"Yes."

"Then this is goodbye."

"Yes," I said. And then, without any conscious decision from me to say them, the words came out. "For now."

Luce gave my arm a squeeze. "I can take for now. I don't accept forever."

I nodded.

She stood up. "Good luck, Van."

"Good life, Luce."

She walked away, toward her home. I didn't watch her go. Instead I studied the rain clouds as they built in size and force. The coming squall would make land before nightfall.

Luce was right. I didn't have to think of it as forever. No choice was irrevocable. Except what I'd done to Jaeger and his men.

Within half an hour, the first drops tapped the cement paving. They sent the few remaining people in the park hurrying for shelter. I watched a shy flicker of lightning touch the upper strata of clouds and listened to the gentle drumroll that followed. More drops fell, more urgently. The next electric flash was bolder, reaching with long sharp fingers toward the bay.

I left the park to the storm. Night would be here soon. I'd take Hollis up on his offer of a lot of food and even more whiskey.

Soon after, I'd try my luck at sleeping. And find out what kind of dreams awaited.

ACKNOWLEDGMENTS

MY SINCERE THANKS TO the following people for letting *Mercy River* flow:

To my agent, Lisa Erbach Vance, of the Aaron Priest Literary Agency, for lighting the path ahead and pointing out the roots and stones which might otherwise trip me up. Her guidance is invaluable.

To my editor, Lyssa Keusch, for her tremendous encouragement and razor-sharp insights into ways to make the tale better. And the whole team at William Morrow: our terrific publisher, Liate Stehlik, Pamela Jaffee, Kaitlin Harri, Richard Aquan, Dave Cole, and Mireya Chiriboga, along with those behind the scenes I haven't yet had the pleasure of meeting. You guys are fantastic.

To editor Angus Cargill at Faber & Faber, with Ruth O'Loughlin, Josh Smith, and Alex Kirby, for their great skill and support. I hugely appreciate my good luck in working with such a deservedly historic house.

To Caspian Dennis of the Abner Stein Agency, for stamping Van Shaw's passport to the UK, and for making that journey both good business and a real pleasure.

To Jerrilyn Farmer, and the rest of our Saturday morning group—

Beverly Graf, Alexandra Jamison, and John McMahon. A brilliant and wickedly talented bunch.

And the technical experts: Christian Hockman, Bco 1/75 Ranger Regiment, for his professional eye on everything from tactics to armament. Áine Kelly, wonderful friend, for gifting young Van with a little Irish Gaelic. Mark Pryor, mystery author and assistant DA, for lending his expertise in legal particulars. They have all made the story richer. The details that make me look smart are their doing, and I own any errors.

My standard disclaimer: This novel is fiction, and I reserve the right to mess with jurisdictions, geography, methods, or anything else that will keep the story moving, keep the lawyers bored, and keep potentially dangerous information where and with whom it belongs. Readers familiar with central Oregon may note that I've taken a few features of that landscape, renamed or tweaked them, and shoved them closer together into the fictional Griffon County. Still, I encourage travelers to go and see extraordinary sites like the Newberry Volcanic Monument or Smith Rock for themselves. I tried to do them justice.

Thanks to every reader who picked up this book and spent the time; I sincerely hope you enjoyed every page. And to every bookseller, reviewer, and fan who might have helped that reader find the book in the first place. You are an irreplaceable part of our community.

And finally: to Amy, Mia, and Madeline, for their love and understanding in letting me live inside my head half the time. Our life together is the real adventure.

ABOUT THE AUTHOR

A native of Seattle, **GLEN ERIK HAMILTON** was raised aboard a sailboat and grew up around the marinas and commercial docks and islands of the Pacific Northwest. His debut novel, *Past Crimes,* won the Anthony, Macavity, and Strand Critics awards, and was nominated for the Edgar, Barry, and Nero awards. He now lives in California with his family, and frequently returns to his hometown to soak up the rain.